To my father, the man who taught me honor, loyalty, integrity, and perseverance. Thanks, Dad, for always leading by example.

Dare and the world yields, or if it beats you sometimes, dare it again and you will succeed.

—William Makepeace Thackeray

Prologue

WITHDRAWN

Black Knights Inc. HQ
Goose Island, Chicago, Illinois...

"THEY SAY HE'S GONE ROGUE."

Like a bad smell, the sentence seemed to hang in the air. Those seated around the large conference table shifted uncomfortably, their expressions varying from wary disbelief to stubborn denial.

Vanessa Cordero found herself falling into that last group. *He wouldn't. Not Rock.*

"Who's they?" Ozzie asked. The guy's wild blond hair and *Star Trek* T-shirt—it read *I beat the Kobayashi Maru*—shouted of his secure position in the upper echelons of Geekdom as loudly as the three microsized laptops open in front of him.

"Official word came down through the DOD," Boss said, pulling out a chair and wearily sinking into it. Frank "Boss" Knight, their esteemed leader, was built like an Abrams tank. Of course, right now he looked more like Atlas—the weight of the world squarely on his big shoulders.

"The DOD?" Ozzie snorted, and Vanessa watched his youthful face contort with skepticism. "Well that makes it all clear as mud, now doesn't it?"

The Department of Defense oversaw all facets of government intelligence and defense from the NSA down to the individual branches of the military. So, yeah, saying the information came from the DOD was ambiguous at best, and downright cryptic at worst.

Boss's jaw hardened. He seemed to hesitate before finally opening the accordion-style folder tucked under his arm. Pulling out a stack of bundled papers, he tossed them into the middle of the table. "Pass 'em around," he commanded.

Vanessa was almost afraid to take one. Afraid of what the information might reveal and—

No. He wouldn't *do this. Not Rock.*

Not the man who'd laughingly and patiently endeavored to teach her to make the perfect roux for a pot of gumbo despite the fact she totally botched and burned the first three attempts. Not the man who'd calmly showed her how to handle a motorcycle even though she kept laying the sucker over on its side. Not the man who'd scooped her up in his arms and carried her two miles back to Black Knights Inc. headquarters the time she twisted an ankle while the group was out jogging.

Not Rock...

The whine of an electric screwdriver sounded below, and Boss pushed up from his chair to stomp over to the railing. BKI's command center occupied the second floor of an old three-story menthol cigarette factory and overlooked the custom motorcycle shop—the cover for their covert government defense firm—on the first floor below. As Ozzie liked to joke, they were grease-monkey motorcycle mechanics by day and Uncle Sam's last resort by night.

And one of them had just been accused of going rogue...

A shiver of trepidation raced up Vanessa's spine. A rogue operator was considered worse than a traitor. And what was the government's stance on traitors?

That'd be death. Pure and simple.

Shitballs. What a nightmare.

"Becky!" Boss yelled as the pages he'd thrown on the table were distributed around the group. His booming bass made her wince, as usual. "Get your ass up here! We have a problem!"

A *problem*? Is that what he called it when every agent and operator employed by the dear, sweet U.S. of A. was going to be gunning for one of their own—when *they* would be required to gun for one of their own? If so, she hated to know what he considered a catastrophe.

The electric screwdriver clicked off and, seconds later, the thump of Becky's work boots pounded up the metal treads. The hollow sound echoed throughout the building and inside Vanessa's tight chest. And, yep, the fact that the room was doing a slow tilt probably had something to do with the fact that she hadn't taken a breath since Boss dropped the bomb. Clamping her eyes shut, she forced herself to rake in much needed oxygen. When she heard Becky arrive on the second floor landing, she cracked an eyelid only to discover the woman's blond ponytail covered in metal shavings. They acted as sparkling accessories to the grease spots staining her shirt.

Becky Reichert was the reason their cover worked so well. Because while most of the guys were pretty handy with a wrench, she was the genius behind the kick-ass motorcycle designs that convinced the general public they were exactly what they were purported to be—simply one of the world's premier custom bike shops.

"Has anyone ever mentioned you bellow like a wounded bull?" Becky demanded, hands on hips, lollipop stick protruding from her pursed lips as she glared at Boss. And, yes, Vanessa would wholeheartedly agree with that assessment.

"Just you, honey." Boss pulled the bright red sucker from her mouth, bending to give her a quick, smacking kiss.

When he straightened away, Becky accurately read his I-really-need-to-hit-something expression, because the teasing light in her eyes instantly dimmed. "What is it, Frank?" she breathed. "What's happened?"

"General Fuller just called to inform me Rock has officially been listed as a rogue operator."

"What the hell!" Becky exclaimed, taking the sucker back from Boss. She bit down on the lollipop and chewed viciously, taking out her shock and disbelief on the innocent candy.

"It's true," Boss insisted, pulling out a chair for his fiancée. "And we need to get to the bottom of it."

"I'm not sure we're going to like what we find once we get there," Mac said in his slow Texas drawl, his bluebell-colored eyes narrowing, his brow furrowing as he flipped through the stapled papers in his hand. "This evidence could be pretty damning."

The coffee in Vanessa's stomach—which never sat well anyway, since most of the Knights preferred their java to have the general consistency of syrup—burned like battery acid. If any of them knew anything about damning evidence, it was Bryan "Mac" McMillan, former all-star FBI agent.

Hesitantly, she looked away from Mac's worried gaze to peer down at the thin packet in her hand, her unease increasing as her eyes skimmed each postage stamp–sized photo and the brief blurb beside it. "All of them?" she croaked, glancing up at Boss in disbelief. "He's supposed to have killed *all* of them?"

"Yep." Boss nodded.

"But most of these deaths look accidental. A heart attack, a car accident, a drowning…Why are they pinning these on Rock?"

"Something about a tip on a PO box in Rock's name that contained a bunch of files on these guys," Boss said.

"And there are untold ways of making a murder look accidental," Ozzie added.

"Here's something interesting," Mac observed, mouth thinned. "Each of these men was kidnapped at one point, and none held for ransom. They all just suddenly reappeared and went about their lives. The local law enforcement was never able to discover who'd held them."

"Yeah," Boss nodded. "I found that extremely odd as well. And since it's the only clue we have to go on, I'm having Ozzie compare the dates of those kidnappings to see if any of them coincide with the times we knew Rock *poofed* out of BKI."

"But *why* would he do this?" Vanessa realized what she said, shook her head, and rephrased. "I mean why are they *saying* he did it? Killing these men…What could possibly be his motivation?"

"Money?" Ozzie posited, frowning at his computer screens. "Says here, these men were all very wealthy. Having Rock eighty-six them might've proved extremely lucrative for some folks. You know, family members, rival business associates…"

"No way," Vanessa jerked her chin from side-to-side, more convinced than ever this was all a giant smelly load of bullcrap. "Have you seen how he dresses? Do you think he'd go around wearing beat-up Levi's, holey T-shirts, and scuffed-up alligator boots if he was sitting on a big pile of cash?" She pointed at the dossier with a finger she was disgusted to find was shaking. Hastily, she clenched her hand into a fist and hid it in her lap. Her number one rule since coming to work for BKI: *show no fear*. The Knights were all hardcore, hard-assed operators who didn't so much as flinch when they were staring death in the face, and she didn't want to find herself labeled the *weak link*. "Now if you told me it was Christian," she continued doggedly, "I might believe you. No offense, Christian." She made a face at the former SAS officer who, as usual, was sporting designer jeans and a cashmere sweater that probably cost more than most peoples' monthly car payments.

"None taken, my dear," Christian said, his smooth British accent a minor balm to her screaming nerves. "As it happens, I tend to agree with you. If Rock had, indeed, accumulated the level of wealth likely to come from performing hits on these men, why was he still messing about with us? Why wasn't he sitting on a beach somewhere, soaking up the sun and ordering umbrella drinks from some bird in a bikini?"

Vanessa glanced around the table at the faces of the people she'd come to love like family. Their expressions gave her little comfort. It was obvious they were as confused and scared as she was, which—*oh dear, sweet, baby Jesus*—had the coffee/acid in her stomach burning its way up the back of her throat.

The Black Knights were *not* supposed to get scared. Hardcore, hard-assed operators who didn't flinch while staring death in the face, remember?

She swallowed hastily and pushed ahead. The silence was deafening...and damning. She couldn't stand it. "Well, one thing we know," she grasped at the first straw to come to mind, "is he wasn't working alone."

"The phone calls." Ozzie halted his typing. "He always got one of those strange phone calls right before he disappeared. Which means he had an accomplice in all this."

"Accomplice? Wait a minute," Becky interjected, yanking a new sucker from her mouth—this one was purple—to point it at Ozzie. "You're making it sound like you think he's guilty."

"I'm not saying anything." Ozzie held up his hands. "I'm just saying he *was* Mr. Mum on the subject of his second job, he *did* have the tendency to vanish at odd times, and he *was* working with someone and—" His laptop dinged, and his face drained of blood. Vanessa's stomach dropped down to the floor in response.

Ozzie turned his computer around. On the screen were two columns. The first one showed the dates of the kidnappings. The second one showed the dates Rock had disappeared off the face of the planet.

The two columns matched perfectly.

Boss let loose with a string of curses that would do any sailor proud. "Okay, so there's obviously a link between these men and Rock's *other* job."

The job that they'd all thought revolved around some shadowy government entity. The job that, according to these recent revelations, obviously wasn't related to the *government* at all.

Holy shitburgers! Vanessa was going to pass out. The room was no longer tilting; it was spinning like a merry-go-round. She lowered her head to the table and tried to slow her breathing as happy little stars pranced on the backs of her eyelids—so much for that whole hardhearted operator facade.

Is it possible? Could he have done it? Just contemplating

the thought made her temples pound in rhythm to her racing heart.

"What?" She heard Becky ask, confusion evident in the woman's voice. "Why does everyone look like they've just seen a ghost?"

"Our government isn't allowed to assassinate its citizens," Boss answered, his voice so rough it sounded like he'd scoured his vocal cords with steel wool. "And each of these guys, down to a man, was an American, born and bred."

A tense silence once more settled over the group, and Vanessa raised her thousand-pound head from the table. "Really? We're really sitting here contemplating the fact that he's guilty? Rock Babineaux? Ex–Navy SEAL? Founding member of BKI and ragin' Cajun who's more patriotic than the whole lot of us put together?"

Rock Babineaux, the man who was witty and courageous and, surprisingly—given his testosterone-laced occupation and training—incredibly self-effacing and modest? Rock Babineaux, the man who'd made her want to throw her rule about not dating operators right out the window?

Her pleading gaze landed on Boss. *Please don't lead us down this path. Please tell me you know Rock wouldn't have done this.*

Boss's Adam's apple bobbed, and for a moment she held her breath. Then she heaved a shaky sigh of relief when he adamantly shook his head. "Hell, no. It's been my experience that when everything is as neat and tidy as this report is," he flicked a scarred finger at the document in question, "then something is way the hell off. Nothing is ever this black and white."

She clung to the certainty she heard in his voice

because, yes, for a second there she'd actually begun to have her doubts.

"I agree, Boss," Ozzie said, closing the lids on his laptops so he could place his forearms on the conference table and lean forward. "And here's something else I don't get: if Rock's second job wasn't government sanctioned and no one in the government save for *El Jefe* and his JCs knows about the true status of *our* organization"—the Black Knights had been run autonomously by the president and his Joint Chiefs for over four years. In fact, their direct report was the head of the Joint Chiefs himself, General Pete Fuller—"then how the hell can the DOD list him as a rogue operator? As far as they know, he's just an ex–Navy SEAL turned motorcycle mechanic. So, what gives?"

Boss whispered a quick profanity that questioned the legitimacy of the births of everyone working in the DOD. And, uh-oh, his I'm-gonna-kill-somebody expression all but screamed that what he had to tell them wasn't going to fall under the happy little banner of Good News.

Great, Vanessa thought. *I knew I should've just gone back to bed this morning.*

When she'd stubbed her pinkie toe on the way to the restroom, run out of conditioner in the shower, and nearly electrocuted herself when her blow-dryer decided to spontaneously combust, she'd had a feeling it was going to be one hellaciously craptastic day.

She hadn't had a clue…

"If you'll look at your dossiers," Boss began, leafing through his own packet, "you'll see the last man Rock supposedly killed was one Fred Billingsworth. Now, Fred was a super high-tech and super-secret private investigator. Which means he didn't spend his time trying to catch cheating spouses or insurance scammers but, instead, was hired out exclusively to major corporations. As far as anyone can tell, his last job was working for some Democratic Party support group. He was supposed to dig up what dirt he could on all the potential candidates for the presidency next election season. As you can imagine, given the tenuous and sensitive nature of his investigations, when he died, the case was quickly taken over from local law enforcement by the FBI. Somehow, and I don't know how, they got a bead on Rock and that PO box which, along with all these other guys, contained a file on Billingsworth. When General Fuller found out, he had to come clean to the powers that be in the Intelligence community about the true nature of our business here or risk having the investigation fall on all our heads."

That got everyone's attention. One of the main reasons the Black Knights had been so effective since they'd opened their doors was the fact that only those few elite men in the highest tier of government knew what they really were.

"What does that mean for our operation?" Ozzie asked.

"According to the general," Boss replied with a heavy dose of skepticism, "it doesn't mean a damn thing. He says it'll be business as usual."

Those seated around the table made varying noises of disbelief.

"What's done is done," Boss muttered, shaking his head. "For now, all we can do is take Fuller at his word."

"And what do we do about Rock?" Ozzie asked, and Vanessa swung her gaze back to Boss. She'd very much like to know the answer to that question herself.

"We find him," Boss declared, nostrils flaring, "before anybody else does."

Chapter One

The edge of Monteverde Cloud Forest, Costa Rica
Six months later...

THERE IT WAS AGAIN...

That tingling between his shoulder blades. That tightening of his scalp. Call it instinct or intuition or some sort of gut reaction brought on by a lifetime of looking over his shoulder, but Rock Babineaux knew someone was watching him.

Friend or foe?

Merde. There was really only one option, wasn't there? Considering he didn't have any friends left.

Slowly, still sipping his *refresco*—the fruity drink he'd fallen in love with the first time he'd come to Costa Rica—he quartered the area around the little outdoor cantina while unobtrusively thumbing off the safety on one of his 9mms.

Where are you? Where are... Ah, there you are.

Over in the corner, a man sat at a small table beneath an arched trellis. The thick vines growing over the top of the structure cast the guy in faint shadow, but Rock didn't need to see him clearly to know he was only *pretending* to read that book in his hand. In reality, the man was eyeing Rock from behind his mirrored sunglasses. They glinted in the evening sun when he leaned forward to take a bite of ceviche, the citrusy fish dish so popular in these parts.

Jet black hair peeking from beneath a baseball cap and olive-toned skin told the story of the man's Hispanic heritage just like his slight frame—Rock would bet his favorite pair of alligator boots that the dude weighed no more than a buck and a quarter soaking wet—and a patchy beard told the story of his youth.

Mon dieu. They're sendin' babies after me now?

A hard knot of resignation tightened in his belly, and his dinner—the one he'd been *so* looking forward to since it was the first food he'd eaten in almost a month that hadn't been picked out of a tree or spooned out of can—turned to bile.

So much for a nice, relaxin' evening in town.

Throwing a wad of colorful money on the bar, he hoisted his heavy pack onto his shoulders, turned toward the dense green growth of the jungle pushing up to the side of the cantina, and made sure his pistols were within easy reach.

Not that he'd actually use them, of course.

Just because every agent and operator employed by Uncle Sam was green-lighted to put a bullet in his brain, that didn't mean he'd return the favor. After all, those folks were just following orders, and he knew all about that, didn't he? It was following orders that'd gotten him into this mess.

Ducking into the jungle, instantly soaked by the warm water clinging to the leaves on the trees, ferns, and vines as he brushed against them, he started up a winding, nearly indiscernible path in the way his father had taught him. Slow, steady, watching where he stepped and how he moved so that he didn't disturb the forest animals around him. Cocking an ear to the sounds behind him, he listened to the symphony of buzzing insects, calling birds, and the wet drumbeat of water falling from leaf to leaf, waiting for that one note that didn't quite belong.

But the seconds turned into minutes, and the minutes turned into an hour and still nothing broke the harmony of the forest's song.

Was I wrong?

The man had been watching him. Of that he was sure. But maybe the guy had just been curious why the tattooed gringo at the bar didn't look like all the other tourists visiting Monteverde Cloud Forest. Rock's heavy-duty cargo pants, faded tank top, and well-worn jungle boots certainly weren't the standard fare of Nike sneakers, jogging shorts, and beer slogan T-shirts. He'd spent the last six months living in the wild...and it showed.

So, *oui,* maybe it was as simple as that.

Raking in a deep breath of relief, he smiled as a scarlet macaw launched itself from a low hanging vine, flying up into the thick canopy. Its brilliant plumage glinted in a rare ray of sunlight that managed to cut through the treetops, its squawking call echoing down to the forest floor below. Adjusting his pack, Rock wiped a hand over his sweaty brow and stepped off the path.

And that's when it happened.

A hundred yards behind him, a howler monkey screeched out a warning and all sound in the jungle, save the murmur of steadily dripping water, came to a record-scratching halt.

Man has entered the forest...

And, okay, now was probably not the time to be channeling Bambi.

Rock quickly shrugged out of his pack and leaned it

against the wet, ivy-covered base of a massive tree. He covered it with the fronds of a nearby fern before silently moving toward the monkey's call. Paralleling the trail, he melded into the jungle's shadows, becoming nothing more than a shadow himself, as the forest slowly came back to life. The insects picked up their droning chorus first, followed by the warbling birds and the grunting chatter of the band of howlers high in the trees.

He hadn't gone very far when a flash of movement caught his eye. Pressing himself against a tree trunk, breathing in the fresh, earthy smell of the lichen growing near his face, he waited. It didn't take long since the guy was sprinting up the trail.

In a hurry to kill ol' Rock, are ya? Well, sorry to say, son, but today is not your lucky day.

He held steady until his would-be assassin whizzed by, then stepped from behind his cover. In a flash, he had an arm around the young man's neck and one of his SIGs pressed into a soft kidney.

Instinctively, the guy began to struggle, flailing around like a June bug on a string, but Rock just applied more pressure. Which elicited a squeak. A very *unmanly* squeak.

Huh?

He didn't loosen his hold on that skinny neck as he tucked his 9mm into his waistband in order to yank off those ridiculous mirrored sunglasses. The baseball cap went next, and he was astonished to watch a long black ponytail unravel in front of him. Rock spun his captive around and nearly shit his own heart.

"Vanessa? What the *hell* are you doin' here?"

She'd found him!

Finally, after months of searching, she'd found him! And the sound of his smooth voice, that sweet Cajun drawl that brought to mind tin roofs and front porch swings, stroked her eardrums like a silken glove.

"I've come to help you," she breathed excitedly, barely resisting the urge to throw her arms around his neck, to touch his dark hair—it was shorter than she'd ever seen it, like he'd been haphazardly cutting it himself, which she was sure he had.

Keep it professional, Van. You have to keep this professional...

Because, yes, it was true she had a little thing for Rock. How could she not? He was just so...so...*natural*, she guessed was the word. None of that bullshit alpha-male mega-ego that so many operators suffered from. Just an unshakable and abiding sense of duty, and a refreshing unpretentiousness that'd attracted her to him from the very beginning. Plus, there was that smooth-as-silk voice...

But he'd made it abundantly clear after she'd sent him all the right signals that he didn't have room in his life for a girlfriend—much less anything more permanent. Now, if all she wanted was to sweeten the sheets, he was her go-to guy. He'd made that readily apparent at a BBQ one night when he'd smoldered at her and told her trouble—and he'd definitely been trouble with a capital T, even before all of this—could be fun.

But she'd been there. Done that. And though she didn't have the T-shirt to prove it, what she *did* have was an empty ring finger with no prospects in sight. And let's be honest here, at thirty, she was beginning to get a bit antsy about the whole thing. Especially since starting a family of her own had always been one of her most cherished dreams.

So, yessir, since she was too old and too jaded to be screwing around—*literally*—with the hot bad boy—*super hot*—keeping things professional was her only alternative, right? Right.

Of course, that was easier said than done. Especially since his tank top exposed the tan contours of his tattooed biceps and accentuated the breadth of his wide shoulders.

Oh, for heaven's sakes, pull yourself together, Cordero.

And, yes, the ridiculousness of her being here, in the middle of the jungle, arguing with her own libido about the man standing before her when every government agency in America had guys out hunting for him, wasn't lost on her. Then again, he'd managed to bring out the ridiculousness in her since day one. For being a communications specialist, she always felt inexplicably tongue-tied around him. Of course, the last time they'd partnered on a mission, he'd done the tongue-tying himself…

And there went her libido again. Memories of his tongue down her throat were not helping the professionalism. Even if at the time it had been strictly business.

"You came here alone?" His expression was flinty, his precisely shaped goatee drooping at the corners of his frowning mouth.

"To the Cloud Forest? Yes." She'd made the four-hour motorcycle ride from the capital city to here all by her little ol' lonesome. *Go, go girl power!* "But the others are waiting in San Jose and—"

"Sonofa*bitch*." He turned and paced a few feet down the trail, cursing in both English and French. Then he swung around and stomped back to her, his hazel eyes glinting even in the deep shadows cast by the forest canopy. "How'd you guys find me?"

It hadn't been easy; that was for sure. When his Burn and Delete notice came over the wires, he'd disappeared faster than a cry in the wind and had proven to be nearly as elusive ever since.

"We were beginning to think we wouldn't," she admitted, letting her eyes run over his face. There were two vertical lines between his dark eyebrows that hadn't been there the last time she'd seen him. And he'd lost weight. He'd been lean and mean to begin with, but now he was nothing but muscle, bone, and sinew. When you combined all of that with the scruffy hair and faded clothes, a girl couldn't help but get a little niggle in her belly. Because the man appeared as volatile and feral as the exotic animals inhabiting this jungle. Still…*keep it professional*, a little voice whispered in her head, to which she responded, *I'm trying, damnit!* "Boss said you cover your trail better than anyone he's ever seen."

Rock grunted, an irritated muscle ticking in his jaw. "I didn't cover it good enough, obviously. You're here, aren't you?"

And, yeah, she'd known he wasn't going to welcome her with open arms, but this undisguised animosity was a bit of a head-scratcher.

Didn't he *want* their help?

"Only because we found that wooden bowl in your bedroom back home. The one displayed above your dresser?" His eyes narrowed further, and she took that to be an affirmative. "After extensive research, we discovered the artist only sells his goods here, at the CASEM store in Santa Elena. And since Boss said you'd never had occasion to do any BKI jobs down this way, that meant you'd traveled here for other reasons. It was a shot in the dark, but it was the only one we had." And luckily it'd paid off, because here he was. *Finally.* "From there it was just a small matter of finding an excuse to come to Costa Rica in order to nose around and—"

"An excuse?"

A large drop of water plopped on her cheek from an overhead leaf, and she held her breath as Rock unconsciously reached forward to brush it off. The pad of his thumb was rough, and, *man,* he smelled good, like fresh foliage, harsh soap, and good, clean, healthy sweat.

Basically, he smelled like he looked. All rough and ready. Wild and exciting. And seeing the look on his face now reminded her of the time he'd interrogated those hit men sent by a crazy Vegas mobster to kill the Black Knights. Then, he'd been tired and worn—performing an interrogation, it appeared, always messed with his head—but the weariness had added a dangerous edge to his expression. It was doing the same thing now. And, boy, oh, boy, did that look go all through her. Because it was the look of man who didn't shirk his duty, the look of a man whom the world had tested time and again, the look of a man who'd know exactly how to handle anything that came his way. How to handle a gun, a terrorist, a woman—

Ack! Seriously, Van?

"The FBI and CIA know about us now," she informed him and watched his jaw harden until the hollows in his cheeks deepened, making his face appear harsh and uncompromising. "When the manhunt started, your association with Black Knights Inc. was discovered and General Fuller had to come clean about our little group.

Since then we've had Company guys breathing down our necks trying to ascertain your location."

"*C'est des conneries!*" *This is bullshit!* he spat in French, turning to pace away once again.

And, yes, a few short months ago she would have agreed with that assessment. But, since then, she'd discovered that having the CIA privy to the true nature of BKI wasn't all that bad. In fact, The Company and its myriad reams of intel had come in quite handy on a few of their more recent assignments. And just because the two groups didn't see eye-to-eye on the culpability of one Richard "Rock" Babineaux, that didn't mean they weren't still batting for the home team and willing to help one another if and when they could in all *other* endeavors.

"They were convinced we knew where you were, which was sorta funny since we didn't have the first clue," she told him, watching the efficiency of his lean-hipped swagger as he once again marched back to her. He moved like a well-built machine. No wasted energy. "They've backed off in the last month or so, and from what Ozzie can gather from hacking into their reports, they've pretty much given up on the idea that we could help locate you." Pretty much, except for that one surveillance van back in San Jose. But she figured she'd keep that little bit of info to herself…for now. Especially since she had the feeling it was going to be hard enough to convince him to come back with her. "But we weren't willing to take any chances. So after we discovered the bowl's origins, and in order not to tip them off to the lead we thought we might have, we tried to come up with a legitimate reason for coming down here."

"And what reason did you come up with?" he

demanded, still looking less like he wanted to fall to his knees and thank his lucky stars they were on his side and had found him, and more like he wanted to clock her upside the head before sending her back home.

She tried very hard not to let that hurt her feelings, especially considering all she'd had to go through in order to locate him.

"Eve has a vacation home in San Jose. You remember Eve, don't you?" she asked. Although, it was probably a stupid question considering Eve Edens was a semi-famous Chicago debutante and drop-dead gorgeous to boot. Anyone who'd ever laid eyes on the woman was not likely to forget the occasion.

"*Oui.* I remember Eve," he said. And, dang, here she'd hoped he may have been blind to Eve's substantial allures.

"Well, since Boss and Becky never got a honeymoon," she continued, trying to ignore the green-eyed monster perched on her shoulder poking her in the temple with a sharp-nailed finger, "we thought it'd be cool and, more importantly, *believable* if some of us came down here as a sort of celebratory vacation and—"

"Wait." He held up a wide-palmed hand. "Boss and Becky are married?"

The momentary look of anguish that passed over his rugged features instantly tugged at her heartstrings. He and Boss had been friends since way back in BUD/S training, and she knew he loved Becky like a kid sister. So, yeah, missing the pair's union had to be a major blow.

And seeing the hurt and regret on his face helped to wash away some of her doubts. Because when the days had turned to weeks and then months, she was ashamed to say she'd actually begun to waffle on the issue of Rock's innocence. But a man who could do what they said he'd done wouldn't be so dejected over missing a simple wedding ceremony, would he? No. No he wouldn't. And she was more than a bit relieved to feel some of her earlier certainty return.

"Yes, they're married." She resisted the urge to give his biceps a comforting squeeze. "Two months ago they went to a justice of the peace. But they're waiting to have the party and reception until this thing with you gets cleared up and you can join in the festivities."

He stared down at the toes of his jungle boots. "You shouldn't have come here. You've put yourself and all the Knights you brought with you in terrible danger."

Stepping forward, she placed a gently persuasive hand on his forearm. "Come home with me, Rock."

The muscles beneath his tan skin bunched at her touch, his prickly man-hair tickling her palm. A stupid woman might find that sexy as hell. Thank goodness she wasn't a stupid woman. Or was she?

Because when he screwed up his mouth, that mouth that was so beautiful and so perfectly proportioned one usually only saw it on renaissance sculptures, she began to think her confidence in her own mental acuity was highly inflated.

"We can help you," she insisted, dismayed when her voice came out all low and breathy. "We can figure out who burned you and determine how to—"

"What makes you so sure I was burned?" he asked, his expression like a chalkboard that'd been wiped clean.

"Because I know you. I know you wouldn't—"

"You don't know a damn thing about me, *chere*," he whispered, stepping away, out of her reach.

Chapter Two

"GO BACK THE WAY YOU CAME," ROCK GROWLED, swinging around on the path to glare at Vanessa after it became apparent she was determined to stick to him like a cocklebur.

"No," she declared, crossing her arms and jutting out her small, stubborn chin, looking madder than a wet hen in a tote sack. Looking like it'd take a jackhammer and two WWE wrestlers to break her away from that spot. "The Knights tasked me with bringing you home, and I'm *going* to bring you home."

Home? He didn't *have* a home. Not anymore. Not since that last fateful mission. Not since he'd started asking questions…

Non. Now all he had was a lonely tree house deep in the jungle and, honestly, he didn't even have that anymore. Now that the Knights had found him, he was going to have to relocate. For their safety and his…

"I'm not gonna say it again." He grabbed her shoulders and gave her a little shake, just so she'd know he meant business. "You *have* to go back."

He couldn't ignore the softness of her flesh beneath his fingers or the way she smelled like mint bubble gum and dryer sheets, so clean and fresh despite the sweat slicking the dusky skin of her chest and neck. He released her shoulders and took a hasty step back.

Everything about her was heart-shaped, from her

face to her mouth to that high, tight ass of hers that was enough to make an atheist believe in God. She was small and exotic and, even dressed like a man and sporting that patchy beard, she was still the most desirable woman he'd ever seen.

For all the good that did either of them.

Because if there'd been no chance of a future for them before this fiasco, there certainly wasn't a chance for one now. And, *oui*, he knew it was a future she was after. It was there in her big, dark eyes every time she looked at him. He could almost see the visions of white dresses and orange blossoms dancing around in her pretty head.

And if things had been different…

But, no. There was no use what-iffing. A man could make himself crazy doing that.

"I'm not going without you," she declared through clenched teeth. "Don't you *want* our help?"

Mon dieu, just the thought of the Knights getting themselves involved in this mess turned his stomach and had the sweat on his skin going cold and clammy.

"Y'all can't help me, *chere*." He was beginning to think no one could. "The best thing is to just forget you ever knew me."

The expression on her face was more determined than that of most four-star generals he'd known. "Impossible," she declared with an angry shake of her head. It caused her long, black ponytail to slip across her shoulder. A few strands stuck to the dampness on her neck, and it took everything he had not to reach forward and brush them away.

Touching her only reminded him of all the things he'd lost in his life, all the things he'd given up when those losses galvanized him into agreeing to become The Interrogator for The Project and—

"There has to be something we can do for you," she insisted.

"There isn't," he growled, giving her the look he'd perfected over the years when questioning bad men about bad doings, the one guaranteed to shrivel a guy's balls.

"There *has* to be," she snapped right back, apparently immune to his expression.

Well, there you go. That's what you get for thinkin' it'd work on someone who doesn't have any dangly bits...

For long seconds they stood and glared at each other, a kind of old-fashioned staring contest. But unlike that childhood game, the stakes here were as high as they came. Because death was stalking him as surely as the jaguars living in this jungle stalked their prey. There was a pretty good chance he wasn't coming out on the other side of this thing alive. So, the most he could hope for was to keep his friends safe while he hunted for the answer to the question of why he'd been betrayed, and while he made whoever was behind that betrayal pay for their duplicity.

"I'm givin' you one more chance, *chere*. Turn around now and go back the way you came."

"Or what?" She dared him with every fiber of her being, looking like a very angry...a very angry...? How to describe her? A very angry sex kitten, that's how. *Oui*. That's about all the mean and menacing she could muster—which wasn't nearly enough for what he was involved in. But she didn't know that. And even her hip shot stance seemed to call his bluff.

So that's how it's gonna be, huh?

"Fine." He spun on his heel and marched back up the path to his pack. Pulling it from beneath the fern, he shook it roughly to make sure all the creepy-crawlies were vamoosed, then he shouldered it and stepped off the trail into the jungle, immediately picking up the pace.

He'd simply outrun her. She'd left him no other choice.

Hopping over bushes, skirting roots, and slipping through curtains of wet vines, he moved through the forest like a ghost—quickly and silently. But much to his amazement and dismay, thirty minutes later he could still hear her crashing through the undergrowth fifty yards behind him, scaring the animals she passed into screams of warning.

The woman had the tenacity of a bulldog combined with the hearing of a bat. Just his damned luck.

Okay, so outrunning her wasn't going to work. Because if he led her too much farther into the jungle, she'd never find her way back out to the trail.

So, the trees it is...

If he scaled one of the monster trees, all he'd have to do was wait. Wait for her to pass beneath. Wait for her to search for him. Wait for her to eventually give up and turn back. And she *would* eventually give up and turn back. Because even though she was proving to have giant brass balls hidden beneath that sweet Latina exterior, nobody, not even hardcore operator and world-class comm specialist Vanessa Cordero, wanted to spend the night alone in the middle of the jungle.

Oui, that was the plan all right. Of course, that plan got shot straight to hell when he went to grab a handhold on the nearest jungle giant just as darkness enveloped him.

That's how it was here in the Cloud Forest. Night fell like an axe blade.

"Zut!" he cursed, glancing around, wondering if she'd

be able to find her way back to the trail and out to Santa Elena in the dark.

Doubtful, considering he could barely see ten feet in front of him and he hadn't noticed her carrying any gear. No food or water. No flashlight…

All of that was confirmed a second later when her tentative voice echoed through the thick foliage. "Rock?" She sounded scared and *that* hit him like an iron-fisted punch in the gut. "I…I can't see where I'm going."

Cursing her, cursing himself, cursing that shadowy bastard code named Rwanda Don who'd gotten him into this mess, he pulled a penlight from one of the pockets on his cargo pants and traipsed back the way he'd come. No sooner had he gone two feet when she called to him again, the fear in her voice now tinged with panic. "Rock? I hear s-something moving behind me, but I…can't really see what it is."

"Just be still!" he yelled. There was no end to the number of four-legged, six-legged, eight-legged, and *no*-legged nasties that could do her serious harm. He dropped his pack in order to turn on the afterburners. The verdant growth of the jungle floor appeared more gray than green in the yellow glow of his flashlight as he raced toward the sound of her voice.

It seemed to take forever and a day, but he finally managed to cover the distance. Shining the penlight around, he called, "Vanessa? *Chere*, where are you?"

Then his light landed on her frightened face, framed by the ropy brown roots of the strangler vines clinging to the tree behind her and the coiled length of a brilliant flash of yellow that could be only one thing.

Eyelash viper.

An arctic blast of fear turned his blood icy, because while the snake wasn't kill-you-on-the-spot venomous, a bite to a hand could certainly result in a lost finger and a bite to a major vein, like, oh, say the one pulsing rapidly in Vanessa's pretty neck where the snake was poised to strike, could definitely cause some major organ damage.

He slowly walked toward her, careful to keep his movements non-threatening. "Don't move," he hissed when she started to take a relieved step in his direction. "Just be very, *very* still."

She stopped dead in her tracks—*good girl.*

"Wh-why do I need to be still?" she asked, her eyes wide and glowing in the beam of his flashlight, her soft voice tremulous.

"Just…" he inched closer, pulling one of his SIGs from his waistband, "…don't move."

"Rock, I—"

She didn't get any further than that because the viper reared up and Rock was suddenly out of time. He raised his weapon.

He was going to shoot her!

She could see his pistol silhouetted against the thin beam of light and for a heartbeat of time, before fear had a chance to kick in, she felt one and only one emotion…

Indignity. She could not believe he was actually going to—

Boom!

His 9mm sounded like a cannon explosion, so loud it rattled Vanessa's teeth. She waited for the punch of mind-numbing pain, for the specter of death to follow quickly on its heels, but all she felt was something fall into the leaves beside her feet.

Instinctively she jumped away, glancing down as Rock pointed his flashlight at the forest floor, spotlighting the writhing, yellow body of the fatally wounded snake. He was at her side in two steps, grabbing the snake by one of its bloody coils and neatly severing its head with the 10-inch bowie knife he'd had hidden somewhere on his person.

"I..." she tried to swallow her heart, which had leapt into her throat the instant she'd seen that big, black pistol pointed at her head. "I thought you were going to..." She couldn't continue. The darkness around her was spinning and if she didn't do something fast she knew she was going to be sucked down into its vortex.

Head between your knees. Put your head between your knees...

She bent at the waist and grabbed the backs of her legs, pulling herself down in a long stretch that impeded the rapid contractions of her diaphragm and kept her from hyperventilating and passing out.

And wouldn't that impress him? If I keeled over in a dead faint?

Um, no. The answer to that was a definite N.O.

She remained like that, doing her best impression of a human taco, for a couple of seconds, pressing her cheek to her kneecaps until the stars stopped spinning in front of her eyes, and then she straightened. In the dim circle of illumination cast by the flashlight, she could just make out Rock's concerned frown.

"Y'okay?" he asked.

"Yes, I—" She raked in a calming breath, appalled to

discover her entire body was shaking. So much for the whole hard-ass operator persona she'd been working on since starting at BKI. "I'm all right," she finally managed.

"What did you think I was gonna do?"

"Oh, uh…" She bit her lip and squinted when he shined the light in her face.

"You actually thought I was gonna shoot you, didn't you?"

"Stop shining that thing in my eyes," she barked, holding a hand up in front of her face. It was a good excuse to *one*, hide her expression from him because she was so totally busted, and *two*, change the subject.

"Sonofabitch! You did!" His tone was incredulous. He spun around, stomping a few feet away. She blinked against the darkness—which was made even worse by the fact that she'd just had a flashlight directed in her eyes—and tracked his movements only by following the thin, bouncing beam of illumination. Then, suddenly, he had the thing aimed at her face, and she was blinded again. "So you believe all that stuff you're hearing about me? You think I—"

"No," she cut him off. Taking a step toward him, imploring him with outstretched hands. "I don't believe it."

He was silent for a long, pregnant moment. The chorus of frogs and the drone of nighttime insects struggled to fill the void, then, "You're a terrible liar."

"Rock, I—"

"Save it."

She snapped her mouth shut. What more could she say? For a split second there, she *had* thought he was going to shoot her.

"You think you can keep up?" The question, so sudden and so far off topic, momentarily befuddled her.

"I—I've done okay so far, haven't I?"

A resonant grunt was his only response. And then there wasn't any time for words, because she was too busy trying to stay close to him and the light in his hand.

The darkness, that stygian, black abyss…It brought back too many memories.

She shivered and tripped over a large root. Flailing, she tried to keep her balance and failed. But before she oh-so-gracefully face-planted into the ground, he was there, grabbing her under her arms, hoisting her up against his solid chest.

And time came to a screeching halt.

It was like someone tipped the hourglass on its side and the grains of sand stopped falling. The sounds of the forest faded away. The oppressive humidity faded away. The unbearable darkness faded away. There was nothing but the two of them, locked in an embrace, faces inches apart, ragged breath mingling.

Kiss me.

The thought slid through her mind, unwelcome and startling. She knew it wasn't right. Knew he wasn't going to change his mind about what he could offer her. Knew she was only wasting her time hoping that he would. But right now, in this moment, that wasn't really a moment at all since it was a brief instant out of time, she wanted to know what it was to hold him in her arms. To feel his passion, taste his essence, and share with him those same things in herself.

He bent just slightly, his full lips so close, his sweet breath so warm…

And then he set her away from him, pressing the pen-light into her palm.

"You take the light," he instructed. "Just make sure to shine it at my feet."

With that, he turned away, and she was left with no recourse but to follow him on knees that'd turned to jelly.

"We think we've found him."

Rwanda Don—that code name always elicited a smile—sat forward, hand tightening around the prepaid cell phone. "Where? How?"

"Costa Rica," announced the CIA agent who'd been working on The Project since the beginning. A tickle of excitement trilled up R.D.'s spine. "And they did it by planting a radio frequency device on Vanessa Cordero. According to reports, she's been in the Monteverde Cloud Forest for a few hours now, and the general consensus *here* is she wouldn't be *there* unless she'd found him."

Could it be? After all these months?

"Are they going in after him?"

"That's the plan." The agent's voice sounded smug. And why shouldn't it? They were very close to their ultimate goal of finally catching and/or killing Richard "Rock" Babineaux, assuring their secret—and illegal—activities over the last few years would forever be kept in the dark.

Let him get killed. Please, let him get killed.

Just the thought of the accusations Rock could make upon capture, and the possibility of the ensuing investigation, was enough to have R.D.'s stomach turning somersaults. Of course, even if someone *did* begin to investigate, it wasn't as if they'd ever find anything.

We took enough precautions. We made sure to cover our tracks.

But only after Billingsworth, that nosy prick, had begun asking too many questions about the origins of certain campaign funds, prompting R.D. and the CIA agent to do some housecleaning. The amount of money lost in process, campaign money that'd been paramount to easily securing R.D.'s future plans, was infuriating.

Still, there was some satisfaction, unsavory as it was, in knowing the only person who knew the true origins of that money was now dead, thanks to two of the boys from The Project…

R.D. raked in a steadying breath. "Keep me informed as the situation unfolds."

The deep sigh on the other end of the line was annoying. "That's been our deal all along."

"Yes. Indeed it has been." With that, R.D. hit the *end* button and sat back, feeling optimistic for the first time in months.

Of course, it wouldn't do to get one's hopes up. Rock was a slippery bastard if ever there was one. And if anyone could slither out from under the wide net the CIA was bound to cast, it was him.

———

She actually thought he'd been about to shoot her…

Rock pressed a hand to his aching chest as he trudged back to the spot where he'd dropped his pack. In the past six months, he'd suffered under the knowledge the Black Knights would be inclined to believe him guilty—why wouldn't they? They'd seen the evidence against him—but he hadn't realized how much it would hurt to bear *witness* to their presumption until this very moment.

And despite all of that, despite the pain in his heart knowing he'd lost their respect and trust, what had he almost done?

He'd almost kissed Vanessa Cordero, that's what.

Which just goes to show what a goddamned *imbécile* he really was, lower than a toad in a dry well. Because kissing her would've done nothing but make a bad situation worse. It would've done nothing but give her hope when there was no hope to be had.

Chancing a glance over his shoulder, he quickly forgot his own misery when he saw the whites of her wide eyes shining like twin beacons through the darkness. It didn't take someone with his particular skills at reading people, or his ability to pick up on subtle facial cues, to recognize the poor woman was scared to death. And her fear didn't have anything to do with the eerie, barking hoot of a nearby mottled owl, because she'd been immune to the creepy, almost ethereal sounds of the jungle before sunset.

Oui, it was as obvious as the nose on his face; Vanessa Cordero was terrified of the dark.

Pourquoi? Of course, the reason behind her fear didn't really matter. The fact that she was this scared at all had him pausing beside his pack, rolling in his lips as he considered his options.

One: He could lead her back to Santa Elena, which would mean two hours of marching through the dense, dark jungle having to listen to her breath hitch every other heartbeat. Or two: He could take her back to his tree house—which was only a fifteen-minute hike—and then send her on her merry way in the morning.

That second option meant he'd have to spend the night with her. Alone. In a somewhat confined space. When he hadn't had a woman in a very, *very* long time…

Vanessa made the decision for him when a noisy clatter sounded behind them and she jumped on his back, her thighs squeezing his waist and her arms wrapped around his neck in a choke-hold that immediately had his eyes bulging as he struggled to breathe.

What in the w—

That's as far as he got before a second loud rattle had her climbing him like a cat climbs a tree, finding footholds and handholds on his knees, gear belt, and shoulders. It was either help her reach her goal or suffer serious injury, so he palmed her ass—*sweet Lord in heaven!*—and gave her a little boost. And, to his utter astonishment, the next moment found her sitting on his shoulders, shining the penlight around the forest canopy with one hand while the other sunk deep into his hair, threatening to rip out the whole kit and kaboodle by the roots.

"What was that?" she breathed as he blinked away the tears that sprung to his eyes. He felt a few hairs pull loose.

And when he fantasized about having Vanessa's thighs wrapped around his ears? Boy howdy, you better believe he never envisioned it quite like this.

"It was just a bird," he assured her as he reached up to gently untangle her fingers from his hair, rubbing his abused scalp in the process. Grabbing her by the waist, he tried to ignore how right it felt to have his hands on her, how taut her flesh felt beneath his fingers, as he lowered her to the ground. No sooner did her toes touch the good ol' terra firma than she latched on to his arm with a claw-like hand.

Okay, so the tree house it is. Because the poor woman would probably need to be fitted for a straitjacket if he tried to march her all the way back to Santa Elena in the dark.

"A bird?" Her voice broke on a frightened edge. "What kind of bird makes *that* noise? It sounds like bones rattling."

Oui, that's exactly what it sounded like, which, he had to admit, was pretty spooky even for someone who wasn't scared of the dark. For someone who was? Sheer, unadulterated terror…and the inclination to climb on top of the nearest solid structure, obviously.

"It's called a Black Guan. And that's just the noise its feathers make when it flies," he informed her reassuringly.

"You're kidding me." She shined the light directly in his face, and he lifted a hand to protect his eyesight.

"*Non*," he said, bending to retrieve his pack. He slapped it a few times for good measure and shrugged into it as he blew out a resigned breath. One night. He could get through one night. "Just stick close on my heels."

"Where are we going?" Her voice was still shaky, the beam of the flashlight she carried continuing to dart up into the canopy on occasion.

"We're goin' to my tree house for tonight. And tomorrow you're goin' back to Santa Elena and then to San Jose."

"And you're coming with me?"

No. But he was finished arguing about it. So he gave her the only answer he could, which was no answer at all.

Chapter Three

THE FACT THAT ROCK HADN'T RESPONDED TO HER LAST question wasn't lost on Vanessa, but she couldn't worry about that now. Not when she was busy trying to slow her breathing and quiet her heart while simultaneously scrambling to keep pace with him.

She felt the darkness closing around her like a hot fist, squeezing her, trying to cut off her air.

Good grief, Van. Keep it together, or you're gonna make an even bigger fool of yourself than you already have.

Of course, making a *bigger* fool of herself might prove difficult, considering she couldn't think of anything more idiotic than climbing the poor man like a light post when that weird bird took flight. She still wasn't quite sure how that happened. One second she had her eyes and flashlight glued to his jungle boots, concentrating everything she had on not thinking about the darkness surrounding her. And the next second? Well, the next second she was on his shoulders.

And, here you are trying to convince him you've come to save him. Fat lot of help you've been so far...

Blowing out a dismayed breath, she focused on putting one foot in front of the other, skirting around the ankle-grabbing vines and giant tree roots. She didn't know how much time passed—it could've been minutes or hours—but suddenly Rock stopped. She lifted the beam of the flashlight to his face only to discover his head thrown back, his gaze focused overhead.

Oh, gosh, I hope it's not another one of those birds...

Hesitantly, she traced the penlight up a huge tree until she saw what had snagged his attention. The distance diffused the beam of light, but even so, she had no trouble making out the proportions of the framework overhead.

Um, okay, so he called *that* a tree house?

He must have seen the astonishment on her face. "I didn't know how long I was gonna be livin' here, so I reckoned I better get comfy."

Comfy. Right.

The mammoth wooden structure spanning the gap between two huge trees came equipped with shuttered windows, a rope bridge, and was that...? Yep, that was definitely an outdoor shower she spied on the landing. It was fed by one of the big plastic rain barrels bolted above the thatched roof.

And here she'd been feeling sorry for him, thinking he'd been huddled in a crude little shack for the last six months. Shack? What a joke. This place looked like the Hilton Hotel of tree houses, like Robinson Crusoe Gone Wild.

"Does it come with cable TV and broadband?" she asked dryly, still frowning up at the structure, marveling at his ingenuity.

"Nothin' that fancy." He led her around the wide, flat, bacon strip–shaped roots of the tree until they came to a long ladder affixed to the trunk with thick steel bolts. "After you," he gestured with a jerk of his whiskered chin.

Vanessa bit her lip and once again shined the penlight up, *waaayyy* up, the trunk of the tree. Now, *normally,* she wasn't afraid of heights. Then again, she'd never been required to cling like a spider monkey to side of a giant rainforest hardwood without benefit of a safety cable and harness either, so…*yeah*…

Forty feet. That's how high she estimated she'd have to climb before she reached the tree house.

Gulp.

Of course, after the snake episode and that weird bone-rattle bird and the subsequent shoulder-straddling thing, she sure as hell wasn't going to let him see her trepidation. She hoped there was still a chance to salvage at least *some* of her whole girl-races-to-the-rescue-of-doomed-operator mojo so, nodding with far more confidence than she felt, she shoved the penlight between her lips and grabbed the first wrung.

Eyes on the prize, eyes on the prize, she mentally coached herself as, hand over hand, she scaled the ladder. By the time she reached what she thought was the half-way point though, that mantra switched to *don't look down, don't look down, just don't look—*

Ah, crap. She looked down.

And as high as it'd seemed while looking up, it appeared a whole hell of a lot higher while looking down. Her eyesight played one of those tricks on her, like in the movies when the camera suddenly zooms back, elongating the field of vision. Just as she was gearing up to have herself a mini panic attack, the beam of her flashlight illuminated Rock, steadily climbing below her, and she forgot all about the likelihood of her breaking every single bone in her body should she lose her grip on the ladder. In fact, all thought came to a full stop. Because the yellow beam caught the play of his muscles, the dips and mounds and planes, casting everything into harsh relief, and it was enough to have a girl's brain turning to mush.

All the Knights were in peek physical condition, but Rock? Rock was almost inhuman.

Not an ounce of fat showed in his bare arms or shoulders as he hoisted himself and his heavy pack up the tree. He was a study in taut, tattooed skin, sturdy bones, and sleek, sinewy muscles. A study in the perfect male form…

And it was a good thing she needed both hands to cling to the ladder or else she might have started fanning herself. Then, as quickly as her synapses went offline, the ol' gray matter rebooted itself and the first thought to spring into her head was, *No man should look that good in a tank top. It's just not fair.*

Disgusted by her inability to control her libido whenever he was around, she went to resume her task of climbing the ladder when suddenly Rock looked up, his fascinating, multicolored eyes flashing in the beam of light and, just like that, she was struck dumb again.

Most people wouldn't consider Rock a handsome man. Save for his tattoos, there was nothing about him that really stood out. At first glance, he had a plain, somewhat forgettable face. But there was just something about him. Something more than his dark brown hair with its auburn highlights, something more than his straight, unexceptional nose and thick, dark eyebrows. Maybe it was his high cheekbones or his square jawline. Or, more likely, it was his lips.

Holy cow, those lips were a thing of beauty. A perfect bow on top and a lush, plump pad on the bottom.

She'd had more than her fair share of fantasies about those lips. A few of which skittered through her sluggish brain right now.

"There a problem, *chere?*" he asked, breaking into her

lurid thoughts, which only worked to remind her of the effect his voice always had on her peace of mind. She supposed it was her propensity for languages, for the tonal quality of words and inflection, that made Rock's fluid baritone, especially when it was infused with the elongated vowels of the South, sound like the most delicious thing she'd ever heard.

She shivered and wished she could blame it on the coolness of the air after sunset. Unfortunately, the oppressive heat and humidity of the jungle hadn't dissipated even one degree. So her shiver had nothing to do with the temperature and everything to do with the fact that she was a goddamned lightbulb when it came to Rock; everything about him turned her on.

And even in the darkness she could see one of his eyebrows begin a steady march up his forehead. For a minute, she worried that perhaps her expression had given away her thoughts. Then she remembered he'd asked her something. What was it again?

Oh, yeah, he'd asked if there was a problem.

And her answer? *Hell yes, there's a problem!*

The problem was that the one man on the entire planet she'd ever gone all goo-goo-gah-gah over also just happened to be the one man on the entire planet who would never return the sentiment. Of course, she couldn't tell *him* that, so she satisfied herself with simply turning and resuming her upward trajectory. And, all the while she was climbing, she was reminding herself she'd come here to help him—to bring him back so the Knights could help him—not to jump his oh-so-delicious bones.

—◦∿◦—

Don't look at her butt, don't look at her butt, just don't look—
Dieu. He looked at her butt.

And how he'd confused her for a man, for even a nano-second, he'd never know. Because Vanessa Cordero had that quintessential Latina build. Her small waist flared dramatically to curvy hips and a high, round ass.

Sir Mix-A-Lot was writing about her with, "*little in the middle but she got much back*," because *merde*!

And when she reached the top of the ladder and hoisted herself onto the landing, effectively shielding her world-class booty from his hungry eyes, he didn't know whether to be relieved or apprehensive. Because even though he was now able to construct a thought that didn't revolve around taking a bite out of each one of her ass cheeks, he knew it was only a matter of time before those ass cheeks would be warming his bed while he lay tossing and turning on a pallet on the floor.

He may never wash his sheets again…

"You need help with that pack?" She interrupted his prurient thoughts, her faux whisker-covered face appearing at the top of the ladder, which served as a reminder of something that'd been bugging the hell out of him.

He shook his head, and she moved back so he could pull himself onto the landing. Straightening, he blurted, "Why the disguise? If the CIA has given up hope that you guys knew where to find me, why'd you need to go dressin' up like ol' Cooter Brown?"

He watched her reach up to finger the tiny hairs still glued to her chin and cheeks. She grimaced and started yanking them off one patch at a time. "I wore the disguise just in case," she told him, scrubbing her hands over her now hair-free face, scratching at a spot that still retained some glue. And, *mon dieu,* why did she have to be so damned beautiful? "Just because we *think* they've mostly given up doesn't necessarily mean they *have*. You know the CIA. They're nothing if not wily. So, I snuck out of San Jose a week ago as Ricardo Ramirez and have been in Santa Elena looking for you as Ricardo Ramirez ever since."

"And you didn't approach me at the cantina because…?"

"Are you that paranoid?" She fisted her hands on her hips. "Don't you trust me? Do you really think I've come here to do anything more than help you?"

He shrugged out of his pack, leaning it against the wall of the tree house. He'd unpack later. For now, he needed a cold drink and an even colder shower. Of course, since air-conditioning and refrigeration weren't really part of the whole Tarzan theme he had going, the odds of getting either were pretty much non-existent. Still, he could dream…and *wish*. Then again, there was a saying that went something like *wish in one hand and shit in the other and see which one fills up faster…*

Opening the door to the tree house, he motioned for her to precede him.

For a brief instant, she hesitated, waiting for him to answer her last set of questions. And only when it became obvious he had no intention of answering anything did she shrug her shoulders and step over the threshold.

He followed her in while *not* looking at her butt. Okay, maybe he snuck one quick peek. He was just a man, after all. Once inside, she glanced around curiously, and he knew what she saw. A slap-dash box-framed bed holding a thick blow-up mattress covered in tangled sheets. A rough-hewn table with one chair. A kerosene stove on a stand. Cooking utensils stacked on a shelf. A pyramid of canned food and MREs. A small water barrel…and a shitload of intel.

Every vertical surface of the tree house was wall-papered with the information he'd been able to find out about himself, his missions, and his targets. And, unfortunately, even given all of that, he still felt no closer to discovering the true identity of Rwanda Don than he'd been six months ago. Maybe if he had his files…

But no. Those files were the main reason he was in this mess. He should've destroyed them and then he—

"You've been busy," she murmured, walking over to the table to pick up a glossy eight-by-ten photo of Fred Billingsworth. The last man he'd interrogated. The last man who'd died.

The *only* man who'd been innocent…

A strange expression crossed her face as she studied that photo, and Rock could tell she was struggling with the suspicion that, *oui,* despite what she thought she knew of him, despite her *wanting* to believe him innocent, the fact remained that maybe he really *had* killed all those men.

"Why didn't you approach me at the cantina?" he asked again. Not that he didn't believe she'd come to help him. All it took was one look at her wide-open, honest face to know she was telling the truth. But he wanted more. He wanted to ascertain her motives. Because, for one, it was his training to go digging around in a person's psyche to see what made them tick. And two, it would give him an idea just how much heat the Knights had been exposed to because of him.

"Because I had to be sure." She dropped the photo back to the table in order to cross her arms and scowl. "If by some miracle I was being tracked, I figured it was best to hang back and see if they trailed you into the jungle."

Okay, so they'd suffered quite a bit of heat if she was having to employ that level of caution. His heart sunk at the thought of what his actions had cost the Black Knights. "When enough time went by and no one took off after you, I followed. But I think maybe I waited too long, because I nearly lost you."

"If only," he sighed, pulling his pistols from his waistband and trudging over to the shelf that held his few pieces of cookware. Placing the 9mms inside a pot and securing the lid—capuchin monkeys sometimes snuck in and messed with his stuff, and the last thing he wanted was to get accidently plugged by some light-fingered primate—he turned back around to find Vanessa's head cocked, her lips pursed.

"And if I *had* lost you, how long would I have had to wait at that cantina before you made a return appearance?"

"A month," he admitted. "Maybe more."

She shook her head in disbelief, blowing out a breath. "Well, thank heavens I brushed up on my Maleku."

"Huh?"

"It was an elderly Maleku man who pointed me toward the cantina. I guess he'd seen you there a couple of times."

And he wasn't surprised the Knights had chosen to send *her* after him. They had to have figured it would take someone with her particular linguistic abilities to decipher the many Chibchan dialects spoken by the locals around these parts.

Just as he opened his mouth to question her further, a subtle sound, a deep muttering, had every single hair on the back of his neck standing on end.

———

Eve Eden's vacation house, San Jose, Costa Rica…

"Oh shit!"

Eve's entire skeleton nearly flew out of her skin at Billy's roared exclamation. The tension around her place had been riding high until a few hours ago when Vanessa Cordero checked in to say she'd finally located Rock. Since then everything had evened out. Calmed down. Which was probably one of the reasons why Billy's sudden outburst scared the bejeezus out of her. It was like a gunshot in the middle of a picnic lunch.

The glass of Chardonnay she'd been in the middle of pouring fell victim to the hand that jumped to clutch her throat. Sparing barely a glance at the shattered glass and gold liquid flowing freely across the granite countertop, she watched as Billy—Wild Bill Reichert to those in the spec-ops community—jabbed a hard finger onto the screen of his phone before launching himself over the back of the sofa and racing toward the hall.

Her natural instinct was to stay rooted to the spot. But just last month, her personal defense instructor informed her, in no uncertain terms, that she needed to *grow a pair*. Which she took to mean when everything inside her yelled at her to get very still and stop breathing—just play the scared rabbit— that's when she should channel a little of her best friend, Becky Reichert, and kick her characteristic reserve to the curb.

So…WWBD? What would Becky do? Becky would be hot on Billy's heels, that's what.

Exhaling a determined breath, she shot out from behind the counter and caught up with Billy just as he was about to throw open the door to the bedroom Boss and Becky were currently in the process of christening.

Oh, no. Bad idea. Because if there was one thing guaranteed to scar a man for life, it was seeing his little sister *in flagrante delicto* with the giant, hairy guy who happened to be his brother-in-law and boss.

She grabbed Billy's wrist before he could finish turning the knob and—

Warm.

His skin was always so warm. That was one of the things she remembered about him. The heat he generated. And even though more than a decade had passed since she'd been in his arms, the mere touch of him brought back the memories as if it was only yesterday...

The way his wide mouth had curved in a smile as the wind blew his shiny brown hair every which way that day they'd sailed her little skiff on Lake Michigan. The way his warm eyes had sparkled that night she finally let him unbutton her blouse in the backseat of his car. The way heartbreak had contorted his young, handsome face that fateful morning he told her he was leaving...

That last one—and the deep ache that always accompanied it—brought her slamming back to the present. "You don't want to do that," she told him.

He shot her a hard look that had her lungs clenching. But she was trying very hard to grow a pair, so she held her ground. "Just yell it through the door. They'll hear you."

For a split second he seemed to hesitate, his expression softening, his dark-chocolate-colored eyes searching her face as if maybe...

But just when she thought he might say something, oh, she didn't know, *nice* to her—like, perhaps, *thank you for keeping me from seeing something that would require me to bleach my brain*—he turned and bellowed into the dark wood. "We've got a problem! Get dressed and get your asses out here!"

Whispered curses could be heard inside the room, followed by the squeak of the mattress and the muffled shuffle of footsteps. Eve wasn't aware she was still holding Billy's wrist until he glanced down at her hand and back up at her face.

Heat climbed into her cheeks before she had the wherewithal to release him.

It'd been this way ever since they'd been reintroduced six months ago. The stilted conversation and wary looks. The subtle jibes. The...*electricity*.

Geez Louise.

Of course, she'd managed to mitigate much of that by avoiding him at all costs. And a *smart* woman would've continued to uphold that status quo. Unfortunately, despite what her professors might say to the contrary, she was discovering she wasn't a very smart woman at all. Because when Becky had called and asked to borrow the San Jose house for a little celebration of her recent nuptials—and as a cover for an operation—Eve jumped at the chance to tag along. To see how it was all done.

Growing a pair indeed. Her defense instructor would be so proud.

Of course, at the time, she hadn't been aware how much being in the same room with Billy Reichert was going to wreak havoc on her nervous system and—

The door to the bedroom flew open, interrupting her thoughts. Boss and Becky stood on the threshold, both wearing fuzzy white robes and sporting hairdos that looked like they'd survived a hurricane.

To Eve's utter chagrin, her blush deepened.

"What is it?" Boss demanded, running a hand over his stubbled jaw.

"Ozzie just intercepted a CIA scramble directive for a couple of stealth choppers over Monteverde Cloud Forest," Billy informed him.

"Fuck me." Boss grabbed the door frame with enough force to crack the wood.

"And Vanessa?" Becky asked.

"She's turned off the signal…just in case." Billy tilted his phone from side-to-side, indicating it was useless as a means of communication.

"Options?" Boss inquired, the big muscle in his jaw beating out a too-fast rhythm.

"There are none," Billy admitted, his expression sickly. "We just have to wait and see if Rock is as resourceful as we all think he is. In the meantime, I think we'd better call in the cavalry. Something tells me we're going to need all boots on the ground here."

"Roger that," Boss said, turning back into the room to grab his phone from the nightstand. He immediately began punching in numbers.

"How many?" Becky's expression was tense as she peered into Billy's face, and even Eve knew what she was after. The odds. Just how many CIA agents was Rock Babineaux going to be up against?

"Eight," Billy replied, and Becky's face relaxed.

"That's not so bad. He and Vanessa can hold their own against—"

"On each team," Billy interrupted. "There are two teams."

"*Oh shit*," Becky breathed, and Eve experienced a disconcerting sense of déjà vu.

Chapter Four

"WHAT IS IT?"

The look on Rock's face was enough to have the ceviche in Vanessa's stomach going rancid.

"They're here," he whispered.

She had a brief flashback to a scene in *Poltergeist* a split second before he grabbed her around the waist and lunged for the open doorway. No sooner had they cleared the threshold than all hell broke loose. A flashbang detonated inside the tree house, momentarily blinding Vanessa and causing her ears to ring.

Of course, she was glad her eyesight wasn't working when Rock yelled, "Hang on!" and looped her arms around his neck.

She instinctively obeyed and was sure as hell glad she did when he grabbed hold of a rope she hadn't seen dangling from an upper branch. Before she knew what he was doing, he stepped off the platform, and then...

Nothing.

Just the thick, wet jungle air between her and a forty-foot drop into oblivion.

Biting back a terrified squeal, she wrapped her legs around Rock's waist and, even though she was still partially blinded by the flashbang, squeezed her eyes closed all the same.

This isn't happening. This isn't happen—

Oh, yes, this was definitely happening.

She was swinging through the jungle, Tarzan-style—uh, Jane-style?—while bullets whizzed by her head. Even with all her senses reeling, she was still painfully aware of the feeling of displaced air near her ear when a round barely missed her.

Holy cow, they were trying to kill her.

Those bastards! They're actually trying to—

And then she didn't have time for thought, because Rock dropped onto a small platform secured to a massive tree trunk opposite the tree house. He landed with enough force to jar the teeth from her head, so it was a good thing she had her jaw clenched. Working solely on instinct, she went to release her hold on him but was stopped when he immediately shuffled around on the barely foot-wide ledge to the back of the tree. There he stopped beside a ladder similar to the one she'd climbed to get to his tree house.

"Swing around to my back, *chere*," he instructed, his tone amazingly calm considering there were groups of men, dressed all in black, repelling from out of the sky while simultaneously *shooting* at them. Of course, Rock and Vanessa's current position behind the humongous tree trunk gave them a moment's reprieve, but she knew it would only be a moment. Now that she'd recovered from the shock of the flashbang, she could hear the rhythmic muttering that'd initially alerted Rock to the approaching trouble. Glancing overhead, she caught a glimpse through the swaying canopy of not one but *two* fabled stealth Chinook helicopters shining bright spotlights into the forest below, lighting up Rock's tree house like a Christmas ornament.

Oh, hell. She nearly swallowed her tongue.

Because there was a legend within the spec-ops community that went a little something like this: if an operator ever makes an error of egregious proportions, then regardless of who he is or where he is, a mysterious black Chinook arrives, and that's the unqualified and unmistakable signal that the spec-ops community no longer requires that particular operator's services.

When a black stealth Chinook shows up on your doorstep, you know one thing for sure—it's time to bend over and kiss your ass good-bye because you're completely and unequivocally fucked six ways from Sunday.

Well, not if I have any say in the matter...

Dropping down to the narrow ledge, she hastily tiptoed around Rock until she was pressed against his back and could once more hook her arms around his neck. He barely gave her time to adjust her hold before he grabbed on to the side rails of the metal ladder. Only he didn't use the rungs to scale down the sucker. Oh, no. That would've been far too *natural* a descent. Instead, he hooked his boots on the outside of each rail and once again...

Nothing but air.

For interminable seconds they were hurtling toward the earth at breakneck speed, the thick air rushing by them, the lush bromeliads growing on the trunk rushing by in a kaleidoscope of colors muted by the darkness. Then Vanessa felt every muscle in Rock's body bunch and strain and felt a deep grunt build in his chest as he tightened his grip on the rails of the ladder. Miraculously, their momentum slowed. And to her amazement, instead of slamming into the ground at terminal velocity, they landed with a soft, controlled *thud*.

She marveled at his sheer strength even as she dropped

to the ground behind him. A split second later, he had her hand secured firmly within his own, yelling, "Run!" as he jerked her into a sprint through the thick undergrowth.

———∿∿∿———

Thirty yards north, and twenty yards west. Inside the hollow of a dead tree whose roots protrude from the ground like little brown fingers...

Oui, that'd be where his nearest cache of gear was stored and, *dieu merci*, thank God his dear ol' daddy didn't raise no fool.

Rock half-carried, half-dragged Vanessa along behind him as he ran, heart pounding steady as a metronome despite the danger, mentally keeping count of his steps while simultaneously cursing himself for putting her through this.

The poor woman was scared to death, realizing for the first time the severity of the shit-storm circling around him, and undoubtedly regretting, with every fiber of her being, her decision to come and find him.

And could he blame her?

Uh, that'd be a big, honking negative.

Because avoiding a ballistic lobotomy was enough to scare the bark out of any dog, even an old hound like him who'd been trained in the fine art of keeping his cool when the world around him was exploding. So, *oui*, if he was nervous—which he totally was; there were *a lot* of men dropping out of the sky—that meant she had to be absolutely terrified.

Because the truth of the matter was, she may be one hell of a communications specialist, but she didn't know jack shit when it came to handling the melee of full-on battle. And that's exactly what they had going here. Battle.

Case in point: the bullet that slammed into the trunk of

the tree not ten inches from his face, ripping away bark and blasting it into a dozen razor-sharp slivers. Vanessa squealed at the same time one of those slivers sliced into his neck. He felt the hot trickle of blood but paid it no mind. He had to get to his gear and secure Vanessa in one of his hiding spots. Now. Five minutes ago…

"Watch the stump!" he yelled, barely seeing the remains of the fallen tree before he was forced to hurdle it. Much to his surprise, Vanessa was right there with him, vaulting the sucker like a gold-medal Olympian as the *pop* and *crack* of automatic weapons fire echoed through the jungle.

Sweat trickled down his face and neck, burning the fresh wound there, but he didn't give it a moment's notice. Because they had a very short window of time—during the initial pandemonium caused by the two helo teams fast roping in—to make their escape. And with each passing second, and each additional set of boots on the ground, that window shrank.

"We're going the wrong way!" Vanessa yelled beside him. "We need to head east if we want to get back to Santa Elena!"

If only it were that easy. One of the fundamental precepts of warfare was to *never go out the way you came in…*

"That's exactly where they'd expect us to head," he hollered above the racket of the firefight just as he was forced to execute a swift juke move lest he run face first into a low-hanging vine. The sudden change in direction caused Vanessa to stumble, but she rallied like a true operator and quickly regained her footing.

And, then, suddenly it appeared the helo teams lost track of their location. Because the rounds were no longer cutting through the foliage all around them and seemed, instead, to be focused more toward the west. But that wouldn't last long. No doubt those boys were wearing night vision goggles, which gave them all the advantages in this little game of cat and mouse.

"Where are we going?" Vanessa panted, now keeping pace beside him as they dodged left and ran smack dab into a thick curtain of wet vines.

This goddamned jungle is gonna get us killed quicker than those helo teams...

"Almost there," he assured her in a whisper. Now that the gunfire was dwindling, he needed to keep their sound signature to a minimum. Wrestling with the vines, cursing under his breath, he reached out to grab her hand. He felt better when he was touching her and, *oui*, he was going to chalk that up to the fact that it was difficult to see and he needed to know exactly where she was at all times and not the fact that...well...he just liked touching her.

"*Where?*" she hissed, calling into question someone's paternity when one particularly spiny vine snagged her ponytail, jerking her back like a puppet on a string.

Unsheathing his Bowie knife took all of half a second. Then he was reaching up to slice through the thickness of her ponytail, effectively freeing her and severing several inches of her hair in the process.

Pity. She had the most beautiful hair he'd ever seen... slick and black as a raven's wing...But they didn't have time to mess around.

Again she surprised him when she didn't so much as utter a squeak of protest. Instead, she whispered, "Thanks," as she lowered her chin and doggedly pushed ahead, breaking into a sprint he was hard-pressed to keep up with.

"This way." He steered her to the right and, *saints be praised!*, there it was.

Dropping her hand, he bent to snatch his pack from the hollow of the tree, briefly overwhelmed by the smell of decaying foliage when he thrust his head into the small space.

"What in the world?" she asked when he backed out.

"Operators, especially those raised out on the bayou, hide gear the way squirrels hide nuts," he said by way of explanation while tearing through the protective plastic bag and digging into the pack to check that both his spare SIGs were just where he'd left them, chambered and at the ready.

Stuffing the pistols into his waistband, he shouldered the pack and turned to her.

"What?" Even in the dimness she must have recognized the look on his face.

"You're bugged, *chere*," he said, and she was shaking her head before the last word left his mouth.

"No. No way. I checked my clothes before I left San Jose. There was nothing that—"

"Then you were tagged at some point in Santa Elena," he interrupted her, taking this small, momentary reprieve in the firefight to catch his breath and mentally run through their dismally few options. Few? What a joke. One. They had *one* option. And it wasn't going to be easy. "It's the only way they could've found us. And you see how they've lost us now? It's because you're out of range. So that means it'll be a low-tech tracking device. Like a sticker or—"

"No, I—" She suddenly stopped, the whites of her eyes glowing in the night as her lids flew wide and she reached into her pocket, pulling out her cell phone. "There was a little boy," she explained quickly, "he bumped into

me at the CASEM store this morning." She handed him
her iPhone, and he was dismayed to see her hand was
shaking—the poor woman was a lot more scared than
she was leading on, *and goddamn you, Rwanda Don, and
what you've brought on us both!* "The screen brightness
is set to dim," she panted, turning around. "Shine it on my
back and see if there's anything stuck to me."

Silently promising slow and thorough retribution to
Rwanda Don, Rock thumbed on the phone's screen, pointing the nearly infinitesimal light it provided at Vanessa's
back and—

There. Stuck to her back pocket. A tiny, metallic-
looking sticker.

A sick foreboding settled in the pit of his stomach. He
peeled the sticker off, raised it and the phone close to his
face in order to see, and…sure enough.

"Oh, shit," Vanessa breathed after turning around, and
Rock couldn't help but think, *oh, shit, indeed.*

Because, pretty as you please, on the back of the sticker
was the tiny wiring indicative of a radio-frequency device.
The thing was incredibly low-tech, likely only detectable
from within a hundred yards, but it was enough. More
than enough. Anyone who'd ever set off an alarm at a
department store knew just how well RFD tags worked.

Vanessa started shaking her head. "Oh, geez. Oh, geez.
I'm so sorry, I—"

"Doesn't matter now," he told her and, as if on cue, a
bullet smacked into the tree they were hiding behind.

Quickly pocketing Vanessa's phone, he bent to grab a
small stone. Attaching the RFD to the rock, he wound up
and sent the sucker flying. A couple of heartbeats later, the
sound of gunfire moved off in the direction of his pitch.

"Now's our chance," he said, once again reaching for her hand.

He tried, he really tried, not to let the fact that she didn't hesitate to lace her fingers with his turn his insides to goo. And, *oui*, if he was being honest with himself, he failed miserably on that front. Because, despite everything, despite the fact that they were running for their very lives, it felt *good* to have someone beside him, to have *her* beside him.

He'd been alone for far too long…

Of course, her intense fear of the dark and trying to evade the masked men whose rate of gunfire exceeded their rate of discussion at about a thousand to one probably had a lot to do with her willingness to participate in the whole hand-holding thing. But at this point he'd take what he could get.

"Where to?" she whispered, glancing around, blinking against the dimness.

And the answer to that question wasn't anything she was going to like. So he simply squeezed her fingers reassuringly and tugged her out from behind the tree. Breaking into a steady jog, keeping one ear cocked to the sounds of the teams scouring the jungle behind them, he threaded his way through the dense undergrowth, using his keen sense of direction and the few landmarks available in the shady mass of grayish-green to help him navigate. A couple of interminable minutes later, they reached their destination…a steep embankment that led to the river below. And after the darkness of the jungle, the break in the canopy and the resultant moonlight beaming down on them seemed bright as a spotlight.

"*Merde!*" It suddenly occurred to him that this might

not have been the best move. "I didn't think to ask before but…can you swim?"

"You're looking at the women's one-meter diving champ at McLane High in Fresno," she said.

Rock breathed a quick sigh of relief while simultaneously wondering if there was anything this woman couldn't do. So far, she'd managed to locate him when Uncle Sam's most skilled agents couldn't, track him through the jungle even when he was trying to outpace her, and outrun the hit squad that'd been sent in to put his head on a platter.

Damn impressive.

And before he could think better of it, he blurted, "If we had more time, I'd be sorely tempted to kiss you smack on the lips right now."

And then it was as if his wish was granted. Because everything came to a stop, the world ceased spinning in its orbit, and she turned to stare up at him, hope and desire and something he dare not name glittering in her dark eyes. "Rock, I…" Her voice trailed away as she took a short, hesitant step in his direction.

Seemingly of its own accord, his chin dipped down.

Right there. Her succulent, heart-shaped mouth was right there, and, *mon dieu*, her breath was warm. Her thigh bumped his, and he leaned forward, and—

The sound of a twig snapping behind them had them jerking apart and leaping over the embankment. Holding on to each other, propping each other up as best they could, they skidded and slid down the sheer grade. Reaching the bottom, they stumbled into the cool, fast-moving water.

Rock had to release Vanessa's fingers as the current took their feet out from under them, and he immediately missed her warmth, the soft feel of her small hand tucked trustingly within his own. But he had only a moment to consider what a colossally dumbass notion that was—what a colossally dumbass move *kissing* her would have been— because the current picked up and, suddenly, it was game on.

For several minutes, all either of them could manage was to tread water as the river took them where it wanted. And even though the water was a welcome reprieve from the stagnant jungle heat, Rock couldn't enjoy the dunking—and the resultant cooling effect it had on his overheated libido—because his heavy pack kept trying to drag him under. He fought it along with the current, all the while scanning the northern embankment for the spot where the rocks protruded into the water. There, in that one particular spot, they could exit the river without leaving any telltale footprints.

Where is it? Where is it? Where—

Ah, there *it is!*

"Head for the rocks!" he managed even though his mouth was full of water. Good thing he was an ex–Navy SEAL and felt as at home in the drink as he did on dry land, or else the repeated pull of his pack against his shoulders would've had him settling to the bottom of the river to serve as food for the fishes. As it was, he had to kick with everything he had in order to keep his head above the water.

"The current's too strong!" Vanessa sputtered, splashing beside him as she fought against the raging river.

No. They couldn't miss this opportunity. Their only hope of survival at this point was escape and evasion. And the first step to accomplishing those tasks was to make sure they got out of this damned river undetected.

The muscles in his legs burned like wildfire, his shoulders threatened to pop right out of their sockets as he battled the heavy current. When he pulled even with Vanessa, he latched on to the collar of her shirt, dragging her with him as he slowly, methodically made his way toward the edge of the river and the quickly approaching rocks. She helped him as best she could, but she was just too light to fight the river on her own.

Still, they only had one shot at this. And the time was...*now!*

Raking in a deep breath, he allowed himself to sink to the bottom a couple of feet down, grabbing Vanessa around the hips. The instant his jungle boots touched silt, he pushed up with every last ounce of strength he had, catapulting her toward the rocks in the process and managing at the last minute, just barely, to reach out and snatch hold of the large branch that'd fallen across the river.

Instantly, the current caught his legs, trying to yank him downstream, but he gritted his teeth and held on for everything he was worth until he was able to hook his free arm around the branch. Straining, feeling the vein in his forehead pulse in time to his heartbeat, he was finally able to pull one leg away from the grip of the river and hook it over the branch. Wrestling his second leg free required much less effort and suddenly, he was hanging upside down, the river foaming and snarling and rushing beneath his back.

A relieved breath punched from his lungs when, after hastily wiping the water from his eyes, he saw Vanessa crawling onto the rocks. Her head was hanging between her shoulders like a drunk in the street, and she appeared to be coughing up a jungle's worth of river water, but the important thing was she was safe. They'd made it!

Well, hallelujah and pass the ammunition!

He'd have taken a moment to pat himself on the back—when he'd brainstormed this particular escape strategy, he hadn't banked on having a woman along for the ride—but he was too busy inch-worming his way along the branch to the water's edge. Carefully, so as not to leave any trace of their passing, he dropped down onto a wide, flat stone.

"Y'okay, *ma petite*?" he panted, crouching beside the still-coughing woman.

She glanced up at him, her black hair—no longer contained in a ponytail thanks to the river—plastered wetly to her neck and face, her full lips trembling ever so slightly. But there was fire in her eyes and, once again, he had to give credit where credit was due. Vanessa Cordero was turning out to be one tough cookie. Then, she proved him correct when she said, "Yeah, I—" *cough, cough,* "I'm okay," right before she shakily pushed to her feet.

"You can take a minute, *chere*. Catch your breath."

"No," she blinked the water from her eyes. "I'm ready."

"You sure?" He bent to peer into her face and, in the glow of the moonlight, he was struck once again by how goddamned beautiful she was. And just like that, his libido—the stupid shit—kicked itself into high gear. Because, you know, it wasn't like he'd just nearly drowned or anything. It wasn't like he'd just missed getting his head blown off. *Twice.*

Jesus. No wonder the females of the species tsk-tsked and shook their heads when the conversation turned to men. As a group, they hadn't evolved much past the caveman stage.

"I'm fine," she insisted. And to prove it, she began climbing up the rocky embankment, which, of course, gave him another eye-goggling view of her perfect ass and…*caveman, indeed*. He was hard pressed not to grab the nearest stick, thump her over the head with it, and drag her back to his cavern so he could have his way with her.

And as ridiculous as that last thought was, it still had his dick—otherwise known as the brainless wonder—twitching with interest.

"Goddamn, sonofabitch," he hissed beneath his breath, disgusted with himself, disgusted with the situation, but, most of all, disgusted by his inability to control his prurient thoughts whenever she was around. Never in his whole life had he reacted to a woman the way he reacted to Vanessa. Maybe it was chemistry, or pheromones, or… hell, maybe it was just the fact that *she* seemed to have a thing for *him.* Which, let's be honest here, was mind-boggling in and of itself. Because she belonged in the centerfold of a men's magazine and he…well, let's just say he wasn't anything to write home about.

"Did you say something?" she turned to look at him, dragging his thoughts back to the situation at hand.

"Nah. Nothin'," he grumbled even as he started up after her. Of course, he wouldn't have to worry about the little thing she had for him for much longer, because as soon as she found out what he had in store for them, any warm fuzzy feelings she might think to send his way were guaran-damn-teed to dry up quicker than spit on an Atlanta sidewalk in the middle of July.

Cresting the ridge, he grabbed her hand—*oui, that feels about right*—and pulled her toward a huge tree that was laying on its side. Pushing the ferns away from the hollow base, he motioned toward the small, dark space with his chin. "After you."

And just as he suspected, she began vigorously shaking her head, murmuring, "No. Oh… Oh, no," while backing away with the stubbornness of an old mule that knows it's headed straight for the glue factory.

Chapter Five

NO WAY. NO HOW. UNDER NO CIRCUMSTANCES WAS SHE crawling into that tree.

"Now, *chere*," Rock coaxed, keeping hold of her hand so she couldn't run screaming in the opposite direction, "don't take off with your pistol half-cocked. I've got tarps coverin' the entire inside of the thing, top and bottom, and, as it happens, I just did my weekly rounds yesterday. Which means that less than thirty-six hours ago I sprayed the sucker with insect repellent. Ain't nothin' living in there that's worse than the guys huntin' us out here."

He might be right about that. But the thing looked like a black hole, a giant mouth open and ready to devour her. And with the sound of the water running nearby it reminded her of—

Her vision began to narrow, her head floating away from her shoulders. And then, suddenly, he was there, beside her, his masculine heat and solidity anchoring her in the moment as he wrapped a heavy arm around her shoulders.

"This is the only way," he whispered in her ear, gently frog-marching her toward the hollowed-out tree.

"But, but—" Her mind raced with a thousand thoughts. The first and foremost being that if she crawled into that abyss she was going to die just like—"They'll still be able to see us using infrared technology, won't they?" She grasped onto the idea like a drowning person grasps a life raft.

Oh, friggin' hell, a drowning person…Why'd she have to go and think of *that*?

"I.T. doesn't work in the jungle when our body heat matches the outdoor temperatures."

Well, duh. She'd known that. Hadn't she? It was hard to remember with her brain floating up somewhere near the canopy. Every step closer to that yawning cavity had her heart threatening to come crashing through her sternum like the alien creatures in those Sigourney Weaver movies. And wouldn't *that* be one more fun thing for Rock to have to deal with?

"We're outgunned, out-equipped, and out of options," he continued, basically carrying her the last foot until they were standing right in front of the downed tree. She thought she could feel the darkness of that hole reaching out to pull her in.

Oh, geez. Oh, geez. Oh, g—

"They'll see our tracks into the river and know which direction we headed," he continued in a calm voice that only managed to make her realize how frickin' close she was coming to a major breakdown. "Now, it's gonna take them some time, probably an hour at least, to come down this far since they'll carefully search each side of the riverbank lookin' for where we got out. And when they can't find hide nor hair of us, they'll start scouring the jungle in earnest. And I can tell you this: with NVGs they have all the advantages. We need to hide out here until daybreak in order to even the odds. By the time mornin' rolls around, they'll be scratching their heads, spread thin, and wondering if maybe we somehow managed to make it to one of the surrounding communities. And that's when we'll make our break for it."

Uh-huh. That all sounded very logical. Except for the teensy, tiny little fact that it meant she'd have to spend the rest of the night crammed inside that tree. In the dark. With the sound of the river running nearby…

"Now I know you're scared." Placing a hand on the top of her head, he half-helped, half-forced her to duck into the crevice. *Oh, geez. Oh, geez.* "But I'm gonna be right here with you the whole time. Nothin's gonna happen to you. I promise."

The darkness inside the hollowed-out log was complete. She couldn't see her hand in front of her face, much less the tarp she felt beneath her knees when Rock tugged her into a kneeling position. They began crawling up the length of the tree and the sides closed in on her, threatening to suffocate her. She should've been comforted by the slightly chemical smell inside the log since it told her she wasn't likely to be overrun by a bunch of critters but, somehow, that just made the claustrophobia worse. "Don't you…don't you have a flashlight in that pack?" Something, *anything* to cut through the blackness. "Or, I know, you could…you could use my phone as a light."

"*Non.*" She couldn't see him, but she knew he was shaking his head. "It just might be enough to shine through the foliage at the base, spotlighting our position. And even though I think we're safe for the time being, I don't want to take any chances. No use temptin' fate if we don't have to."

So, okay. No light. She could do this. She could do this. She could—

Oh, my God! I don't think I can do this…

"*Bon, chere*, you're doin' fine," he crooned softly, and the smooth sound of his deep voice took the tiniest edge off her nerves. We're talking microscopic. "Now just lie on down there," he helped her onto her side in the tight space, "and I'll be right back."

"*What?*" she squawked, scrabbling into a sitting position and banging her head in the process.

The overhead tarp crackled on contact, but she couldn't worry about her sound signature right now. Not when the only person keeping her sane was threatening to leave her all alone. *In the dark!*

"What do you mean?" She reached into the blackness, relieved when her fingers landed on Rock's warm forearm. She followed the muscular expanse up and over his bulging bicep, past his big shoulder, until she could wrap her hand around the back of his neck and pull him forward. Pressing her forehead to his, she panted, "You can't…you can't leave me."

His rough hands reached up to cradle either side of her face, his breath feathered along her lips and, had she not been so terrified, she'd probably have melted into a slurry of hormonal sludge on the spot. As it was, it was taking everything she possessed not to pass out flat. "I have to go conceal our tracks from the rocks to here," he told her, gently running the pads of his thumbs along her cheeks. "I'll be right back. I promise you." And with that, he slipped from her grip, and any terror that'd abated while she'd been in his arms returned ten-fold.

"Rock, I—"

"What's your favorite song?" he asked, and the sudden change in topic combined with the darkness and her nearly paralyzing fear to make her dizzy. Er, *dizzier*. Because she already felt like she was sitting in the middle of a merry-go-round while some sadistic mofo pushed the ride faster and faster and *faster*…

Her stomach dropped down to hang somewhere in the vicinity of her knees.

"I don't—" She shook her head, wondering if there were fireflies inside the tree trunk or if those flashing lights were simply tricks her mind was playing on her. She *was* holding her breath, after all, and the ol' gray matter had to be getting frighteningly low on oxygen.

"When you're alone in the shower, what do you sing?" he pressed.

"Uh," she wracked her under-oxygenated brain and could come up with only one thing. "I guess…" She raked in a deep breath and, yep, no fireflies. But the world was still spiraling out of control. "I guess I always sing 'Sweet Child O' Mine.'"

She was surprised by the sound of his deep chuckle. Really? He was laughing and talking inanely about what songs she sang in the shower? At a time like this? Was he insane?

"Guns N' Roses, eh? Somebody's been spending too much time around Ozzie."

And, oh crap. Just the thought of the Black Knights' resident techno-geek—and his penchant for '80s hair bands—made her miss home so much that tears burned behind her eyes. What she wouldn't give to hear Boss and Becky arguing right now, or see Steady Soto thumping out an unconscious rhythm with his pencil as he sat hunched over a medical journal at the conference table, or taste the foulness that passed for coffee back at the chop shop. Instead, she was here, inside this decaying tree. In the capital D-A-R-K.

Her heartbeat, which had begun to slow just a tad with thoughts of home, kicked itself into overdrive once again.

Then the sound of Rock's soft voice drifted from the blackness. "*She's got a smile that seems to me…*"

She'd heard him sing before, knew he had the voice of an angel. In fact, anytime he'd taken out his guitar to strum and sing around the fire pit in the courtyard back at BKI headquarters, she'd found herself mesmerized. But here? In the confines of this hollowed-out log? Man, that sweet baritone sounded like a benediction. She closed her eyes, concentrating on the sound of his voice with every fiber of her being.

And, surprisingly, it helped. Her heartbeat slowed, her lungs filled with oxygen, and the world around ceased doing its best impression of a carousel.

"Come on, *ma petite*," he coaxed. "Sing with me."

She opened her mouth, not surprised by the wobbliness of her voice when she joined him in the second verse. And by the time they came to the chorus, she was feeling much better. Much…*stronger*.

"That's good," he said. "Now you just keep on singin'. And by the time you get to the last line, I'll be back."

He slipped away and her voice broke, but then she heard him murmur in the dark. "Just keep on singin', *chere*."

Pulling her knees to her chest, squeezing herself into a ball, she kept on singing.

Just singing and singing and singing. Concentrating on the lyrics. Keeping the beat inside her head. Listening to the rustle of foliage as he worked outside to cover their tracks. And just as the last *sweet child o' mine* slipped past her lips, she felt him beside her. Still, she jumped when he wrapped an arm around her shoulders to give her a reassuring squeeze. "Shhh," he whispered soothingly before quickly moving away again.

A *clacking* sound told her he was checking his weapons, probably emptying them and the clips of water. A soft *clinking* indicated he'd found some sort of rag and was hurriedly wiping the pistols down.

Which was rule number one for any operator: take care of your weapons first, the hysterical woman about to have a conniption fit second.

She tried; she really tried to keep it together. But the darkness was still there and it was suffocating her, and just as she was about to lose it, his pack dropped to the tarp with a soft *thud*. A second later he was coaxing her to lie back and stretch out beside him. Wrapping his arm around her, he pressed her cheek against his chest, and his shirt, even though it was wet, was warm. It smelled comfortingly of healthy man, laundry detergent, and clean jungle water.

"How did you know to do that?" she whispered, her voice amplified by the close walls of the hollow tree.

"Do what?"

"Get me to sing. How did you know that would help me?"

For a long moment, he said nothing. Then, slowly, "It's…it's all part of my education and training. See, I studied psychology in college and after that I was…*disciplined*, I guess is a good way to say it, to watch people, to look for clues as to what makes them tick. So, I noticed how sound affects you, how you wince when Becky fires up her grinder, or how you jump and beat back a shiver whenever Boss bellows in that deep voice of his. Tone, pitch, resonance…You pick up on all those subtle variations. Of course, even without the training, I'd have known you had quite an ear on you. I mean, how could you be so phenomenal at learnin' new languages if you didn't? But it's more than that. You actually *feel* sounds.

Like other people feel pleasure or pain, you have a visceral, physical reaction to noises."

She stilled, her breath hitching, because…that was the first time anyone had ever described it to her that way. And it was so spot-on she wondered how she'd never thought of it before.

"Which is why music, why harmony soothes you," he went on. "You probably don't even realize the way your shoulders relax whenever someone turns on the radio, particularly if it's a song you like. Your whole demeanor changes, becomes calmer."

Amazing. He was absolutely amazing.

"Who…who taught you to do that?" she asked. "Who taught you how to see those things?"

"Truth of the matter is, I don't know."

"What?" she pushed up from his chest in order to look at him, which was completely silly since she couldn't see a damned thing.

And suddenly the darkness was back, reaching inside her, squeezing her heart and lungs in a black fist.

Oh, geez. Oh, geez. Please, Lord, not again.

The fear made her weak and useless, and she absolutely *hated* that. But, try as she might, there was nothing she could do about it.

Rock must have sensed the change in her, because he pressed her head back to his chest and whispered, "Shhh. It's okay. We're all right."

Uh-huh. Sure. *He* might be all right. But she was definitely *not*.

The chattering of her teeth must've clued him in to this fact, because the next words out of his mouth were, "You wanna tell me about it?"

"About what?" She fisted her hands together, trying to keep the memories as bay.

"About what happened to make you so afraid of the dark," he murmured, his voice so quiet it was only audible because her ear was a few inches from his mouth. "You want to tell me about that?"

No. She most certainly did not. She didn't talk about the accident. Ever. With anyone. Which was why she was so surprised when the words, "I was with my parents when they died in a car wreck five years ago," tumbled out of her mouth in one long, shaky breath.

Whoa. Had she really just said that? Out loud?

She waited for him to respond, to say the words she'd heard so many times, from so many people, especially in the days after the accident...*I'm so sorry, Vanessa. How awful for you...*Sorry? Awful? That didn't come close to describing it. And because those words were all so ineffectual, because in the end they were meaningless since nothing could change what had happened, they had become a knife, slicing into her brain and slashing her composure to pieces any time someone offered them up.

But dreadful seconds ticked by and Rock didn't say anything, just pulled her closer, anchoring her against his warm, reassuringly solid side as his thumb gently rubbed a circle in the fabric of her sleeve.

So, okay...

Maybe she could...maybe she could do this.

"We were..." she licked her suddenly dry lips, trying and failing to slow the rapid slideshow of images burning through her brain. "We were in Doylestown, Pennsylvania, visiting my aunt for Christmas. On the way back to the hotel, we...we hit a patch of ice on a bridge. My dad was driving." And she remembered the sound of her mother screaming in the passenger seat as they blasted through the guardrail and catapulted over the edge, remembered the look of horror and soul-tearing regret on her father's face as it was reflected in the rearview mirror. "We went over the side and into the river. I was in the backseat and that's—" Her voice hitched and she had to swallow the lump of torment and grief that lodged in her throat. "That's the only thing that saved me."

Again, he said nothing, just held her close, rubbing that circle on her arm. The motion, and the accompanying soft rasp of the fabric of her sleeve, was soothing, almost hypnotic. It gave her the strength to go on despite the fact that the memories were so close to the surface her skin actually crawled, like she was covered with fire ants.

"The nose of the car buried itself into the riverbed and stuck there. The water was only about six feet deep, slow moving, and with a thick layer of ice covering the top. I slammed into the door and window on impact. It knocked me out."

And, oh, the horror of coming to. Of knowing…

"When I regained consciousness, I was hanging from the seatbelt, my arm broken, the water only a foot from my face."

She heard him exhale slowly in the darkness. And, yeah, he could probably guess what came next. "I knew my parents were under that water, but my seatbelt was jammed. No matter how hard I tried, I couldn't get it undone. And, with my arm so severely broken, I couldn't slither out of the straps either. I struggled so hard for so l-long—" Her voice broke. The memories of the crushing ache in her arm—that hadn't come close to the debilitating pain in her heart—washed over her in a tidal wave. Even though her rational mind had told her there was nothing she could do for her parents, some instinct inside her, some animalist drive had spurred her to fight with everything she had. She'd understood in those moments how wild animals chewed through their feet to free themselves from hunters' traps. The urge to live was as intrinsic as it was intense. And the urge to save those she loved was stronger still. But, in the end, she'd been helpless. Infuriatingly, pathetically helpless…

"But I couldn't get free," she finally finished. "So I just…I just h-hung there, slowly freezing to death."

He lowered his chin to place a soft kiss on the crown of her head but didn't so much as utter a sound. No words of sympathy or condolence. And it was like he somehow knew this was the first time she'd been brave enough to speak of the accident, been brave enough to relive it. As if he understood that any little thing, any word or sudden movement, would make her lose her nerve again.

"I…I stayed that way for an hour, in the pitch black, listening to the water trickling by beneath me, knowing all the time…" She had to stop. Had to take a second to slow the dizzying excess of oxygen entering her lungs with every rapid breath. Because if she didn't get control right now, the next stop on this crazy train of emotional upheaval was a little place she liked to call Dead Faint. So, she closed her eyes, held her breath, and slowly counted to ten.

It was a trick she'd learned as a child and, more often than not, it actually worked. This was no exception. By the time she reached nine, her head no longer felt as if it was floating away from her shoulders. "Knowing all the time that my parents were dead only a couple of feet away."

And she'd screamed. Screamed until her throat was bloody. Screamed for help. Screamed in horror. Screamed at the gut-wrenching sorrow that'd invaded her soul like a foul, acrid disease. Just...screamed...

But no one had heard her. And when she couldn't scream any more, when no more sound could escape her swollen, ravaged throat, she'd silently continued screaming in her head.

"Finally, a passing car saw the broken guardrail and called it in. The local fire department cut me loose and fished me out of the river but, of course, it was too late for my parents." She finished the rest in a rush. "And ever since that night, anytime it's dark like this, I feel like I'm back there. Stuck in that car. Unable to see, but knowing all the same that the two people I love most are dead and gone."

And, there. She'd done it. She'd told the story. She couldn't *believe* she'd actually had the guts to finally tell the story.

She was in the middle of congratulating herself, blowing out a relieved breath and patting herself on the back, when Rock finally spoke. But his words were not what she expected. "Go on. There's more."

More? There wasn't any more. She'd told him—

"Tell me more about the darkness," he said, and despite the sultry heat inside the log, a harsh chill slipped up her spine.

She swallowed, the sound clicking in her dry throat. He grabbed her hand and flattened it over his chest until she could feel the firm beat of his heart against her palm. It steadied her. And when she pressed her ear to his chest, the slow, unwavering drum of his heartbeat grounded her enough to admit, shakily, "I...I feel like it's...I don't know, out to get me or something. Like it missed me that night on the river, and it's just...just *waiting* to finish the job."

And until she said the words, she hadn't realized that was what she was afraid of.

Her racing blood slowed to a halt, and she stilled, searching inside herself. And the harder she looked, the more she peeled back the thick layers of her psyche, the more she realized, *yes*. Yes, that's exactly what had been haunting her for the last half decade...

Okay, and *seriously*? She'd installed nightlights all over her loft-style bedroom back at BKI, broke out in a cold sweat anytime she was inadvertently caught out in the night, and squirreled away flashlights all over the shop because she was afraid the dark was, like, what? *Alive?* That it was a sentient being purposefully and personally stalking her?

Jesus Christ! Was she crazy?

Abruptly the fingers of darkness that'd been squeezing her heart and lungs withdrew. The weight of the blackness pushing in around her suddenly felt less oppressive.

Holy crap! That's all it took? Just to put a name to it and, *poof*, the fear was gone? She looked inward again, seeking that paralyzing terror, the sense of impending doom, but...nothing.

Oh, the pitch black wasn't comfortable by any means. It still brought back stark memories of that night. But now she could look at the whole experience without nearly blacking out from fear. Now she could view it rationally and see it simply for the heartbreaking tragedy it was and—

Holy, holy, *holy* crap!

"How do you *do* that?" she breathed.

"Like I said, it's my training."

"It's more than that," she whispered, awed and grateful at the same time. "It's a gift."

She felt him shrug.

For long seconds after that mind-blowing revelation, they remained silent. Then, he murmured, "I *am* sorry about your folks. It's tough to be an orphan, no matter what your age."

Orphan…And, yep, that's all it took for the dam to break.

The tears she hadn't realized she'd been holding back threatened to overflow. Turning her face into his chest, she fisted the fabric of his wet tank top into balls beside her cheeks and tried to steady herself. But she couldn't. Especially not when Rock whispered softly, "It's okay to let go, *chere*. There's no one here but you and me."

Uh-huh. And, just like that, she could no longer pretend she was tougher than she really was. Then Vanessa did something she never, *ever* allowed herself to do in front of anyone…

She cried.

And it wasn't one of those tragic, lip-quivering, slow-crocodile-tear cries either. The kind most actresses perfected. Oh, no. This was a full-on, ball-your-eyes-out, tears-and-snot-everywhere kind of deal.

It was humiliating and liberating at the same time.

Humiliating because, come on, this was *Rock*. The one man on the entire planet she wanted to impress with her grace and poise and strength. Liberating because finally saying the words out loud, telling the tale and admitting to the root of her fear was freeing in a way she could have never imagined. Letting someone else share in the horror of her experience, having someone hold a mirror up in front of her face so she could address the foolishness of her irrational fear, relieved her of a burden she hadn't known she'd been carrying around like a two-ton bolder of shame.

Pushing up from his chest, she wiped a shaky hand across her eyes and beneath her nose. "Thank you," she breathed.

"*De rien*," he whispered—*you're welcome*—and, oh, sweet merciful Lord, his mouth was right there.

She couldn't see it in the dark—she couldn't see *anything*, which for the first time in years didn't scare the living crap out of her—but she could feel his lips moving, could feel the heat of his breath.

And, suddenly, she didn't care about the impropriety of the situation. She didn't care that he'd made it quite clear there could never be anything permanent between them. She didn't even care that there were men skulking through the jungle outside, looking for the first opportunity to blast an extra hole in each of their heads. All she cared about was this moment, when she had him exactly where she'd always wanted him.

Without a second thought, she reached up to fist her hand in his short hair and pressed her lips against the lush pad of his mouth. His stubble tickled her nose and chin; she could taste hints of the papaya he'd eaten for dinner on his breath, and—

Okay, so this was obviously a big mistake.

Because the man did a pretty good impression of a brick wall. He didn't move. He didn't even appear to breathe. And his lips were sealed shut like he'd applied the ChapStick version of Krazy Glue.

Yep, in the Great Handbook of Kisses, this was going to go down under the title *Worst One Ever*.

And just as she was about to pull back and apologize for what was obviously a stupendously dumbass move, his mouth softened and the tip of his tongue swept over the seam of her lips. A hot flower of desire bloomed low in her abdomen, and opening her mouth to him was instinctual. Of course, the part where she sucked on his tongue was totally deliberate. And what had started out as tame quickly became tumultuous.

He growled deep in his chest—the resulting rumble against her breasts was delicious—and slid his hand down her waist in order to pull her on top of him. Her thighs fell to either side of his lean hips, her pelvis cradling the stark evidence of his desire. And, just like that, the traffic light blinked from red to green, and they were a *go*!

Teeth and tongues and hands everywhere.

Sucking, licking, laving…

He grabbed her ass with both hands and ground her against his erection. The friction was unbelievable and so delicious it had her toes curling inside her boots.

Once he realized she was more than happy to oblige him in the bump-and-grind they had going, he released her ass to snake a hand between their bodies so he could undo the buttons on her shirt. She lifted herself slightly, to give him room to work, and then…

Bliss.

The rough pad of his thumb found the aroused bead of her nipple even through the ACE bandage she'd wrapped around her chest in order to flatten her breasts. He pinched it gently, coaxing it into an even harder point, and a longing whimper sounded in the back of her throat.

This was what she'd wanted for months. To push past his barriers. To get him to drop his guard. Because she'd always known it would be like this between them. Explosive and succulent and—

A rustling outside alerted them to the fact that they were no longer alone in this part of the jungle…

Chapter Six

"SHIT, EVE," BILL GROWLED AS THE LADY OF THE HOUSE bent to set a plate full of little sandwiches, all with the crusts cut off—*how sweet*—on the coffee table. He slammed shut the copy of *To Kill a Mockingbird* he'd be reading—or, more accurately, *trying* to read. Usually losing himself in a classic calmed his nerves, but he figured nothing short of a lobotomy was going to come close to mitigating his anxiety when Eve was in the same room. "This isn't a goddamned cocktail party, so you can stop playing the attentive hostess."

"Leave her alone, Billy," Becky snarled from her position at the other end of the sofa. Her livid expression crowned him King of the Assholes more eloquently than any words could. Still, she felt the need to follow that up with, "And quit being such an asshole."

"It's okay, Becky," Eve said in that cultured voice of hers that always just…just *got* to him. And that was the kicker, wasn't it? That despite everything, despite the fact that she'd booted him to the curb well over a decade ago, he still hadn't found another woman who could get to him the way Eve Edens could.

Not that he hadn't tried. Especially in the six months since she'd crashed back into his life…

Oh, yeah. It was official. He was quickly outpacing both Ozzie and Steady when it came bagging babes, which was really saying something since, between the two of those bastards, there wasn't a barmaid or hostess left in Chicago who hadn't taken a…*ride*, if you will…on one or both of the Black Knights. And yet for Bill…?

Nothing. Nada. Zilch.

Not *one* of the women who'd shared his bed in the last six months, not to mention the scores—okay, maybe not scores, but certainly more than his fair share—who'd shared his bed in the last ten or so years had inspired the kind of passion that Eve managed to inspire just by walking into the room.

"Billy can't help himself where I'm concerned," she finished, smiling down at him sadly and, yeah, so maybe he *was* king of the assholes. Because it wasn't her fault he'd been young and dumb and unable to see that she'd only been tiptoeing on the wild side, taking a little spin around the block with the bad boy from the wrong side of town before settling on someone more appropriate.

God*damn*it!

"But just so we're clear," she continued, holding his gaze, and *that* was something new. The Eve he'd known years ago was as shy as a church mouse on a Sunday morning. But this new Eve? Well, *she* was showing a backbone made of pure, forged steel. And, *sonofabitch*, that just made him want her more. "I cook because it soothes me. I'm not yelling at you for reading that book and telling you this isn't a…a *gosh darned*"—now *that* was the Eve he knew; the one who blushed anytime she tried to curse—"library visit."

"You're right," he told her, meeting her wide eyes unhesitatingly. Eve had always reminded him of a china doll. Milky-white skin, jet-black hair, eyes as clear and deep as sapphires, and a fragility that brought out the

Neanderthal in him. "I'm sorry. I shouldn't take out my frustration on you."

She blinked like he'd just sprouted a second head from his ear. And, yeah, so he was probably overdue on quite a few of the apologies he owed her.

"Well...I...well...okay, then," she sputtered and turned to make her way back toward the kitchen. He watched her walk away and gave himself over to the sheer joy of examining the graceful movement of her long, tan legs. That is, until his sister interrupted his pursuit.

"I don't understand why you have to do that," she said. When he turned to glance at her, Becky was wearing "the look." The one that informed him a lecture was coming.

He hoped to head it off. "You heard me apologize, right?"

"I heard you. I'm just not sure I believe you. Why can't you just forget about it? It was a lifetime ago."

"Maybe I'm just no good at letting go of grudges," he admitted. But he knew that was only partially true. Because no matter how hard he'd tried, the fact remained that what he wasn't good at was letting go of Eve.

"Yeah. And maybe you're just an asshole."

He shrugged then fought a smile because he knew just how to derail his sister from this current line of badgering. Clearing his throat, he said in his best orator's voice, "You never really understand a person until you consider things from his point of view—until you climb into his skin and walk around in it."

Becky rolled her eyes. "And that would be from...?"

He picked up the book from his lap and turned it so she could see the cover. "Atticus Finch, baby. A man of inordinately wise words."

"That's a really annoying habit you have."

"Which one? Being an asshole or quoting classic literature?"

"Both."

He winked and was rewarded when one corner of her sullen mouth twitched. She could never stay mad at him for very long. That was the thing about Becky. She could blow up quicker than a stick of dynamite, but her anger always burned out just as quickly.

She reached for one of the sandwiches Eve had delivered, just as Boss strolled into the room. Bill went on instant alert. Boss's face looked like a thundercloud on a good day—thanks, in part, to a bevy of scars—but today? Well, today it looked like an F5 tornado.

A stone of dread settled at the bottom of his stomach, and he figured it wouldn't be long before his ulcer started acting up again.

"General Fuller confirmed a CIA operation over Monteverde Cloud Forest," Boss announced. "Says there's nothing he can do about it. His recommendation is for us to convince Rock to turn himself in."

Yeah, right.

"Not likely," Bill snorted. "Even if there was a way to contact him, Rock would rather die in the jungle with a bullet in his brain than rot away in an eight-by-ten."

"Dying in the jungle with a bullet in his brain is looking more and more likely," Boss scowled. "Those teams have orders to shoot on sight."

"Sonofabitch." Bill shook his head, wondering, again, how it had come to this. Surely Rock wouldn't—

"Still no word from Vanessa?" Boss asked, breaking into Bill's thoughts.

"Nope," he glanced over at the end table and the blank

screen of his cell phone. "It appears she still has her phone turned off."

Boss nodded and ran a big hand back through his hair. Then he turned to survey the room as if it had the answer to the question he asked next. "Any idea how they, the CIA, I mean, found them?"

"If I had to guess," Bill mused, running a finger under his chin, "I'd say that despite her disguise, and despite all her precautions, somehow Vanessa was followed. And then maybe she got herself tagged while she was in Santa Elena."

"That was my thinking, too," Boss nodded. "I guess we didn't give those spooks enough credit, huh?"

"Guess not," Bill agreed. "Which is why we need Zoelner"—the Black Knights' resident ex-CIA operative—"down here to fill us in on their operating procedures. Any luck getting in touch with him?"

Besides the General, Boss had put out a war cry to all the Knights. Telling those who weren't currently on a mission to get their asses to Costa Rica ASAP.

"Nope. He's incommunicado in Syria. And even if he could manage to cross the border to Turkey, it'd take him nearly forty hours to get here. And I don't mean to go all Han Solo on your ass, but I got a bad feeling this is all gonna be over long before that. Goddamnit!" His jaw hardened until the scar cutting up from the corner of his lip went stark white. "I knew we never should've let Vanessa go in there alone. She isn't trained for this shit."

At this point Becky piped up with, "Now, come on, Frank. You know that was the best option we had at the time. We couldn't *all* go traipsing over to Santa Elena after she jumped the gun. And she was right, you know.

She *was* the only one of us capable of speaking the native languages, of blending in with the locals and asking the right questions."

Boss had nearly shit a brick when Vanessa decided to pull a Lone Ranger—minus Tonto—on them. Taking it into her fool head to track Rock on her own before they'd agreed on the specifics of an exfiltration strategy. But to follow her would've raised more than a few eyebrows, so they'd been left with no other option but to let her do her thing. And, miracle of miracles, she'd actually found the guy.

Unfortunately, it appeared the CIA had found *her*.

Boss was right. She wasn't trained for this shit. But there was nothing to be done for that now.

Boss blew out a hard breath, "Yeah? And now I not only have one, but *two* operators out there with their heads on the chopping block."

"Rock won't let anything happen to Vanessa," Bill assured him, as certain of that fact as he was that Eve was in the kitchen cursing him to hell. Because no matter what Rock had done…scratch that, no matter what the government was *saying* he'd done, he would never let harm come to a woman under his protection. "He'll die before he allows her to get hurt."

"Yeah," Boss grimaced. "And that's exactly what I'm afraid of."

Snap. Crack. The sound of footfalls in the undergrowth drew closer.

And it was back to being a brick wall for Rock. He stilled beneath Vanessa, his chest, which moments before had been heaving with passion, barely moved. She followed suit, raking in a shallow, silent breath as her heart clenched into a tight ball of fear.

Had Rock been wrong? Had the hit teams already made it down this far? Or was that just an animal out there…?

The air inside the hollow tree felt too dense to breathe, like she was sucking molasses into her lungs.

Schick. Tick.

Oh, shitballs, whatever it was, it was big. And, as if on cue, a snuffling sound reached her ears, followed closely by a barking grunt.

Jaguar.

Vanessa's stomach flipped as every hair on her head stood on end.

Just an animal? *Just?* Had she really been foolish enough to have that thought? Because there was no *just* when it came to a friggin' two-hundred-pound jungle cat with razor sharp teeth and two inch claws.

"Don't. Move." Rock whispered.

Yeah, she hadn't planned on it.

She felt him reach down beneath her thigh, and for a moment she entertained the crazy notion that he was going to try to pick up where they'd left off. And if they were, indeed, seconds away from being devoured by the big cat, she couldn't say she really blamed him. At least they'd both die happy, doing something pleasurable. But then the hard steel of a gun barrel kissed the inside of her leg.

Okay so they'd likely survive the cat. A couple of slugs from Rock's SIG would insure that. Unfortunately the resulting gunfire would undoubtedly bring hell raining down on them in the form of the teams of men currently scouring the jungle.

It seemed their luck was holding steady. Because this was definitely a lose/lose situation.

"He smells the blood," Rock murmured.

Blood? What blood?

"What are you talking about?" she breathed into the darkness, her nearly silent words still managing to sound like a shout inside the hollowed-out log.

"From my neck."

Huh?

She reached up, careful not to make so much as a sound, and felt the neck in question. Her fingers raked across a long, deep gash and came away sticky with blood. "*Jesus*, Rock," she hissed, "are you hit? Why didn't you tell me?"

"No." She could feel him shaking his head. "Just a sliver of wood from a tree."

Like that was *so* much better. Because bullet or wood-chip didn't make a damned bit of difference when it came to nearly severing your jugular.

"Slowly," he instructed, "I need you to slide off me. I hear him comin' 'round to the base of the log."

And that was bad. Because if *they* could squeeze inside the tree, the jaguar would have no problem doing the same. The thought of that big cat in here with them was just too horrifying to contemplate.

Vanessa carefully rolled off Rock onto her side, barely completing the maneuver when she felt him scoot down toward the mouth of the log.

"Be careful," she whispered, and immediately rolled her eyes as she thought. *Well, that's ridiculous advice.* Like what else would he be?

"Don't scream," he retorted, which had her heart— the sucker had just recovered from the initial shock to start beating again—once more screeching to a halt. She actually fancied she could hear a *scriiiiitch* echo in the darkness.

When someone warned you not to scream, it was generally followed up by something truly scream-worthy.

She bit her lip until the pain made her eyes water, but even then, she didn't unclench her jaw. She figured it was better to chew the sucker right off than take a chance of letting so much as a peep slip out of her mouth.

The seconds ticked by, and the snuffling around the entrance to their hideout grew louder until Vanessa thought she'd go crazy waiting for whatever it was she wasn't supposed to scream at to happen. Then she heard a loud *thump* followed immediately by an earsplitting yowl.

And *that* was what Rock had warned her about. Because the unholy, pissed-off roar that echoed outside was enough to raise the hair on the back of her neck and make goose bumps break out on her arms while a reactionary shriek lodged in the middle of her throat.

"After that boot to the head, he'll think twice about sticking his nose in here again," Rock said. She could make out the soft shush of his cargo pants brushing against the tarp as he scooted back to her. "Now, I'm gonna have to go out and erase the big cat's tracks. If those teams heard that yowl, they're gonna wonder if it has to do with us."

"Y-yeah, okay," she said, heart beating a mile a minute.

"You gonna be all right in here by yourself?" She could hear the worry in his voice.

"Yes," she was proud to say. Even prouder when she realized it was the truth. For years she'd lived in constant terror of a place and situation exactly like this, but all it'd taken was ten minutes of being subjected to Rock's astonishing brand of psychoanalysis and she was, maybe not cured, but at the minimum drastically improved.

Of course, that didn't do a thing to alleviate her terror for the safety of the man's hide when he exited the hollow tree to begin silently covering the jaguar's tracks. The whole time he was out there, exposed, images of the big cat launching itself from the nearest tree to sink razor-sharp fangs into Rock's jugular played like a horror show inside her head. Over and over again, she saw it happening. Cat. Launch. Claws. Teeth. Blood. And just when she'd had enough, when she was going to have to go out there and see for herself that he was okay, the greenery at the mouth of the log rustled and the air thickened as Rock scooted inside.

"Is he…" she began but stopped when she discovered someone had dumped a bucket of sand down her throat. She swallowed, trying to work up some saliva to battle the dryness, and tried again. "Is he gone?"

"For now." She closed her eyes, whispering a silent prayer of thanks into the darkness. "And one good thing about his arrival: now we know the hit squad isn't anywhere close. That cat wouldn't come within a hundred yards of a big group of men like that."

Okay, as far as silver linings went, she guessed that was a pretty good one. Blowing out a blustery breath, tilting her head from side-to-side to try to work out the kinks in her neck, she reached for him in the darkness. Now that they'd averted one crisis, it was time to deal with another. "So I guess it would be a good time to get a bandage on that cut before you bleed to death."

Chapter Seven

VANESSA'S SMALL HAND LANDED ON HIS FOREARM, AND Rock tried and failed to ignore the fact that her palm was warm and smooth and sending little electrical jolts all through his body.

He should *not* have kissed her. And the last thing he should be thinking about right now was kissing her again. But that's exactly what he was doing.

Thinking about kissing her. Kissing her and a whole hell of a lot more.

Mon dieu, but she'd been hot. A burning flame in his arms. Sexy and lusty and...*feminine.* She was soft in all the right places, firm in all the rest, and it boggled his goddamned mind that she'd even stop to give him the time of day.

Oh, not because he wasn't used to getting attention from women, even beautiful women. He may not have Snake's surfer-boy good looks or Ozzie's movie-star profile, but he'd gotten more than his fair share of *les jolies filles* over the years, especially when he'd been with the Teams...

Oh, mama, had those ever been the days. When there'd been plenty of base bunnies only too happy to overlook his thick Cajun accent and lean, rangy body in order to say they'd bagged themselves an honest-to-goodness Navy SEAL.

But, unfortunately, since starting Black Knights Inc., his pace in the, uh, *bunny* department had slowed considerably. And more recently, ever since he'd been on the run—no, that wasn't true; it was ever since they'd hired Vanessa—that pace had screeched to a full stop. Because every time he tried to take a woman home from the bar or local cantina, he was stopped by visions of long, inky-black hair, dark, flashing eyes, and an ass that didn't know the meaning of the word *quit*.

And *that* scared him like a hound pissing peach pits. Because had that jaguar not showed up when it did, he'd likely be buried balls-deep in her sweet feminine warmth right at this very moment. And though the act would've undoubtedly been one of the most pleasurable experiences of his entire sorry life, it would've also been a mistake on too many levels to count…Because despite the fact that her actions had been screaming, *Ride me, cowboy. Hard and fast*—which, wouldn't you know, just happened to be his particular specialty—he was fully aware that, deep down inside, Vanessa was the "forever" type of girl. So if he'd given in to the lust that'd momentarily grabbed hold of them, he'd have given her hope there could be a future for the two of them when there absolutely could *not*.

He pulled away from her gentle touch, shaking his head even though she couldn't see him. "The wound is nothin'," he told her brusquely. Was that his voice that sounded like a rusty hinge? "The blood's already drying."

"Yes," she dragged the *s* out on the end of the word. "But here in the jungle, the smallest cut can lead to massive infection. We need to get that thing cleaned, dried, and bandaged."

She had a point. But if she put her hands on him again…Good Lord. He reckoned he'd be toast.

"All right, fine. But I'll do it myself."

She made a tsk-ing sound, and her hand landed on his forearm again only to start on a slow, agonizing journey up his bare arm. The erection he'd managed to beat back when the jaguar arrived on the scene swelled with new life.

Merde. This woman's gonna be the death of me!

He grabbed her hand and tossed it away, trying to ignore her surprised hiss. "I'm serious." His harsh tone declared the topic closed for discussion. "I'll do it myself."

The resounding silence following that statement let him know more clearly than words ever could that he'd gone and hurt her feelings.

Well, *bon*. If she considered him a prick of legendary proportions, she'd be only too happy to see the backside of him once he returned her pretty ass to the Knights. And it was better to suffer some hurt feelings now than all-out heartbreak later on.

"Suit yourself," she finally huffed, and he figured it was mission accomplished on the whole getting-her-to-think-he-was-a-prick front. A rustling sound alerted him that she'd picked up his pack, but he was still caught off guard when it slammed into the center of the chest. The breath shot out of him in a harsh *oof* and, despite himself, he felt a smile curve his lips.

Mon dieu, he liked her. Considered her damn near perfect, in fact. Because along with being tough and beautiful and lusty, she was also spunky as hell. The combination was Kryptonite to his Superman. Which was just one more reason why he had to make sure he didn't encourage any more bouts of tongue wrestling—*Lord have mercy, can that woman ever kiss*! He was already too far gone where she was concerned.

"Thanks," he wheezed, digging into his pack, fishing for the antibiotic wipes and self-adhesive bandages he'd packed.

"Oh, you're very welcome." The sneer on her face was apparent in her tone, and it occurred to him, as he broke open a pack of wipes, that since she was already pissed, it was probably a good time to go all in.

"And about that kiss," he said, hissing when he wiped the antibiotic cloth across his cut. It burned like the fires of hell.

Appropriate, considering that's probably where he was headed someday.

"Yeah? What about it?"

For a moment, he was too busy blinking back tears of pain to speak. Glad, for once, for the complete darkness inside the log lest she realize what a goddamned sissy he really was. *Zut! Just give me some bubble bath and a tampon. I think I'm officially part of the estrogen party.*

Then he managed, "It can't happen again."

"Don't you worry about that," she snapped. "The way you're acting right now, not only do I have no plans to kiss you again, but you'll be lucky if I don't suffocate you in your sleep."

He smiled.

Funny. He'd forgotten to add that to his list of reasons why he thought she was perfect. Tough and beautiful, lusty and spunky...and funny.

Goddamnit!

"I'm serious." He had to work hard to keep his voice stern.

"So am I," she shot back without missing a beat.

"Vanessa," he warned.

"Richard," she mimicked his tone, but the sound of his

given name on her lips had his stomach turning a fast, dizzying somersault.

No one called him Richard. Not anymore. Not after his parents. Not after Lacy…

Words abandoned him, so he busied himself with the bandage's adhesive strips. Carefully peeling them away, he found the outer edges of the cut on his neck and centered the dressing over the top of it. Pressing the medicated pad in place, he wondered what she was doing. She was awfully quiet over there. Too quiet.

What's she thinking?

Of course, when she opened her mouth, he decided he'd have preferred it if she kept her thoughts to herself. "Just out of curiosity, *why* can't we do that again?"

He knew what she was after, but he still asked, "Do what?"

"Kiss."

And just the word, spoken from those heart-shaped lips of hers, felt like an intimacy, like a single finger running up the length of his dick, like a wet tongue sliding—

Jesus! He was a lost cause.

"Because we're coworkers," he said and wished he could call the excuse back the moment it left his mouth. It was so lame it only opened up an avenue of argument. And, *oui*, just as he expected…

"That's ridiculous," she huffed. "Just look at Boss and Becky. And, last I checked, we aren't coworkers anymore. You haven't drawn a BKI paycheck in months."

She had him there. So that left…the truth. Even though he knew it was going to hurt.

"Well, then, we can't do it again because you've got orange blossoms in your eyes, *chere*. And since I'm not the kind of man who would take advantage of a woman, it's best we just keep our hands, and everything else, to ourselves."

"Who says you'd be taking advantage?"

She was like a goddamned dog with a bone. The stubborn, willful, *wonderful* woman.

"I do," he insisted. "I'm not likely to make it out of this mess alive and—"

"Pfft," she cut him off. "Don't be ridiculous. *Of course*, you're going to make it out of this thing alive. Now that we've found you, we'll all help you clear your name. And once that's done—"

"What makes you so sure my name *can* be cleared?" He made sure his tone was unmistakable.

For a long moment, silence echoed more loudly than a gunshot through the hollow log.

"I don't believe what they're saying about you," she finally whispered. But he could hear the note of hesitation in her voice. Good. As long as she had the slightest hint of a doubt, letting him go once he got her back to San Jose would be just that much easier. "And you're trying to change the subject." Um, busted. "We were discussing the reason why we can't act on this…this *thing* that's between us."

Thing.

Sweet Lord have mercy! It was more than a *thing* for him. It was a goddamned *obsession*. He couldn't shake it. Because every other thought in his head seemed to circle back to the fact that he wanted to know her body.

Every detail of it…

The shape of her hips. The smoothness of the skin behind her knees. The taste of her desire on his lips when he kissed her where she was hot and wet. He wanted to know the way she responded when she was being loved. How she breathed when he kissed her nipples. How she arched when he entered her body. How she moved beneath him, above him. He wanted to know her. It. All of it. All of her...

Which was why he had to nip this thing in the bud. For her sake *and* for his own. It was time, as his dear ol' daddy used to say, to deliver the coup de grâce.

"Okay, let me make it very clear to you, *chere*," he said, his heart pounding for the pain he knew he was going to inflict. But that's the thing about the truth. It hurt. "You have some romantic notion in your head that we could act on this *thing*, as you call it, and then it would grow into something more from there. But I can assure you it won't."

"Why?" The word wasn't timid; it was demanding. The woman had the heart of a lion and he wished, oh how he wished, things could be different.

"Because while I have no doubt I could give you the thrill ride of your life, I can guarantee that's all it'll be. You see, *ma belle*, no matter what, you can't let yourself fall in love with me."

"Why?" That one word again.

"Because I'll never fall in love with you."

––––—*w*––––—

"They've lost contact with the targets."

It was not the news Rwanda Don had hoped to hear upon answering the phone. Squeezing the untraceable device in an angry fist caused the cheap plastic casing to crackle warningly.

"What do you mean? What happened to the RFD on Miss Cordero?"

"It was found attached to a stone some sixty yards from Babineaux's tree house," the CIA agent relayed. "He obviously discovered the thing and disposed of it. And, while the teams were busy following the device's signal, he and Cordero managed to slip away."

Slip away.

Indeed. Just as R.D. suspected might happen.

Goddamn Rock! The man was too smart for his own good. Definitely too smart for R.D.'s peace of mind.

"Any idea where they're headed?"

"Tracks lead into the river, but the teams have found no point of exit. It's suspected Babineaux and Cordero rode the sucker all the way back into Santa Elena…or else they drowned. Parts of that river are very dangerous."

"No." R.D. wasn't sure of many things, but the impossibility of Richard "Rock" Babineaux, all-star ex–Navy SEAL, drowning was one of them. "You know as well as I do, there's no way he drowned. He's still there. Somewhere."

"Mmph," the agent made a noncommittal sound before continuing. "They've called in a backup team to search Santa Elena, and the other two teams are tearing the jungle apart. Don't worry. If Babineaux and Cordero are still alive, they'll find them. We've got three more hours until daybreak in those parts, and they can't hide forever."

R.D. was beginning to have doubts in that respect.

Beginning? What a joke. There'd *always* been doubts that Rock could be caught. The man was too well-equipped and too well-trained. To put it simply, he was *good in the woods*. Which was the military's cutesy way of saying he was a veritable prodigy when it came to jungle recon, battle, and survival.

As a rule, R.D. didn't have much respect for the armed

services. They were too loud, too extravagant, fighting all-out wars when a few well-placed bullets in the heads of very specific people could accomplish the same task. But, occasionally, Uncle Sam popped out a specimen of inordinate intelligence and skill.

Unfortunately for R.D. and the CIA agent who'd personally helped pursue The Project after The Company decided to put the kibosh on it, Rock Babineaux happened to be one of those...

"There's more," the agent went on. "Inside Rock's tree house was a shit-load of intel."

The small seed of fear that'd taken root in R.D.'s stomach upon hearing the initial news that not only was Rock alive and well, but he'd had managed to disappear like a goddamned ghost, bloomed into an ugly flower of chill-inducing terror.

"Wh—" Grabbing a glass of water from the edge of the desk, R.D. took a quick swallow and tried again, "What sort of intel?"

"Reams of information on his targets," the agent declared, discomfort in every word. "I'm talking thousands of documents with red strings connecting this piece of information to that. It looked like *A Beautiful Mind* in that place. Very concerning."

"I want copies of every piece of intel and—"

"Now, hold on a second," the voice on the other end of the line sounded alarmed. "You know I like you and I think it's a shame The Company shit-canned The Project all those years ago. And I've been happy to help you out up until now. But this thing we had going is done. It's over. And I'm only keeping you in the loop now as a favor and because—"

"You're keeping me in the loop because your ass in on the line just as much as mine is. And you *helped me out* because you were greedy and wanted the money The Project could provide you with. So don't try pulling that self-righteous bullshit on me. You forget who you're talking to."

"Fine." The word was spat out like a hunk of rancid meat. "But it's one thing to keep you up-to-date on our activities. It's another thing entirely to funnel copies of top secret documents your way. It's my neck on the line over here."

R.D. sighed in exasperation. "I understand that ever since we sacrificed the funds we took—"

"Stole," the agent interrupted. "Have the balls to call it what it is. We stole those funds."

A blood vessel in R.D.'s temple began to pound. "Fine. I understand that after we had to sacrifice the funds we *stole* from The Project's targets by anonymously donating them to those charities—"

"A goddamned waste of good money, if you ask me," the agent grumbled, and R.D. had the urge to reach through the phone and strangle the fucker.

"Would you stop interrupting me?"

"Why did you have to use that money for the campaign? You know that stuff always gets vetted time and again. It was a stupid—"

Now it was R.D.'s turn to interject. "Shut up! We've gone over this. I made sure to cover my tracks. I spread it out over legitimate sources—"

"Not legitimate enough, obviously. Billingsworth smelled the stench and started nosing around."

Yes, he had. And it was a crying shame.

"What's done is done," R.D. insisted with a growl.

"Now we just have to clean up the mess. Which brings me back to the point that even though you no longer have monetary incentive to continue helping and sharing information with me, you certainly have a personal one. I need to see that intel. You don't have time to go through it piece by piece to make sure Rock didn't find anything that points back at us. I do. Get me the documents."

"Nothing points back to me," the agent announced, a chilling sort of certainty in his voice. "It was *your* twin brother's murderer who was The Project's first target. It was *your* use of the funds for campaign purposes that resulted in Billingsworth needing to die."

It took everything R.D. had to maintain calm. "Have you forgotten it was *you* who pointed the CIA to Rock's post office box after he started nosing around? And, believe me, *partner*, if I go down for this, I'm not doing it alone."

"Are you threatening me?"

R.D. leaned forward, sighing heavily. "Just get me that intel, will you?"

"I'll do what I can," the agent declared, but R.D. detected a note of indecision.

Shit! It couldn't fall apart now. "We need to stick together on this. I…" What R.D. was about to do rankled so badly it necessitated a pause. "I have some money left over from my brother's life insurance policy if that will help you come to the right decision."

"How much?" the agent asked curiously.

A hard stone of hatred settled at the bottom of R.D.'s stomach. "How much will it take?"

Chapter Eight

VANESSA JERKED AWAKE AT THE FEEL OF A HAND ON HER shoulder. She would have squealed, too, had not a warm palm immediately settled over her mouth.

Who? Where—

And that's as far as she got before the memories came flooding back. She was in a hollowed-out log, in the middle of a Costa Rican rainforest, being hunted by the CIA with a man who had no qualms telling her that, while he thought she was hot-to-trot and he wouldn't mind letting her polish his rocket—so to speak—he had absolutely no plans to start anything permanent with her because...and get this...he would *never*—that would be with a capital N, his tone had made that very obvious—fall in love with her.

When he'd blurted that out the night before, she'd sat in the dark struck completely mute. Because, really, what *did* one say to a declaration like that? *Ow*? And, yeah, it had hurt so badly she'd been unable to breathe for long seconds afterward.

But to admit as much to him would've only added to her humiliation, so she'd done the only thing she could think of. She'd pulled herself together, bolstered her tattered pride and said, "Well, okay then." And immediately followed that up with, "Do you have anything to eat in that pack?"

Not that she'd been hungry, of course. Quite the

contrary. The granola bar he'd handed her had gone down about as easy as a handful of woodchips dipped in habanero sauce, but she'd managed, by God. Because she'd been determined not to let him see how much he'd wounded her.

And in keeping with that line of thinking, this morning she pushed his hand away from her mouth and whispered in what she was proud to say was a completely firm and completely *non*-pride-shredded voice, "Holy shitburgers, I can't believe I actually slept." *Especially not with you stretched out beside me, each one of your breaths echoing in the darkness and reminding me that, no matter what my fantasies, you'll never be the man for me.*

Yeah, she went ahead and left that last part out.

"It's the adrenaline wearin' off," he murmured, and *his* voice was rock steady, too.

Well, goody. We're both just hunky-dory after last night's little Come-to-Jesus chat.

Great. Perfect…

Goddamnit!

She pushed into a sitting position, trying to beat back the humiliation that threatened to choke her even as she blinked owlishly in the dimness. No longer was the inside of the hollowed-out tree pitch black. Subtle light drifted through the small breaks in the dense foliage over the opening. And despite her having named her fear—and, in the process, found a way to, maybe not *beat* it per se, but at least mitigate it—the break in the inky blackness was a welcome reprieve.

Well, at least one thing seems to be going my way…

"We need to get movin'," he declared, stuffing all the trash, the granola bar wrappers and empty pouches of antiseptic wipes, into his pack.

Vanessa highly suspected his actions had little to do with the fact that he was conscientious about leaving the jungle unspoiled and more to do with the fact that rule number one when trying to outfox a hunter was *don't give him a place to start*. If for some reason the men gunning for them happened to stumble upon this log, Vanessa knew Rock didn't want to leave any trace that they'd passed the night here.

Which was fine by her. She'd rather there not be any telltale reminders of this place left lying about either, reminders that *this* was the spot where she'd offered herself up, body and soul, and been soundly rejected.

A hot morsel of shame and indignation burned in her chest, but that was nothing compared to the city construction workers operating jackhammers inside her skull.

"I have a headache so big it makes the Sears Tower look like a domino," she admitted, lifting a hand to her temple.

"It's dehydration and heat exhaustion," Rock said, shouldering into his pack and checking that the clips for his SIGs were loaded before slamming them back into the grips with his palms. The maneuver flexed the large, stylized skull tattoos with their crossed swords and the words *sea, air, and land* that were inked on each of his bulging biceps, and emphasized the barbed wire and thorny rose tattoos ringing his muscular forearms.

Grrrr. Why did he have to be so damned sexy?

I mean, seriously? He had a voice like an angel, a heaping helping of that oh-so-delicious Southern charm, a dangerous streak that was guaranteed to have a girl squirming in her seat, *and* a body like an Adonis? Not to mention that, while she smelled like she'd spent the night in wet clothes on the inside of a hollow log, he still managed to emit a…well, not necessarily a clean scent, but it was definitely a hot *manly* scent. Manly enough to have desire swirling through her belly and her toes curling inside her boots.

Frickin' frackin' shitballs! It's just not fair!

"Well, don't you just have the answer for everything this morning?" she griped then wished she could call the words back. One sure way to let him know that her whole *hey, I'm cool you just want to bone me and toss me aside* demeanor was all just a big fat act was to turn into Lady McBitchesAlot. "Sorry," she added hurriedly, wincing and rubbing a thumb in the center of her forehead. "Headaches turn me into a total bear."

"Take this," Rock passed her the canteen. They'd emptied it last night—scratch that, *she'd* emptied it last night; it was the only way she'd been able to choke down the woodchips and habanero granola bar—but Rock must've already made a trip down to the river to refill it.

And it was good thing she *hadn't* been sleeping like a baby with a whole group of CIA agents out to kill her or anything. Sheesh! She hadn't even heard him leave, much less return.

Then again, she comforted herself with the knowledge that Rock *was* incredibly stealthy. Maybe not scare-the-holy-crap-out-of-you silent like Ghost, the Black Knights' crackerjack sniper, but he could still hold his own against the best of them. And let's admit it, she *wasn't* the best of them.

Tilting the canteen to her lips, she hesitated when she remembered the number of untold microscopic organisms that bred in these jungle waters, most of them nasty enough to cause an otherwise healthy person to turn into a sweating, convulsing, shitting machine.

"Did you add iodine tablets to this?" she asked.

Rock slid her a look that questioned the validity of *both* her college degrees. "This isn't my first rodeo, *chere*." And, okay, so she wasn't the only one who was cranky this morning. He was doing a fairly decent impression of *Lord* McBitchesAlot.

Raising her brows, she eyed him over the top of the cantina as she let the cool, slightly chemical-tasting water slip down her parched throat.

"Sorry," he winced. "Playing hide-and-seek with two hit squads obviously makes *me* a bear."

And… there was that.

Okay, so the truth of the matter was that she had much bigger things to worry about than her bruised pride and wounded ego. Number one being she was running from a group of operatives bent on putting a bullet in Rock's brain… and hers, too, if last night's shoot-out was any indication.

She guessed that's what she got for consorting with a supposed rogue operator…

And she still believed in the *supposed* part, didn't she? *Yes. Yes, I do.*

Although, in the short time they'd been together, he'd made two cryptic remarks—*you don't know a damn thing about me,* and *what makes you so sure my name can be cleared?*—that, admittedly, caused her to once again entertain a sliver, just a teensy, tiny, ever-so-little sliver of doubt.

And she *hated* that feeling. Hated looking at this man she'd grown to both respect and like—yes, *like*, even if he had shot her down like a duck hunter shoots a mallard, because at least he'd been honest, and a gal had to appreciate that—and wonder if maybe she'd been wrong about him. If maybe he *was* capable of cold-blooded—

"You ready?" he asked, and she raked in a deep, bracing breath.

"Ready as I'll ever be, I suppose." She searched his eyes, looking for something to let her know she was mistaken in harboring any doubts. But his expression was unreadable.

"Then let's do it." Even in the low light, she caught the flicker of chagrin that quickly passed over his face at his choice of words. And a little part of her, an *evil* part of her, was glad he was suffering at least *some* discomfort after last night's discussion.

After all, what's good for the goose is good for the gander… and what is with *all the water-foul references bouncing around inside my head this morning?* It gave whole new meaning to the expression bird-brained. Obviously Rock was right. She *was* suffering from heat exhaustion…

He pressed a finger to his lips, calling for silence—had her thoughts been that loud?—before quietly scooting down to the base of the log. She followed suit, crab-walking in the tight space until she had to stop to wait for him to push the foliage aside. He did so slowly, the barrels of his 9mms peeking through the green curtain first. After what seemed eons, he shoved the guns in his waistband and brushed the ferns and small shrubs aside before climbing out.

Vanessa was right on his heels. And even though the jungle canopy was dense and the sunlight filtering through weak, the brightness outside when compared to the interior of the log had her squinting and blinking. She raised her hand to shield her eyes just as a shadow moved in her peripheral vision.

She barely had time to turn before Rock burst into action, moving so quickly he was nothing but a blur. With a round-house kick, he booted the black-clad agent's M4 machine gun out of his hands, dodging blows aimed for his head as he landed a few hard punches that sounded loud and obscene against the natural buzzing chatter of jungle life.

The agent responded with moves to rival Jet Li, but Rock somehow countered each one. Ducking, swaying, blocking…

For a moment, Vanessa was stunned, staring in slack-jawed horror. But she quickly regained her wits and raced around the grappling men toward the discarded weapon. Bending to snatch it off the ground, she ran through the steps of her weapons training…

One: slap the magazine to ensure it's fully seated. Check. Two: pull the charging handle to the rear and watch to see a live round or expended cartridge eject. Check. Three: release the charging handle and tap the for-ward assist assembly to make sure the bolt closes. Check. Four: turn and fire.

But when she spun to aim the M4 at their would-be assassin, it was to find that her help was no longer needed. Because Rock had the guy in a choke hold, applying a buttload of pressure to the arm he'd wrenched behind the man's back. The agent was up on his tiptoes, aiming ineffectual body blows at Rock with his free hand, but it appeared Rock barely felt them.

Vanessa's heart thundered, the blood pounding in her ears, so she was equal parts stunned and impressed when she heard Rock say, in a remarkably calm tone, "Hurts like hell, doesn't it?"

Their assailant answered with a high-pitched grunt, his face turning red and his eyes bulging from their sockets.

"How long before your team arrives?" Rock asked, and when the man garbled, "Fuck you!" Rock bent the dude's arm up and back even further.

Vanessa winced in sympathy as the agent's face contorted with pain.

"F-fuck you!" the man bellowed again, a little louder.

"Sorry, but you're not my type." Rock released just enough pressure so the man stopped turning purple but not enough to give him a chance to escape or enough oxygen to launch an effective counterattack. It was sort of amazing how quickly and easily Rock had mitigated the threat. No muss, no fuss, no blood. Just one very pissed-off CIA agent. "And since you're making a pretty good racket, and since I don't hear any of your folks racin' to the rescue, that must mean you're all by your lonesome out here. If I had to guess, I'd say you've fanned out far enough that you're all spread, what? Twenty, thirty minutes apart from one another? This is a big jungle, after all. *Non?*"

Something in the agent's face must've clued Rock into the fact that he'd hit the nail on the head, because a knowing smile curved his lips before he said, "Now the way I see it, *mon ami*, you got three options here. One, I can make sure you never shoot with this arm again—which will *certainly* put a damper on your career. Two, I can let my lady friend over there put a bullet in your leg that'll guaran-damn-tee you don't walk right for six months—which will *likely* put a damper on your career." The agent's bulging, bloodshot eyes rolled toward Vanessa. She raised a brow, indicating that, *yes*, she would have no trouble doing exactly what Rock said. "Or three, you can be a good boy and stop fighting so we can tie you up, real quick like."

"You…you're not gonna kill me?" the man panted, beads of sweat sliding down his forehead.

"Come on now. Why would I do that?" Rock frowned. "You're not doin' anything but what you've been ordered to do."

Vanessa watched the agent's gaze dart about. Then he looked up and back into Rock's face, frantically searching his eyes. And he must've found what he was looking for, because he managed a jerky nod, saying, "Okay. Tie me up."

"*Bon*," Rock winked. "Good choice. Now, *chere*," Rock turned to her, "I need you to hurry and get in the main compartment of my pack and pull out that bundle of zip ties."

Looping the M4's strap over her shoulder, Vanessa felt a little like Rambo—sans the spiffy red bandana—and did as Rock instructed. Less than ninety seconds later, the operative was tied to a small tree. His ankles and wrists secured by plastic zip ties and a strip of duct tape over his mouth.

She stepped away from the trussed-up man and turned to Rock, a wonderful lightness filling her being despite the fact that they were still in a shitload of trouble.

"What?" he demanded, frowning so fiercely the corners of his goatee drooped, his lush bottom lip pouting in the most delicious way. "Why are you grinning at me like a possum eatin' a sweet 'tater?"

"You *didn't* kill all those men, did you? You really didn't."

He blew out a deep breath, rubbing a hand over his goatee and turning away to squint into the distant foliage. "'Course I didn't," he muttered.

—⁓—

"I *knew* it!" Vanessa shot a fist in the air—that's right, a fist. Rock felt one corner of his mouth twitch. He'd never seen someone—outside of the stoner dude at the end of *The Breakfast Club*—actually do that.

"I knew those charges were trumped up." She nudged the tied-up operator with her foot and pointed a finger in Rock's direction. "And when your buddies find you, you should tell them to leave Rock alone. He's innocent. I mean, if he'd really killed all those men do you think he'd think twice about killing you? No." She shook her head adamantly. "And another thing—"

"We don't have time for this," Rock cut her off because he could tell she was about to get herself on a roll. "We need to get goin'."

"Oh," she blinked at him. "Uh...yeah. Sure." But instead of coming to his side, she once more nudged the operator's foot. "I'm serious," she hissed. "You're going to tell them, right?"

And seeing her, with her inky black hair—shorter now, thanks to his knife work—all down around her shoulders, and an M4 strapped to her back, railing in his defense, a veritable tigress determined to help him clear his name, he felt himself fall...just a little. Because, *mon dieu,* she was something.

But he shook his head and reminded himself of all the pain and suffering that resulted from loving someone, reminded himself of Lacy's sunken eyes and sallow skin in those last months, and his resolve once more hardened to stone.

Vanessa was obviously satisfied when the operator vigorously nodded his head, because she smiled triumphantly and strolled over to Rock. And when she glanced up at him, the dreamy look in her eyes disturbed him more than if she'd chucked a grenade in his direction.

"Get that thought right out of your pretty head," he warned, adjusting his pack and turning into the jungle.

"What thought?" she inquired, following close behind him.

"The one that says, *oh, Rock*," he raised his voice into a terrible falsetto, "*you're my knight in shinin' armor, my hero*."

"Pfft. For one thing, I've known a lot of heroes in my life, so don't go thinking you're anything special."

And *that* caught him off guard. Because it was the first time he considered the fact that Vanessa had spent most of her career as a linguistics and communications specialist in the spec-ops community surrounded by men who tended to not only come equipped with far more than their fair share of testosterone, but also the ability to bag just about anything that moved—and it occurred to him to wonder just how many of those *heroes* she'd invited into her bed.

And following right on the heels of that thought was a burst of jealously so intense he actually lost his footing. Had a vine not been handy, he'd have face-planted into the forest floor. As it was, he had to grab onto the sucker and breathe past the hot vise gripping his chest.

Just the thought of her arching into some bastard who grunted above her was enough to have red easing into the edge of his vision.

And he knew it was absolutely ridiculous to feel that way. He had no claims on her. Didn't *want* any claims on her. But he still couldn't shake the images in his head or the way they made him want to tear some nameless, faceless A-hole's head clean off his shoulders.

"And secondly," Vanessa continued, unaware that he was about to burst an aneurism on the spot, "your *armor* isn't all that shiny. In fact, if you must know, it's actually pretty dingy and, I'm not trying to pick a fight or anything, but you could use a washing machine and a healthy spritz of cologne."

Just like that, the green-eyed monster that'd perched on his shoulder disappeared, and a surprised laugh burst from him.

"Wow," he said, trudging through particularly dense undergrowth, wincing when he crushed some of the plant life beneath his boot since it was basically the same thing as waving a semaphore flag for the guys who were hunting them. Of course, if his calculations were correct, and he was right about how far back that agent's teammates were, they had enough of a head start to make it to the old Rio Verde road and the rusting 1966 Bultaco Metisse dirt bike he'd squirreled away there, before the spooks caught them. "Now, doncha go holdin' back on me. I want you to tell me how you really feel."

She snorted. "I just thought I should drag you down off that high horse you climbed up on. Wouldn't want you to start suffering from altitude sickness or anything."

He chanced a glance over his shoulder and—

Mistake.

Because her cheeks were red and rosy from the heat, her eyes dark and half-lidded from weariness, her hair all mussed and crazy from letting it dry without brushing it, and he realized…

*This is what she looks like after making love…Warm and blushing and messy and…*merde, merde, merde!

"You're really beautiful, you know that?" The words hopped out of his mouth like they were attached to springs.

And the statement, blurted with absolutely none of his usual Southern finesse, caught her off guard. She stopped in her tracks, her chin jerking back on her neck as if she was a marionette and someone yanked her string. She stared at him for a long moment, her dark eyes searching for something in his face as the jungle around them chattered and buzzed and dripped, as the air hung heavy with the smell of wet foliage and exotic orchids. But when it became obvious he wasn't going to give anything else away, she shrugged her shoulders and pushed forward, brushing aside a long vine that hung in the path. "I don't get you," she observed quietly.

"You wouldn't be the first," he retorted, cursing as his boot snagged on a root, causing him to stumble. Again.

Goddamnit! Twice in as many minutes he'd lost his footing. Which was saying something since he usually had the reflexes of a whole herd of cats.

But this woman, this one, small, *spectacular* woman muddled his thinking, caused him to lose his focus and—

"Seriously," she pressed, "one minute you're all *stay back, Van; I'll break your heart* and the next you're telling me how beautiful I am. What's with that? Are you, like, some sort of sadist or something?"

No. More like a masochist. At least when it came to her. Which was just one more reason on his very *long* list of reasons why it was imperative he keep her at arm's length.

"I didn't tell you that to hurt you, *ma belle*," he admitted, taking out his Bowie knife to slice into a vine. They were running dangerously low on water. And besides the ass-load of hostiles after them, the next biggest threat in the jungle was dehydration.

Unscrewing the cap on his canteen, he gripped the severed end of the vine and aimed it at the opening, allowing it to unload its precious cargo of water. Once the canteen was full, he dropped two iodine tablets inside before replacing the cap and re-hooking it to his pack.

Vanessa was silent through the process, but once they were moving again she asked, "Then why *did* you tell me?"

Why indeed…

He considered all the possible answers he could give her and decided on the truth. "I suppose because chances are pretty good I'm not gonna make it out of this thing alive, and I…*merde*…" He felt the air thickening around him. Rain was coming. Soon. "…I guess I…I guess I wanted you to know that while what I said last night was true; it has nothin' to do with you and everything to do with me."

"*Not make it out of this thing alive.* You keep saying that," she snapped at his back. "But I don't get it. If you didn't kill those men, then there *has* to be a way to clear your name. There has to be some sort of evidence that proves you weren't—"

He stopped and swung around, surprising her when he grabbed her by the shoulders. Now, normally he didn't cotton to laying hands on a woman without her permission, but right now he needed to make sure she understood what he was saying. And that required him having her full, undivided attention.

From the diameter of her wide eyes and the way her mouth was hanging open, he had it.

"I might not have been the one to pull the trigger, *chere*," he growled, hoping she could see the truth in his face. "But I'm the reason they're dead all the same."

And right at that moment, the sky opened up.

Chapter Nine

VANESSA'S HEART BEAT WITH A TERRIBLE RHYTHM AT Rock's declaration, and the torrential rain instantly soaked her to the skin.

The reason they're dead? What does that mean?

Had he…had he participated somehow? Maybe…hired the person who *had* done the deeds?

But that last one didn't make any sense. She wasn't sure about much when it came to Rock—not anymore; the man was an enigma wrapped in a riddle surrounded by beard stubble—but one thing she was certain of was that he wasn't one to let another do his dirty work.

So…what? What was with that cryptic statement?

She opened her mouth to demand he explain himself, but he'd already turned and was trudging quickly away. Left with no other recourse, she clenched her jaw and followed, her mind spinning with exactly two thoughts…

Is he innocent? Or is he guilty?

She'd gone back and forth so much on the issue in the last sixteen hours she felt like a yo-yo.

But even when she caught up with him, she couldn't ask what he meant, because it took everything she had to keep pace as he wound his way through the jungle. She stepped where he stepped, avoiding the things he avoided, stopped to grab a quick drink from the iodine-laced water in the canteen when he stopped to do the same.

For an hour, maybe two—she'd lost the ability to

accurately gauge the passing of time—they fought their way through the undergrowth, the rain steadily falling all around them but doing nothing to mitigate the heat. Vines clung to clothing and hair, shrubs grabbed ankles, and tree roots jumped up to snag the unsuspecting toe. Her muscles began to ache, her empty stomach began to make itself infuriatingly known by grumbling and growling, and the headache she'd awoken with that morning remained stubborn as a mule, kicking her in the cranium every couple of minutes.

She was just about to call for a break—her legs were Jell-O, and she'd tripped three times in the last five minutes—when suddenly the rainforest opened up and she found herself on the side of a mountain. The ground dropped off in a steep decline that was traversed some thirty feet below by the long, snakelike track of an old jungle road.

Without the protection of the canopy, the rain came down in sheets, running into her eyes and mouth, but she didn't care. It felt so *good* to be at the edge of the jungle, to be out in the open. She drew in a deep breath and spread her arms wide, reveling in the freedom of being able to stretch out without touching vines or ferns or bushes or trees or—

"What are you?" Rock shouted beside her, the heavy patter of raindrops on foliage muffling his voice and obscuring his face, but she could still make out his lopsided smirk. "Queen of the World?"

She scowled up at him, in no mood to joke—even if the reference *did* include the oh-so-delicious Leonardo DiCaprio—just as the ledge of dirt she was standing on gave way. And then it was yeehaw! She flew down the mountainside on the jungle's version of a Slip N' Slide. Only there was no smooth, plastic sheet beneath her bottom. Oh, hell no. It was just a river of mud and root-balls and the occasional rock.

She bounced and skidded and bounced some more. And every time she landed back on her ass, her teeth clacked together causing her headache to grow to the relative size and shape of an aircraft carrier.

By the time she hit the flatness of the roadway with her stomach, arms and legs all akimbo, mouth full of mud and M4 gouging into her side, she was thinking it might've been easier, and certainly less painful, if she'd just stepped in front of one of those rounds aimed at her head last night.

"*Blech*," she hacked, repeatedly spitting until most of the mud that'd been in her mouth was sitting on the road in front of her in a wet, disgusting heap. Then, she managed to—*painfully*—heave herself onto her back, keeping her eyes closed as the rain pelted the dirt from her face and filled her open mouth.

She turned to spit just as Rock landed with a *humph* beside her. Slowly, as if every bone in his body ached, he pushed into a kneeling position, raking the rain and mud from his face with an ungentle swipe of his hand.

"*Mon dieu*," he breathed, shaking his dark head until dirty water flew from the spiky tips of his short hair. "That was unexpected."

"Yeah," she agreed, still flat on her back, wondering if she'd ever be able to move again. "And it looked a lot more fun in *Romancing the Stone*." She blinked the water from her eyes only to have it replaced by more.

"You okay?"

She lifted her chin—and, yep, the ol' noggin weighed in at a cool metric ton—and shot him a look that not only questioned his intelligence, but his sanity.

He winced. "Sorry. Stupid question. Let me rephrase; is anything broken or irreparably damaged?"

"My pride?"

"I'm serious."

"So am I," she insisted, slowly pushing into a sitting position. The horror of the last day combined with the worry of the past six months caused unexpected tears to pool in her eyes.

Oh, great. Perfect time to have a breakdown.

She hoped he couldn't tell, not with it raining so hard. But then her stupid lip began to quiver and suddenly she was back in his arms.

"Ah, hell, *chere,*" he crooned, rubbing a gentle hand over the back of her head. "I'm so sorry to put you through all this."

All? Did that include last night's rejection? Did that include his declaration that he'd never—capital N—love her?

Oh, great, and now she was crying—again, she was crying *again,* for Pete's sake!—for a whole new reason. He must think her a total pantywaist. Here she was, supposed to be *helping* him, and so far all she managed to do was lead the guys who were after him right to his door and break down in his arms. Twice.

Geez, Van, pull yourself together!

But try as she might, she couldn't stop the tears that slipped down her cheeks, hotter than the raindrops. And that's when it occurred to her—as she sat covered in mud on a remote jungle road while being chased by government agents who'd been given orders to kill her—that there was no other place she'd rather be.

Because no matter how badly she hurt, or how much she longed for a shower, or how scary it was to actually get shot at, nothing mattered as long as she was with Rock.

Her tears dried up quicker than a mirage in the desert, and she stilled in his arms.

No, no, no. This can't be happening.

Her impression of a two-by-four obviously wasn't lost on him, because he tilted her chin up and brushed her sopping hair back from her brow.

"What?" he asked, his lovely hazel eyes searching her face, his perfect nose dripping water from the tip, his luscious, swoon-worthy lips tilted in a frown. "What is it? What's wrong?"

What was wrong? *What was wrong?*

She just realized she *loved* him, *that's* what was wrong!

She loved him for his courage and his honesty, for his loyalty to his friends. She loved him for his strength and determination and, yes, even his stubbornness. She loved him like she'd never loved any other man, and he was determined, no, absolutely *convinced*, he'd never love her back. Which had all been fine and good when the idea of the two of them together was more fantasy than feeling, more lust than anything close to love. Last night it'd been a blow to her pride when he made that declaration, but now…?

Oh, sweet Lord, his words replayed through her head—*I'll never fall in love with you*—and this time the blow, quick and deadly as a stiletto strike, went straight to her heart.

Tears once more burned up the back of her throat, but this time she refused to let them fall. If she let them fall when he was looking her smack-dab in the face, he'd know, he'd use that crazy skill of his to figure it out…

"It's nothing," she said, sliding from his arms—it felt like she left her heart behind. "Just one hell of a headache."

Creakily, she pushed to a stand and rearranged the M4 so the magazine no longer threatened to take out her left kidney. And as quickly as it had started, the rain stopped. In the relative silence that followed, she could feel Rock watching her.

She tried to act nonchalant as she stretched the kinks from her neck and busied herself with a missing button on her shirt. Then the sun came out, and the world around them turned into a steam bath. Sweat broke out all over her already wet body, but still Rock sat there. Looking at her, undoubtedly trying to see inside her head.

She bent to retie the lace on her boot, tucked the bottom hem of her cargo pants more securely inside her sock, and realized she was quickly running out of distractions when, finally, he pushed to his feet. Taking a step toward her, her heart played the part of Mexican jumping bean and hopped into her throat.

No, no, no. Don't press me for answers, she silently begged him.

And it was almost like he heard her thoughts, because he quickly changed direction and headed toward the side of the road with that loose-hipped swagger so many Southern men learned to perfect.

She cocked her head and watched as he pushed aside the lush foliage growing next to the road like he was searching for some sort of treasure hidden beneath.

What the—

Her curiosity took the slightest edge off her heartbreak,

or at least allowed her to focus on something else, and she was amazed to find herself limping—her left ass cheek was going to be black and blue for a week—over to him, "What are you looking for?"

"A *cipó cabeludo*," he said, shoving aside a huge fern.

"A what?"

"It's a plant and it—ah, there's one." His face was triumphant when he straightened and handed her a...was that a leaf?

Yes. Yes, it was.

"Uh," she frowned down at a tear-shaped piece of plant life sitting green and glossy in the center of her palm, "*okay*?"

"Chew on it," he instructed, and she turned her head so she could regard him from the corner of her eyes, pursing her lips.

"Whatchu talkin' bout, Willis?"

He grinned, and the expression went all through her. Because even though most folks wouldn't label Rock as handsome, they'd have to agree that, when he smiled, he was absolutely beautiful. Those perfect lips, those flashing eyes...

"Chew on it," he insisted again.

"And *why* would I want to do that?"

"Because of your headache. It'll help with the pain." He winked, hooking an arm around her shoulders like they were best buds.

And suddenly the sharp edge was back on her heartbreak. In fact, her heartbreak felt like nothing *but* sharp edges. Like there was a ball of shattered glass banging around behind her breastbone. And she knew there wasn't a plant on the planet that could help with that...

―᠁―

Bam! Bam! Bam!

Bill almost spilled the glass of lemonade in his hand and, from the corner of his eye, he saw Eve nearly jump through the roof when someone pounded on the back door with a heavy fist.

"Who the hell is—" But that's as far as he got before Ozzie burst onto the scene, followed quickly by Steady and Ghost.

"We hear you guys are up the Rio de Caca without the proverbial oar," Ozzie announced with his usual, dramatic fanfare. "But never fear; the cavalry is here!"

"Lord, save us," Becky muttered, pushing up from the table where she'd been in the process of downloading all the information she could find on Rock's supposed targets onto her laptop. They'd already exhausted that avenue, but she'd needed something to occupy her time because none of them—her included—were used to sitting around with their dicks in their hands. Well…Becky didn't have a dick, but the point was still valid. "With your IQ, I'll never understand how you manage to not only mangle, but completely mix your metaphors."

"It's a gift," Ozzie grinned then spied Eve behind the kitchen counter. He dropped his duffel bag on the clay-tiled floor and slapped a palm over his heart. "I swear Eve," he crooned in what Bill had come to recognize as his panty-removing voice, "you get more beautiful every time I see you."

Eve blushed, a hand fluttering to her throat as Ozzie skirted the center island and snatched her into his arms, smacking a kiss on her cheek and squeezing her until she smiled and batted ineffectually at his shoulder.

"Put me down, you big goof," she laughed, her sapphire eyes sparkling.

Bill discovered that he was grinding his teeth so hard he was probably in the process of pulverizing his fillings. Any second now, there'd be little shards of metal alloy shooting out of his ears.

"I'll put you down when you agree to marry me," Ozzie retorted, nuzzling her neck.

"You ask every woman you meet to marry you," Eve giggled, squirming in his arms. "Now put me down!"

"Yes!" Bill shouted, tossing aside the report he was reading on the latest brand of plastic explosives and slamming his lemonade on the end table. He pushed up from the plush sofa and glared at Ozzie until it was a wonder the kid didn't spontaneously combust. "Put her down!"

Ozzie dropped Eve, lifting a questioning brow at Bill. The guy's sandy blond hair was even wilder than usual, thanks in part, Bill suspected, to the fact that upon hearing Boss's demands to get their asses down here ASAP, the boys had hopped the first military transport they could find. Which probably meant they'd spent most of the night in the cold belly of a cargo plane trying to find a comfortable spot among the shipment of whatever was being transported and the high-grade netting holding it all in place.

"Well, who pissed in your Post Toasties?" Ozzie inquired, coming around the island so he could bend and dig something out of his duffel bag.

Despite himself, Bill felt one corner of his mouth twitch. "Are people still saying that?"

"Oh, yeah," Ozzie's nod was vigorous. "I am. You can't go wrong with a classic." He pulled out a digital camera and started snapping pictures of Eve's lavishly decorated living room.

Bill jumped when Ghost said from beside him—the man was stealthier than anyone should be—"Give the kid a break, Wild Bill. He's sufferin' from a double whammy of excess bravado and testosterone. And we all know that particular combo is eventually fatal."

Staring at Ghost—a guy renowned for being aloof and taciturn—Bill's jaw slung down to hang somewhere in the vicinity of his chest. "Doth mine ears deceive me?" he finally managed to ask. "Or did you just string, like, twenty words together? What *has* Ali been doing to you?"

"Probably has more to do with what *he's* been doing to *Ali*," Ozzie quipped, hooking the string on the camera around his wrist so he could beat out a three-stroke rhythm in the air—*bah-dah-bum*.

"Jesus," Bill shook his head and leveled Ghost a look, hooking a thumb over his shoulder. "How many hours have you been cooped up with him?"

"Too many," Ghost replied. "Wonder Boy is on a Pat Benatar kick. The idiot sang 'Heartbreaker' the entire way here. And, I swear, if I hear one more *doncha mess around with me* I'm gonna shoot myself in the head. And then I'm going to shoot *him* in the head."

Ozzie opened his mouth to point out the preposterousness of this particular plan, and Ghost pointed a warning finger in his direction. "Don't even think about it, kid!"

"*Heartbreaker, dream maker, love taker*," Steady sang as he dropped his duffel and hopped up on one of the barstools surrounding the kitchen island. He grinned evilly at Ghost, and even bedraggled, unshaven, and unshowered, Carlos "Steady" Soto still managed to resemble a *GQ* ad.

In fact, his swarthy, Latin looks had once prompted Becky to accuse him of being pretty enough to simply melt his enemies' bullets. "What?" He pasted on what Bill suspected was supposed to be an innocent look and shrugged his shoulders. "I didn't sing the headshot-worthy part."

"That's what I'm talkin' about," Ozzie nodded, slapping a high-five with Steady before the two bumped knuckles.

Bill caught a glimpse of his sister standing in the middle of the room, her hands planted on her hips, her mouth stretched in a wide grin. She absolutely *loved* having "her guys"—as she called them—together. Ate up all the quips and banter with a soup ladle. And, not for the first time, he patted himself on the back for suggesting to Boss all those years ago that she and her custom motorcycle business be the ones to provide the cover for Black Knights Inc.

Since a very young age, he'd known that whatever made his kid sister happy, made him happy, too. With the exception of one thing: her best friend, Eve. And speaking of…He turned to find the woman in question rummaging through the refrigerator, loading up her arms with all the food she'd been preparing over the past few days.

The cooking was a new thing. When he'd dated her all those years ago, she hadn't known how to boil water much less whip up a tasty batch of chicken tetrazzini.

You've come a long way, haven't you, sweetheart? And for a moment he forgot all the heartbreak she'd caused him, feeling nothing but pride for her. Pride for how she'd broken away from that spoiled rich girl stereotype to really make something of herself. Pride for the way she'd come out of her shell, overcoming the nearly debilitating shyness that'd plagued her as a teenager.

Then she turned and their eyes clashed—like, seriously

clashed; Bill was surprised a loud *clink* didn't echo through the room—and, once again, painful memories sliced like a bayonet strike through his brain.

Still, he couldn't manage to drag his gaze away, and for long seconds they both simply stood and stared. The air between them vibrating with an awareness that was nearly palpable. Or maybe there was no *nearly* about it, because Ozzie piped up with, "Good God! You two have *got* to quit that. You're making my boy parts get bigger!"

With that, the spell was broken.

Bill glanced away, his heart throbbing like an open wound, just as Boss sauntered into the room.

"I thought that was the scent of bullshit I was smelling," the big guy said, grinning that lopsided grin of his, slapping Steady on the back as he passed him, punching Ozzie on the shoulder, and stopping to shake Ghost's hand before finally throwing an arm around Becky's shoulders. "And I sure am glad you guys are here. We're going to need all the—"

The affable expression on Ozzie's face disappeared. He made a slicing motion across his throat with one finger, and Boss stumbled to a stop.

Ozzie might be an epic pain in the ass, but he was also one hell of an operator and a veritable whiz with all things technical or electronic. And right now, he was staring at the digital display screen on his camera, and the look in his eye was one of pure, unadulterated disgust.

He made a rolling motion with his finger, indicating they should keep talking and Boss picked up with, "We're…uh…we're gonna need all the mouths we can find in order to get rid of this food Eve's been cooking."

Ozzie nodded and made another rolling motion with

his finger even as he bent to grab a notepad and pen from his duffel. Becky picked up the ball and ran with it. "And speaking of, what's on the menu tonight, Eve?"

"Um…I," Eve looked around, baffled. And when her eyes landed on him, Bill nodded and gave her an encouraging wink.

"Please tell me it's some more of that Mediterranean pasta salad," he said, widening his eyes to prod her into playing along.

"Oh, well…I…" she stuttered but then seemed to physically pull herself together. Her shoulders straightened, her expression firmed, and she stood just a little taller. "I hadn't planned on it. I thought maybe I'd start with a green salad, and then some lasagna and garlic bread. What does everybody think?"

Various noises of indecision were made by all as Ozzie hastily scribbled something on the notepad. When he turned the message around, there were exactly two words written there: OPTICAL BUG.

Oh, shit.

For a split second, silence filled the room. Then everyone played the game like a champ and started debating the merits of lasagna over pasta salad. And all the while, the goddamned CIA was listening in…

Chapter Ten

"Aren't we going to stop and call to let them know we're coming?" Vanessa shouted over Rock's shoulder.

For the last three and a half hours, they'd been speeding—first down the rutted-out jungle track and then the pot-holed road—toward San Jose on a rusty old motorcycle that Rock had miraculously produced from thin air.

Okay, maybe not thin air. He'd produced it from out of the jungle. On the opposite side of the road from where he'd picked that leaf for her to chew—which had worked wonders, by the way—he'd scrounged through the shrubs, pulling away vines, and came away pushing what looked like an old dirt bike, but was, in reality, a pile of gears and rusty steel attached to a whining engine that truly belonged in the scrap metal pile at a junkyard.

Compared to the shiny paint and sparkly chrome on the custom choppers back at BKI, this thing would be ashamed to even call itself a motorcycle. And the ride? Holy hell, she'd thought the long skid and bounce down the side of the mountain was hard on the ol' ass cheeks, but it was nothing like sitting on the back of, what she'd affectionately come to think of as, Sir Rusty RidesLikeATank.

"No," Rock yelled back at her. "I'm gonna leave you at La Sabana Park. From there, you can either catch a bus or call them to come pick you up!"

What?

After *everything* they'd been through together over the

past day, he was *still* determined to do this thing without her help? Without the Black Knights' help?

"You're kidding me!" she barked, then had to grind her teeth together when he leaned into a tight turn. The way the dirt bike sounded, she expected the poor thing to disintegrate beneath her, just explode in a cloud of oxidized dust. But then Rock straightened out, and old Rusty miraculously held itself together, so she continued, "We can *help* you, Rock! Come in with me!"

He shook his head before taking another curve, this one in the opposite direction. Once again, she clamped her jaw and tightened her grip around his waist, pressing her face into his back. And she was startled to realize how badly she wanted to plant a kiss there, just push her lips into the shallow divot of his spine so she could feel his hard muscles flex on either side of her face. Just breathe in the smell of him, the warmth of him, the—

And it was official; she was a total goner.

Because it didn't matter what hurtful things he'd said or that he was mixed up in something likely to get him killed—and maybe the rest of them along with him. It didn't matter that he was stubborn and willful and altogether too quick to take matters into his own hands or that he was determined to toss her away like last week's takeout Chinese. It didn't even matter that he swore he'd never feel for her all the things she felt for him.

What mattered was that *she* loved *him*. Loved him with everything she had and, because of that, she was going to help him whether he thought he needed it or not. And if there was one thing she was sure of beyond a shadow of a doubt, it was that he stood a better chance *with* the Black Knights than without them.

When they came out of the curve, she scooted forward, pressing her thighs more tightly around his hips, pushing her bound breasts into his back, and tried, somewhat unsuccessfully, to ignore the hot stab of excitement that exploded between her legs just by being this close to him with ol' Rusty vibrating away beneath her. It helped when she felt Rock stiffen in response to her sudden shift in proximity.

Step one complete. Now, step two...

Flattening one palm against his washboard belly, she made sure her pinky finger lay no more than a centimeter away from his penis, and the ache between her own legs throbbed like a bad tooth. But, as anticipated, Rock sucked in a hard breath that allowed her to keep her focus.

And... step two complete. Step three?

While he was distracted, she surreptitiously moved her other hand to his hip and carefully slipped her cell phone from his pocket, stealthily transferring it into her own.

Mission accomplished.

Hastily, she scooted back, shifted her hand, and felt him relax.

And, holy smokes, he wasn't the only one. Because the feel of him pressed all along her front, so hard and warm and completely, utterly male was making her ridiculously lightheaded. And he was certainly right about one thing: she *was* hot-to-trot where he was concerned. One touch, one look, and she was ready to toss off her panties and ride him like a amusement park rollercoaster.

Of course, if he'd been unwilling to humor her in that endeavor before, he'd be even more adamant about keeping her at arm's length here in about half an hour. A little morsel of remorse lodged in the pit of her stomach for what she was about to do, but she ignored it.

This is *what's right,* she told herself, though there was an annoying voice inside her head whispering how Rock may never forgive her for what she was contemplating doing.

Well, if that's the case, so be it. I'd rather Rock hate me and be alive, than like me and be dead...

The little voice pointed out the idiocy of the thought, because, really, how could Rock like her if he was *dead*? And it was at this juncture in her internal debate that she told the perturbing little voice to fuck off.

Hardening her resolve, she started wiggling in her seat like maybe she'd contracted a severe case of jungle ass-rot. And just as she'd hoped, a couple of seconds later, Rock glanced over his shoulder concernedly.

"What's gotten into you?" he yelled above the engine's sickly, earsplitting whine. "You're squirmin' around back there like you've got a whole colony of leaf-cutter ants in your pants."

She pasted on an expression of embarrassment and chagrin. "Sorry!" she hollered, then she added, "It's nothing!"

He turned back to the road, but only after sliding her a long look of disbelief from the corner of his eye.

Vanessa bit her lip and writhed around on the torn-up leather seat, wincing only slightly when the maneuver made the bruises on her butt start barking like a pack of wild dogs.

Rock swung back around, his dark brows pulled down in deep V. "Okay, that's it! What the hell's wrong with you?"

"I gotta pee!" she blurted, making sure to wince convincingly.

"You can't hold it?"

She shook her head, and he sighed heavily before

turning to scan the narrow expanse of roadway in front
of them. After about a mile, an old dirt path appeared on
their right, and Rock throttled down. Pulling the rusty bike
onto the track, he motored up a short distance, until the
mountain forest pressed in on them from either side. Then
he stopped and cut the engine.

Sweet, blessed relief. Vanessa's ears started celebrating, and she was surprised she didn't feel them happy
dancing on either side of her head.

"I'll be quick," she promised him as she hopped from
the bike.

"Here," he said, digging into his pack, pulling out a
couple of packs of antiseptic wipes and handing them
to her.

"Seriously?" She lifted a brow. "That'll probably burn
like crazy."

"*Mais, non.* They're not for…" he looked down at her
crotch and then glanced away quickly. Was that an actual
blush she saw staining his cheeks? "… for *that*," he finished, clearing his throat. And, yes, that *was* a blush.

Huh. Will wonders never cease?

The devil in her couldn't help but press him. "Then
what *are* they for?"

"They're for," he turned back to her, his hazel eyes
roaming over her muddy face, "cleaning up a bit. Not that
you need to. You're fine. You're always fine. You could
be covered in cow manure and you'd still be fine. You
could be wallowin' in pig slop and you'd still be fine. I
just thought that—"

He suddenly stopped, obviously realizing he was bab-
bling. Vanessa couldn't help herself; she was grinning
from ear to ear. "Never mind," he groused, reaching

forward to snatch the wipes from her hand, but she held them out of his grasp.

"No, no," she told him. "I'll definitely take them." Because, truth of the matter was, the thought of scrubbing some of the dirt from her face and hands sounded divine. "And you might think of doing the same." She looked pointedly down at the wide, dirty palm extended in her direction. "I've seen cleaner fingers on a diesel mechanic."

Rock glanced at his hand, frowned, said a really filthy word in French, and hid his fist behind his back.

"Not that I wouldn't still think you were fine, too, even covered in cow manure or pig slop," she added, watching delightedly as his jaw slung open.

Deciding that was the perfect time to make her exit, she didn't wait for him to respond—simply turned and ran into the trees. Immediately, she was overwhelmed by the sound of insects buzzing, birds chirping, and monkeys screeching in wary alarm. Of course, compared to the noise pollution that was Sir Rusty RidesLikeATank, the jungle's cacophonous song was a symphony.

And it was just what she needed for the next few minutes. Because the loud, buzzing hum of the rainforest was guaranteed to drown out the sound of her voice.

Traipsing through the undergrowth, she stopped when she figured she'd gone some thirty yards or so from the trail. Leaning against a tree, dragging in the rich smell of wet foliage that was a welcome reprieve after sucking in the dirt bike's rank exhaust for the last three-plus hours, she opened up the packages of wipes Rock had given her and scrubbed her hands and face. The medicated cloths smelled stringent but, more importantly, clean. So she used the last bit of moisture on each to swipe at her armpits. Then she figured she'd stalled for about as long as she could, so she slipped her cell phone from her pocket and thumbed on the device.

Oh, look at you, you three big, beautiful bars!

But, still, she hesitated. If she did this thing…

A myriad of thoughts spun through her head, all of them resulting in Rock losing what little trust he had in her.

But this is what's right, she told herself. So, raking in a determined breath, she took one more moment to still her shaking fingers—*he's going to kill you for this*, that pesky voice insisted—and punched in a number she knew by heart.

A series of beeps and clicks established her secure connection, and then there was no turning back.

Is this really happening?

Eve glanced at the faces surrounding her and decided, *yes*. Yes, this was really happening.

She was really crammed in her master bedroom closet with a half-dozen hardened operators watching Ozzie finger one of her silk slips while licentiously wiggling his eyebrows at her. "Nice," he said, nodding appreciatively.

"Uh…thanks," she told him, rolling her eyes when he winked as if to say, *I can think of a lot of other ways you can thank me, sweet britches.*

And, yes, he'd actually called her that once. Sweet britches.

Who did that?

Ozzie apparently. But, in spite of herself, and in spite of Ozzie's general inclination to toss out ridiculously demeaning pet names, Eve couldn't help but like the guy. He was just so…so…*easy*, she guessed was the word. Easy to get along with. Easy to brush off. Easy to *not* take seriously.

Unlike Billy…where *everything* was serious.

And speak of the devil. Right on cue, Billy slapped Ozzie's hand like one would a recalcitrant child. "Cut that shit out."

"Why?" Ozzie demanded in a stage whisper.

"Because it's annoying."

"*You're* annoying," Ozzie snapped back.

"Jesus!" Billy hissed, once more having to smack Ozzie's hand away because the Black Knights' computer whiz kid was now in the process of lifting her slip up to his nose in order take a deep whiff. "I said, cut it out!"

And even though she knew Ozzie was just trying to get a reaction from her and Billy and anyone else who might want to jump into the fray, Eve couldn't help the blush that stood out like two red flags on her cheeks. The combination of fair skin and a tendency toward almost debilitating shyness was the bane of her existence. Of course, she was working very hard on that last one…

"Party pooper," Ozzie whispered, sticking out his bottom lip and rubbing his hand as if Billy actually hurt him.

"Both of you guys need to zip it," Boss commanded and, despite herself, despite her determination to "grow a pair," the man's booming bass, especially echoing in the small space, made her jump.

She jumped again when Billy reached out to lay a gentle hand on her shoulder, "Easy, Eve. We're okay."

Crimeny. The way she was hopping around, you'd think she was standing on live electrical wire. And all those gathered in the closet with her had to think she was the world's biggest wimp. Yep, she could almost see the circus sideshow advertisement now…

Come one, come all! See the woman with the amazing backbone of a squid!

Great. Just…great.

Taking a deep breath, promising to smack herself upside the head should she jump for no reason again—a little aversion therapy never hurt anyone—she glanced around the group, briefly registering the fact that she missed the warmth of Billy's hand when he removed it. "Are we really okay? Because if that's the case, I don't understand why we're all crammed in the closet. And just what the heck *is* an optical bug anyway?"

After Ozzie held up that message, to her utter befuddlement, they'd talked inanely of food for the next couple of minutes until Steady—she'd learned he was the equivalent of the Black Knights' doctor-on-staff—strolled over to her Bose iPod dock and jacked in his iPhone. Seconds later, the booming beats of Los Lobos blasted through the house, and Boss motioned for everyone to follow him.

Here.

To her closet…

"An optical bug is a high-tech listening device undetectable not only to the naked eye but also to standard bug detectors," Ozzie explained. And it was amazing how quickly he could go from class clown to engineering professor. If he'd been wearing a pair of glasses, this is the part where he'd shove them up the length of his nose. "What it does is shoot a high-powered beam of light at a window where it picks up on vibrations in the glass. It then turns those vibrations into audible speech. But as James Bond as that sounds, an optical bug has a fatal flaw."

She lifted a brow, feeling the need to pinch herself. Who would ever believe the Chicago debutante whose sixteenth birthday party ran on the front page of the society paper was in a closet with a group of clandestine government defense warriors, trying to help a supposed rogue operator, all while being bugged by…who was bugging them exactly?

That was going to be her next question.

"If you turn off the infrared filter on a digital camera," Ozzie continued, "and snap a photo, the light beam shows up as a red dot."

He handed her his digital camera, and there on the display screen was her living room. And there in the middle of her living room window, was a big, glowing dot.

"I knew," he went on, "given Boss's general tendency toward paranoia—"

"It's only paranoia if they're not out to get you," Boss interrupted, his expression surly, which caused Ozzie to grin like a little kid.

"Like I was saying," he continued, "given Boss's general tendency toward paranoia, I knew you guys had swept the premises for bugs, so I couldn't figure out how they picked up Vanessa's trail. I knew they couldn't have tagged her leaving the house. We're all too good for that. And I've seen her Ricardo Ramirez disguise. That thing's a beaut. So, no way, just by seeing her, they'd realize who she was. Which meant they had to know what to look for and where to look for it. And the only way they'd know that was if they'd somehow been listening in on the goings-on around here. That's when I realized…optical bug."

Eve couldn't stand it anymore. "Who are *they*?" she asked.

"The CIA," Becky, Boss, Ozzie, and Billy all answered at once, while Steady simply muttered, "The Company."

Uh-huh. She raised a hand to her spinning head.

Geez freakin' Louise! She'd known the U.S. government was after Rock. That'd been made very clear to her when Becky first approached her about appropriating her vacation home as a base. But she hadn't realized that by agreeing to help the Knights try to clear Rock's name, she'd also be making *herself* a target of "The Company." Which probably showed exactly how naive and gullible she really was.

"It's okay, Eve," Becky assured her, reaching forward to squeeze her fingers.

"Um," she blinked, this time not worrying about the fact that her squiddy backbone—or lack thereof—was showing, "*how* is it okay? The freakin' CIA is after us."

"Not us," Becky said. "Just the information they think we have."

"And that's different because…?" She was hoping someone would assure her she wasn't hours away from finding herself locked in a federal prison cell. Not that she didn't think she could survive it, mind you. Because with her tragic lack of street skills, not to mention her somewhat dubious local celebrity status, she was pretty sure she'd be quickly taken under the wing of—and forced to become the bitch of—someone named Big Bertha or Crazy Carla or Hot Knife Hattie. But, see, the thing was, Eve would desperately like to avoid that scenario if at all possible…

"Because," Boss said, and she turned to look at his scarred face, taking comfort in the certainty she saw in his eyes, "so far, we haven't done anything wrong."

So far...

Yeah, she hadn't missed that little caveat.

"I'm surprised an optical bug would work on those windows," Steady said, scratching his head.

"What?" Eve glanced around. "Why? What's wrong with my windows?"

"He's talking about the fact that they're those fancy double-paned contraptions, with the blinds between the glass," Ozzie said.

"I didn't want big heavy window treatments to obscure my view," she said, defensively, not that she'd been able to enjoy it on this trip since all the shades in the entire house had been drawn upon their arrival. Still, *what* exactly was the problem with her windows?

"Good thinkin'," Ozzie winked reassuringly. "And it also makes using an optical bug more difficult since the beam of light has to cut through a pane of glass and the plastic blinds before reaching the window where it can pick up the noise vibrations of our speech. Difficult," he nodded toward Steady, "but not impossible."

"*Mierda*!" Steady cursed in Spanish.

"You said it." Ozzie agreed, before adding, "What we need are vibrators." The sudden change in subject had Eve blinking rapidly and glancing around like maybe she'd misheard.

When no one seemed to bat a lash at this statement, she asked the time-honored and oh-so-eloquent question of, "Huh?"

"Vibrators," Ozzie repeated and, yep, she hadn't misheard. "We can tape them to all the windows and turn them on. Their resonance will screw with any optical bugs The Company tries to employ."

And it was at this point, much to Eve's consternation, that all heads turned toward her.

"What? Why are you looking at me?" she demanded, her stomach filling with dread. Being the subject of such close scrutiny, especially when the scrutinizers were a group of hardened operators, made her feel like a bug under a microscope. Like, at any moment, someone was going to reach out and pull off one of her wings, like she was about to—

"This is your house," Steady piped up.

"Yes. So?"

"So where's your stash of sex toys?" he demanded, completely deadpan.

She couldn't have stopped the hot blush that burned up her chest and neck to explode in her cheeks if she'd shoved her whole body in a barrel full of ice water. "I…I…don't…" She shook her head and coughed, unable to go on since there was a gigantic lump of embarrassment in the middle of her throat.

Seriously? Had he just asked where she kept her stash of *sex toys*? Like it was a foregone conclusion she had one? Of course, what made it even more humiliating was the fact that—

"I brought Mr. Blue with us," Becky announced eagerly, and Eve wondered if the closet was suddenly spinning or if it was just her.

"Mr. Blue?" Billy questioned. "Do I even want to know?"

"He was my stand-in for Frank before Frank decided to pull his head out of his ass and make an honest woman of me." She winked at Boss.

The big guy picked up the conversational ball and started to run with it, "And now he's fun to use to—"

"Nope," Billy held up a hand, cutting the Black Knights'

leader off mid-sentence. "I was right. I didn't want to know. Holy good God almighty, I'm never going to get that image out of my head." He shuddered like someone had just poured a bucket of spiders down his shirt.

Steady gave Boss a *way to go, man* punch, which had a smug smile spreading across Boss's harsh face. The guy was the picture of someone completely sure of both his woman and his manhood. And when he wrapped a possessive arm around Becky's shoulders, Becky smiled up at him, and the heat in her eyes was enough to have Eve looking on with longing.

She wished she had that much confidence, that much chutzpah, to admit that she—

And, just like that, her defense instructor's encouragement whispered through her head. *You need to grow a set of balls, Eve. Come out of your shell. The whole world isn't going to judge.*

And it was good advice. She *knew* it was. But the truth of the matter was, the world *had* judged her and very harshly at that.

Unfortunately, a man's life might depend on what she did right now, so she swallowed her humiliation, locked her stupid knocking knees together, opened her mouth and admitted, "I have one of those lipstick-tube shaped vibrators in my purse, and another one in the bedside table in the master bedroom. Will those help?"

The urge to go find some sand to bury her head in was strong, especially when Billy slowly raised one sleek brow. But she lifted her chin and held her ground even as every single eye in the closet landed on her crimson face.

Chapter Eleven

"Why, Eve, you naughty, naughty girl," Becky chuckled, reaching into the pocket of her shorts in order to pull out a cherry Dum Dum. Bill watched with his lungs frozen, his head buzzing, and his dick thumping against his zipper—just the thought of Eve pleasuring herself with a little vibrator was enough to shoot the mercury level on his horny-meter all the way to the tip-tippity-top—as his sister handed the sucker to Eve with the fanfare and care someone might use to pass off a newborn babe.

"What's this for?" Eve asked, and Bill didn't need to see the heat in her face to know she was far more embarrassed for having made that…uh…little confession—*fuckin'-A!*—than she was letting on. Because the tremor in her voice, and the way she tried to cover it up by delicately clearing her throat, said it all.

It was all so endearing and *goddamnit!* It was sexy as hell!

"For once again proving how badass you really are under that ballerina exterior of yours," Becky explained.

Bill wouldn't have thought it was possible, but Eve's blush deepened. "I don't know how admitting that I have a couple of…" She trailed off, seemingly at a loss for words.

Ozzie had no trouble jumping into the void. "Self-pleasuring devices?" he offered helpfully.

She winced, clearing her throat again. "Yes. I don't know how my admitting I have a couple of *those* makes me a badass, more like a Super Freak. But I guess I'll take what I can get."

Super Freak? Well, maybe. But that was the kind of Super Freak he could really get behind…or on top of… or beneath, come to think of it. And before Bill could stop it, his mind conjured up an image of her lying in that big feather bed out there, head thrown back against the cool, white pillow, black hair fanned out, mile-long legs spread wide. She was pink and slick and open as she—

Christ! He had to shake his head in order to jangle the thought loose before his erection grew as big as the Trump Tower. As it was, he had to do one of those covert stance adjustments or suffer some serious discomfort.

Of course, it turned out it wasn't all *that* covert, because Ozzie caught his move, glanced down at his fly then quickly back up to his face, and shot him a wide, shit-eating grin. Bill responded with a smirk that could be read only one way…*Yeah? Well, go fuck yourself.*

"Three," Ghost announced in a low voice, and Eve jumped like someone poked her with a cattle prod. Not that Bill could blame her really. Ghost had a certain quietness, a weird stillness about him that sort of allowed him to blend into the background, making one forget he was there. And, thankfully, the frightened movement and the look of intense embarrassment on Eve's pretty face was enough to take the tiniest edge of his ardor. Of course, what happened next assured he wasn't thinking about her, or feather beds, or lipstick-shaped vibrators at all, because the silly woman clenched her eyes closed and proceeded to do something completely preposterous.

She reached up and smacked the middle of her forehead with her palm.

Every eye in the closet zeroed in on her, the expressions

on the Knights' faces varying from concern to amusement to consternation.

"Aversion therapy," she said by way of explanation. "My personal defense instructor says I need to…um…grow a pair of balls." She bit her lip. "Which I take to mean includes not jumping like a scared rabbit at the slightest thing."

And despite himself, Bill felt the wall he'd built up around his heart—the one Eve had provided the mortar for—begin to crumble. And when she glanced over at him, her face awash in embarrassment and uncertainty, but with…

What was that glowing in the depths of her eyes?

It looked suspiciously like the same flame that ignited the gazes of hardened operators right before they crossed the wire and jumped into the danger zone. It looked suspiciously like the fire of determination…

Wow. You're really coming into your own, aren't you, sweetheart?

Again, he felt that sliver of pride for her. Because if there was one thing he'd learned in life, it was that seeing yourself clearly, baring witness to all your faults and foibles and trying to do something about them, took a level of courage most people never attained.

"You think that kind of therapy would work for Ozzie's annoying habits?" Becky asked.

"*What* annoying habits?" Ozzie demanded, and all the Black Knights groaned in unison.

"Seriously, though," Ghost brought the conversation full circle, "Will three be enough…um…devices?"

"Three will be enough to cover the picture windows in the living room," Ozzie said, all serious again. The kid had a wacky ability to play the village idiot one minute and don his superhero clandestine operator mask the next.

Bill would never understand it. "But we should still be careful what we talk about. From now on, or until we can scrounge up some more vibrators, all mission-related issues should be discussed in here."

"Agreed," Boss said as Bill furtively watched Eve unwrap the Dum Dum in her hand and shove it between her lips. And whatever sadistic genius invented the lollipop should either be shot or sainted—at this particular moment, he couldn't decide which.

"And I think Ozzie should probably pay a visit to our CIA friends in the van across the street," Boss continued.

"Why?" Becky asked, frowning.

"Two reasons. One: to let 'em know they're not fooling anyone. And two: to maybe see if we can't get a bead on any other nifty devices the fuckers—" The big guy winced and smiled apologetically at Eve. "Er...sorry for the language."

Becky groaned and rolled her eyes. "Jesus, Frank. Nobody gives a shit right now. It's not like we're at a fucking cocktail party or something."

Boss slid her an exasperated look before slowly grinning and squeezing her close to his side. "It would be good," he continued, "to know what other nifty devices the spooks might be utilizing; not to mention we need to know if we're being watched by satellite."

"Not as of twenty-two-hundred last night," Ozzie answered. "I checked all Eyes In The Sky. One was focused on Santa Elena, but none here."

"Good. That's good," Boss nodded.

"Wait a minute," Eve held up her hand, moving the sucker to her cheek with her tongue, and the flash of pink had Bill's gaze lasering in. Oh, how he remembered the taste of her. So sweet. The feel of her in his arms. So lithe and trembling and… *Jesus!* "Are you trying to tell me you *knew* all this time the CIA was out there?"

"Of course," Boss and Becky answered in unison.

Bill watched the slideshow of emotions flit across her face. First disbelief, then realization, and finally confusion. Two jobs Eve should never attempt: government operator or poker player. "But, but," she sputtered, shaking her head.

"We knew they were keeping an eye on us," Becky explained. "But it didn't matter since we hadn't planned on actually *doing* anything here. Of course," she frowned, "that's before we knew the *fuckers*," she emphasized the word and grinned up at Boss, who only rolled his eyes and leaned down to kiss the tip of her nose, "were listening in."

"Right," Boss nodded, straightening. "And I think we should—" Right at that moment, his cell phone blasted the opening bars to "Don't Fear the Reaper," and the big guy was cursing and pulling the device from his hip pocket. "Go," he said by way of answering. Then, "Thank God, Vanessa! We've all been worried sick!"

At this point, every eye in the closet was focused solely on the Black Knights' leader.

Boss ran a big hand back through his hair. "Yeah… yeah…Shit! Are you sure?" He looked around, spotting the notepad in Ozzie's hand, and snapped his fingers indicating he needed something write with. Ozzie handed over the notepad and slipped the pen that was clipped to the collar of his faded *Star Trek* T-shirt into Boss's hand.

"How long until you get there?" Boss asked, turning his wrist to check the time on his diver's watch before jotting down the name of an intersection and San Jose's major metropolitan park. "Yeah, we can make it. You just make sure Rock doesn't shoot us once we come barreling in."

Bill couldn't help but smile. Because he didn't care what was being said about Rock, the ragin' Cajun could never harm a single hair on any one of their heads. Of course, Eve didn't know this, because she glanced over at him, sapphire eyes as big as saucers.

"He's joking, Eve," he assured her on a whisper. "I promise," he emphasized, inwardly shaking his head at himself.

Why am I always reassuring her?

And not that he really wanted an answer, but from somewhere deep within, a voice whispered, *because you still care*.

No. He frowned. He didn't care about her. At least not any more than he cared about the next person. *Any* person.

Liar. The little voice taunted, and Bill had the sudden urge to strangle the bastard.

"Will do," Boss said, once again dragging Bill's thoughts back to the situation at hand. Goddamnit! Being this close to Eve, shoved in a closet and smelling the sweet perfume lingering on all her clothes, was seriously screwing with his ability to keep his mind on task. "And good job, by the way," Boss finished before clicking off. Then, addressing everyone gathered in the closet, he announced, "It's time to roll."

"What's up?" Steady asked.

"We're bringing him in." And considering that was good news, Boss's face looked suspiciously stony. Then Bill understood why when he added, "But he's not going to come willingly."

Oh, shit.

"Ozzie," Boss barreled ahead, "did you do like I asked and check to make sure both of our secondary vehicles were secure before you got here?"

Before heading over to Eve's house, they'd purchased

a couple of old beater pickup trucks from a Costa Rican farmer who'd allowed them to use his hot-as-the-surface-of-the-sun barn to overhaul the engines before secreting them away in the garage of an abandoned house down the street. Because, you know, there was always the off chance they might need to make a clandestine escape. And one thing Bill could say for the Black Knights, they were nothing if not prepared for every eventuality. A man learned early on in his spec-ops training that it was better to sweat more now, so he could bleed less later…

"Affirmative," Ozzie nodded. "Locked up safe and sound. Checked them and the house for any bugs or surveillance gear. Nada. No one's the wiser on our secondary base."

"Good," Boss mused, rubbing a hand back through his hair again. "Okay, so while you distract the spooks and see just what type of gear they've got going in that van of theirs, the four of us," he pointed to himself, Bill, Steady, and Ghost, "will sneak out the back to the secondary base, grab the vehicles, and go apprehend Vanessa and Rock. Becky," the big guy turned to his wife, and Bill beat back the protestation that jumped to his lips. His little sister was no longer his sole responsibility. Sometimes he had a hard time remembering that.

"Don't you dare leave me out of this, Frank," she hissed, hands on hips, nostrils flaring.

The big guy rolled his eyes. "Wouldn't think of it, love," he chuckled. "I want you and Eve to take her Land Rover and tear ass out of here about twenty minutes after me and the boys are gone. I want The Company guys following you, and—this is important—you gotta make sure you give 'em one helluva race. If it looks like they're losing interest, you'll need to stop. Preferably somewhere seedy or strange, so they'll wonder what you're up to and stay with you. You need to keep them occupied until after we get back here with Vanessa and Rock, which should be no more than half an hour, tops. You think you can manage that?"

"Done," Becky nodded, her eyes alight with excitement. Bill chanced a glance at Eve and found her face just the opposite of Becky's. Now he knew what people were talking about when they described someone's complexion as ashen. The woman was so pale she was gray.

"Uh," he felt it was time to pipe up. "I'm not sure Eve—"

"I'll do it," she interjected, turning to him and lifting her chin. The move might have looked convincing had her lower lip not been trembling like a leaf in the wind.

"Eve, you don't have to—"

"I *said* I'll do it," she declared, and he couldn't help but admire her determination. The woman had courage, he'd give her that. Because while most people thought courage came from facing danger without fear, the truth of the matter was *real* courage was doing what needed to be done even when you were scared shitless to do it.

"Okay," he nodded, trying, really trying, to remember all the reasons why he disliked her.

"One last thing," Boss said. "Ozzie, once you've distracted the spooks, I need you to scramble all satellite feeds. I don't want *anybody* knowing what we're about to do."

"No problemo," Ozzie declared, and Bill knew this wasn't one of the times the kid was boasting. If Boss wanted every satellite on the planet out of commission, Ozzie, aka The Wizard of Oz, could probably make it happen. Which, when Bill took the time to think about it, scared him half to death. He couldn't help but fear the fate of the world when a twenty-seven-year-old kid who loved bad '80s music and had a weird affinity for cheesy sci-fi shows wielded that much power at the tips of his fingers. He just thanked God Ozzie was on their side…

"Good," Boss jerked his chin once. "Everybody clear on their tasks?"

"Affirmative," the Knights answered in unison, with Eve shakily whispering, "Y-yes."

"Then let's toss back some concrete milkshakes, harden the hell up, and do this thing. We've got half an hour before Vanessa and Rock reach the city limits."

Bill shook his head at another one of Boss's inspirational speeches—*concrete milk shakes; where did the guy come up with this stuff?*—as the group shuffled out of the closet. Once they were gathered in the center of Eve's bedroom, Ozzie opened his mouth, a mischievous twinkle in his eyes.

Boss was quick to cut him off with, "If you make a joke about all of us coming out of the closet, Ozzie, I swear I'll kill you in your sleep tonight."

"Aw, man! You're *all* party poopers," Ozzie pouted.

And, just like that, the Black Knights were in full effect and back in action…

―――⁓―――

Rock used an antiseptic wipe to clean the last vestiges of mud from his fingers before glancing down at his watch and then back to the obscure jungle trail down which Vanessa disappeared.

Thirty minutes, he thought dejectedly as he opened a new pack and pulled out a second medicated cloth, scouring his face with it until the smell of alcohol burned his nose. Just thirty measly minutes, half an hour, a mere drop in the bucket on the timeline of his life. That's all he had left with her...

Mon dieu. It hurt more than he ever thought it would. And scared him down to his very bones that it should be that way.

So, it's good you only have thirty more minutes with her.

That's what he told himself as he wadded up the used wipes and shoved them in a side compartment of the pack looped over the dirt bike's handlebars. Unfortunately, he just couldn't make himself believe it. And when he saw her crashing through the undergrowth, dirty, bedraggled, and so beautiful he could barely breathe, making him hotter than a billy goat in a pepper patch just by stomping toward him with that unconsciously sensuous gate of hers, he knew he was a lost cause.

And he knew he was about to do something colossally stupid. Because it suddenly occurred to him that this was his last chance. His last chance to do something for himself. His last chance to experience something wonderful and pure. And, *oui*, he knew it was a mistake, but no matter how hard he tried, he just couldn't seem to make himself care.

He *wasn't* going to make it out of this thing alive. The secrecy of his second job—hell, even after all these years he didn't have the first goddamned clue who his contact was—combined with the speed with which the evidence in all those killings was laid on him, assured him he was up against one or more very powerful, very elite, and very *connected* people. And chances were pretty good he was eventually going to find himself on the wrong end of a bullet or a syringe loaded with enough polonium-210 to drop a horse.

But for now, for the next few minutes, he was going to forget about all of that and live his life. Live it like he'd dreamed of living it before he was dragged from his BUD/S class in order to be trained as a master interrogator. Live it liked he'd dreamed of living it before the black specter of death shrouded everyone and everything that'd made his life worthwhile. Live it like he'd dreamed of living it when he'd been a young man, poling his pirogue out on the coffee-colored waters of the bayou.

And just the thought had Mr. Happy, the brainless wonder, pounding impatiently against the zipper of his cargo pants.

Tu es stupide. This is for her. This is going to be all for her, so she'll remember us...

Vanessa finally made her way to him, and some of what he was thinking must've been written across his face, because she turned and watched him warily from the corner of her eye. "What? Why are you looking at me like that?"

"Like what, *mon ange*?" he asked, not surprised his voice came out a low rumble. And, just like always, her sensitive ears picked up on the subtleties of his tone, because she shivered despite the heat. Quickly, efficiently, he transferred his pistols from his waistband to his pack, and she watched the maneuver with wide eyes.

"Like I'm a six-course meal and you haven't eaten for a week," she finally answered, swallowing, her lovely, dusky-colored throat working delicately.

He held out a hand to her, and she looked at it like some people might look at a loaded weapon. "I want to kiss you," he told her.

Unlike what most folks believed, honesty was *not* always the best policy—at least not in his line of work.

But he'd learned early on, it could get a man very far with the right kind of woman. And Vanessa Cordero was certainly the right kind of woman.

"But I thought you were in a hurry—"

"We can take a few minutes."

She shook her head, but she didn't back away. It was a good sign. "But you said—"

"Now I want to make sure you understand what it means," he interrupted her again, lowering his chin, peering out at her from beneath his brows. "I want you to understand that it doesn't change anything. That I'm still gonna drop you back in San Jose and then we'll likely never see each other again."

"Rock…" This time she even took a step forward, her eyes pleading. But she still didn't take the hand he offered. "Don't do that. We can—"

"I want you to understand that I've wanted you from the first time I saw you, and this is assuredly my last chance to do somethin' about it. And I know it's selfish of me, and I probably shouldn't ask this of you, but I want something…something *good* to take with me before I go. Do you understand, *chere*?"

For a moment she did nothing but search his eyes, her chest rising rapidly with each breath, then…bingo.

She placed her small hand in his and nodded her head, taking another step toward him. "I don't know how you manage to make me agree to things I damn well know I shouldn't." *Thank you, sweet, baby Jesus.*

He closed his eyes on the prayer, because this woman, this fierce, beautiful, *wonderful* woman was essentially granting a dying man's last wish. "I'll make sure you won't regret it," he promised, pulling her to him.

And Lord have mercy, he tried to be gentle, but she came against him with her mouth open, seeking. And when his lips found hers, when his tongue delved into the dark, wet mystery of her, he lost it. Just a little bit. And the next thing he knew, he was leaning against the bike, her world-class ass cheeks cradled in his palms, overflowing his hands as he rubbed her against the length of the erection that sprang to life the minute she got within two feet of him.

She was succulent, ripe and sweet and oh-so-wantonly willing, kissing him to within an inch of his life, sucking on his tongue in the most maddeningly delicious way, giving him an idea of how she'd suck—

He groaned when she speared her fingers into his hair, opening to him further, moving against him in that fervent way that only made the ache pulse harder for both of them. He was filled with a kaleidoscope of emotions. Elation. Longing…*Dread.* Because this was going to be over too soon, and then there'd be no more. Nothing more. His past was going to catch up with him or he was going to catch up with his past. Either way, the end result would surely be his death, but in the meantime…

Vanessa…

She hooked the toe of her jungle boot on the dirt bike's gearshift in order to get closer to him, in order to more completely align their bodies and—

Hot.

He could feel the heat of her womanhood, even in the jungle's steamy atmosphere, press against his pulsing dick, and all rational thought flew from his head. In one quick move, he turned and lifted her until she was sitting on the dirt bike's torn, leather seat, grabbing her behind the knees and jerking her toward him even as he stepped forward, wrapping her thighs around his hips. He seated himself at the apex of her legs, reveling in the warm welcome he received.

And, *oh Lordy*, he knew he should use more finesse. After all, this was what she was going to remember about him for the rest of her life. And he wanted it to be a memory she'd take out and savor, like a fine piece of dark chocolate, all smooth and rich and wonderful. But his suave Southern charm eluded him, and all he could seem to evoke was Genghis Khan. He was overcome with the intense desire to pillage, conquer, claim...*mark?*

Oui, mark. He wanted to imprint himself on her heart, on her soul. And he realized how unfair that was, realized the last thing he should want was to leave an indelible impression on her psyche, because he knew she was already halfway to falling in...maybe not love, but it was something very close to that emotion—a second cousin, if you will—with him. But, bastard that he was, he couldn't help himself. This was the last woman he'd ever know, the only woman who'd ever made him wish things could be different, and was it too much to ask that she look back on this, on *him*, fondly?

No. It wasn't. But if he wanted all of that, he needed to take it down a notch. Do her really right. She'd undoubtedly had her fair share of fervent groping and tactless fondling. Beautiful women like her always did. So, if he was determined to give her something to remember, something to *really* remember, he needed to *sloooowwww* it way down.

Chapter Twelve

"WHAT'S WRONG?" VANESSA WHISPERED WHEN SHE FELT Rock pull back, when his frenzied hands stopped running all over her body like he was trying to memorize each one of her curves.

"Nothin' in the world, *chere*," he assured her in a low, delicious rumble, skating his lips across her cheek and down to her throat. At her pulse point, he stopped and sucked, and she could swear she felt it right between her legs, right where he was throbbing against her. "I just want to savor this. Don't you?"

Savor. Yeah. She could totally go for some savoring. Of course, she'd savor it more if his pants were undone, if she could feel him in her hands, so hard and smooth, so much a man…

"Yes," she breathed in his ear, delighted when she felt a harsh shiver cascade through his big body.

Sooo, Rock has sensitive ears, does he?

She gently bit on his lobe, sucking it between her lips, laving it delicately with the tip of her tongue. He groaned, the sound equal parts torture and rapture.

Yep, sensitive ears…

She blew softly, nibbled lightly, and was rewarded when he once more grabbed her ass, grinding his erection against her. Rubbing her just right. And she couldn't help but think, *if we weren't wearing clothes, he'd be in me right now. Hot and throbbing and thrusting…*

And, yeah, she knew he'd said all he wanted was a kiss, but it had already gone *well* beyond the simple stage of kissing. And if he was determined this would be the one and only time he dropped his guard, the one and only time he allowed himself to give in to his lust, then, by God, she was going to take it as far as she could.

All the friggin' way, if he'd let her. Because she *loved* him, and after he found out what she'd just done, she was pretty sure—probably close to 100 percent certain, as a matter of fact—he'd never allow himself this chance again. Very likely wouldn't *want* this chance again. You know… given he was going to hate her…

She pushed the thought aside, knowing there was no undoing what'd been done, so there was no use worrying about it now. Especially not when he was in the process of granting her most fervent wish. Not when she was poised to do the one thing she'd dreamed of doing since the first day she walked through the doors of Black Knights Inc.

His mouth returned to hers, his male lips, so plump and firm, so knowledgeable. Yes, she'd always known Rock would be a good kisser. With a mouth like his, how could he not be? But even though she'd gotten a taste of his skill last night, she was still taken aback by his technique. Like the way he sucked her bottom lip between his teeth in order to bite down gently, or the way he filled her mouth with his tongue, coaxing her to follow suit and then, when she did, the way he softly sucked until she could feel each pull low in her belly, making her moan and writhe and ache.

Everything a woman dreamed of when she dreamed of kissing, Rock did. And it didn't feel contrived or intentional. It just felt sensuous, like he instinctively knew what was good, what it took to make a woman burn.

And, baby, was she ever burning. The air in her lungs was a gasoline fire; the blood in her veins blazing so hot that every inch of her skin was ultra-sensitized. Each of her nerve endings was exposed, and everywhere they touched felt like coming into contact with an open flame…

She wanted more. More of him. More of this. Just more, more, *more*…

As their mouths tasted and their tongues mated, she scooted back just a fraction of an inch. Snaking an eager hand between their bodies, she unhooked his gear belt and barely registered the fact that it fell to the ground at his feet because she was too busy reaching for the button at the top of his fly. She smiled against his lips when it popped open without much effort. His zipper was next, and the metal teeth *scriiiiitching* against one another was some of the sweetest music she'd ever heard. And then she delved her hand inside and…

Whoa.

She wasn't surprised to find him hard and hot. She'd known he'd be both of those things. But she was taken aback by his thickness, by the feel of the large vein pulsing against her palm and, suddenly, she had to see, had to look…

She pulled back and ducked her chin, sucking in a heated breath when she saw him spearing unrepentantly from the V of his cargo pants. He was so rigid, standing almost vertical. So engorged, the skin of him almost purple. His plump, weeping head stared at her defiantly and she'd have reached for the snap on her own pants, thinking only of impaling herself on all that unapologetic maleness, had Rock not started working the buttons on her shirt, distracting her.

She watched as he slipped undone one button, then another and another. He had such wonderfully dependable-looking hands. Broad and tan, with artistically long fingers.

It was hard to imagine those hands had caused that CIA agent to squeal like a little girl, but she knew they had. And she also knew they were minutes away from giving her intense, unspeakable pleasure…

A shiver of anticipation slipped up her spine as he pushed the last button through its hole, finally spreading the halves of her safari shirt wide. She lamented the fact that there wasn't a red lace bra to meet his penetrating gaze, because there was absolutely nothing sexy about the Ace bandage wrapped around her chest, smashing her breasts flat.

"Sorry," she breathed, licking suddenly dry lips, her hand stilling against him.

"For what, *chere*?" he glanced up at her, his multifaceted eyes glowing in the dimness of the shade, his head cocked.

"For…for not having on sexy lingerie, I guess," she shrugged, abashed and at the same time so horny she could barely stand herself. And speaking of…

She moved her hand up his length and watched, fascinated, as he caught his lower lip between his square, white teeth, sucking in a startled breath, but never dropping her gaze.

It was erotic as hell, seeing the emotions play across his usually stoic face, getting a glimpse of the pleasure she was giving him, watching as a wave of bliss tripped up his spine, causing him to shudder, making him pulse heavily in her hand.

But just when she was about to get into a rhythm, he grabbed her wrist, gently removing her fingers. She frowned when she realized he was forcing her to stop, and a small grin played at his mouth as he leaned forward to nip at her pouting lower lip. Then *she* was the one sucking in a startled breath, because he manacled both of her wrists behind her back with one hand as he used the other to reach into the sheath clipped to his loosened waistband, pulling out that 10-inch Bowie knife.

The breath sawed from her lungs when the tip of the ultra-sharp blade slipped beneath the bottom edge of the Ace bandage. He was still watching her, keeping her a prisoner of his gaze. And, in response, her heart beat hungrily, pounding out a rhythm that echoed down the entire length of her body.

"Hold still," he told her, eyes locked with hers and sparkling with dark secrets. They were the secrets of a man who'd made it his business to know what a woman wanted…

She ground her teeth together, not daring to breathe, barely daring to move, as that blade slowly, ever so maddeningly slowly slipped up the wrappings, slicing through them like they were nothing. And only after the last binding slipped free and fell to the side did he drop his gaze in order to look down at what he'd uncovered.

She thought she saw his pupils dilate. Thought she saw him rake in a ragged breath. Then, "*Tu es tellement beau*," he whispered, his voice no more than a low rumble in his wide chest.

You are so beautiful. That's what he said. And when she saw the heat in his eyes, caught the rapid tick of the heavy muscle in his square jaw, she *felt* beautiful. Even sweaty and bedraggled, hair all messy and without a stitch of makeup, when she looked at Rock looking at her with a sort of reverent awe, she felt like the most beautiful woman in the world…

"Touch me," she pleaded, closing her eyes, letting her head fall back on her neck…

"*Parfait*," Rock whispered, telling Vanessa she was perfect in his first language as he reached forward with one finger to touch the tip of an exquisitely formed breast. He swallowed, the brainless wonder jumping in the V of his undone pants when her nipple hardened to a little nub on contact.

As Ozzie would say, she was five feet, five inches of *boom* and *pow*. She had it all, a fine ass, flawless breasts that were neither too big nor too small, and a tiny little waist that was the perfect fit for a man's hands.

Oui, she had it all. And it was all explosive. To a man's senses, that is.

And that was before he got to her nipples…

Whowee, he reckoned she had the most delicious nipples on the planet. Round and brown and a little bit puffy, just like he liked, standing out slightly from the rest of her breast. And he would bet his daddy's old 'coon-skinning knife that she tasted as good as she looked.

Leaning forward, cupping her breast in his palm, lifting it like an offering even as he ran the rough pad of his thumb over her nipple just to see it tighten more, he sucked it into his mouth. She was salty and sweet. He could taste the sweat on her skin, but beneath that was the minty lotion she used.

Yep, just as he'd thought. Delicious.

Vanessa moaned as she worked one hand free from his grip in order to palm the back of his head and press him more tightly against her. Her heels dug in just above his butt as she pulled him close, the material of her cargo pants hot and damp and—

Jesus, Mary, and Joseph! *Damp!*

The woman was wet clean through her pants. And that was it. The momentary control he'd managed to wrangle suddenly snapped, and all the gentleness he'd forced on himself was gone in an instant. He sucked at her breast, flicking his tongue fast and hard, feeling her breath hitch even as a slow keening whine sounded in the back of her throat.

It was a plea. A sweet, feminine entreaty for more.

And, *oui*, you better believe he was going to give it to her.

Snaking a hand between their bodies, he managed to unsnap her fly and slide her zipper down. Then he delved inside and realized why she was damp clean through her pants.

The woman wasn't wearing any underwear.

He pulled back, grumbling with delight when her nipple popped free of his mouth, all wet and shiny and begging for more kisses.

I'll come back to you, he promised before looking up to find Vanessa watching him with that particular look a woman gets when she knows she's got a man eating of her hands, when she knows she has him just where she wants him because he's stopped thinking with that round thing on his shoulders and has started thinking with that hard thing between his legs.

"You're not wearin' any panties," he murmured, his fingers finding nothing but smooth, wet flesh.

Apparently, Vanessa shaved. Everything.

Mon dieu. How the hell was he supposed to keep his head about him, make this all for her, when she was both panty-less and hairless? Had she intentionally come to the jungle to drive him crazy? Or...get him killed? Because he'd certainly lost track of time—it could've been minutes or hours since they'd started this—and that was oh-so dangerous.

But no matter how hard he tried, he couldn't seem to make himself care. All he knew was that there was no stopping now.

"They chafe in this humidity," she breathed, even as she worked her second hand free from his grasp in order to reach down and grab him. She wasn't shy about it either. She clamped on and started stroking him in a firm, fast rhythm that had his eyes threatening to roll back in his head.

Since he figured turnabout was fair play, and since it was either get going on her or he was going to make a big ol' fool of himself by popping off like a pubescent boy, he slammed his lips over the top of hers and sucked her tongue into his mouth at the same time he slid a finger inside her.

Damn, she was tight. Smooth as satin, hot as sin, and oh-oh-*oh* so wet.

"More," she demanded against his lips.

He aimed to please, so he worked a second finger inside of her and was rewarded when she tightened around him, squeezing gently, giving him an idea of what kind of heaven he'd find if he used his knife to slice off her pants, if he took a step forward and spread her wide, if he pushed himself…

But he wasn't going there.

Oh, no.

He may have made the decision to take a taste of what she was offering since it was likely going to be his last meal, but he was damned well going to stop before the main course. Because he knew she had feelings for him, and he knew she talked big about not thinking he'd be taking advantage of her if he…well…fucked the shit out of her like he wanted to. But the truth of the matter was, despite her bravado and protestations to the contrary, Vanessa Cordero was a bleeding heart romantic. And if he let this thing between them reach the pinnacle of physicality, he knew she'd regret it.

She'd regret it when she realized he wasn't lying about keeping his emotions locked away. She'd regret it when she knew he really wasn't coming back for her no matter what. And, she'd definitely regret it once he was dead and buried and there'd be no way for her to salvage her pride and tell him off for the previous two infractions.

So he'd offer her what he could, and take from her what he felt she could afford to give without suffering any self-recrimination, and he'd hold what they shared in—maybe not his heart; he was making damn sure to keep that particular organ out of the equation—but, perhaps, his soul. *Oui,* somewhere safe. Somewhere where he could take it out and cherish it when the end was near.

"Oh, Rock," she gasped, stroking him so expertly it took everything he had not lose it right then and there. In fact, he needed to make this thing happen. Now.

He found the hard, slippery knot of nerves at the top of her sex with the pad of his thumb. Rubbing it gently from side-to-side, he worked his fingers, pumping quickly.

"Rock, Rock…" His name became a chant she whispered over and over against his lips and then…

Sweet Lord in heaven, she came.

With one long cry of triumph, she clamped down on his fingers, sucked his tongue into her mouth, and moved against his hand with the kind of wild abandon every man dreams of. Rocking her hips, her inner muscles spasming, hard at first, and then more softly, she rode out her orgasm. And all the while her hand was still working on his raging cock, sliding, stroking, spreading his own wetness down the length of him until it felt so good he knew he had to stop her.

With his free hand, he grabbed her wrist, but she refused to let go, refused to stop that maddening stroking. Pulling back on a strangled gasp, he found her watching him, a dark, feminine knowledge glowing in the depths of her eyes.

"S-stop." That's what he said with his mouth, but his body demanded more, more, *more*. Evidenced by the fact that his pelvis tilted slightly forward, seemingly of its own accord.

"I'll stop," she breathed, still working him, still looking up him, the very picture of female provocation, "if you make love to me."

"N—" For an instant the pleasure was so intense he couldn't make his vocal cords work. But when he squeezed her wrist, managing to slow her movements, he found it within himself to shake his head. "*Non, chere.* I can't do that. I *won't*."

For a long second, she just watched him and...*oh, Lordy, is she ever somethin'!* With her cheeks all flushed from desire, her lips swollen from his kisses, and her dark eyes half-lidded and lazy from spent passion. Then she seemed to come to some sort of decision, because her expression changed and—

Oh, hell. I know that look!

It was the same one she'd given him when they'd been standing in the middle of that jungle trail back in Monteverde Cloud Forest. And that look was, in a word: determination.

He had a moment to feel a skitter of apprehension slip up his spine, but that was it. Just one, all-too-brief second to try to decide how to best remove her firm grip from his cock without doing himself serious harm, before she leaned up and snagged his lips, licking slowly into his mouth as she did something crazy with her hand. And then he not only forgot that he was supposed to be stopping this thing, he also forgot his own name.

Zut alors! He didn't know what she was doing, some sort of magical twist and tug, but it was the best damn thing he'd ever felt. And before he could try to wrangle his scattered thoughts, before he could pull his wits about him and take back control, she released his lips, only to kiss her way back to his ear and whisper, "Come for me, Rock," right before she bit down on his earlobe.

His orgasm exploded through him like a landmine, quick and startling and completely debilitating. Colors flashed, sounds echoed, the world around him condensed into a tight ball of sensation, and Vanessa worked at him until she'd wrung every last drop of the pleasure from his body.

And only when he slumped against her, his forehead on her shoulder, his breath sawing out of his lungs like he'd just wrestled an alligator, did it begin to sink in what had happened.

Sonofabitch! This isn't what I wanted. This isn't—

"Your thoughts are incredibly loud," she whispered, placing a series of gentle kisses on the bandage that covered the wound on his neck.

He pulled back to look at her, at the beauty of her face, at the perfection of her small, triumphant smile, and something in him threatened to soften. For a brief moment, he once more found himself wishing things were different. Wishing he'd chosen another path all those years ago when his family died, when Lacy died, and the specter that was The Project and Rwanda Don offered him a chance at another life.

But then an image of his parents' bodies, bloated and unrecognizable, flashed through his brain, an image of Lacy, looking up at him from her hospital bed with such sadness, skewered through his mind, and his heart hardened once again.

Life was about loss. He'd learned that lesson the hard way. And loving someone only compounded that loss…

So, no. There was no use in wishing things were different.

Because even if they were, he'd never be able to give her what she wanted. He'd never be able to let himself love her; he couldn't suffer that kind of hurt again. And he'd certainly never allow her to fall in love him, to know she'd suffer after his death the way he'd suffered after Lacy's.

"We need to get goin'," he grumbled, pulling away from her even though it caused a startling ache to set up shop in the center of his chest. His jaw worked like a stone grinder as he dug in his pack to pull out the last package of antiseptic wipes, handing them to Vanessa so she could clean up as he shoved himself back in his pants, adjusting his knife in its sheath before bending to retrieve his gear belt.

"Rock." She tilted her head, watching as he stood, her expressive eyes confused, pleading. "I...I don't understand..."

And, *oui,* why would she? He felt like a giant ass.

"I didn't want it to go that way, *mon ange,*" he admitted, buckling the belt in place as he stared down at his jungle boots like this was the first time he'd seen them.

"What? Why?" He glanced up to find her ripping open the pack of wipes with her teeth before putting them to use. A deep blush warmed his cheeks as she cleaned the evidence of his blunder from her hand and the tank of the old dirt bike.

Christ, he'd popped off like a champagne cork at a New Year's Eve party, and he hadn't lost control like that in years.

What a colossal goatscrew!

"Because I—" he began, then suddenly stopped.

"Because you what?" she asked, stuffing the used wipes into his pack before passing him his 9mms. "Why didn't you want it to go that way?"

He shoved the weapons in his waistband, giving himself a moment to try to explain to her. But the moment passed and...

Nada.

He had nothing.

"I just wanted it to be all about you," he finally said, and one sleek black brow slowly climbed up her forehead. He had the inexplicable desire to lean forward and kiss it.

Non, non, non. Bad idea. Colossally bad idea. Because he was absolutely certain that one kiss would set them both off again. One kiss and this time they wouldn't stop at a couple of hand jobs. Hell no. They'd take it all the way to the finish line.

"Well, why in the world would you want that?" she demanded, buttoning her shirt, covering up those exquisite breasts of hers which—*whew!*—allowed him to stop acting like that tree behind her was the most fascinating specimen of plant life on the planet.

"Because I wanted it to be a good memory for you," he said, watching covertly as she tucked the tail of her shirt into her pants before zipping them up and clicking the snap closed. "Because I wanted you think back on me, on…on this moment, with fondness."

"And you think me giving you a little reciprocal pleasure would…what? Diminish that somehow?"

No. No, that's not what he was thinking. But he didn't dare tell her what he *was* thinking because he was scared to death to admit it fully to himself. In fact, he was very afraid he might be skating precariously close to an epiphany he in no way, shape, or form, wanted to have…

So he simply shook his head and shrugged.

She snorted. "Well, that was just silly of you, wasn't it? Because in case you haven't figured it out yet, it's a point of pride for me to give just as good as I get."

And, *oh Lordy*, she wasn't kidding about that…

Chapter Thirteen

"YOU SURE YOU DON'T WANT ME TO DRIVE?" BECKY asked as Eve tightened her seatbelt and started the Land Rover's engine. The vehicle came to life with a loud rumble that echoed inside the closed garage and inside Eve's quaking chest.

"I know this city a lot better than you do," she said, surprised her voice came out as steady as it did considering there was a whole colony of butterflies fluttering around in her stomach, threatening to come crawling up her throat at any minute.

Was she really about to involve herself in a car chase with the CIA?

She adjusted her rearview mirror, caught a glimpse of her reflection, and frowned at the look of wide-eyed terror on her face.

Oh, come on! It's not like you're about to engage in a gun battle or anything. You're just going to drive…fast… with the CIA hot on your tail. Oh, good gracious…

Okay, and she turned off the internal pep talk since it obviously wasn't working—typical, really, of most of her internal pep talks…

With a shaky finger, she reached up to press the button on the garage door opener, watching as the contraption ascended inch by excruciating inch. And, yes, there it was. That white van. Just sitting there. And behind those tinted windows, it was filled to the brim with government agents.

Government agents whom she was about to lead on a wild goose chase.

Geez Louise...

"You sure you can handle this?" Becky pressed, eyeing her bloodless face with concern.

In response, Eve took a deep breath, drank that metaphorical concrete milkshake Boss spoke of, and reached over to yank Becky's seatbelt tight. "Just hold on to your hat, sister," she said as she threw the Land Rover into reverse and burned rubber down the driveway.

Once she was on the street, she shifted into drive and took off like a bat out of hell, her tires squealing on the pavement and leaving a thin puff of gray smoke in her wake. The Land Rover's big engine growled as it shifted through the gears, and Eve took a moment to lament the fact that she'd purchased an automatic. For this little endeavor, a standard would've been better, but she'd have to make do with what she had.

"Come on, come on," she muttered, watching the rearview mirror with one eye even as she kept the other on the road. Her vacation house was on a mountainside, and the road leading to it was curvier than a coiled snake. "Can't you CIA guys see we're up to no good? Why the heck aren't you following us?"

"Jesus!" Becky yelped, grabbing the bar above the passenger window as Eve took the next curve on two wheels. "Where the hell did you learn to drive like this?"

"My father sent me to defensive driving class a couple of years ago when I was having problems with that stalker," she answered through gritted teeth as she wrestled the wheel back to the right, hugging the edge of the road until Becky glanced out her window and down a mountainside so sheer it defined the word vertigo—why the world's most beautiful views also happened to be the most dangerous, Eve would never know.

Unconsciously, Becky leaned away from the window and toward the middle of the vehicle, as if her puny five-foot-two-inch frame could really affect any change in the vehicle's trajectory should Eve lose control—which sooo wasn't going to happen. Eve wasn't good at much, but she'd taken to driving like a fish to water.

"Defensive driving?" Becky gulped. "This…this is more than d-defensive driving, Eve, this is—Holy shit! Look out!"

A herd of peccaries, Costa Rica's infamous wild pigs, raced across the roadway, and Eve was forced to slam on the brakes. The Land Rover shuddered and skidded, necessitating her to go against instinct and turn into the slide. But just as her instructor had promised, and just like she'd practiced a million times, the maneuver allowed her to control the vehicle and bring it to a jolting stop a mere foot from the squealing pigs.

"He was an ex-Hollywood stuntman," she explained, breath sawing from her lungs, heart racing at breakneck speed, even as she tapped an impatient finger, waiting for the nasty-tempered swine to make it across to the opposite side of the street.

"Who?" Becky breathed, foot up on the dashboard to brace herself, both hands now closed in tight fists around the bar above the passenger side window.

"My defensive driving instructor," Eve explained as the last pig crossed the road—she was certain there was probably a joke in there somewhere. And right at that instant, the white van appeared around the bend behind them.

"They took the bait!" she squealed delightedly and pounded a victorious fist on the steering wheel before stomping on the gas.

"Who the hell *are* you?" Becky demanded as they proceeded to blast down the mountain like a bullet from a gun.

―⁓―

"They're late," Boss grumbled in the driver's seat, checking his watch. They were sitting across the street from the green expanse of La Sabana Metropolitan Park where the Inter-American Highway led into downtown San Jose. The smell of tobacco from the nearby smoke shop filled the air coming in through Bill's open passenger side window, competing with the more pungent aromas of the fish cart on the corner and dozens of car exhausts. But that didn't distract him from the fact that, according to what Vanessa told them, they should've seen her and Rock blazing into town on the back of a dirt bike fifteen minutes ago. Bill already had his cell phone out before Boss finished with, "You need to call and tell your sister, so she can keep those damned spooks away from the house for a little longer."

"On it," he said, punching in Becky's number and listening as his secure connection was made. After the first ring, Becky picked up with, "Holy shit! You're never gonna believe where I am."

"Becky―" he tried to interrupt her, but she just talked right over him.

"After one hell of a car chase…By the way, did you know Eve can drive like a Hollywood stuntman?"

"Huh?"

"Doesn't matter," she quickly went on. "The important thing is, I think the spooks were clueing-in to what we were doing, making them run after their own tails and all, because they started to back off. And that's when Eve had a friggin' epiphany. Guess what she did?" Before he could even open his mouth, his sister sailed ahead. "She decided we could kill two birds with one stone, and that brings me back to where I am. Which is standing in line at a seedy-as-hell sex shop watching Eve purchase a whorehouse's worth of vibrators."

"Huh?" Okay, so apparently his vocabulary had shrunk to that one word. And it might have something to do with the fact that his brains had ostensibly turned to mush. Just plain, gray mush. It was the only thing that could account for the fact that none of what Becky had just said made damned bit of sense. Hollywood stuntman? Sex shop? *Eve?*

"Oh, shit!" Becky breathed. "They're coming in the door. I gotta go."

And that was enough to joggle some sense back into his slushy cerebrum. "Beck—" But she'd already hung up on him. "Goddamnit!" He clenched his fists before once more dialing her number, grumbling to Boss as he listened impatiently to the click and beeps, "I don't know how you put up with her. She is the most exasperat—"

"Save it," Boss interjected. "Here they come."

And, sure enough, when Bill leaned past Boss to glance out the driver's side window, he spotted Rock and Vanessa barreling toward them on a loud, rusty dirt bike. And, even at a distance, it was easy to see they'd been through hell. From what he could make out, Vanessa's hair was a wild rat's nest, and Rock looked like he'd taken a bath in mud, the tattoos on the guy's bare arms nearly obscured. The only clean part on the Cajun appeared to be his face, and that was fixed with grim determination.

No doubt Rock didn't like being here in the middle of the city. And Bill couldn't blame the guy, considering the entire free world was out for his hide. Thumbing off his phone, Bill tucked it back in his hip pocket—he'd have to make that call to his sister a little later, because right now they had to get this party started—and opened the passenger door.

Hopping out, he gave a hand signal to Ghost and Steady parked in the pickup truck behind them before climbing into the bed of the first truck. Once Steady mimicked his maneuver, Bill slapped on the back window, alerting Boss they were ready to go.

And go they did.

Boss hit the gas, shooting through the cross traffic and slamming into the park where Rock had stopped the dirt bike. Steady and Ghost were hot on their back bumper until they crossed the street, then they pulled even and Bill, hanging on to the lip of the truck bed for all he was worth lest he find himself bounced right out, glanced across at the other vehicle to see Steady grinning gleefully. Because he was happy to be seconds away from having Rock back among their ranks, or because the crazy sonofabitch loved it when things got fast and dangerous? Bill didn't know. Figured it was probably a little of both.

And, then, in a move straight out of the Operators' Tactical Driving Handbook—if there wasn't such a thing, there should be—both trucks sandwiched the motorcycle between them, pointing their front ends toward each other to form a V before rocking to stop.

Dust swirled up around them in a brown cloud, and Bill took that to be his cue. He stood up in the bed, his hand on the butt of the pistol tucked in his pants. Not like he'd use it, of course. But there was nothing wrong with a little showmanship.

"Hello, Rock," he said as the dust—it smelled dry and tasted acrid on his tongue—began to settle. "We've missed you, man."

Rock's face contorted with betrayal as he glanced over his shoulder at Vanessa. "Get off the bike," he enunciated slowly, concisely, his deep voice clearly legible even over the growl of the three vehicles' engines. And it was a good thing Vanessa wasn't fragile, because that tone, not to mention the I'll-never-forgive-you-for-this look plastered all over Rock's face, was enough to shatter the backbone of a lesser woman.

"Rock, I—" Vanessa began, but Rock cut her off when he roared, "Get off the fuckin' bike, Vanessa!"

She hopped off the rusty motorcycle like it suddenly grew teeth and bit her in the ass, plastering herself up against the bed of Bill's truck. And then Rock did what they all assumed he would. He torqued the throttle, spun the bike in a tight one-eighty, and took off, head low between the handlebars. Which is when Bill and Steady jumped into action.

Jump being the operative word.

They both planted a foot on the side of their respective truck beds and launched themselves at Rock, yanking the guy backward as the dirt bike shot out from beneath him. From the corner of his eye as the three of them hit the ground in a tangle of arms and legs, Bill saw the motorcycle careen a short distance before slamming into the base of a big tree and toppling to its side.

Sonofa*bitch!* He grunted as Rock managed to land an elbow to the bridge of his nose.

"Get off me!" Rock howled as Bill and Steady worked to gain the upper hand. "You don't know what you're gettin' involved in!"

"We're getting involved in saving your goddamned life, you crazy, Cajun sonofabitch!" Bill growled just as Rock managed to snake an arm free and clock Steady in the jaw.

"*Pendejo!*" Steady cursed, wrestling to get Rock's arms secure.

It wasn't working. The slippery bastard managed to break every hold they momentarily got on him and, *goddamnit*, they were losing him!

"Little help here!" Bill yelled, ragged breaths sawing from his lungs, pulse pounding in his temples due to the mighty struggle. He was relieved when Ghost sprinted around the back of one truck to lend a hand. And it was un-freakin'-believable, but it took all three of them to subdue Rock. Even then, it was still one hell of a fight.

Bill managed to scramble on top of the bucking man, pressing a knee between Rock's shoulder blades as Ghost struggled to keep Rock's hands behind his back. Steady whipped out a couple of zip ties and, in a flash, secured the Cajun's wrists.

"Don't do this," Rock begged, heaving, trying to unseat Bill and doing a pretty good job of it. The guy was whip thin, with the physique of an Olympic swimmer, but his appearance was deceiving. Because the ragin' Cajun was strong as an ox. "You'll all wind up puttin' your fool heads in the middle of someone's crosshairs! Don't do it! It's not worth it!" His voice broke, and everything in Bill stilled. Breath, blood, thoughts. Just...full stop. Because, was Rock actually...? "It's not worth it!" Rock choked again, his voice sounding like he'd sent his vocal chords through a meat grinder.

And, yeah, Bill was pretty sure the guy was sobbing.

Jesus.

A hard lump settled in the middle of his throat, and the ulcer he was so certain he'd finally kicked to the curb acted up and started gnawing on his stomach lining. Because Rock was one of the toughest bastards he'd ever known, with a hard set of emotional calluses built up over the years of bearing witness to the repeated horrors of war, and for him to be openly losing it now...

Well, not to put too fine a point on it, but shit must be really bad.

Worse than any of them imagined.

And it only made it all the more terrible that, in order to keep them safe—and Bill was certain that's what the deal was—Rock had been determined to go it alone. Was still determined to go it alone if the continued bucking and cursing and screaming was anything to go by, the big, stupid, self-sacrificing prick.

"And putting our fool heads in the middle of someone's crosshairs would be different from every other day because...?" Steady huffed, and Bill was glad to see he wasn't the only one sucking air. Wrestling with Rock was tantamount to kickboxing a kangaroo. Steady moved to secure Rock's kicking feet by sitting on the guy's calves and lacing together two zip ties.

Rock continued to struggle with everything he had, grunting and wailing and, even though Bill couldn't understand French, he was pretty sure Rock was begging them not to do this.

"Hurry it up," Boss called, leaning an arm out the window of the truck. "We're starting to draw a crowd."

And, sure enough, when Bill glanced up, running a forearm under his bloody nose—*goddamn, stubborn Cajun!*—it was to find a woman grasping the hand of a small, dark-headed boy, looking on in terror.

"We're good," Steady declared, throwing his hands in the air like a steer roper who'd just completed his final knot.

"Get 'im in the truck," Boss commanded, and Bill and Steady each grabbed an arm and a leg, hoisting Rock up—good God, the man was heavier than he looked, too. As gently as they could, they transferred him into the bed of the pickup truck and all the while Rock continued to fight them as if his life depended on it...or, more likely, as if *their* lives depended on it.

And then Bill felt like crying too, especially when Vanessa turned around to peer into the truck bed, tears flowing down her dusty cheeks. "Stop struggling," she pleaded, choking on a sob as Bill jumped up alongside Rock in order to carefully flip the guy onto his back. "P-please. You're going to hurt yourself if you—"

"How *could* you!" Rock roared once he was on his back. His face was wet with tears and snot and blood, and it was obvious that at some point during their struggle he must've taken a blow to the nose.

Shit.

They hadn't wanted to hurt him.

"How could you do this to them!" he continued to scream at Vanessa. Bill had to press a hand to the center of his chest as stomach acid started inching its way up the back of his throat. "How could you do this to me! I trusted you! And now you've killed us all!"

"Hey, now—" Bill began but was cut off when Vanessa shook her head and backed away, muttering, "No. No, Rock, I—"

"Get in the truck, Vanessa," Boss commanded, but she just continued to stand there, openly sobbing, shaking her head and staring at Rock with…was that?

Yep. That was definitely her heart in her eyes. And, shit, that made what she'd just done so, *so* much worse.

Bill glanced down at Rock, wondering if the man knew that BKI's sexy little Latin communications specialist was in love with him. Hard to tell, given the guy was busy struggling while simultaneously staring poison-tipped daggers at the woman.

"Get in the goddamned truck, Vanessa!" Boss thundered, and she jumped a good foot in the air. Then, as if she suddenly remembered where she was, she wiped a forearm over her eyes and sprinted around the back of the vehicle.

Bill watched her crawl into the passenger seat before glancing down at Rock, ready to give the asshole a piece of his mind for one: not letting them help him figure this thing out from the very beginning, and two: taking his hurt and frustration out on Vanessa when she'd only done what any one of them would have done in the same situation.

But one look at the guy's face and…

Christ. Every thought flew from his head. Because Rock's eyes were pleading, frantic, almost wild with fear. And it was seeing that fear—the bone-deep terror in a man he respected the shit out of and had grown to love like a

brother—that had a lone tear slipping from the corner of
his left eye to run into the groove beside his nose.

"Please, Bill," Rock begged even as he continued to
buck ineffectually against his restraints. "Please don't do
this. You hafta let me go. I'll never forgive myself if—"

He stopped the man from saying anything more by
slapping a palm over his mouth. He used his other hand to
press a finger to his lips. And when Rock only continued
to struggle, he wiped away that ridiculous tear—come
on, steel-balled operators weren't supposed to cry—and
whispered, "Stop, my friend. We gotcha now. And we
don't plan to let you go again."

"Stop crying, Vanessa," Boss commanded, and she tried
to obey. She really did. But the look on Rock's face...

Disbelief, hatred, betrayal. It'd all been there. Flashing
up at her like a neon sign.

"I sh-shouldn't have—" she sputtered, wiping at her
wet cheeks, but it was useless. The tears just kept on
coming. "I shouldn't have done this," she finally managed, choking on a hiccup, grabbing onto the door handle
when Boss sped into a turn as they raced out of the city.
Concernedly, she glanced out the back window to find
Bill lying in the truck bed beside Rock, his arms and legs
wrapped around the man, obviously trying his damndest
to keep him from bouncing around too much since he was
trussed up like a Thanksgiving turkey.

And all of this was happening because she'd
betrayed him...

Him. The man she loved. The man who'd saved her
life, helped her conquer her nearly debilitating fear, and

sacrificed his own safety in order to bring her back here where *she'd* be safe. The man who'd trusted her…

Oh, good God, what have I done?

"Bullshit," Boss spat, shifting down when they started to climb the mountain road that led to Eve's vacation house. "You did what was right. He may not think so now, but in the end he's gonna thank you."

Even through the dirty back windshield, she could see the tears mixing with the blood on Rock's face.

Tears. Holy shit, she wouldn't have believed it if she hadn't seen it with her own eyes. But it was true. Tough-as-nails, big-balled, take-no-guff Richard "Rock" Babineaux had lost it. And it had nothing to do with his busted nose. Nope. No way. Because in the time they'd worked together, she'd seen him shrug off two broken fingers, a knife wound through his side, and a hairline fracture to his shinbone.

Thank her? Boss thought he was going to *thank her*?

"He'll never forgive me for—" She was interrupted when Bill reached up to slap a hand on the window. Frowning, she watched as he held up his cell phone. Or, should she say, what was *left* of his cell phone. The thing was cracked right down the middle, an obvious casualty of that scuffle with Rock.

Scuffle?

Jesus, it hadn't been a scuffle; it'd been an all-out brawl. And for a minute there, she'd been sure Rock was going to come out the victor, even against three very skilled, very big, very *determined* operators. He'd fought with everything he had, and it'd been heartbreaking to watch when he was finally brought down. Almost like witnessing the death of a heavyweight in the ring. All that courage and valor and determination just suddenly…beaten.

New tears gathered in her eyes, but she managed to hold them in long enough to inform Boss, "Bill's phone is broken. Does that—"

"Fuck!" Boss cursed, checking his rearview mirror to make sure Ghost and Steady were still keeping pace in the pickup truck behind them. "You need to call Becky. Tell her we're running late. Tell her to keep those goddamned spooks away from the house for a little while longer."

Vanessa was in the process of pulling her phone from her cargo pants when Boss's cellular buzzed in his pocket. "Goddamnit! First get that for me, would you?" he said, grinding his jaw as he flew into another turn, using both hands to control the speeding vehicle on the narrow mountain pass.

Gingerly—because, come on, this was *Boss*; she wasn't sure she'd ever actually *touched* the guy and now she was about to go rooting around in his pocket—she used her thumb and forefinger to pull his jeans pocket wide. Then she slipped her hand inside and snagged the vibrating phone.

"Speak of the devil," she said after seeing Becky's coded number on the screen. Thumbing on the device, she bounced into the passenger side door when Boss swerved around another bend, hitting her funny bone in the process. She cupped her screaming elbow, grimacing in pain, as she held the phone to her ear. "Hello?"

"Vanessa?" Becky's voice sounded harried. "Are you guys back at the house?"

"No. We're on the mountain road right now and—"

"Damnit!" Becky yelled that one word so loudly Vanessa was hard pressed not to yank the phone away from her ear—her likely *bleeding* ear. "Tell Frank to gun it! The spooks lost interest in us, and we think they're on their way back to you guys. We lost track of them when we got cut off by this goddamned train!" As if on cue, the high, lonely wail of a train whistle echoed through the receiver. "And why isn't Billy answering his phone?"

Ignoring that last question, Vanessa turned to Boss. "Becky says to punch it," she quickly relayed. Adding, even though she didn't know exactly what it meant, "She says the spooks lost interest in them," *What interest?* "and are heading our way."

"Perfect," Boss grumbled sarcastically as he slammed his boot down on the gas. But they'd only gone another 100 yards when Ghost began laying on the horn behind them.

"What in the world?" Vanessa asked at the same time Boss let loose with a string of curses so blue they blistered her ears. He was glaring at his rearview mirror, the hard muscle of his jaw twitching spasmodically. And when she turned in her seat to look behind them, she caught a glimpse of a plain white van blazing up the hill behind Steady and Ghost.

Oh, shitburgers.

That looked suspiciously like the van that'd been parked outside Eve's house before she made her trip to Santa Elena, and it didn't take a genius of Ozzie's caliber to figure out these were the spooks Becky was talking about.

"Get Ozzie on the phone!" Boss bellowed, wrestling the truck around another curve, shifting like a racecar driver. "Tell him to have the garage door up and ready. We're coming in hot!"

Chapter Fourteen

PAIN.

That was Rock's entire world. Pain in his shoulders where they were wrenched behind his back. Pain in his nose where Ghost had inadvertently ground his face into the dirt road back at the park. Pain in his hands as the pickup slammed into another curve and, unable to control his momentum, he rolled onto them, squashing them between his ass and the corrugated metal of the truck bed.

Pain in his heart…

"I'm gonna have to cut you loose!" Bill yelled from beside him, and, just like that, all his maladies were forgotten. Had he convinced Bill he wasn't screwing around? That letting him go was the only way to keep everyone safe? His heart soared with relief, only to come crashing back to Earth when Bill continued, "We've got the CIA on our tail, which means we need all hands on deck!" The truck swerved into another curve, and Bill squeezed him tightly, trying to keep them both from doing the whole slide-and-slam routine against the top of the rusted wheel well. "We can't fight with you hog-tied!"

Fight…

They were determined to fight the CIA.

For him.

Goddamnit!

The military had a warm and fuzzy acronym to describe this situation. FUBAR. Fucked up beyond all recognition.

Because not only were the Knights now involved in this god-awful mess, but it also appeared his worst nightmare was coming true. The stupid, loyal *connards* were determined to put their reputations, their freedom, and more than that, their very lives on the line.

For him.

He wanted to howl with frustration and fear, just have himself a good ol' fashioned tantrum. But he'd already indulged in that, and look where it'd gotten him. Exactly where he'd always sworn he'd never be…

As Bill sliced through the zip ties shackling his hands before scooting down to tackle the bindings at his feet, Rock wondered if it was possible just to jump out and save everyone the trouble.

If he died on impact with the road, so be it. At least his friends would be alive.

And if he didn't? Well, undoubtedly he'd be in the hands of the CIA, which was as good as dead since they considered him a rogue operator and traitor. But again, his friends would be alive…

So as the world around him exploded into chaos, as Boss continued to drive like a madman—about three times faster than anyone should attempt on this winding, mountainous road—and as some stern-sounding voice echoed through a loudspeaker and up into the canopy of trees, "Pull your vehicles to the side of the road unless you want us to open fire!" everything inside Rock screeched to a standstill.

His decision was made.

And even though it meant Rwanda Don would remain at large, even though it meant he'd never clear his name and that Fred Billingsworth's real murderer would go unpunished, nothing mattered except the men with whom he'd he spilled countless drops of blood—an ocean of blood. And, as if in agreement of his decision, every scar on his body ached in memory.

Knife wounds, bullet wounds, broken bones. The Knights had been there through it all. Carried him when they needed to, donated blood when they had to, and always, *always* risking everything they had in order to ensure he made it out of every grisly, gut-wrenching situation alive.

But not this time.

This time he'd brought trouble down on himself, and he'd be damned if he'd let the Knights give up their reputations, their *lives* for him.

Oui, he was going to do this. The instant his ankles were free, he pushed to his knees and, holding onto the edge of the truck bed, managed to clamber unsteadily to his feet.

"What the hell are you doing?" Bill yelled, looking up at him in alarm, trying to scramble into a kneeling position even as the truck rocked and bounced.

"Tell everyone I'm sorry!" Rock said, planting one of his jungle boots on the side of the bed, wishing that he could see Boss and Becky grinning at each other with love in their eyes just one more time, wishing he could taste some of Shell's homemade pasta, or…or hear the husky timbre of excitement and desire in Vanessa's sweet voice when she spoke to him.

He took out the memory of the two of them locked together back on that narrow access road, mouths fused, hands hungry and searching, and held it close, held it in his mind's eye. Reveling one last time in the feel of the humid Costa Rican air tunneling through his hair just like her soft fingers had done, sucking in the tart smell of damp foliage and wild orchids that reminded him of her salty sweet taste. Through the truck's back windshield, he saw the back of her messy, dark head, realized it was the last time he'd likely lay eyes on her, and lamented the fact that he'd yelled at her earlier.

She'd only done what she thought was right. What *he'd* have done if the situation were reversed…

"Tell Vanessa I'm sorry and I understand why she did it!" he yelled as he made his final peace and allowed his muscles to bunch. The next instant, he pushed off the truck with everything he had.

But instead of going airborne, instead of the whole human-flight-that-would-inevitably-result-in-a-deadly-crash move he'd planned, he found himself being slammed onto his back in the middle of the truck bed, Bill's hand clutching his waistband, the man's face looming above him and contorted with fury.

"What the hell's the matter with you!" Bill roared, eyes filled with rage and disbelief even as they slid and smacked against the top of the wheel well—*bam!* Rock's ribcage felt that one—when Boss raced into another curve.

"Let me go!" he shoved at Bill frantically, wondering idly if he had a cracked rib. It was suddenly hard to breathe. "I won't be able to live with myself if—"

But that's as far as he got, because huge vacation houses appeared to the right of them and that deep voice once more sounded over the loudspeaker, "This is your last warning! Pull over or we *will* open fire!"

And a solution suddenly presented itself. Rock didn't like it, but he'd take it.

Snatching one of his SIGs from where Bill had stored it in his waistband after disarming him, Rock pressed the cold circle of the barrel it into the man's thigh. "If I have to shoot you in the leg in order for you to let me go I will," he promised.

"You're too late!" Bill grinned gleefully, and the next thing Rock knew, the truck was shifting down through the gears, the tires screaming against the asphalt, and he was sliding up the truck bed and crashing into the cab. He barely had time to gather his wits before Boss executed a hard right, gunning it one last time and then slamming on the brakes.

The truck came to a shuddering halt inside a well-appointed garage. A split second later, Ghost and Steady screamed to a stop on their right, and the garage door rolled down behind them.

Tick, tick, tick...

That's all that could be heard for a few interminable seconds. Just the loud clicking of the overheated engines once Boss and Ghost switched off the ignitions. Stars spun in front of Rock's eyes from the introduction his skull had had with the truck cab. It was very shades of Wile E. Coyote after the Roadrunner dropped an anvil on his head and, *oui,* he'd obviously watched way too many cartoons as a kid. But when he managed to blink them away and push up into a kneeling position, it was to find Ozzie standing by the door that led into the house, one hand on the control for the garage door opener, the other gently cradling an Mk-43 Mod 1 machine gun like a mother cradles a baby.

And the kid was grinning from ear to ear.

"Boy, is it ever good to have you back, Rock," he said, chuckling. "Things were getting mighty dull without you."

"They're holed up in Ms. Edens's vacation house," the CIA agent relayed, causing Rwanda Don to sit forward, heart beating out a too-fast rhythm, breath coming in short, staccato bursts that resulted in the cell phone slipping.

Fumbling with it, R.D. managed to get it back in place before, "Is he with them? Rock? Is he with them? Did they get visual confirmation?"

Jesus. Get a hold of yourself. You're blathering like an idiot.

R.D. forced a little self-control, as much as was possible given the situation, and leaned back in the leather chair.

"Affirmative." Hearing that one word had R.D.'s breath rushing out silently and relief washing like a benediction through clenched muscles. "Babineaux was spotted standing in the back of the truck bed before the vehicle disappeared inside Ms. Edens's garage. The team on site is doing their best to surround the house, but there aren't enough of them. So we're waiting on the choppers to pick up the two units still in the Cloud Forest and bring them back to San Jose. Once that's done, offensive maneuvers will commence."

Offensive maneuvers that likely would not have been needed if that stupid CIA observation team had stayed put, like R.D. had advised, instead of chasing after the two women!

Damnit! It was days like this that made R.D. happy to no longer be a part of The Company.

Bumbling imbeciles...

Of course, now was not the time for *I told you so*.

"You realize the Knights have friends in high places, too. They could call in—"

"They won't be calling anyone," the agent interrupted. "The observation team has activated the cell phone jammer. It'll be nothing but hiss and static over the airwaves around that place."

Good. That was good. So no more of Rock's friends and colleagues would be racing to the rescue.

"You mentioned offensive maneuvers. What, exactly, will those entail?" R.D. asked anxiously.

This thing needed to be over. The sooner, the better. And then things could start getting back to normal. Well...the *new* normal. Because with Rock out of the picture, The Project, R.D.'s baby for the last half decade, was officially dead.

But maybe, just maybe, if everything continued to work according to plan, there would be a resurrection of it one day. All it would take was a *tiny* policy change, and The Project could once more be breathed to life. But that required the party nomination, which required campaign funds, which required—

Christ. It was all so complicated and messy.

"It's simple," the agent interrupted R.D.'s spinning thoughts. "Either Babineaux gives himself up without a fight, or the CIA teams storm the castle, killing everyone inside. After all, as far as the CIA knows, they *are* aiding and abetting a rogue operator and known serial killer."

Serial killer...

If The Company only knew the caliber of men Rock had supposedly murdered, they'd likely saint him instead of sacrifice him.

R.D. leaned forward once more, picking up the end ball on the stainless steel Newton's cradle sitting at the edge of the maple wood desk. It'd been a gift from a grateful patient—the Newton's cradle, not the desk. And, unlike the other gifts received over the years, this one hadn't been thrown directly in the trash.

Why?

Probably because it was a reminder that for every action, there was an equal and opposite reaction. Releasing the ball, R.D. watched distractedly as it slammed into the row of stationary balls, causing the one on the opposite end to shoot out. Kinetic motion at work.

Click, click, click.

Rock was like that ball. He had the power to affect a cascading change that could eventually blow up everything R.D. had worked toward for years. Already, he'd caused a series of ripples that were spreading…

Storm the castle. Kill everyone inside.

That would certainly solve most, if not all, of R.D.'s problems. But, unfortunately, it'd never come to that. *Rock* would never let it come to that…

"You know as well as I do that Cajun bastard will give up everything, fight to his last breath to protect the innocent, to do what he thinks is right. And if given a choice between sacrificing himself or watching his friends fight a battle they have no hope of winning, he'll choose the first option each and every time. We can't have that."

Click, click, click.

The balls continued to bang against each other, their cadence keeping time to R.D.'s rapidly beating heart and—

"Which is why I've secured an alternate ending."

"What do you mean?"

"I have a hit man in place to take Babineaux out if he decides to do the honorable thing and give himself up."

Jesus. He said it without any remorse, without any

thought to the good work Rock had done for them over the years. Still, R.D. had to appreciate that pragmatism. This was a situation that required one and only one solution.

"The Cleaner?" R.D. asked hopefully. "Have you found him?"

"No. The Cleaner is still off the grid." Which was just one more thing R.D. needed to worry about. "I have another man in place. No worries. This is almost over." With that, the line went dead, and silence reigned in the wood-paneled office, broken only by the *click, click, click* of the balls on the Newton's cradle.

Chapter Fifteen

"WHAT DO WE DO NOW?" VANESSA ASKED ANXIOUSLY, blowing like a racehorse and glancing around Eve's plush living room at the harried faces of the Knights.

Harried…except for Ozzie. He didn't look the least bit harried. Quite the opposite, in fact. The big goofball was grinning like a loon, chomping on his gum to beat the band, and squeezing Rock with one arm while clutching a mean-looking machine gun with the other.

"First things first," Boss said, running a hand through his hair. "We need to call Becky and Eve and tell them to hold back. We don't want them blowing in here and giving those CIA pricks a reason to open fire."

"I'm on it," Ozzie said, releasing Rock in order to dig his cell phone from his hip pocket.

"Please, don't do this, Boss," Rock pleaded, briefly closing his eyes. "Just let me go. Let me—"

"I'll let you go if you tell me you're responsible for what happened to those men," Boss said.

And, oh, no. Oh, *crap.*

Quite unintentionally, Boss had posed the question in such a way that Rock could answer in the affirmative. If what Rock had told her, about being the reason those men were dead, was true. And, yep, right on cue…

"*Oui*," Rock said, opening his eyes and nodding, his hard expression even more stony than usual—which probably had a lot to do with the fact that his face was covered in dust and blood. "I'm the reason they're dead."

Everything in the room came to a standstill.

No one moved, no one blinked, no one so much as dared to breathe. The Knights just stared at Rock, their expressions varying from absolute shock to wary disbelief. And Vanessa was about to open her mouth to refute Rock's claim when, suddenly, in the resounding, pin-drop silence, she picked up on a gentle whirring she hadn't realized had been nibbling on her subconscious since they'd barged into the living room.

Now, it burrowed under her skin like a chigger, driving her batty.

What is *that?*

It wasn't the air conditioner or the clothes dryer. It wasn't the subtle hum of the refrigerator. No...this sounded familiar. It sounded like...

She glanced around, and that's when she saw a big blue dick taped to one picture window. She blinked, but there was no mistaking what she was seeing.

Big. Blue. Dick.

And not only that, but the other two windows in the room were equipped with a tube of lipstick. Except each tube of lipstick appeared to be vibrating.

What in the—

"So *now* will you let me go, *mon ami?*" Rock asked, his tone tinged with desperation as he stared at Boss's ravaged expression, which dragged Vanessa's attention away from the plastic cock and oscillating lipsticks and back to the crisis at hand.

"Bullshit, Rock!" she spat, clenching her hands into fists in order to keep from grabbing him so she could shake some sense into him. "You told me yourself you weren't the one to pull the trigger."

And boy, oh boy! If she'd thought the look he shot her when he'd been in the back of that pickup truck was enough to boil her blood, it was nothing compared to this one. Because she'd take the fire of hatred any day—after all, Rock had once told her that love and hate were two horns on the same steer—over this ice cold derision.

Was it just her? Or did the temperature in the room drop twenty degrees?

"It doesn't matter!" he hissed through clenched teeth, frosty daggers shooting from his eyes, his tone glacial.

"Of course it does," Boss asserted at the same time Ozzie said, "Uh, yeah, dude. It kinda does."

"*We have you surrounded!*" That deep voice sounded over the loudspeaker once again, and Vanessa was astonished to see Ghost—the man whose face was usually fixed in unreadable lines—actually roll his eyes.

"Are they kiddin'?" he asked, shaking his head. "There are, what? Six guys in that van at the most, and they think they've got us surrounded?"

"They're CIA," Steady replied completely deadpan. "Full of their own pomp and circumstance. If there were only two of them, they'd think that was enough to do us in."

"But that won't be the case for long," Boss added. "They've got to be calling in backup, so what's our plan? Any ideas?"

"Boss," Rock said, then implored, "*Frank.*" And, oh, hell no. Nobody called the big man by his Christian name save for Becky and his sister. Vanessa turned to the Black Knights' leader and, yep, sure enough. The muscle in Boss's square jaw ticked out a hard rhythm, and there was actual fear in his eyes. Fear that Rock might say something to change his mind. "You have to let me go, *mon frere*. It's the only way to keep everyone alive."

And *that* would be the something…

She held her breath as she watched Boss consider Rock's statement, then the big man shook his head "I…I refuse to believe that."

That's what he *said*, but Vanessa wondered if Rock could hear the uncertainty in Boss's tone. To her, it was as clear as a struck bell.

"It's true," Rock whispered, stepping forward to lay a hand on Boss's big shoulder, nodding in that way a person does when they're trying to convince someone to agree with them and, *yes,* obviously he *had* picked up on Boss's kernel of doubt.

"Rock—" Boss began, but he was cut off by Ozzie swearing loudly.

"What the hell is the fucking matter with you?" Steady asked the question they were all thinking.

"Cell phone jammer," Ozzie said, looking ready to throw his phone on the ground and stomp it to smithereens. Of course, with his love of technology, he only glared at the offending piece of equipment like it had personally betrayed him, before shoving it back in his pocket. "So what now? How do we keep Eve and Becky hell and gone from here?"

And, suddenly, all eyes turned to Vanessa.

A deep foreboding throbbed in her chest before deciding to make like a Canadian goose and migrate south to the pit of her stomach.

"What? What am I supposed to—"

"You need to go out there and keep them away from the house," Boss said, and she was shaking her head even before he finished. "Those spooks wouldn't dare shoot an unarmed woman."

"No way. I'm not tucking tail and running." At this, she turned to Rock, stuck out her chin, and glared. He might hate her guts, but she loved him and she damned sure wasn't going to leave him right when the CIA was poised to blow him and everyone with him to Kingdom Come—wherever *that* was.

"Go, Vanessa," Rock nodded, and…was she imagining it? Or did something in his eyes soften, just for an instant.

She decided to pretend that was the case even if it wasn't, and she stepped forward, placing a tentative hand on his arm. His lean muscles bunched beneath her fingers, reminding her of how hard he'd been against her, how knowledgeable he'd been when giving her pleasure. Reminding her of…too much. "No," she whispered. "I'm not leaving you."

"Don't you think you've done enough?" he hissed. His jaw was clenching so hard, she marveled he could speak at all. And, yessir, she obviously *had* been imagining that softening of his eyes. "You've doomed us, so the least you can do now is go save Becky and Eve."

She flinched like he'd hit her, but, in truth, his words—and specifically his hard, cutting tone—felt more like a knife, slicing her to the bone.

Ozzie frowned at Rock, "Hey, that's not fair. She only—"

"Save it, Ozzie," she interrupted, stepping back and shaking her head, a deep sadness pervading her body and weighing down her limbs. "He might be right."

In Black Knights vernacular, she might've fucked them

all. Her love for Rock, her desire to have him back with her, back with the Knights, might've blinded her. Kept her from seeing what was really the right move. Which was probably leaving him the hell alone to try to figure out and clean up this mess by himself.

Rock was nothing if not capable of dealing with his own problems. But despite what he'd told her time and again out in that jungle and on the long ride to San Jose, she thought she'd known better. She thought she'd known what was best.

What an asshole she'd turned out to be…

"But—" Ozzie tried again.

"No buts. If I need to go out in order to keep Becky and Eve from barging in here and making the situation worse…" If it was possible to make this situation worse, considering her decision to betray Rock had backfired so fantastically that he was now cornered by the same group of people he'd managed to elude for the last six months. And, oh yeah. She'd simultaneously managed to put all the Knights in the middle of the CIA's crosshairs, too. "…Then that's what I'll do."

And even though it took everything she had to turn away from Rock, even though her instinct was to throw her arms around his neck and tell him exactly what she was feeling, she knew he wouldn't welcome the gesture, nor would he want to hear her words. So, with a deep, fortifying breath, she started to march out of the living room only to be stopped by a callused palm on her forearm.

For one brief moment, her heart sprouted feathers and soared. Did Rock…?

But, no. It was only Boss.

"I'll walk with you," he said, his expression solemn, that kernel of doubt still in his eyes.

"Yeah," she swallowed, amazed to discover she was about to completely blow her cover as a hard-assed operator—*again*—and burst into tears. But she sucked it up. Literally. She made a snorting sound as she raked in another breath. "You have to know he's not telling us everything, right?" she whispered lowly, keeping the conversation private. "He wouldn't have played even a tiny part in killing innocent people. He…he just *wouldn't* have."

"Hell, I know that," Boss grumbled quietly. "But as right as you are about that, *he* might be right in that the only way out of this thing now is to give him up."

Oh, geez. Just the thought of what the CIA would do to him if they got their hands on him…

The walk to the front door was the longest she'd ever taken, especially since each step took her further and further away from the only man she'd ever loved. But when they finally reached their destination, Boss didn't give her a moment to second-guess herself. He opened the door the barest inch, shouting out, "I've got a woman exiting! Don't shoot!"

"Affirmative!" That loud voice echoed over the speaker and down the side of the mountain in the opposite direction, an effective death knell to the part she was going to play in the rest of this operation.

But just before she squeezed through the door, hands up, palms out, she heard Steady yell to Boss the four most fantastic words ever spoken in the history of the world…

"I've got a plan!"

Rock stood by the front door to Eve's vacation home, listening to the eerie sound of those black Chinooks muttering overhead, aware of the fact that the original six CIA agents had now ballooned to over twenty, and trying to guess what the odds of this thing actually working might be.

Because Steady's big plan?

His death. Pure and simple. Richard "Rock" Babineaux needed to die.

And with his head aching like a rotten tooth and the room spinning ever so slowly due to the fact that he was a pint and a half low on blood, he figured he was pretty close to accomplishing that goal.

"Two to one," Ozzie said from beside him. Because in all the years they'd worked together, the two of them had made a game of weighing the odds.

Unfortunately, this wasn't a game.

And he was starting to get that feeling…

The one that told him things could go really wrong, really quickly. And he absolutely hated that feeling. Especially since he'd left Vanessa with the impression that this was going to be all her fault.

He hadn't wanted to be so hard on her, but he'd needed her out of the house. Safe. And the quickest way he'd known to accomplish that feat was to blame her for their current predicament and guilt her into leaving.

Of course if this thing went sideways, those were going to be the last words she ever heard out of him and…

Sweet Lord almighty!

When she saw him go down, she was going to flat-out lose her shit—all the women were—and he hated that. He hated knowing she was going to think, just for a little while, that his death was on her. Because, yes, she'd betrayed him, and by God he may feel like holding her down so he could wring her neck, but he in no way wanted her to suffer under the impression that—

"Naw," Steady scoffed, interrupting his thoughts. "It's way better than that. I'd say it's closer to fifty-fifty."

Way better?

Steady considered it *way* better that he only gave this thing—*his* plan—a fifty-fifty shot of working?

Rock closed his eyes and girded his loins to do… well…what he was about to do. Because the truth of the matter was, they'd run out of options. So when Steady had piped up with, "You need to die, Rock," before laying out a plan to make that happen, on *their* terms, they'd decided to give it a go.

But now that he was here, about twenty seconds away from opening that door and stepping into the abyss, he was beginning to regret his decision to go along with this harebrained scheme. Of course, that probably had a lot to do with the fact that, besides there being twenty-plus agents stationed outside with direct orders to shoot him dead if he put up any kind of resistance, he had three small capfuls of plastic explosives taped to his chest.

That's right.

Plastic explosives. Taped. To. His. Chest.

Mon dieu, he could only pray Wild Bill was on top of his game with those charges—way the hell at the very pinnacle of his game, in fact. Because when dealing with explosives of any kind, especially C4, you didn't just check your work once—you checked it three times. And, by God, you better never let your attention wander while handling them or you might wind up missing a few digits at best, a few lifetimes at worst. And if Bill hadn't calculated those percentages just right...

Merde. He couldn't think that way. These men had had his back for years, and he trusted each of them implicitly. Still, that didn't stop the breath from shuddering out of him as Boss opened the door and shouted, "He's coming out! Hold your fire! He's unarmed and coming out! Do I have your word you will *hold your fire*?"

A long, interminable second passed, then that deep voice that'd been issuing commands and yelling threats for the last forty-five minutes sounded over the loudspeaker mounted to the top of the van.

The van that was now parked across the street. The same one the women were huddled in front of, being held at gunpoint—and, *oui, that* particular situation completely coddled his balls. "This is Special Agent Patrick Wilhelm! And you have my word, Mr. Knight, that as long as there's no funny business, we will hold our fire!"

Boss turned to Rock then, and the expression on the man's face was enough to have Rock shaking his head and grinning. "Don't worry, *mon ami*. We're the Black Knights." And harking back to their days with the SEALs, he added, "Hoo-ah?"

"Hoo-ah, Rock!" Those Knights gathered around him barked in unison before he threw the door open and stepped over the threshold.

The first thing to hit him was the pungent smell of aviation fuel. The choppers overhead were perfuming the jungle and neighborhood beneath them. The second thing to hit him was the setting sun. It was a bright, orange ball, glowing low along the horizon, and he blinked against its molten brilliance. It was beautiful, perhaps the last sunset he'd ever see…And too soon, a sound to his left diverted his attention. The people from the house next door were standing out on the road, watching the unfolding drama with wide, worried eyes.

Of course, that was nothing compared to Vanessa's expression.

When his gaze zeroed in on her, held securely between Eve and Becky, he felt like keeling over then and there. Before his cue. Because the woman was bawling her pretty eyes out, pulling against the two women and shouting over and over again, "Rock, I'm so sorry! I'm so sorry!"

"It's okay, *chere*," he whispered, knowing she couldn't hear him. "It's gonna be okay." Then he closed his eyes and waited for his end…

Chapter Sixteen

WHAT HAPPENED TO THE PLAN? VANESSA THOUGHT frantically.

Steady was supposed to have a plan! But this wasn't a plan. This was Rock giving himself up in order to save all of them, which *wasn't a plan*!

"He can't do this," she sobbed, noting that now instead of her holding Becky back from rushing into the house to be with Boss, both Becky and Eve were having to hold *her* back from sprinting to Rock. "There has to be another way. There has to—"

"Stop it, Vanessa!" Becky barked in her ear, wrestling her back toward the van's bumper like a pint-sized bar brawler. "If you go flying up to him like some sort of wild banshee, the CIA just might kill both of you. Use your friggin' head, woman!"

And, yes, Becky was right. She wasn't using her head; she was listening to her heart. And she'd already done enough of that today, hadn't she? Because it was her heart that'd insisted she bring Rock back here…

Gulping down the hard knot of fear and remorse that'd been steadily growing in her throat ever since Bill and Steady tackled him off that dirt bike, she forced herself to stop struggling. But, it was obvious both Becky and Eve didn't trust her as far as they could throw her, because each woman kept a restraining hand on her arm.

She didn't care. Nothing mattered right now except the

man who was standing on that threshold, looking so brave and honorable as he sacrificed himself for all of them.

She wanted to yell at him to come down from that cross he'd climbed up on, but she knew it'd do no good. Once Rock made a decision about something, it was nearly impossible to change his mind. And he'd obviously decided, along with the rest of the Knights—and you better believe she was going to rip every single one of them a new asshole for agreeing to this—that giving himself over to the CIA was the only solution. The only way out. For *them.* Not for him.

Jesus, what did I do by bringing him back here?

Doomed him, that little bastard of a voice answered.

She closed her eyes, hoping beyond hope that when she opened them again she'd discover it had all been a dream. A very, *very* bad dream…But, no. No such luck. Because when she took a deep breath and blinked against the brightness of the sun glinting off the whitewashed stucco house, he was still standing there. Still looking so brave and honorable and…and so goddamned *sacrificial*.

She could not believe she'd *done* this to him, brought him this point of no return, of no more options except to give himself up. She'd destroyed him and any chance he had of clearing his name by trying to save him. And she'd never, never as long as she lived, be able to forgive herself. She'd just made the biggest mistake of her life, and what made it all the more terrible was the fact that the biggest mistake of *her* life might very well result in the end of *his* life.

The world around her dissolved into nothing but a blur as she allowed her eyes to linger on his wonderfully plain and, at the same time, wonderfully beautiful face.

He was pale. Even at a distance, she could see that. His dark goatee stood out in harsh contrast to the skin of his face. And the clean bandage he'd applied over the wound on his neck was almost indiscernible against his pallor.

And, yeah, who wouldn't be pale? He was about to turn himself over to the CIA as a traitor, and The Company wasn't exactly known for its leniency toward traitors.

Pale, but clean, she noted distractedly. At some point he'd washed off most off the mud and grime they'd accumulated from their trek through the jungle, and she didn't doubt that was because he figured he was in for a very long, very rigorous examination—both mental and physical—and why add sweat and dirt to the discomforts he was sure to suffer at the CIA's hands?

He'd traded in his tank top for a loose, gray T-shirt, which only emphasized how much weight he'd lost over the last few months. He'd definitely been running on empty when she found him.

But at least he'd still been running, that taunting voice whispered.

A hard sob shook her as she watched him take a step forward at Agent Wilhelm's command. Then a gunshot rang out, loud and shockingly obscene. It was followed by three more in quick succession, and that's when her world ended...

—❧—

When the first charge blew, Rock didn't need to pretend to stagger back as blood sprayed out from his chest and up into his face. The C4 packed quite a little punch and, even though they'd put protective tape beneath the cap containing the small amount of explosive and a good amount of his blood, it still managed to sear his skin.

The second and third blasts were a little harder to fake, but he did his best.

Of course, the fourth shot caught him completely off guard and had him landing flat on his back with a loud *umph*. His left ear felt like it'd been sheered clean off the side of his head.

Had Ghost decided to take one real shot? Make it count? Maybe to help Rock out with his bid for an Academy Award? If so, Rock was certainly going to give the man a piece of his mind, because...

Merde.

He'd didn't remember the part where he signed up to be Picasso.

Then again, going through the rest of his life minus one ear was a small price to pay if this thing actually worked. And that was the last thought he had before utter confusion exploded around him.

Suddenly Boss was screaming, "You bastards promised not to shoot!" at the same time Agent Wilhelm shouted, "Hold your fire! Hold your fire! Which one of you assholes is firing!"

And Vanessa?

Well, Vanessa was just screaming her head off. Even through all the pandemonium, Rock could hear the agony in her wail as Boss hooked strong hands beneath his armpits and, with a mighty heave that had every single one of Rock's sore muscles protesting, began hauling him back into the house. He let his head loll back on his neck, kept himself completely boneless. And once the soles of his boots cleared the threshold, Steady, ready and waiting at his predetermined spot, slammed the door shut with a loud *bang*.

Then it was Ozzie's turn in this little sideshow they'd scripted. The kid, after receiving his cue from Boss, squirted some of the blood Steady had drawn from Rock's vein not more than thirty minutes ago onto the floor. Boss dragged Rock back through it, creating a huge bloody trail indicative of a man who'd just sustained three shots to center mass and a fourth one—four, really?—to the head. At the designated location, about fifteen feet down the hall and mostly concealed by the partition leading into the kitchen where they'd faked a humongous pool of blood, Boss dropped him.

Rock opened one eye, caught the concerned look on Boss's face, and gave him a thumbs-up. The C4 had managed to singe him, and he thought he smelled the pungent aroma of burning hair—which told him they should have shaved his chest before taping the explosives on—but, other than that and the god-awful ringing and burning in his ear, he appeared to be in one piece.

Huh....

He hadn't really believed it would work. Then again, Wild Bill Reichert *did* know more about the esoteric use of all things that go *boom* than any man in the world.

Agent Wilhelm's voice sounded again over the loudspeaker, only this time he was relaying his intention to enter the premises and ascertain the condition of the rogue operator.

Rogue. Rock detested that word. It was synonymous with a cheater, a blackguard. And, while technically he was operating outside of orders—had been for the last six months— none of those descriptions accurately portrayed him.

"Come on in, you sonofabitch!" Boss shouted after he'd run back to the door, throwing it wide open. Rock figured now was the time to pull out his best Meryl Streep as a beam of golden sunlight slipped in through the opening, highlighting the back of his head where he lay in that sticky pool of fake blood and…

Sweet Lord. The sound Vanessa made when she saw him.

He was certain he'd hear it in his nightmares from this day forward. Because if heartbreak, guilt, denial, and grief all combined together into one huge, ugly lump, it would make the awful noise tearing out of Vanessa's ravaged throat.

It's not real, chere.

But for her, unfortunately, it was. And there was nothing he could do to reassure her. In fact, he felt a little guilty when it occurred to him that the scene she was causing likely went a long way in helping convince the CIA that what they'd just witnessed was, indeed, his death.

And, as if Boss could read his thoughts, the big guy continued yelling, "You've killed him!" And even though Rock had his eyes closed, he imagined Boss was standing in the doorway like an avenging angel, all two hundred forty pounds of pissed-off operator, puffed up and looking ready to shoot someone. "You might as well come and see your handiwork!"

Uh-huh. Rock could just imagine Agent Wilhelm jumping right on that, especially since it would require him to approach Boss.

A couple of interminable seconds passed before heavy footsteps pounded up the steps of the front porch. Rock tried to pay attention to the direction those steps moved, but it was difficult given he was distracted by the noise of all three women sobbing hysterically. And the guy who'd been holding the gun on them, who was *still* holding the gun on them by the sounds of it, kept shouting, "Get back! Stay put!"

Rock silently promised to kill the *morceau de merde*—piece of shit—if he so much as twitched that trigger in the women's direction, but his attention was soon diverted by the conversation taking place at the front door…

"Who took the shots?" Boss demanded, his tone filled with enough authority and rage to make most men curl into a protective fetal position. "Because I want that bastard's balls on a platter!"

"It wasn't us," Wilhelm declared vehemently. His voice sounded far less official when it wasn't booming at them over the loudspeaker. "Swear to God, it wasn't. One of my men saw a flash from a scope coming from the trees across the way. I've got part of my team in pursuit of the shooter."

Shooter. That would be Ghost, and no way in hell would the CIA catch him. That man came by his nickname honestly. If he wanted to disappear? He did. Period. End of story. Just… *smoke.*

"Bullshit!" Boss thundered, sounding like he was vibrating with fury. *Go Boss! Way to sell it.* "You just killed an innocent man. And when we find out who was *really* behind all those murders back stateside, I'm going to see that you're stripped of your position and the only job you'll get in the intelligence community is that of urinal cake replacer in the men's bathroom at Langley's detention center!"

Urinal cake replacer? Was that even a real job?

"It *wasn't* us!" Wilhelm shouted ferociously, and, okay, so *there* was that official tone.

For a couple of minutes, obscenities were exchanged, and Rock imagined the two men were face-to-face like a couple of rabid dogs, snarling and barking and slathering. Then Wilhelm said, "I need to examine the body."

Body. *Mon dieu*, it was bizarre to be referred to as such.

"You lay one finger on that man," Boss rumbled, his voice pitched so low you could feel it in your chest like the boom of fireworks on the Fourth of July, "and I'll personally put a bullet in your brain."

"You wouldn't dare," Wilhelm scoffed. And Boss must've made a face that begged the CIA agent to call his bluff, because a couple of seconds ticked by before Wilhelm opened his mouth again. And this time, his tone was far less assured. "Look, Mr. Knight, my men *didn't* kill Babineaux. Someone else did. As a rogue," there was that despicable word again, "he probably made a lot of enemies. Someone was waiting to take him out."

And, as Rock's dear ol' daddy used to say, *B.I.N.G.O. That spells bingo*!

Because that was *exactly* the conclusion to which they'd hoped the CIA would jump.

"Even if what you're saying is true, you're not touching him," Boss declared, his uncompromising tone saying it all. Rock was pretty positive the guy's Rock-of-Gibraltar expression probably said it even better. "That man lying dead over there," he imagined Boss hooking a thumb in his direction and he held his breath, "has done more for the safety and for the sovereignty of our country than you and all those men you've brought with you combined. He bled red, white, and blue since the day he was born," mostly just red, Rock could vouch for that, "and I won't have you poking and prodding at his corpse, defiling him more than you already have."

"I've got orders—"

"You've got orders to confirm his death," Boss interrupted. "Well, as I'm sure you can see, the man is dead. If you want confirmation that that's really Richard 'Rock' Babineaux lying over there in a pool of blood, you can just scoop up a sample and take it back to your fancy-schmancy lab at Langley. I'm sure you have a DNA profile on him from his time with the SEALs."

And hadn't *that* been a fun day in the Teams? When they'd all filed down to the infirmary where an automaton-looking asshole with a needle and some plastic tubes took their blood, swabbed their cheeks, and removed a follicle of hair from each of them? Funner still was the fact that it'd all been done on the not-so-unlikely chance that their bodies were so badly burned or shredded or *whatever* that normal means of identification wouldn't work.

Of course, he never thought he'd be using those tissue samples to help *fake* his own death. But if there was one truism in the spec-ops community, it was always expect the unexpected.

The silence while Wilhelm considered Boss's decree stretched until it was palpable. Like a rubber band pulled to its breaking point. And Rock's heart, usually pretty good about keeping a steady beat, began thundering in his chest so loudly he thought it a miracle Wilhelm couldn't hear it even from thirty feet away. And wouldn't *that* be the way to blow this whole can of worms wide open?

He fancied he could actually hear the second hand ticking on Boss's big diver's watch. Everything hinged on Wilhelm accepting this particular edict.

And just when he was sure the guy was going to balk, Wilhelm yelled, "Dietz, bring me the collection kit! We've got samples to take!"

—∿—

He was dead. She'd killed him.

She might not have been the one to pull the trigger, but

she'd killed him just the same—and, yes, at any other time she'd have appreciated the fact that those were the exact words Rock had used to describe the deaths of those men and...

Had used...

She was already thinking of him in the past tense.

Oh, God! She fell to her knees as two words spun around and around inside her brain.

Rock's dead. Rock's dead. Rock's dead...

But even though her head knew it was true—she'd seen him take three shots straight to the chest and...oh, sweet Lord...the blood; the blood had been terrible—her heart was another matter entirely. Her heart couldn't accept the fact that he was really gone. It was throbbing against her ribs, aching, denying what she'd seen with her own eyes.

And there was a part of her, an overwhelming part that wanted to scramble to her feet, run to Rock and gather him in her arms. Just squeeze him and kiss his lips before the warmth of vital, vigorous life left his body forever. Because that part of her, irrational as it may sound, believed that if she could just hold on tight enough, if she could just hold on long enough, he wouldn't really be gone.

But this stupid CIA agent refused to let her go...

Then, from the front porch, she heard Wilhelm, that sonofabitch who'd let Rock get shot, ask Boss if he could pull a hair from Rock's head and the tenuous thread that'd held her broken pieces of sanity together snapped.

"No!" she screamed, struggling to her feet, flinging away Becky and Eve's hands, ignoring the CIA agent who yelled, "Halt!" as she ran toward the house...toward Rock.

She no longer cared if she lived or died. All she cared about was getting to him.

And even when she felt the evil eye of that agent's

machine gun settling between her shoulder blades, she didn't stop. Her feet flew across the street. "Don't you touch a hair on his head, you *motherfucker!* I'll kill you! I swear to God, I'll kill you!"

Her voice was nothing but a high-pitched shriek. And it was official. She'd completely lost it. But even though she *knew* she'd completely lost it, even though a part of her was standing outside of herself, watching herself do and say these things and not believing it, she couldn't stop.

Rock's dead. Rock's dead. Rock's dead...

The mantra kept time with her boots pounding up the porch steps. And she was amazed she wasn't already sporting a hot piece of lead between her shoulders, especially when she shoved Agent Wilhelm, who was standing by the front door, watching her in wide-eyed astonishment, aside.

"Ma'am, I—"

But that's as far as he got before her boots crossed the threshold, and she was immediately stopped by Boss's big arms. He closed them around her to form of a huge, human straitjacket.

"Let me go!" She sobbed, struggling in his unyielding grip as the fire of remorse and denial scorched through her veins and turned each breath she managed to rake in to hot ash. "Let me go to him!"

"Leave him be, Vanessa," Boss said in that bearlike growl he'd perfected. "There's nothing you can do for him."

And that's when her heart caught up with her head. Hearing those words...*There's nothing you can do for him...* was the final nail on the coffin of her hope, her...denial.

Rock's dead.

And right at that moment, darkness consumed her and she knew no more...

Chapter Seventeen

"HE'S DEAD."

They were the two most comforting words Rwanda Don had ever heard, which made up for the fact that R.D. was stuck in a coat closet, having been pulled away from the benefit dinner by the ringing phone. "You're sure?"

"According to reports, he took three slugs to center mass and one to the head," the agent relayed without the slightest bit of remorse.

R.D. couldn't quite feel the same. After years of working with Rock, it was hard to take pleasure in the man's demise. Especially since that demise would not have been warranted if the high-minded sonofabitch had just left well enough alone.

But Rock wasn't one to leave things alone.

And now he'd paid the ultimate price.

"The Agent in Charge has collected DNA evidence, and the teams are pulling out, on their way back home," the agent continued, and R.D. batted away one particular overcoat that smelled like it'd been washed in expensive Burberry cologne. New money. You could always spot them by their overwhelming use of designer fragrance and their need to wave their wealth around with couture labels and excess bling. But, new or old, money was money. And, unfortunately, ever since the dissemination of those funds into the charities, that was something R.D. needed to keep the campaign going. "We'll have the test results in twenty-four hours, but visual confirmation is at one hundred percent. It's over."

Yes, *that* part was over.

"We still have The Cleaner to worry about," R.D. reminded the agent. "Where *is* he? Why has he suddenly gone AWOL? And, most importantly, do you think it has something to do with those trumped-up charges against Rock?"

"We watch and wait on that front," the agent said. And though it was extremely aggravating, R.D. had to admit that was probably the right strategy. No need to start jumping at shadows.

"I'm assuming you're still interested in receiving copies of the intel we acquired from Babineaux's hideout?" the agent asked.

Yes, and then there was *that*.

R.D. needed to see those documents. Needed to make sure none of the information led back to The Project and, by extension, the person code named Rwanda Don...

"Yes. Forward everything to me."

"The money—"

R.D.'s face filled with blood. "We've already agreed on a price! Now get me the goddamned information before everything we've *both* worked for goes up in smoke!"

Slamming a finger down on the phone's *end* button, R.D. took a deep breath, smoothed bunched facial muscles, straightened a seam, and exited the coat closet. Nodding to hotel staff standing at attention along the hallway leading to the Mayflower's ballroom—one of DC's most respected hotels—R.D. pushed through the doors just as raucous cheers erupted from the crowd of well-dressed and well-coifed attendees.

Governor Ward was on the podium, having just made a wonderful speech sure to elicit donations from wealthy pockets, and R.D. beamed with approval.

The nomination was nearly in the bag…

————

Eve hadn't really had the opportunity to get to know Rock before he pulled his Polanski act and quit the country over six months ago. But that didn't make watching the man get shot to death any less horrific.

As she stood in her foyer, the sound of helicopters revving up and leaping into the air behind her—it was amazing how fast the CIA could load up and get the heck out of Dodge once they'd accomplished their mission—she couldn't take her eyes off the man's body. Or what she could see of it, that is. Most of his torso was concealed behind the partition leading into the kitchen, but the back of his head was visible, and there was so much blood. It was everywhere. Spattered against the front door, in a big ugly streak down the hall, and pooled around Rock's head in a grizzly, sticky puddle.

It had been touch and go for a while there, the CIA insisting on taking the tissue samples themselves, even though Boss had apparently threatened to shoot anyone who tried to touch the body. Then Boss made a call to some general in DC before handing the phone to Agent Wilhelm. Eve thought she heard Wilhelm say, "Yes, sir, General Fuller," which would make sense since Pete Fuller was the head of the Joint Chiefs and likely the only person on the planet—besides the president himself—who was capable of convincing the CIA agents to simply stand by the front door and watch while Steady carried out the dubious tasks of gingerly plucking a hair from Rock's head, scooping up some of the spilled blood, and taking a scraping of skin cells before handing all the specimens over to the waiting CIA agents.

Agent Wilhelm had grumbled about still needing to take the body with them to the States, but Boss had threatened at that point to not only call General Fuller back, but also to put a bug in the ear of the Costa Rican government, which, from what Eve could gather, would've guaranteed an international dick-measuring contest because the United States wasn't supposed to engage in covert operations in the Central American country without explicit approval from the host country's government, which the CIA had *not* obtained.

In the end though, she didn't think it was legal, political, or job-related worries that had Agent Wilhelm settling for the samples they'd collected. It was the look each Black Knight wore. The look that said, *Over our dead bodies*.

And speaking of dead bodies. There was Rock. So still…so *lifeless*…

Oh, geez Louise. It was too awful to contemplate.

She didn't realize she was openly sobbing until Billy grabbed the back of her head, pulled her into his arms, and pressed her face into his warm shoulder.

He smelled like leather and sunshine and something faintly chemical. Except for that last thing…he smelled just like Billy. Just like she remembered him smelling all those years ago. During the best and worst summer of her life…

"Shh, Eve," he whispered in her ear, his breath hot against the side of her cheek. "It's gonna be all right."

His deep voice should have been comforting. But it

wasn't. Because she'd just witnessed a man being gunned down on her front porch. And she was beginning to have her doubts that anything would ever be all right again.

"Why?" she snuffled against his shirt, aware she was probably covering the thing with snot, but she'd be embarrassed about that later. For now, all she could concentrate on was the resounding silence in the house now that the helicopters had flown away. The silence that was broken only by Becky's soft sobs. And her own, come to think of it. "Wh…why would they d-do that?"

Hadn't Rock deserved the right to defend himself? Wasn't he an American, after all? How could his own government just kill him in cold blood? And, yeah, she'd heard that CIA agent claim it was some mysterious shooter—whom they had never been able to find, by the way—but she knew it had to have been them. The men who were supposed to uphold the country's laws, not crap all over them in the absolute worst possible way.

"Shh, Eve," Billy soothed again, but it did nothing to console her, especially when she heard Vanessa—the woman had fainted dead away; she'd never seen someone actually *do* that—come to with a horrific shriek.

"Rock!" she screamed, and Eve pushed out of Billy's arms in enough time to watch Vanessa spring into a sitting position from where Boss had laid her out on the floor. Then she was scrabbling over to Rock, slipping and sliding on her hands and knees in the man's blood and another hard sob clawed its way up the back of Eve's throat.

Oh, it was terrible. She couldn't watch. But she couldn't tear her eyes away either. Because Vanessa, tears running down her face in a terrible mess, grabbed Rock's head from the puddle of blood and lifted it, hugging it against her chest before bending to place a gentle kiss on the man's lips…

And what happened next didn't make a bit of sense.

Because Billy settled his hard, callused palm over her mouth, and from the corner of her eye she watched Boss do the same thing to Becky. Then, before Eve could begin to struggle, Boss asked, "We clear?"

And that's when she noticed Ozzie over in the corner tapping away like crazy on a laptop keyboard. "As far as I can tell," the wild-haired man answered, frowning at the screen and then shooting a pointed look toward the windows of the adjacent living room. "But let's stay vigilant."

"Affirmative," Boss said, then, "Okay, let's get the body cleaned up and ready for transport."

And that's when Rock's shoulder moved, and Eve saw his wide hand emerge from behind the partition to settle on the back of Vanessa's head.

Eve understood then why Billy had placed his palm over her mouth, because before she could call it back, a shriek of surprised terror rippled up from the depths of her shaking chest.

"Shh," Billy whispered into her ear again. "It was all a hoax."

"Vanessa, *chere,* just breathe," Rock crooned, and the sound of that slow drawl and silken baritone kissed her ears and had another hard sob ripping up the back of her ravaged throat. It felt like she'd swallowed industrial-strength bleach. But she couldn't bring herself to care.

Rock was alive! He was alive!

But how…?

She'd seen those bullets hit him. She'd seen him go down. Yet, here he was. Sitting at Eve's dining room table after having grabbed a quick shower and change of clothes, reaching over to run a reassuring hand through her messy hair even as he held a tea towel against his ear.

And in the ten minutes since he'd been lying in that pool of blood, in the ten minutes since he'd pulled her to him and kissed her back with everything he had—probably to keep her from screaming her fool head off at the first sign he wasn't dead—she hadn't been able to stop crying.

It was like something inside her had broken and couldn't be fixed…

Oh, she'd think she had herself under control, the tears would dry up, the shaking would stop and then, suddenly, off she'd go again, proving what an incredibly *un*hardass she really was.

Jesus.

"Done." Becky walked into the living room, dusting off her hands like she'd been chopping logs instead of putting batteries into an amazing assortment of vibrators before taping them to all the windows in the house—along with Eve's help. Which was another thing Vanessa had yet to fully process, the sight of Eve Edens, Chicago's reigning socialite, with huge, ridiculously colored plastic cocks in her hand. "No more optical bugs up in this joint. Bam!" Becky acted like she was spiking a football before she broke into a little victory dance.

"Let me get a look at that ear," Steady said, grinning and shaking his head at Becky as he sauntered over to Rock, his camouflage Army-issued medical kit held loosely in one tan fist.

"Nothing to be done for it," Rock said, pulling the tea towel away. There was a shallow, half-inch wide chunk of flesh missing from the outer edge of his ear.

"At least we can stop the bleeding," Steady muttered, setting his kit on the table and unzipping a pocket. He reached inside and came out with a package of QuikClot.

"*Merde*," Rock groused, his goatee drooping at the corners. "That stuff burns like the fires of hell."

"Quit being a baby," Steady teased, ripping open the pack to shake some of the powder onto Rock's torn ear. Rock hissed and grimaced and Steady rolled his eyes. "It's better than losing any more blood and—"

Blood.

There'd been so much blood…

Vanessa couldn't help it; another loud sob shuddered out of her.

"What's up with her?" Steady asked, one black brow arched in question.

"I think the dam's developed a major structural crack," Rock replied, frowning over at her even as he held still so Steady could tape a makeshift bandage around the wound on his ear. "*Chere*," he murmured again, grinning and giving her a reassuring wink. "It's okay. *Je suis bon*."

Yeah, he might be good, but she was definitely *not*. Because she could have *killed* him. And she could *not* get the image of him taking those shots to the chest out of her head. The gruesome sight of blood spraying in a terrible shower, of watching as he—

Just then, the back door inched open, and Ghost slid into the house, fluid like a shadow, quiet as a whisper.

"We good?" He posed the question to Ozzie, who was

at the other end of the dining room table, alternately typing on the keyboards of two humming laptops.

"Seem to be," Ozzie nodded, never taking his eyes from the screens. "Looks like the satellites have been repositioned, and I'm not picking up any other signs of surveillance."

"Yeah," Ghost nodded, approaching the group in order to carefully place his sniper rifle—he called it Sierra, of all things—on the table before lowering himself into a seat opposite Vanessa. "I didn't see any sign of continued surveillance, and I made two passes 'round the property before enterin'. Maybe we're good t'go."

And that's when Rock leveled Ghost with a hard look. "What the hell, man? Why'd you shoot my ear off?"

"First of all, it's not off, it's just missin' a chunk," Ghost said.

"Oh, goody. I love it when we argue over semantics," Ozzie snorted, grinning even as he continued to type and watch his computer screens.

Ghost shot the guy an exasperated look before turning back to Rock, finishing with, "And secondly, I didn't do it."

The room fell silent as Ozzie quit typing, his fingers hovering over the keyboards.

"Then who did?" Boss asked from his position in the doorway. The concerned expression he wore made his scars stand out white against his tan skin. Of course, when Becky strolled over to hook an arm around his waist, his face softened slightly before he bent to place a kiss in her hair, next to her temple.

The exchange was so natural it was almost instinctual, and Vanessa, watching with envious eyes, was dismayed when another hard sob threatened. Try as she might, she couldn't hold it in. But because of her clenched jaw and tightened lips, it came out sounding less like a sob and more like a hysterical little *eep*.

"What's wrong with you?" Boss demanded, glowering. "Are you sick? Did you catch something in the jungle while you—"

Desperately, she shook her head, hoping he'd leave well enough alone.

Geez, Van, you're really impressing the hell out of your boss and your coworkers today, aren't you?

"The dam's sprung a leak," Steady offered, and Boss's brows slid down his forehead, his expression all but screaming *ah, women's theatrics; I get it*.

But he didn't get it at all. Nobody did.

"So who tried to smoke Rock?" Ozzie asked, oblivious to the fact that she was sitting there suffocating under the guilt of knowing her actions could have very well gotten Rock *really* killed instead of only *pretend* killed.

"Dunno," Ghost shrugged. "I heard the shot directly to my left after I'd fired off the blanks, and I tried to track him. But by the time I'd eluded those CIA boys, the sonofabitch was long gone."

All eyes, including Vanessa's—red-rimmed and still brimming with tears, no doubt—turned to Rock. And, oh, he was so beautifully alive. Looking much worse for wear, but alive. She couldn't help herself, she reached over and squeezed the hand that was closest to her, needing to assure herself that he was real and warm and vital, half-expecting him to pull away because he was so rightfully *pissed* at what she'd done.

But he didn't.

Just the opposite. He turned his palm and laced their

fingers together, and her heart pounded against her ribs until she fancied everyone seated around the table could see it fluttering the fabric of her safari shirt.

"*Non*," he shook his head. "You all stop makin' eyes at me. I haven't the first clue who that might've been. Unless Rwanda Don didn't want me talkin' to the CIA and decided to hire someone to take me out. Which I wouldn't doubt, come to think of it."

"Rwanda Don?" Boss asked as he toed out a chair and settled his bulk into it, pulling Becky down onto his lap.

Bill walked into the room right at that moment with Eve directly on his heel, and it was obvious from the man's stony expression and Eve's red cheeks that they'd had yet *another* disagreement about something. Vanessa wasn't sure what the story was with those two, but it was obviously long, convoluted, and painful. And speaking of...

Rock must've decided the whole hand-holding/reassuring thing had gone on long enough, because he returned her hand to her lap and gave it a judicious pat before planting his tattooed forearms on the table. And so much for her momentary, desperate hope that maybe he'd forgiven her for bringing him here, for nearly getting him killed.

But how could she really expect him to do that? She couldn't even forgive herself.

Oh, God. If she started crying or...or *eeping* again, she was sorely tempted to grab Ghost's sniper rifle and just put herself out of her misery.

Fortunately, Rock's next words interrupted the world-class pity party she was in the midst of throwing for herself. "Rwanda Don is a long story. You sure we have the time for it?"

Boss frowned as he glanced at his watch. "Hell no. General Fuller arranged transport for us back to the States, and the van should be here any minute."

"Well, if we don't have time for this Don person," Becky piped in, "then would someone mind telling me what the heck happened out there?" She flung a hand in the general direction of the front door.

And, yep, that was just the distraction Vanessa needed, because she was way past needing an explanation herself. After all, she *had* seen Rock get shot. Four. Times.

Yet here he sat. Not a scratch…er…not a bullet hole in him.

"Steady," Rock nodded toward the Knights' resident medic, "you want to take this one, *mon ami*. It *was* your idea, after all."

The smile that lit Steady's face was blinding, and it occurred to Vanessa why everyone—including Steady himself—had tried to pair the two of them together when she first joined the group. After all, they both had that hot Latin blood, and Steady possessed the kind of dark beauty all women found irresistible.

All women except her, obviously.

Because the moment she'd walked into BKI headquarters, she'd only had eyes…er…*ears* for Rock. All it had taken that first day on the job for her to start salivating and imagining Cajun French–speaking babies was for Rock to open his mouth, and Carlos "Steady" Soto hadn't stood a chance. From that very first word, she'd been toast. Complete and total toast.

She was *still* complete toast.

And he was never going to love her. *Never.* Capital N…And why should he? If he hadn't had a good reason before, he certainly had one now. She'd nearly gotten him *killed*.

Another ravaging sob threatened in her chest, but this time she managed to hold it back.

"I just figured," Steady began, tugging on his ear as he set out to explain his grand scheme, "that if we had any hope of making this thing work, of helping Rock out, we had to get the friggin' Company off our backs. And the only way that was gonna happen was if Babineaux kicked the bucket. So we drew some blood, had Wild Bill fit him with explosives, let Ghost go out and simulate sniper shots, and voila!" he snapped his fingers, "Ding, dong, the Cajun's dead!"

For a long moment after that rather short monologue, there was nothing but silence, each of the women staring at Steady, trying to determine if what he'd said made a lick of sense. Becky was the first to come to the conclusion that, *no*. No, it didn't. Because she shook her head rapidly, like a cartoon character without the resulting *eye-ee-eye-ee-eye-ee* sound effect, and said, oh-so-eloquently, "*Huh?*"

"Yeah," Vanessa nodded, a million questions spinning through her brain, but the most important one Becky seemed to have nailed. "What she said."

Bill rolled his eyes. "I don't know how the hell you managed a medical degree when you can't explain yourself for shit."

Steady's face was wallpapered in big dollop of *what-the-hell-dude*. "I hit the high points."

"Yeah," Bill nodded then quickly shook his head. "Like that time you told me to take the high ground and cover you while you recon-ed that leafy foxhole in Colombia? When you just happened to leave out the part where you planned to toss a grenade in the sonofabitch, blowing it to Kingdom Come and bringing every FARC guerrilla within a quarter-mile radius down on our heads?"

"Ooh, ooh," Ozzie raised his hand like a kid in a classroom. "I've got one. Like the time you told me to distract that Taliban warlord with my witty repartee so you could scout his compound for the location of his weapons stash. Only instead of marking the location of said stash, you called in an airstrike and watched it go *kaboom* while I was left to make like Usain Bolt and hightail it on outta there. That was classic."

Steady waved an unconcerned hand. "Details are superfluous."

"Jesus," Bill's expression was filled with disbelief, then he shrugged and turned back to the group at the table. "Steady drew Rock's blood because we figured the CIA would want DNA evidence. Then I took a portion of that blood, put it into three bottle caps along with a small amount of plastic explosive, and set each with a charge before taping them to Rock's chest. Ghost," he pointed a chin at the man in question, "armed with blanks and the remote detonator for the charges, snuck out before The Company sent in backup. When Rock stepped out on the porch, ostensibly to give himself up, Ghost pulled the trigger on his sniper rifle and the remote detonator simultaneously, which resulted in the sound of gunshots and the high-powered bursts of blood you saw shooting out from Rock's chest. Add a little more blood in a smear down the hall, fake a giant pool of blood with red food coloring, oil, and some thickening agent, and voila!" He snapped his fingers, grinning at Steady, who was now the one to roll his eyes. "Ding, dong, the Cajun's dead."

"Like I said," Steady sighed, "superfluous details."

"But—" Vanessa was trying to wrap her head around the complexity and brilliance of the plan. It wasn't really working. Her head. Not the plan. Obviously, the plan had worked perfectly.

"Plus," Ozzie added, "we figured they'd assume Rock had made enemies, being rogue and all—"

"I hate that word," Rock grumbled, and Vanessa, even with her head spinning, once again experienced the overwhelming urge to reach over and grab his hand. But she figured she'd pressed her luck about as far as she could with that little move, so she laced her fingers together in her lap, squeezing them until the her nails bit into her knuckles.

"—so it'd be easy for them to jump to the conclusion there was an assassin out there looking to put an end to his life, which," Ozzie frowned, "come to find out, is probably true. Dude," he turned to Rock, eyes wide, "you're unbelievably lucky you were already flopping around from those explosives, making yourself a moving target, or you'd probably be sporting a new hole in your head."

"Don't remind me," Rock grunted, drawing a design on the tabletop with one long finger, frowning concernedly.

"And since we're talking about that flopping around…" Ozzie continued, grinning like the cat who'd swallowed the canary. All he was missing was a feather sticking out of his mouth. "You could use some serious acting lessons. Daniel Day-Lewis you are not, my friend."

Rock opened his mouth, probably to refute Ozzie's aspersions upon his acting ability—after all, he *had* managed to fool the CIA and all the women present; Vanessa would *not* think about that—just as Boss's phone began blasting the opening bars to "Don't Fear the Reaper."

"Our ride is two minutes out," the big guy announced after glancing at his iPhone's screen. "Ghost, grab the body bag."

"Body bag?" Eve interjected for the first time since they'd all gathered around the table, a definite hint of horror in her tone. "Why do we need a…a…*body bag*?"

"Because Rock's dead," Boss shook his head, frowning at the poor, obviously overwhelmed woman like maybe she'd been absent the day they handed out extra IQ points. "We can't very well let him walk out of here. No one but the people in this room, not even General Fuller or the other Knights, know what we've pulled off. And they won't. Not until we get home. And Fuller won't know until after we clear Rock's name. Which begs the question, Ghost. You gonna be all right not telling Ali what's going on?"

"She's at her parents for the next two weeks, and she knows I'm on a mission. She doesn't expect t'hear from me for days," Ghost said, bending to pull a thick, black body bag from a duffel bag, laying it out on the floor and unzipping it.

Eve's gulp was audible. And seeing that monstrosity there, watching Rock push up from the table, Vanessa felt herself on the precipice of bursting into tears yet again.

So close. She'd been so close to really losing him. Had that bullet that'd taken a bite out of his ear been two inches to the right…

This time, it was *her* gulp that was audible.

"*Chere*," Rock leaned down to whisper in her hear, his hot breath tickling her lobe. "You didn't do anything wrong today. You gotta stop beatin' yourself up, okay?"

No, she couldn't stop beating herself up for almost getting him killed. No way. No how.

Then he grabbed her chin and forced her to look at him. "I'd have done the same thing if I were in your shoes," he insisted, and Ozzie piped in with, "He's right. We all would've done the same thing."

"But how c-can you forgive me after I almost got you—"

"Vanessa," he held her gaze until she could see the truth of his words in his eyes. It warmed her heart like nothing else ever could. "I don't hold anything against you. You did what you thought was right. That's all any of us can ever do."

And a little bit of the weight that'd been pressing on her shoulders lifted away. Because if Rock could forgive her for what she'd done, then maybe she could begin working toward forgiving herself. Sucking in a shaky breath, she nodded. And Rock must've been satisfied with what he saw in her face, because he winked and then strolled over to lay down inside the body bag.

And, okay, seeing him there like that, inside that retched thing, had tears threatening again. But she figured she used up her allotment of everyone's patience when it came to hysterics, so she held them back.

"You…you c-carry body bags around with you?" Eve asked, watching with wide, terrified eyes as Ghost zipped Rock into the thing.

"Of course," Boss said, bending to grab four duffels, shouldering two on each arm. "This isn't a game of Risk we're playing here. Men die in this business. But one thing's for certain: if they do, we never leave 'em behind."

"Hoo-ah!" Ghost, Bill, Steady, and Ozzie all answered in unison. And hearing that call to arms, that battle cry to duty and brotherhood, sent a shiver streaking down Vanessa's spine.

Chapter Eighteen

Black Knights Inc. Headquarters
21 hours later...

"WHY CAN'T I GO HOME NOW?" EVE ASKED.

Bill watched as she glanced warily around at the hard faces of the Knights. Everyone who'd been down in Costa Rica was now gathered around the conference table on the second floor of the shop, anxiously waiting to hear the sit-rep—situation report—from Rock. Everyone except for Ozzie, that is. He was over at his bank of computers monitoring all CIA activity to make sure no one was second-guessing the show they'd seen down in Central America.

Of course, after the eighteen-hour, two-plane-ride journey north to Chicago, and the three-hour power nap each of them had taken upon arriving home—they'd all been fall-on-their-faces tired—it was a pretty sure bet if they hadn't heard anything from The Company by now, they were in the clear in that respect.

Still...the Knights never took chances. Case in point, the next words out of Boss's mouth. "You can't go home because you know too much." The big guy's jaw looked hard as a rock, his gray eyes flinty.

A hand jumped to Eve's throat as she swallowed... loudly.

Becky punched Boss on the shoulder, glaring at him.

And when Eve turned to Bill beseechingly, he had to fight hard to keep from reaching across the table to grab her hand. Consoling her, protecting her, reassuring her had been his job…once.

But not anymore.

"What the hell?" Boss demanded, glowering at his wife, rubbing his shoulder as if her puny swipe actually hurt him.

"The way you said that, *because you know too much*," Becky lowered her voice, frowning lopsidedly, and it was actually a pretty good impersonation of Boss at his most badass, "made it sound like there was an unspoken *and now we have to kill you* tacked on to the end."

"It did?" Boss turned to Eve, his scarred brow arched in a ragged line.

"M-maybe," Eve admitted. "Sort of…"

Boss glanced around the table, his expression asking the rest of the Knights for verification of the ladies' assessment. He frowned fiercely when he was met with various winces, shrugs, and nods.

"*See*," Becky stressed, never one to pass up an I-told-you-so. "You could use a little work on your delivery."

"That's not what you said last night when I—"

"Jesus, God, please spare me," Bill held up a hand. *Erp.* The thought of Becky and Boss getting in on made him throw up a little in his mouth. One thing a big brother never wanted to picture was his little sister doing the nasty.

"You need to stay here because the CIA might try to make a grab for you as soon as you leave," Ozzie added, swiveling away from his computers in order to face the group, for once not being his usual irreverent and obnoxious self.

"What?" Eve glanced at him in alarm. "Why? I thought you said they bought the ruse, so—"

"Just because they bought it doesn't mean they won't think to double-check. And you're an easy target, Eve." Ozzie's serious expression—yes, the kid could pull one out on occasion—softened. Although, Bill had to admit, the fact that the guy was wearing T-shirt with a picture of Spock that read *Trek yourself before you wreck yourself* sort of ruined the whole hardened-operator persona he'd suddenly donned. "All it'd take is ten minutes with them poking and prodding at you before you'd fold like a cheap lawn chair."

"Well I—" Eve began, but Bill decided it was time to interject. They didn't have time to sit around pacifying Eve's fears, and they really needed to get moving on, what he suspected was going to be, the monumental task of figuring out how to clear Rock's name.

"Ozzie's right," he declared, making sure his harsh tone brooked no argument. When Eve turned to blink at him rapidly, raking in a shaky breath, he figured he'd nailed it. "You've still got a week left on the vacation time you took, so it's best if you spend it here with us." God help him. "Hopefully, by the end of that week, we'll have either cleared up this misunderstanding with Rock or we'll at least be well on our way to doing so. Then you'll be free to leave."

And, yes, that sounded a bit autocratic, even to his own ears. He figured it sounded autocratic to hers as well when her eyes narrowed to slits and her lips tightened.

"You can't hold me here against my will." She pinned him with a determined stare, one she wouldn't have been able to pull off a decade ago.

"No, we can't," he assured her, allowing his face to

soften. "But we're asking. Nicely. Pretty please with a cherry on top?"

And, yes, he'd pulled out the big guns. Because that little phrase was one they'd used between the two of them that summer when they'd been young and dumb, when they'd mistakenly confused their mutual lust for something more. And maybe he was an asshole for whipping it out now, but he knew it would work like a charm. Because it always had…

"O-oh…" She looked flustered, just as he'd hoped. "Okay, but I—"

"Good," he cut her off. He couldn't stand it when she looked at him like that, so trustingly, so…innocently. She *wasn't* innocent. Sheltered, yes. But not innocent.

Although she had been.

Once.

And he'd been such a goddamned idiot to try to protect that innocence and—

"All right," Boss interrupted his thoughts, which was just as well. He needed to get his mind off the woman who'd— *spurned*, he guessed was the word—him, and get the sucker back in the game. "And since we're talking logistics here, Ozzie, how goes the plans for Rock's funeral?"

Okay, and how bizarre was that? To be talking about a guy's funeral when he was sitting catty-corner from you?

"It's good," Ozzie nodded. "The Connelly brothers have a guy who works in the city morgue. He's tagged a John Doe with Rock's name and entered it into the system." The Connelly brothers were a quartet of burly Chicago boys who manned the guardhouse by the main gate at BKI headquarters. And the crazy, Irish bastards had enough connections around the city—both legitimate and illegitimate—to make Bill's head spin. "We've got a

casket on order from Lakeview Funeral Home, and we're
negotiating a plot in Lincoln Cemetery. All BKI personnel
are putting the finishing touches on their various missions,
or abandoning them completely, and should be trickling
home in the next seventy-two hours, give or take."

And wasn't that going to be fun? When the Knights
walked in expecting to attend a funeral, only to realize
Rock wasn't really dead? If the Connelly brothers' reac-
tions to the news were anything to go by, Rock was going
to be sporting some cracked ribs. Which was another
thing Bill was still trying to get his head around, the fact
that the Geralt, Manus, Toran, and Rafer Connelly could
manage to simultaneously wrap a guy in a bear hug. Talk
about one hell of a weird sight to behold. It'd looked like
a human boulder pile, all huge and lumpy.

"If anyone is watching," Ozzie continued, "it'll look
like we're doing what we should be doing. Making all the
arrangements to bury one of our own."

And *bam!* As always, the I's had been dotted and the T's
had been crossed. There were days when Bill still felt the
need to pinch himself to make sure he wasn't simply dream-
ing up the well-oiled machine that was Black Knights Inc.

"Fantastic," Boss declared. "So now it's time to get
down to brass tacks." He turned to Rock, and Bill watched
the ragin' Cajun blow out a deep breath. The man still
looked dead-dog tired, but there was no mistaking the
determination in his eyes or the hard set of his jaw. Rock
was finally ready to explain just what the *hell* was going
on. "You wanna tell us why the fuck our government is
saying you killed ten hardworking Americans?"

-∿∿-

And there it was.

The question Rock knew the Black Knights had been dying to ask from the first second they had him back in the fold.

He glanced across the table at Vanessa. And even after everything, after all the terrible things he'd said to her, after the way he'd pulled her close with one hand while simultaneously pushing her away with the other, she still looked at him with such trust in her beautiful, dark eyes, such…*conviction*. Like no matter what he had to say, she'd never stop caring for him, never stop believing in him.

Dieu, she was some kind of woman.

The *best* kind of woman. The kind that deserved a loyal, honorable, trustworthy man who'd worship the ground she walked on and love her with all of his heart. Too bad Rock could give her everything on that list except for that last thing.

The most important thing…

"First of all," he began, slowly, then found himself stopping almost immediately in order to wrangle his erratic thoughts into some kind of order. This explanation was going to be long and laborious and, truth be told, he was probably going to step all over his dick trying to lay out the intricacies of the whole sordid tale. Not to mention the fact that he was as nervous as a long-tailed cat in a room full of rocking chairs over how the Knights were going to take it. He wasn't sure whether they'd see what he'd chosen to do as something worth glorifying or reviling. Since, honestly, he reckoned it fell somewhere in the middle of the two.

"First of all," he tried again, and this time he was able to finish his thought, "I want everyone to know, I didn't kill those men. In fact, some of those deaths I wouldn't have the first clue how to manage. I mean, how *do* you give a guy a heart attack?"

The question was meant to be rhetorical, but Ozzie interjected with, "Atropine."

"What's that?" Vanessa asked, her dark brows pulled down in a sharp V. While her attention was diverted, Rock found his gaze drifting over her pretty profile. And lower…to her breasts. Those beautiful breasts he'd kissed and caressed, those perfect nipples he'd licked and sucked and watched furl into little brown nubs. They were covered now by a lipstick red T-shirt that worked to emphasize the beauty of her black hair and olive skin, but he could remember them perfectly and—

Merde. Now his dick was hard.

Way to go, dipshit, he chastised himself even as he shifted uncomfortably in his seat. Dropping a hand, he tried to inconspicuously adjust himself into a more comfortable position, but when he glanced up, he found Ghost watching him with one black brow quirked in question.

He rolled his eyes and jerked his chin in Vanessa's direction—better to admit the truth than have Ghost thinking he was some sicko perv who got wood from discussing all the esoteric ways to kill a man. Realization dawned in Ghost's eyes, and he nodded once, sliding Vanessa a surreptitious glance before turning his attention to Ozzie.

And, *oui*, maybe Rock should take a page from Ghost's book and pay attention, too. After all, it was his job, his *life*, they were in the middle of discussing.

"…derived from the nightshade plant," Ozzie was saying. "It's incredibly dangerous. Just a minute amount sprayed on the skin—"

"Great. Good," Boss cut him off, coming as close to

rolling his eyes as Boss ever came. "You're a genius. We get it." The big guy turned back to Rock. "Continue, will you?"

"*Oui*." Rock didn't relish the thought of laying everything out on the table. But as his dear ol' daddy used to say, *It's time to shit or get off the pot*. He'd been keeping secrets from the Knights for long enough, and it was time they knew the truth. "So, while I didn't do the actual killin', I *did* interrogate them. I was the one to extract confessions from them." And, oh, the horror of digging around inside those men's heads. Of discovering what made them tick, what made them happy or sad or horny or scared…

If it was possible to catch sociopathy from the scum of the Earth, then Rock was doomed. Because he'd gotten closer to rolling around in the psychological muck with those men than anyone ever should.

"That's why your vanishing acts meshed with their kidnapping reports," Ozzie said. "You were interrogating them."

"*Oui*."

"But interrogating them for what? Get them to confess to what?" Steady asked, leaning forward on the conference table, lacing his fingers together. Everyone liked to give Steady shit for being flaky, but the truth of the matter was, the man had a mind like a steel trap. He was the only Knight in residence who had a chance of giving Ozzie a run for the money in the IQ department, which was probably why the two of them got on so well. A case of über brain meeting über brain…

"The better question would be, what *didn't* they confess to," he said, trying to push away the memories of some of those confessions, of hearing the filth that spewed from the men's mouths, of seeing their utterly inhuman lack of remorse for what they'd done.

Until they'd been caught, of course.

They'd always been sorry as hell to have been caught.

"Drug traffickin', weapons deals, slave trade, child prostitution, murder, rape, extortion, money launderin', the selling of military secrets." The list went on and on. "You name it; these men did it. But in order to get a visit from me, they had to have knowingly participated in, or ordered the murder of, an innocent. That was a rule."

Boss turned a page in the dossier in front of him. The one that listed all ten of the men Rock was accused of killing. And, oh yeah, there was the added benefit of having the guys' pictures printed there as well.

Like Rock really needed any reminders…

The name, date of birth, face, and list of crimes of each of those men had been etched on the back of his brain with a dull knife.

"Nothing in the files suggests these men were involved in anything illegal," Boss muttered, slowly flipping pages.

"Of course not," Rock snorted derisively. "And that's because the world's greatest crooks are nearly impossible to catch and prosecute." He looked around the conference table at the people he'd come to think of as family. The people who'd never stopped believing in him and who'd put their lives on the line, who'd gambled their reputations—who were *still* putting their lives on the line and gambling their reputations—to help him clear his name, and hoped like hell they'd be able to understand why he'd done what he'd done. "*Connards* like these men, men with connections and money and power, cloak themselves behind dummy corporations and under layers of cover. It's the middlemen who get caught in sting operations. But these guys at the top? They almost always get away to either start another racket or simply amp up their current ones."

"Seriously," Ozzie concurred, nodding sagely. "You guys watched *The Wire*, right? The head honcho always seemed to slip away and—"

"Must it *always* come down to music, movies, or television with you?" Boss interrupted exasperatedly. "I mean, not all of life's problems can be boiled down to pithy lyrics or witty dialogue."

"Says you," Ozzie snorted, shaking his head. "From an anthropological point of view, pop culture is a way to express the—"

"Ozzie's right about the head honchos," Rock cut in before the conversation digressed any further—as it had the tendency to do when Ozzie was in the room. "And because our justice system is both righteous on the one hand and flawed on the other, these guys are left to go about their business, killin' and maimin' and generally wreakin' havoc on humanity. These men were domestic terrorists in every form of the word. And it was my job to apprehend them and get them to confess to their crimes, to make them spill their vile guts, catching the filth they spewed on tape."

"And after the confessions?" Boss asked.

"I let them go," Rock shrugged. "But not before I sent the tape to Rwanda Don. And from there I washed my hands of it."

"What do you mean?" Ozzie asked. "You didn't know they were being killed?"

"Oh, I read in the paper how a couple of them died, seemingly of natural causes, but I didn't know the rest were six feet under until I got tagged for killing them and started doing my own investigations. Up 'til that point, I just assumed my interrogation tapes were being used in open and ongoing cases to bring the sonsofbitches to justice."

"And you don't know who killed them? If it was this Rwanda Don person or—"

"*Non*." Rock shook his head. "Don was the brains behind The Project, not the muscle. Maybe he was the one who did the research on the men, found the ties to black market operations or murders…I don't really know. All I know is, I was given a thorough, *incredibly* thorough file on each man. These files would not only document what information could be gleaned about this individual's nefarious activities, but also his personal habits. His likes, his dislikes, his familial ties. Everything. And that's what I'd use to get inside his head."

"These were the same files The Company found in your PO box?" Boss asked. "The ones that implicated you in the men's deaths?"

Rock shook his head. "*Merde*. I don't know why I kept them. It's almost like I wanted them for proof. Proof of what I'd managed to get those monsters to admit to. Proof that The Project was working. But you take those files and the fact that all those men are dead, some later proven by foul means, and it's pretty damnin' evidence, even if I do say so myself. Somehow, Rwanda Don knew about the PO box. Knew just where to point the CIA so I'd get fingered for it all."

Boss sat back in his chair, his eyes narrowed on Rock's face. "Why do I get the impression the word *project* is capitalized?"

Rock lifted a shoulder, his lips twisting. "Probably because you've been in the spec-ops community long enough to smell the stench of a hush-hush, backdoor operation when it's sitting in the same room with you…"

Chapter Nineteen

R.D. FROWNED AT THE NUMBER ON THE CELL PHONE'S screen.

Why is he calling? They'd agreed to sever ties unless The Cleaner showed up and—

The Cleaner…*Oh, shit.*

"Hello?" R.D.'s hand was shaking. Just the thought of what that man was capable of, combined with the fact that he'd gone missing soon after Rock's Burn and Delete notice went out over the wires, made R.D. incredibly wary.

No, wary wasn't the word. Maybe *downright terrified* was a better turn of phrase.

"My guy didn't kill Babineaux," the CIA agent said, disregarding a salutation.

For a long moment, R.D. was speechless. Then, finally, "What? What do you mean he didn't kill Rock? I thought you said—"

"I know what I said," the agent spat. "But I got that information from the CIA, not the actual man in the field. My guy called me not five minutes ago to say he wasn't the one to make the kill. That it was the other guy."

Now R.D. was *really* confused. "What the hell are you *talking* about? *What* other guy?"

"The other shooter," the agent stressed, and R.D.'s heart stopped. There wasn't supposed to *be* another shooter. Unless…

Could it have been The Cleaner?

But why? Why would The Cleaner go after Rock? Unless the man had heard of the charges leveled against Rock and wanted to make sure he actually took the fall for them. But that didn't jive with what R.D. knew of the man…

"What did he look like?" R.D. demanded. "This other shooter? Did your man get a look?"

"Nope." There was heavy disgust in the agent's voice, and R.D. could picture the man frowning fiercely. "He said he was already in the process of pulling the trigger when the first three shots hit Babineaux mid-chest. He said his round only glanced off Babineaux's ear because Babineaux was already stumbling back like a drunkard from the other shots. Then, according to his story, he had to hightail it outta there or risk The Company boys coming down on his head. So he didn't have time to get a look at the other triggerman."

Oh, shit. Oh, *shit. Other* triggerman? What did this mean? What did—

"Do you…" R.D. had to swallow before trying again. "Do you think it was The Cleaner?"

"Why? What purpose could the man have for going after Babineaux?"

"To make sure Rock took the fall for the murders, of course."

There was silence on the other end of the line, and R.D.'s pounding heart caused blood to rush hot and fast. Then, finally, "If that's the case, then he's probably looking to tie up all the loose ends."

Yes. And that was exactly what R.D. was afraid of…

"Wait a minute, wait a minute," Becky cut into the question Boss was poised to ask, and Rock turned his attention toward her. She was frowning around the lollipop sucker protruding from her mouth. "Why'd somebody have these guys killed? I mean, I understand why they *needed* to be killed…" And Becky didn't know it, but that simple phrase helped alleviate some of Rock's trepidation. "…but if you got them to confess, and you had it recorded, couldn't your contact, this Rwanda Don person, just turn them and the tape over to the police? Let them face a judge and jury?"

"No way in hell," Ozzie answered before Rock could. "A confession coerced from a man under duress would be nothing more than empty words. I mean, how would the police know whether Rock had tortured the guy or not, forcing him to admit to whatever Rock told him to admit to?"

"You didn't torture them, did you?" Becky turned to him, dark eyes wide.

"*Non.* Of course not." He hadn't needed to use any physical force, because the CIA had taught him ways of peeling back the layers of a person's mind, of wheedling and picking and prying until the individual being interrogated almost begged to confess.

"So let me get this straight," Boss interjected. "Are you telling me this *Project*," he made the quote marks with his big fingers, "was a government-sanctioned endeavor that assassinated those American criminals who were either too slippery or too careful to be caught by standard police methods? Is that what you're saying?"

"In a nutshell. Although, like I said, I didn't know about the assassination part until after I was burned." But he hadn't looked very hard. Truth was, after delving into their degenerate minds, he'd tried very hard to forget they existed. "Sometimes these guys didn't die until months, even a year later."

"Fuck me." Boss shook his head at the same time Ghost grunted and Ozzie let loose with a string of profanities.

"What?" Becky asked, glancing around the table. "What's so bad about that? I mean, if there'd been a way to prove their guilt, and depending on what state they lived in, they'd have likely ended up with a needle in their arm so—"

"Posse Comitatus is a document forbidding the use of Federal troops inside the U.S.—which Rock certainly *was* when he was part of the SEALs." Boss explained. "Then, of course, there's our Constitution, which prohibits the government from taking action against any individuals outside of what can be proven by law."

"So you're saying this Project was…what?" Becky blinked. "Illegal?"

"According to everything I know about how our judicial system works," Boss said.

"But these were terrible men," she argued. "I mean murder? Slave trading? Child prostitution? These guys were bottom feeders. No," she shook her head, her blond ponytail whipping across her shoulders, "they were worse than that; they were friggin' slopsuckers."

"No denying that," Boss agreed, and another thread of anxiety that'd been tied around Rock's heart loosened. Of all the Knights, that he'd been most worried about how Boss would react to the news that he'd been involved with The Project. Because even though Boss had been known to bend the rules with the best of them, the fact remained, the man rarely broke them.

And The Project? Well, to his utter regret, it appeared
The Project had broken *all* the rules…

"Which brings us around to the question of *who* exactly
you were working for in the CIA," Ozzie said.

And now they were getting to the meat of *one* of
Rock's problems. Because the truth was… "I don't
know," he admitted.

"You don't know?" Boss frowned, his brow furrowed
in a series of deep lines. "So then who set up the interrogation rooms for you? Who helped you snatch these guys? I
mean, they were all wealthy, right? Their security had to
be ultra tight."

"The location of an interrogation room, always in some
abandoned building, was part of their file. It was ready
for me when I needed it. And as far as kidnapping them?"
He lifted a shoulder. "You always did say I was a slippery sonofagun. I just bided my time, slipped into their
inner circle, and grabbed them when they least expected
it." And there were a few times he'd almost been caught.

"Jesus, Rock," Boss breathed, shaking his head in disbelief. *Oui*, sometimes Rock had a hard time believing it
himself. And saying it all out loud? Well, it sounded even
more preposterous than it did in his head. "Okay," Boss
continued, "so then who the hell was this Rwanda Don
person you told us about?"

And again, all he could answer with was, "I don't know."

Boss growled, running a hand through his hair. "Okay,
man, so let's start at the beginning. How did the CIA
recruit you into this…this Project?"

And so it begins… The sad, complicated, *twisted* tale
of his life.

Rock took a deep breath, laced his fingers together on

the table, and started in on a story even *he* sometimes had a hard time believing. Because it was the stuff of B-rated spy films and really bad thriller novels. And, in his case, it also happened to be true…

"After I applied for BUD/S, I was contacted, via telephone, by a guy from the CIA callin' himself Rwanda Don," he began. "His voice was altered, using one of those gizmos that made him sound like he was a throat cancer survivor."

For a second, his eyes snagged on Vanessa's. And there it was again. That look of absolute conviction. Even after all he'd just told them, there was no censure, no judgment in her eyes. *Non.* There she sat, steadfast in her belief that what he'd done was right. And he had the thought again…

Mon dieu, she's some kind of woman. And he wished…

Hell, he didn't know *what* he wished anymore. And then an image of Lacy popped into his head. The way she'd looked in those last days, so skinny and sickly, and his heart hardened.

Non. *Don't second-guess yourself,* mon ami. *You know what loving someone can cost you. And you can't put that kind of burden, that kind of pain, onto someone else.* Because his job with the Black Knights—not to mention his affiliation with The Project—all but guaranteed the likelihood of him meeting an untimely death, and he refused to allow someone who loved him to suffer the kind of loss he'd suffered after Lacy died. The thought was simply unbearable…

He shook his head and continued, "Well, anyway, I was asked if I was interested in comin' in for an interview."

"Coming in where?" Boss asked.

"That's the thing. I was interviewed right there in

Coronado. It wasn't Langley or the Pentagon or somewhere in DC. I went to an abandoned building where I was shown a bunch of CIA credentials before I was hustled into a room by a couple of dudes wearin' face masks. Once there, I was questioned by Rwanda Don and a few other people who were sitting on the other side of a two-way mirror, with all their voices disguised. I'd heard The Company could be pretty loopy when it came to recruiting new agents for new projects, so I went along with it and answered all the questions as honestly as I could."

"And what kind of questions were you asked?" Ozzie said, rising from his chair to stroll over to the conference table. He pulled out a seat to join the group but not before plunking a razor-thin laptop down in front of him.

"The standard fare," Rock admitted, thinking back on that day and how nervous he'd been. It was the first clue he'd had of what a crazy, almost *unbelievable* world the spec-ops community really was. "I was asked about my reasons for wantin' to join the SEALs. About my thoughts on certain government policies. How I felt about the possibility of having to take a life in the line of duty, yada, yada. And then it got weird."

"Weird?" Becky asked, crunching down on the sucker in her mouth. "How so?"

"They started askin' me about my folks' deaths. About how I'd feel if I discovered they hadn't died in an accident. About what I'd do to the man who'd killed them if I could get my hands on him."

"Whoa, whoa," Boss held up a hand. "I thought your parents died in a boating accident down in Louisiana."

"*Oui,*" Rock nodded. "So did I for the longest time. But

at this interview, they showed me information that pointed the finger at Halsey Chemical Company."

Ozzie's fingers began clicking on the keyboard of his laptop before he mumbled, "Halsey Chemical Company. Why does that ring a bell?"

"Probably because fifteen years ago, and then again twelve years ago, they made the headlines," Rock said. "See, Halsey had been dumpin' waste into the bayou near my parents' home for years. Everyone who lived in those parts knew it. A class action lawsuit was brought against the company while I was still in boot camp."

"*Two* class action lawsuits," Ozzie said, eyeing his screen, no doubt having pulled up boatloads of information about Halsey Chemicals and the lengthy trials.

"I'm talkin' about the first one right now," Rock clarified.

"Which was won by the plaintiffs."

"*Oui*," he nodded. "A few mid-level administrative types within the company copped to knowing about the chemical dumps, and they received pretty hefty sentences. The company paid restitution to those families who'd suffered physical ailments, but, you know," he shrugged, his heart thudding slow and hard against his ribs, just like it did every time he thought of the awful injustice perpetrated down in Louisiana, "how do you put a price on a life?"

And for the first time since they'd gathered around the conference table, no one tried to answer a question when it was posed. Probably because the answer was obvious.

You didn't. You didn't put a price on a life. It was impossible...

After a long silence, he murmured, "My best friend, B.B. Fournier, was one of the ones who fell ill. And after several rounds of chemotherapy, an amputated arm, and a shitload of radiation, B.B. finally succumbed to the disease those bastard chemical company suits had given him with their negligence and ambivalence. And then there was my uncle Leon and my cousin Jenna and… and Lacy…"

Sweet, soft Lacy. The girl who'd promised to wait for him to finish his military stint so he could go to college on the G.I. Bill. The girl who'd been long dead, the victim of a rare and aggressive brain tumor that'd metastasized into her lungs and liver by the time his four years in the Navy were up.

"Who was Lacy?" Becky asked quietly.

Rock glanced across at Vanessa and saw realization dawn in her big, dark eyes. "My fiancée," he whispered.

"Jesus Christ, Rock!" Boss rumbled. "Why the hell didn't you ever *say* anything about this to us?"

Probably because it wasn't something he liked to talk about. The fact that everyone he'd ever loved was moldering away in a dank, dark crypt down at the edge of the bayou. But instead of admitting as much, he simply shrugged. "I guess because, as my daddy used to say, the only thing you get from digging up the past is dirty."

"Yeah," Boss said, "but still…"

"I didn't want or need pity. There was nothin' to be done for it. My family and my fiancée were all dead, and that was that."

But it still sat like a bitter pill in the bottom of his stomach, even all these years later, that the only thing the families of the victims of Halsey's carelessness and malfeasance had to show for their lost loved ones were some old photographs and a little pile of money that'd surely run out by now.

"Anyway, I thought everything was settled with Halsey," he continued, shaking away the memory of Lacy's red hair and blue eyes. The love they'd shared had been young and green as an unripe strawberry, but it'd been true nonetheless. And her death had changed him, made him into the man he was today. A hard man. A... *ruthless* man. Vanessa might even call him heartless, and he wasn't sure he'd be able to argue to the contrary. "But, come to find out, Halsey hadn't stopped dumpin' their chemicals. My father caught onto to what they were up to and approached Martin Halsey himself. The man acted all shocked and outraged, assuring my father he'd look into it. 'Course it wasn't until two days later that my father and mother were dead, their boat wrapped around a cypress tree, their bodies lost in the waters of the bayou for nearly a week."

And sweet Lord have mercy, by the time they'd been discovered, there was hardly anything left that was recognizable. Had DNA not proven their identities, Rock would *still* be wondering what had really happened to them....

"Martin Halsey," Boss murmured, flipping to the first page in his packet. He lifted a brow when he read the name that was second to the top of the list.

"*Oui,*" Rock nodded. "He was the second man who confessed his sins to me, which I can promise you were far more prolific and grandiose than orderin' the deaths of my parents. You see, along with knowingly and willfully poisoning the people of Terrebonne Parish, he was also runnin' drugs in from the Gulf...and girls." He shook his head, remembering the disgusting spark of excitement that'd lighted Martin's eyes when the man confessed about the girls. "Thirteen-, fourteen-year-olds...

He'd sell them on the black market for a pretty little penny. And I can assure you, Halsey wasn't just pond scum; he was the muck that lived on the filth that grew on the sludge at the *bottom* of pond scum."

"What happened to him?" Becky asked.

Rock shrugged. "Don't know. I turned in my interrogation tape. Time passed. Then I heard scuttlebutt that local PD were investigating him on charges of kidnappin' and child molestation."

"Says here," Boss pointed at the dossier, "that he got drunk, fell overboard on his fan boat, and found himself in the path of an alligator."

"Yeah," Rock mused. "And even though I was pissed at the time because he hadn't been brought to trial before he died, I satisfied myself with the knowledge his death was appropriate."

"How so?" Becky asked.

"The man *was* cold-blooded, after all." Although in hindsight, maybe prison would've been preferable. Inmates did have a very unsavory way of punishing child molesters…

There was silence around the conference table as that little bit of logic sunk in. "And, of course," he continued, "it wasn't too long after that, Halsey's company got pinched for dumping chemicals *again*—that second trial Ozzie mentioned—and got shut down. I always kinda assumed my interrogation was used to help in that endeavor somehow."

"So, in the end," Ozzie said, "it was a win for the good guys."

"Here's what I don't get," Eve said, and it occurred to him he'd completely forgotten she was listening in. It was one thing for the Knights to know what he'd done, but Eve? What would *she* think of all this? He held his breath as he waited for her to finish. "I don't get how you can't know who you were working for within the CIA?"

Seriously? After all he'd just admitted to, kidnapping, forced interrogation, false imprisonment, *that* was her question?

He made a face and shrugged. "Sometimes in the government-engineered secret interrogator/spy world, there are no clear associations. You see, durin' all my years of trainin', when I'd get leave from SEAL work, the only people I ever came into contact with—outside of office administrative types, that is—wore black masks. *I* wore a black mask. At the time, I reckoned it was supposed to help protect everybody involved with The Project. I mean, *come on,* I was being trained to kidnap and interrogate U.S. citizens. If that story ever leaked…" He whistled between his teeth, shaking his head. "And then, after the training was over, I received a message saying The Project had been put on hold, and I was to await further instructions. A few months later, Rwanda Don contacted me, tasking me with interrogating the first man on that list, and Rwanda Don's been my only connection to Langley ever since."

"So how'd you get paid?" Ozzie asked. "Surely there's a way to trace the money back to its source, to the specific department within The Company…"

Rock looked at the kid and smiled. "I didn't get paid, *mon frère*."

"*What*?" Ozzie wasn't the only one to squawk the question. Rock heard at least three distinct versions of it.

"It was my understandin' that because the work I was

doing was technically illegal, there was no way to compensate me for my time. Not that I'd have taken payment for my services in this particular endeavor anyway."

"Why you?" Vanessa asked. "Why did they choose you?"

"Why'd they choose to burn me?"

"No," she shook her head, her dark hair swishing against her shoulders, which caused one long, inky lock to curl invitingly around her right breast. Her perfect, *perfect* right breast. And, *merde,* there went the brainless wonder again, stiffening up like a reprimanded corporal. "Why did they choose to recruit you in the first place?"

"Like I told you," he said, "I studied psychology in college, but more than that, it was criminal psychology. So I already had a pretty good idea of how a corrupt mind worked. Plus, the psych tests I took while applying for BUD/S training probably showed I was keen on justice and not averse to personally playing a part in handing out that justice when the occasion called for it. Of course, I'm sure it helped that I'd come from a town decimated by exactly the type of man The Project intended to go after. Add to that the fact that I had no family left, nothin' to keep me from going in as deep as it gets, and I was the perfect candidate for the job."

"And everything was going along fine until Fred Billingsworth," Boss mused.

"*Oui,*" Rock nodded. "Out of everyone on that list, he was the only one who was innocent. And I *knew* he was innocent. After interrogating the guy for only thirty minutes, that much was clear."

"So why is he dead like the other nine men on this list?" Ozzie queried.

Rock shook his head, the kernel of bitterness that'd taken

root in his belly over six months ago and had since grown to the relative height of a cornstalk, threatened to choke him. "If I knew the answer to that, I think I'd know the answer to who burned me. See, after I interrogated Fred and determined his innocence, I tried to get in touch with Rwanda Don. Fred was different. He wasn't guilty like the rest. And I wanted to make sure I hadn't screwed up somehow. But, no sooner had I started trying to find a way to contact Don, to make sure he understood Fred was innocent, than I hear Fred is dead. Supposedly from falling asleep at the wheel and running off the road. Which got me to thinking about those *other* two men I'd interrogated whom I knew were *also* dead, presumably by natural causes. I began to wonder if this thing, The Project, wasn't simply a means of gathering information and evidence against these guys, but also a way of having them deleted. You all know what I discovered." He nodded toward the dossier still clutched in Boss's big hand. "That document there says it all. Of course, after I found out about the deaths, then I *really* started to ask questions. I mean, this wasn't what I'd signed on for, right?" He made a face, shaking his head. "Less than four hours after my first phone call to Langley, my Burn and Delete notice came over the wires."

"So then the question becomes," Ozzie mused, "what was Billingsworth investigating that made this Rwanda Don character, or whoever Don works for, so nervous that they'd turn their backs on everything The Project had previously stood for—deleting high-class criminals—and go after an innocent man?"

"My information says Billingsworth was investigating the candidates for the upcoming election," Boss said.

"So you think his murder was politically motivated?"

Ozzie posited. "You think he found something on one of the candidates, and whoever was running The Project from within the CIA commanded this Rwanda Don person to take Billingsworth out? And then when Rock got nosy they decided to take him out, too?"

"I'd say that's a good possibility," Boss said, and Rock couldn't help but agree. That was the avenue he'd been trying to investigate on his own, but he'd run out of leads weeks ago…

For a long moment no one said a word, all of them digesting the ramifications of everything that'd been discussed. Then, once again, Eve broke the silence, quietly asking, "If you don't know who Rwanda Don is, then how did you get the tapes of your interrogations back into his hands?"

And out of all the questions posed today, this was the easiest one to answer. "Before each mission, I'd receive a phone call where Rwanda Don, always with that disguised voice, would give me the address and number of either a PO box or a train station locker or some such thing. I'd go there, pick up one of the files, and then it was up to me to secure the confession. After doing so, I'd drop the confession tape back at the spot where I picked up the files and redial the phone number—which was different every time, by the way. After two rings, I'd hang up, and my part was over."

"So you can't find this Rwanda Don that way," Eve mused, her smooth brow beetled.

And that was the whole problem. As far as Rock could figure, there was *no* way to find Rwanda Don.

"I say we look harder at everyone Billingsworth was investigating," Ozzie said, frowning in consideration. "That seems to be the key."

"Agreed," Steady nodded. "And, Rock, if you could get me the locations of those train station lockers, and anything else you can remember, I can start making calls to see if we can find whoever rented them. Can anyone think of anything else we could try?" he asked the group.

There was silence while everyone considered options, but after a couple of minutes, when no one offered more ideas, Boss slapped a hand down on the conference table. It was his standard signal the sit-rep had come to an end. "Well," he boomed, "I'd say we've got a couple of good threads to pull. So let's start yanking and see what unwinds."

As the Knights pushed up from the conference table, each intent on helping him get clear of this whole, sordid mess, Rock couldn't help but shake his head in wonder. He may've lost his parents and Lacy down in Louisiana, but the Black Knights were his family as surely as if they'd shared a womb together, bonded not by the blood running through their veins, but by the blood they'd spilled together in the field.

When he pushed up from his chair, there was a hard lump of affection and gratitude throbbing in his throat.

Chapter Twenty

VANESSA LIFTED THE PILLOW SHE'D THROWN OVER HER head and glanced at the glowing red numbers on her digital alarm clock.

Oh-two-hundred.

And Rock had yet to stumble up to bed. She knew this because for the last three-plus hours she'd been listening for the telltale *clank-clop* of his cowboy boots on the metal stairs. But if she'd counted pairs of footsteps right, everyone *except* for Rock—and Ozzie—had hit the hay long ago, gone to get a little shut-eye after one hellaciously frustrating day. Between the lot of them, they'd been unable to help Rock come any closer to clearing his name. So, the plan was to tackle the problem again tomorrow, with fresh eyes.

But, first, Vanessa had something to settle with Rock. *Tonight.* If the uncooperative sonofagun would just come up and go to his room and—

The sound of footsteps stopped her mid-thought, and she cocked an ear.

Nope. That wasn't Rock. That soft plodding sounded like Ozzie's Vox sneakers, not the hard wooden heels of cowboy boots. Still, Ozzie might have news...

Vaulting from the bed, she padded barefoot across the room before throwing open the door and catching Ozzie just as he was about to stroll past. A startled hand jumped to the Springfield Armory XD-45 he always had strapped to his side, but as soon as he saw her, he relaxed and leaned a hand against the doorjamb, one blond brow winged up his forehead.

"Well, finally," he grinned. "I've been waiting for you to come to your senses and invite me into your bedroom for—"

She rolled her eyes and shoved a finger over his mouth. "Can it," she said, shaking her head. Ozzie hit on everything with two legs. He absolutely *personified* the term man-whore.

"What did you find out about the folks Billingsworth was investigating?" she asked impatiently. Since they'd hit a brick wall concerning Rock's pick-up and drop-off locations—apparently whoever rented the lockers and such had paid in cash and used an alias, go figure—Ozzie'd been trying to found out everything he could about Billingsworth's investigation. It was now their only hope.

A hope that was squashed when Ozzie shook his shaggy head. "Not much. I know Billingsworth was hired to find dirt on the candidates, but other than a messy divorce, one child born out of wedlock, and an arrest made during a pro-life demonstration outside an abortion clinic, none of the candidates seem to have gotten their noses dirty. I certainly don't believe any of the stuff I just listed would warrant one of them having Billingsworth killed. "

"Shit."

"You said it."

"Have you told Rock?"

"Just now," he nodded

"How'd he take it?"

"About how you'd expect. Seems the guy can't catch a break. Did you know about all that stuff with his family?"

She shook her head. No. She hadn't known. But she should've guessed. Because it all made sense. Those moments when he thought no one was watching and he'd get that thousand-yard stare. Or those times when he'd be joking and carrying on and then, suddenly, go quiet. Then, of course, you had his assertion that he'd never love her…

And though a small part of her worried that was because his heart was still with his dead fiancée, a much larger part suspected he'd simply built a wall around the organ in order to protect it. And could you really blame him? Everyone he'd ever loved was dead, so why would he want to open himself up to that kind of heartbreak again?

She could certainly understand that kind of thinking. After all, she'd suffered despair and loss, too. And, yes, there had been times since her parents' deaths when she'd contemplated the notion that it would be easier if she just never allowed herself to get close to anyone again.

"But don't you worry," Ozzie assured her by laying a hand on her shoulder just as a flash of lightning blazed through her bedroom window and a crash of thunder sounded overhead. Instantly the sky opened up and the steady *thrum* of rain against the roof tried to muffle Ozzie's next words. "We'll figure something out. After all, there isn't anything the Black Knights can't do once we put our heads together."

That seemed to have been the case in the past…but in this instance? Well, suffice it to say, she was beginning to have her doubts. Which meant *Rock* had to be having *his* doubts, and that just sucked so hard.

"Now," Ozzie continued, wiggling his eyebrows enticingly and raising his voice above the sound of the rain. "You gonna invite me in or what?"

"Um," she cocked her head, grinning up at him. It was impossible not to like Ozzie. "I think I'll go with *or what*."

He clutched his heart like she'd shot an arrow straight through it, stumbling back dramatically. "Selfish, hard-hearted woman."

"Goodnight, Ozzie," she said pointedly.

"Goodnight, beautiful," he winked. "But if this ol' thunderstorm scares you, you know where to find me." She snorted and watched as he sauntered toward his bedroom at the end of the hall. Once he closed the door, she turned back into her room and raced toward her bedside table. Ripping open the box she'd stored there, she peeled off some of its contents and turned to check her reflection in the mirror above her dresser.

Um, not good.

Because, for one thing, her hair was a mess—thanks in part to the haphazard, cut-and-go trim job she'd received from Rock out in the jungle. And, for another, it looked like she was carrying enough luggage beneath her eyes to keep herself geared up for an around-the-world vacation…

Running a hasty brush through her hair, she tamed what flyaway locks she could. The under-eye baggage? Nothing to be done for that, so she waved an exasperated hand at her reflection and tiptoed out of her room and down the stairs to the second floor.

It was dark, the stygian blackness breached only by the dangling florescent lights hanging down from the three-story ceiling, illuminating the shop floor below. But, amazingly, the darkness no longer held any fear, even when a crack of thunder rattled the windows and rumbled deep in her chest. And she had one man to thank for that. Rock.

But first…

Walking to the rail, she leaned over, and her eyes immediately snagged on his ass, hugged ever-so-snuggly in his faded Levi's as he bent over his Harley, using a shammy to polish a bit of chrome. The bike was simpler than many of custom choppers in the shop. Not a lot of flash and gizmos, just one fantastically intricate red, white, and blue paint job—the beast was appropriately named Patriot—a long stretch, and a whole hell of a lot of chrome.

Of course there was the occasional flare here and there. Like the leather seat made out of alligator hide and the lid covering the battery box styled with the words *Laissez les bons temps rouler! Let the good times roll!* It was a nod to his Cajun heritage, as were the little crawfish emblems carved into the chrome exhaust.

Then there were the hydraulics...

Patriot didn't lean on a kickstand like some bikes. Oh, no. With the push of a button, it lowered to the ground, supporting itself on its sturdy chassis, which resulted in a motorcycle that was almost impossible to push over. And with a paint job as intricate as that, one could totally understand why Rock would want to ensure nary a scratch marred the surface.

Vanessa loved that bike.

The clean lines and sparkling paint had spoken to her on such a visceral level that when it'd come time to sit down with Becky to conceptualize her own motorcycle, she'd taken a page from Rock's book. Designing something that was as beautiful for its simplicity as it was for its artistry.

You better do this thing before you lose your nerve, that annoying voice whispered through her head, punctuated by a flash of lightning that briefly illuminated the second-floor loft. This time, she chose to heed its advice. After all, too much more standing here, gawking, and she'd need someone with a shovel to scoop of the puddle of estrogen-y goo she'd melted into because… Oh. My. God…the way Rock's shoulders filled out that T-shirt, the way his large, western-style belt buckle lay flat against his washboard stomach, and the way his dark goatee drooped at the corners when he skirted the bike in order to wipe down the gleaming front forks, was just too much.

Patting the packages she'd hidden in her bra, she made her way toward the staircase and quietly descended to the shop floor as thunder echoed overhead. The smell of motor oil and freshly ground metal assaulted her nostrils, but she'd become accustomed to the odors after all these months working at BKI and, more than that, she'd actually grown to *like* them. They reminded her of everything she loved…her job, the Knights…Rock…

The stained cement was cold beneath her bare feet when she stepped off the stairway, but it did nothing to mitigate the fire in her heart. She now knew why he'd been holding her at arm's length, knew why he maintained he could never fall in love with her. And seriously? It was all a giant load of crap.

She was determined to make him *see* it was all a giant load of crap. Tonight. Tonight she was going to push past his defenses, shove all her chips on the table, and go all in.

"Rock?" When she whispered his name, he leaned around the front of the motorcycle, his eyes sparkling in the overhead light, his short hair sticking up from the fingers he'd undoubtedly run through it, and, oh crud, was he hot.

Hot and stubborn and so, so, *so* much in denial.

"What's wrong, *chere*?" His tone was concerned. "Couldn't you sleep? Did the storm wake you?"

She shook her head, her tongue feeling like it'd swelled to ten times its normal size. He stood—a series of bunching muscles and fluid movements—and walked around the side of Patriot.

"You're not having nightmares about that run through the jungle, are you?" His brows angled down toward his perfect nose. "I knew I shouldn't have—"

"No," she interrupted him, surprised to find she could actually *talk* with that swollen tongue. "It's not that."

Then what is it?

She expected him to ask the question, which would give her a lead-in to her proposition. But he remained frustratingly mute, lifting a dark brow in question as a flash of lightning screamed through the tall windows, highlighting the colors of the tattoos on his arms, delineating the hard lines of his biceps.

Well, fine. *Fine.* She'd just do this the hard way—or the easy way, depending on how you looked at it.

"I want to make love you," she blurted just as thunder cracked nearby.

And it was obvious by Rock's narrowed eyes, by the way he cocked his head, that her statement was completely drowned out by the racket.

Crud. To work up the *cojones* to utter those words once was one thing, but to have to repeat it? Good grief, it was like Mother Nature was playing the world's cruelest joke on her. Mentally flipping the bee-yotch the bird, Vanessa took a deep breath and tried again. "I want to make love to you, Rock."

And, yep, he definitely heard her this time…

Oh, how she wished she had a camera, because the expression on his face was priceless. If she'd told him she wanted him to smear himself in motor oil, roll around in glitter, and then let her spank his ass with raw fish fillets, he couldn't have looked more dismayed.

"You know what we discussed in the jungle," he said, his deep voice even lower than usual, rippling up her spine, a form of thunder in and of itself. "About you havin' stars in your eyes and about me not wantin' to hurt you."

"It's bullshit," she spat. "Because no matter what you *think* you know about me, the truth is I don't expect this thing to end in a white wedding and orange blossoms. It's simply this…I want you. I've wanted you since the first moment I saw you." She shook her head. "No, that's not true."

His square chin jerked back on his neck, and a little grin tugged at the corner of his mouth. "Now doncha go holdin' back on my account, *ma belle*."

"Hey," she planted her hands on her hips, "you're not one to lecture me on how to sugarcoat things." Because she remembered what *else* he'd told her in the jungle. *I'll never fall in love with you…*"The *real* fact of the matter is, I haven't wanted you since the first moment I *saw* you; I've wanted you since the first moment I heard you *speak*." She caught her lip between her teeth before grinning and wiggling her eyebrows. "*Your voice, it's like butta*," she said, doing her best impression of Mike Myers's *Saturday Night Live* Coffee Talk character.

She could tell that, despite the seriousness of the conversation they were having, he was having trouble holding back a chuckle. Which was what she'd aimed for. To inject a little levity into the electric atmosphere.

Rock was easier to coerce—which, yeah, that's totally what she was doing—when he was feeling amiable. "You *kill* me woman," he said, his eyes sparkling.

She shook her head. "I don't want to kill you. I want to make love to you. And I'm tired of your excuses."

With that, she threw caution to the wind and took a step in his direction. Followed by another. And another...

Mon dieu, she was stalking him like a hungry lioness and if he didn't do something quick, he was screwed. Metaphorically and *literally*.

And, *oui*, it was getting harder and harder to dissuade her—and himself—especially since the brainless wonder had swelled to let's-get-it-on proportions the minute he saw her standing barefoot on the shop's cold concrete in that lipstick-red T-shirt and those tight black yoga pants that were enough to give him an eye-gasm.

He held up a hand he was disgusted to see was shaking, but, *thanks be to Jesus*, the move stopped her mid-stride.

"I don't want this, *chere*," he insisted as she stood there looking at him, refuting him with the spark in her eye, the quirk of her brow, and the sexy tilt at the corner of her delicious, *too* goddamned delicious mouth.

Then she did something unbelievable and glanced, rather *pointedly*, at the bulge behind the fly of his Levi's. "You're lying," she breathed in that sex-operator tone she'd donned upon first propositioning him.

And, *oui*, she was right about that. Because the truth of the matter was, he wanted it more than he remembered wanting anything in his whole sorry life. He wanted *her* more than he remembered wanting anything in his whole sorry life. But this *wasn't* right. He was trained to figure out what people were hiding, to discover their true motivations, and though Vanessa talked of simply wanting him, in reality, she was operating under the harebrained impression that if she could get him to succumb to her physically, he'd succumb to her emotionally as well.

And that *wasn't* going to happen. It *couldn't* happen. Because then *she'd* succumb emotionally—more than she already had, that is. And he'd be left knowing when he died—and chances were still pretty good that could happen sooner rather than later—she'd be left with nothing but heartbreak and loss. He couldn't do that to her. He just couldn't...

He tried shaking his head, but it was hard given he appeared to be paralyzed from the waist up.

"I know what you're afraid of," she said as she took another step toward him. It was followed by another and another until she was standing in front of him, close enough to touch. Close enough to grab and kiss. Close enough that her cherry-red toenails were almost touching the tips of his alligator cowboy boots. And after one craptastically tough day—oh, who was he kidding? It'd been a craptastically tough *six months*—she still somehow managed to smell good enough to eat. Clean and fresh, slightly minty and *very* womanly.

The brainless wonder in his pants certainly appreciated her nearness. The stupid bastard started pounding against his zipper like a convict pounding against the bars of his cell.

"I'm not afraid of anything," he managed, even though someone, at some point, had shoved a giant fist down his throat.

"You're lying again," she whispered, reaching forward

to run a finger—one soft, delicate finger—down the length of his arm. Goose bumps exploded in the wake of that finger. "I can hear it in your voice. You're afraid that if you give yourself to me, if you let me give myself to you, then that brick wall you've built up around some of your...*softer* emotions will come crumbling down."

"You're dead wrong about that," he growled, grabbing her hand to stop the motion of that maddening digit. "It's not *my* softer emotions I'm worried about. It's *yours*. The last thing I want to do is hurt you, *chere*."

"That's just an excuse. You're hiding behind this oh-so-honorable notion that you have to protect me from myself, when the truth of the matter is you're scared to death that I might be right and you might be wrong."

"I'm not wrong."

"Prove it. Take off your clothes." She said the words clearly, decisively. And, pig that he was, that authoritarian tone went all through him. In that instant, he could totally picture her in a leather catsuit, wearing six-inch heels, and slapping a satin-tipped whip against her palm while she stalked toward him—he'd be tied to her bed with fuzzy pink handcuffs, of course.

Mon dieu, I'm in some serious trouble here.

"Vanessa," he warned, but she just cut him off.

"It's time to put up or shut up, Rock. I want you. I know you want me. You've warned me away multiple times. And, yet, here I am. So...Take. Off. Your. Clothes."

He opened his mouth, only instead of words coming out her tongue went *in*.

He hadn't seen her move, hadn't seen her take that last step toward him, but suddenly she was in his arms, up on her tiptoes, her cool palms on either side of his face, her lush lips planted over the top of his mouth, and her sweet, agile tongue trying like hell to memorize the exact dimensions of each and every one of his teeth.

And that's when it happened.

That's when the tenuous hold he'd had on his self-control, on his *self-denial,* broke. God help him, but he was going to take what she was offering. Because she was right. He'd done his best to dissuade her, but he was finished fighting his own wants and desires…He was finished fighting *her.*

Grabbing her amazing ass in both hands, he leaned back against Patriot's seat and lifted her until they were aligned. *Dieu.* He could feel the heat of her through her yoga pants, surrounding him, hinting at the silky, sultry bliss he was sure to find between her legs.

He kissed her with everything he had. He *loved* kissing her. Because kissing her was absolutely breathtaking, like oh-my-God-I'm-about-to-come breathtaking. Except they still had all their clothes on, which come to think of it, was a definite plus since he'd undoubtedly already be balls-deep inside her if they didn't, and they happened to be missing one very important component.

Tearing his mouth away, he started to say something then completely forgot what that was when she immediately kissed her way back to his ear, tugging his lobe between her teeth and licking sweetly.

His eyes crossed, and his toes curled inside his boots. How did she know to do that? How did she—

It took everything he had to grab her shoulders and push her back. And when she looked up at him, her eyes half-lidded, sparkling with dark feminine triumph because, *oui,* she'd certainly won this battle—he was a goner, no more fight left in him—he nearly forgot, *again*, what it was that'd made him stop in the first place. But then she moved, rubbing herself against his throbbing erection, and a mere wisp of sanity returned. It curled like a thin line of smoke through his passion-hazed brain and set fire to just enough synapses to have him gritting one word through clenched teeth, "Condom."

Then, even with most of his brain focused on the place where their bodies were sliding together, he had the where-withal to wonder if he'd be able to hold off long enough to even make a condom necessary because, *merde*, she felt so damn good in his arms. All smooth skin and soft curves. Feminine in every sense of the word.

His gaze was riveted to her movements when she lifted a hand and reached into her T-shirt. Then he was surprised he didn't start drooling, tongue hanging out and eyes bulging like a cartoon dog, when she began pulling out the accordion-folded length of condoms she'd stored between her breasts.

Belle ange—his beautiful angel—had come equipped, had she? And Lordy, just the thought of her upstairs, stashing those condoms in her bra because she was bound and determined to seduce him, ratcheted his desire to another level. He wouldn't have thought it was possible, considering right at this moment, he was hornier than he'd ever been in his life, but the way she pulled those condoms out of her shirt, slowly, seductively, had his breath sawing from his lungs and his knees going weak.

Thankfully, he was supported by Patriot's sturdy chassis, or he might've proven just exactly how much of a goner he really was, how wild she really drove him, and taken a header into the shop floor because...

"*Merde*, woman," he breathed, "that might be the sexiest thing I've ever seen." And it reminded him of the time she pulled a pistol from a thigh-high holster beneath her skirt. It'd been during a hotel stakeout, and he hadn't thought it could get much better back then…

Whowee, had he been wrong.

The corner of her mouth twitched just as another flash of lightning illuminated the shop, electrifying the air around them to a fever pitch. He actually felt the hairs along his arms and the back of his neck lift as she leaned forward to whisper against his lips, "Oh, honey, you ain't seen nothing yet."

And then she did it. She took a step back, whipped her T-shirt over her head, reached around to unfasten her bra—damn, he barely got a look at it, just a quick peek of ball-tightening red lace before she tossed it over her shoulder—and pushed her yoga pants down the smooth, tan expanse of her legs.

And, as if that move needed a symphonic accompaniment, thunder boomed overhead, an auditory exclamation point to emphasize the sweet spectacle in front of his eyes.

Holy, holy, *holy* shit. He wanted to prostrate himself before her and swear fealty to all things woman. Because she was the very picture of femininity: round hips, round breasts, high, round ass. Her sex—her *bare* sex, Lord help him—was swollen and plump, and looking at her, he couldn't help but feel awkward and gangly, made up of sharp corners and hard planes. The very opposite of her lush ripeness. And he was so overwhelmed by the beauty that was Vanessa Cordero, by the temptation she represented just by standing there, he was surprised he could talk. Yet somehow he managed, "*Tu es magnifique.*" And it was the first time since he'd left the bayou that he didn't have to translate when he told a woman she was magnificent. "But, *chere*," he had to rip his eyeballs away in order to glance around the shop, then up at the dark second-floor balcony. "Here?"

"Right here," she breathed, stepping back up to him, winding her arms around his neck, sealing their lips once more.

Chapter Twenty-one

VANESSA'S HEART WAS A SLEDGEHAMMER, POUNDING, drowning out the sound of the occasional thunder clap over the wet city outside. She'd done it! She pushed past his defenses, and she was in his arms and—

Oh, was she ever in his arms. His solid chest was a warm wall against her breasts, his strong hands anchoring her to him even as she dug her fingers into the deep divot of his spine, reveling in the hard line of muscles on either side.

They were so close, touching everywhere, but she wanted to get even closer, she wanted to absorb him into herself. Since she couldn't do that, she satisfied herself with reaching down to grab the hem of his T-shirt, releasing his lips just long enough to whip it up and over his head, tossing it aside before clutching him to her again, reveling in the feel of his pectoral muscles, warm and hard against her furled nipples, glorying in the sensation of his flat stomach cushioning the gentle curve of her own. And then she reclaimed his wonderfully wicked mouth.

Holy cow, could Rock ever kiss. And simply kissing him was more pleasurable than many of the full-on sexual encounters of her life. And she didn't want it to stop. She *never* wanted it to stop. But she had to. Because she couldn't figure out how to undo his stupid belt.

Ripping her mouth away, she frowned down at the offending accessory. "What the hell? Does this thing have a combination lock?"

Rock was breathing hard, and his rough chuckle tickled her ears and sent a frisson of pleasure skittering down her spine where it exploded at the base of her belly. Oh, man, she could listen to him do that all day. And if he did it while he was inside her…?

Of course that would require her getting off this ridiculously stubborn belt!

Sonofa—

"Here," his long, tan fingers brushed hers aside, and she watched, for future reference, how he grabbed the big buckle, pulling it in the opposite direction she would have guessed. And then the belt was undone and it was her turn to push his hands away.

"Let me," she said. And they both watched as she undid the top button on his Levi's and slowly, tooth by hard, *scritching* tooth, unzipped his fly.

"Ah, there you are," she breathed when she shoved his jeans and his boxers down the length of his legs and his erection sprang free, thick and violently red, the tip swollen and weeping.

"Indeed." His voice was like a rusty hinge when she reached forward to stroke him. And, oh, *hot*.

He was so hot, burning her hands, scorching her brain as she watched her fingers move over him, around him.

"*Non, chere*," he pulled her hand away. "I'll never last if you start doin' that thing again."

"What thing?" she asked, tearing her eyes from the unapologetic jut of his impressive sex in order to drink in the corrugated ridges of his flat stomach and the delicious line of muscles that formed a V above his hipbones. A smattering of hair grew in the center of his chest and narrowed into a path that trailed down his belly. There were a couple of raw patches on his pectoral muscles, no doubt from the plastic explosives—plastic explosives…Jesus!—that'd been strapped there. And tattooed over his heart in big, loopy cursive? The words *Always Remember*.

She'd seen the ink before, of course. But now that she knew what it meant? Now that she knew all he'd suffered? Well, just throw on the scuba gear and air up the tanks, because she was sunk. Completely, totally, sunk. In over her head.

And she wasn't going to think of what it'd mean, or how bad it'd hurt, if by tomorrow he didn't realize he was in the same sunken boat with her. Because for now? Bliss…The bliss she was feeling, the elation and passion, was all she could concentrate on.

Just look at him. With his pants bunched down around his alligator cowboy boots and all that maleness on display, with his dark hair messy and his hazel eyes heavy-lidded and sparkling, he looked like he belonged on a *Cowboys Gone Wild* beefcake calendar. And, oh, how she wanted to touch him again. To feel him pulse and throb and fill her hand…

"That thing you do that shoots me to the moon," he grumbled, reminding her she'd asked a question. And, okay, so he wasn't in the mood for a repeat of what happened out in the jungle. Which was just fine by her. Because she wanted more this time, too.

Hell, she wanted it all. And she wanted it fast and hard. She wanted it *now*…

"Touch me," she breathed, realizing she'd never craved anything as badly as she craved Rock's touch. His hands were so big and hard, so knowledgeable…

"My pleasure, *chere*," was what he said. But what he did? *Oh, good grief!*

He spun her until she was bent over Patriot, her stomach cradled on the alligator skin seat, one hand braced on the back fender, the other on the big gas tank. And her ass? Well, her ass was there on display. And the sight must've pleased him, because he sucked in a ragged breath before making a low growling noise that tickled her ears—she could swear she felt the resultant rumble in the wet, aching spot between her legs.

His erection brushed her hip when he leaned forward to smooth a hand over her ass, and it was so hard. So hard and so hot it nearly burned her, branded her. And she welcomed it. She wanted to be marked. By him. And screw the feminist movement, because right now she was glad she was a woman and he was a man, stronger and bigger and able to bend her to his will. The operative word being *bend*.

"Poor, *chere*," he crooned, rubbing a callused palm over her butt cheeks. "Too many bruises on this beautiful, beautiful ass."

And until he mentioned it, she'd forgotten. Forgotten she was sore, forgotten she was discolored, forgotten everything but the mesmerizing feel of his hands on her and the way they made her womb pulse and throb until she thought she couldn't stand it another second.

"Please, Rock," she begged. "Please touch me."

And he knew what she was after, because he used one booted foot to spread her legs wide and then...

Holy cow!

His hand slid over her ass one last time before traveling farther. Down to the swollen lips of her sex where he cupped her in his palm. Then, when she was about to open her mouth to beg him for more, he used two fingers to gently grind her lips against her aching clitoris. Her eyes crossed, her head fell to the side, and she moaned.

It felt so good. So good and almost enough. *Almost.*

"Rock," she panted, pressing back against his hand. Wanting more. *Needing* more. "Please."

And, delightful man that he was, he gave her what she needed. With one hand, he reached under her braced arm to cup her breast, stroking her beaded nipple with the edge of his rough thumb. And with the other, he spread her lips, finding her entrance with two thick fingers and pressing, ever so gently but ever so surely, inside.

Three pumps was all it took. Just three forceful pumps of his fingers in and out, and she lost it.

She came hard and fast, her inner muscles squeezing and pulsing and aching. Stars danced on the backs of her eyelids, every follicle of hair on her head felt like it lifted, and she rode the waves of her orgasm with abandon. Reveling in the intense pleasure, celebrating the joy that was the human body brought to the sexual brink. And when she crested that last wave, when her body spasmed for the final time, she realized that low, keening wail that'd been filling her head was actually her.

Good God almighty.

Rock had never been with a woman who had a hair trigger before, and he had to admit, he'd been missing out. Because watching Vanessa go off like a bottle rocket every time he touched her was sexy as hell. Too sexy.

And all he could think was that he wanted to be inside of her. Now.

Catching hold of her waist, he spun her around and hoisted her onto Patriot's seat, stepping between her thighs as she braced her bare feet on the chrome exhaust. And then she was grabbing him with one hand while she used the other and her teeth—*sweet Lord have mercy*—to rip open a foil condom wrapper.

A second later he was sheathed and she was using him against her. Rubbing the swollen, aching head of him like a sex toy up and down the length of her until she put the very tip of him inside…

And even though his eyes were crossed in ecstasy, he couldn't rip them away from what he was seeing. Because if he'd thought watching her go off like a bottle rocket while he'd used his fingers was hot, it was nothing compared to watching the length of himself disappear inside of her. Inch by slow, steady inch.

Hot and tight and wet…

"I just want to…" She hooked her heels above his butt and jerked him forward until he was seated to the hilt.

"Unh," he exhaled, and she moaned, "Oh, that feels good."

Good? It felt better than good. It felt transcendent. She was holding him so snugly while simultaneously melting all around him, and she looked like every fantasy he'd ever had come to life. Because she was once again bracing herself with one hand on the gas tank and the other on the back fender and her dark head was thrown back, which made her breasts stand up all pretty and round.

He bent to suck one of those proud peaks into his mouth, and the taste of her combined with the minty, clean smell of her had his orgasm threatening at the base of his spine. He felt his balls pull up close to his body even as they were smashed against the smooth globes of her ass.

And then he did something he hadn't done in years...

He forgot about finesse and cadence and skill. He simply placed a hand at the small of her back so that her pelvis tilted forward and proceeded to pump into her with everything he had.

It was a hard, driving rhythm, a single-minded determination to sate the hunger of his desire. Of hers.

Each stroke ended with his name on her lips, each withdraw was a harsh, indrawn breath. And then she was coming again. Moaning and tightening around him, and he let her nipple pop free of his mouth so he could clench his jaw against the mind-numbing pleasure.

Too soon. He didn't want it to end, but...

A litany of French curses spilled from his lips as he came and came and came some more, the storm raging outside, lightning flashing and thunder roaring. *Dieu*, it seemed endless, and yet it wasn't enough, because it was the best orgasm of his entire life, and he never wanted it to stop.

He never wanted to be separate from the sultry grip of her body, never wanted the pleasure to end. But end it did. Finally. After many long seconds.

And when the world stopped spinning and his head stopped floating somewhere near the ceiling, he pulled back to find Vanessa watching him. Her succulent bottom lip caught between her teeth. A tentative little smile making the corners of her dark eyes crinkle. And for a moment, he was dumbstruck.

Because this woman, this incredible, wonderful, smart,

beautiful, funny, lusty woman wanted him again. It was there on her face, in the question in her eyes.

"You're insatiable," he declared, chuckling and shaking his head. His chest was still rising and falling like he'd run a race, he was still shivering from the unbelievable orgasm he'd had, and she wanted him again.

"Hey," she shook her head and tightened around him for emphasis. "If this is going to be the only night you tear down those walls, I want to make sure I take full advantage."

God love the woman; she was nothing if not audacious. Honest to a goddamned fault.

"Well, how about we take that full advantage upstairs, to my bed, *non*?" he asked, then a tickling on the back of his leg had him frowning.

"What? What is it?" Her brow crinkled adorably.

"Is that your toe?"

"Huh?"

"On my calf?"

She dropped her chin and stared up at him like maybe he'd finally gone around the bend. And to add emphasis to their current position, she tightened her legs around him, reminding him that one: they were still locked together— *dieu*, she was so tight and wet and wonderful—and two: her ankles were still securely fastened together just above his ass.

So…"What the hell *is* that?" he asked, almost afraid to look.

Pushing aside his shoulder, she glanced around and down, and then sat back on the bike, her lips rolled in, her eyes sparkling with suppressed laughter.

He sucked his teeth and lifted a brow. "Is that a cat's tongue?"

She nodded, but this time there was no suppressing

her laughter. A snort turned into a giggle, which quickly morphed to a hiccupping chortle.

Rock glanced over his shoulder and down to find Peanut, the world's ugliest, fattest, most odor-ific tomcat—and the Black Knights' acting mascot—licking the back of his leg while one severely crooked tail swished back and forth happily.

"*Fiche moi le paix.*" *Get the fuck away from me*, he said, trying to nudge Peanut and his rasping tongue away with one booted foot. But his wide stance combined with the grip of Vanessa's vice-like thighs and the fact that his jeans were still down around his ankles to preclude the movement. And then the stupid cat made everything so much worse by rising up on his back legs—quite a feat given Peanut's substantial girth—in order to lick the back of Rock's knee.

Vanessa lost it. She hooted with laughter and, had he not been being molested be an overzealous tomcat, he could have appreciated the way it made her wet sheath tighten around him. But really? This thing had just gotten weird. And he'd had some pretty funky fantasies over the years, one in particular that involved candy corn and a feather duster, but a fat cat with a sandpaper tongue was too much, even for him.

"Little help here?" he grumbled, turning back to Vanessa, making sure both his tone and his expression accurately displayed his displeasure.

"What?" she asked innocently, batting her lashes and looking too sexy for words, all tousled hair and rosy cheeks. "I thought you liked puss—"

He slammed a finger over her lips and shook his head. "Don't say it."

She just grinned evilly around his finger as the rain

suddenly let up, no longer lashing against the leaded glass windows. That's how it was here in the Midwest: thunderstorms rolled out as quickly as they rolled in. And it was almost like their lovemaking had been, maybe not so much caused by the electricity in the air, but certainly enhanced by it.

As least that's what he was going to tell himself. Because the other alternative was that it was, hands-down, no-holds-barred, the best sex of his entire goddamned life, and he just couldn't go there. Not now. Maybe not ever. Because it scared the shit out of him to contemplate exactly *why* that might be the case. I mean, *oui*, there was the whole getting-it-on on the back of his bike that was undoubtedly super hot, but he highly suspected his level of excitement and enjoyment had less to do with the fantasy-worthy situation and location, and more to do with the fact that it was…well…*Vanessa*.

"Is the big, bad operator put off by a little feline lovin'?" she taunted once he removed his finger, her light tone and teasing eyes jerking him out from under the weight of his heavy thoughts.

In answer, he grabbed her hips and stroked into her. Hard.

And that accomplished exactly what he hoped it would. Because all the laughter left her face and her mouth opened on a quickly indrawn breath.

"Upstairs?" she asked after a long second of staring into his eyes, her breasts rising and falling rapidly.

"Indeed," he concurred.

And then the race was on.

He pulled out of her and bent to shove Peanut away while simultaneously yanking up his jeans and twisting off the used condom. She hopped off Patriot and leaned over—*mon dieu*—to gather up her clothes before sprinting for the stairs.

God love her, she didn't even attempt to drag on a stitch before she was hauling ass up to the second floor.

Running after her, he barely heard Peanut's baleful wail of desertion before he was on the second-floor landing, chasing her around the conference table, delighting in her teasing laughter as she headed for the stairs leading to the third-floor living space, totally engrossed in watching the bounce of her round butt cheeks and the occasional glimpse he had of her jouncing breasts.

He made a grab for her on the stairs—all that tan, jiggling flesh was too much to resist—but she twisted out of his grip, and he was left to stumble up after her. Once they made it to his room, he tossed the used condom in the trash, caught her around the waist, and heaved her onto his bed.

She landed with her thighs spread, all that was wet and warm and womanly on display, and he jumped on top of her, settling between her lovely legs, reveling in the fact that she instantly claimed his mouth, sucking and laving and...*sucking*.

The woman was doing her best impression of a Hoover on his tongue, and the thought of how unbelievably insane that would feel on his dick had the top of his head lifting away.

"You gonna keep your boots on again, cowboy?" she giggled when he kissed his way down her fragrant neck.

He glanced up at her and Mr. Happy once again pounded against his fly because, *merde*, she was so goddamned beautiful. "Depends," he smirked. "Would you like me to?"

She caught her plump lower lip between her teeth and

nodded, her dark eyes glinting mischievously. "But lose the jeans, will you?"

"I aim to please," he said, catching one brown nipple between his lips and chuckling when she speared her fingers into his hair, breathing, "Oh, Rock…"

Oui, ma petite, it's Rock making you feel so good, so hot, making you burn from the inside out.

And then she did it again, astounded him and left him breathless all at the same time, because she hooked a finger under his chin, forcing him to release her delicious nipple and stare up into her pretty face. "Richard," that name went through him like a lightning strike, "I said, *lose the jeans*."

And, boy howdy, in the next second you better believe he set the world record for shucking britches.

———

Two things woke Vanessa.

One was the fact that, despite the glowing numbers on the clock reading oh-nine-hundred in the morning, it was pitch dark inside Rock's bedroom. At some point, he must've inadvertently switched off the bathroom light which had been burning during all three—yes, count them, *three*, and the last time in the shower should really count twice—of the absolutely delicious love-making sessions they'd indulged in. The man was a veritable prodigy. They'd done it every which way imaginable and a couple she'd never even dreamed of.

Who knew turning her head toward the foot of the bed and hooking her heels over the headboard while Rock straddled her and stroked into her would result in her thighs squeezing together, which, in turn, allowed his penis to rub…Just. The. Right. Spot?

And that brought her around to the *second* thing to wake her...

The feel of Rock's erection, hot and pulsing against her hip.

She grinned into the darkness and turned toward him, reaching down to palm the smooth, warm length of him. And he was awake instantly, the steady cadence of his breathing coming to a sudden stop.

"Oh, shit," he said.

"Not exactly the response I was hoping for," she frowned, stilling her hand.

"*Non, non, chere.* Not that. I was talkin' about the light. I didn't mean to switch it off. It's just habit."

"Don't worry about it," she said, stroking him again and loving the way his hips thrust up into her hand and the way he sucked in a harsh breath. "After that conversation we had in the jungle," stroke, twist, stroke, "I'm not afraid anymore. Funny how easy it was to overcome once I actually knew the root of the issue."

"I'm so glad." His sleepy voice was a warm tongue licking up her spine.

And she couldn't stand it. She had to kiss him. But morning breath was always an issue, so she satisfied herself with leaning forward to place tender kisses up the column of his warm neck and back farther, to his ear.

Stroke, twist, stroke. She kept up the rhythm she'd learned would shoot him to the moon as she sucked his lobe between her teeth, licking it softly.

"Mmm," he said, and she smiled because she'd rendered him speechless. Or so she thought, because in the next second he said in that low, rumbly voice of his, "Climb up here, *ma petite.*"

"Condom?"

"Hmm, mmm," he murmured. "I want to use my mouth on you."

And despite herself, despite the numerous things they'd done together, done *to* each other, that request had heat climbing into her cheeks. Because it was such a vulnerable position to be in, vulnerable and powerful all at the same time. But she trusted Rock like she'd never trusted any man. And, more than that, she wanted to please him, to make him understand how good they could be together, how good they already *were* together.

She kicked away the covers and pushed to her knees. Throwing a leg over him, banging her knee—*ow*—on the headboard in the process, she straddled his wide shoulders. Then she wasn't thinking about her poor knee at all. Because he said, "Turn around."

"Turn around...? Oh." Oh!

She felt herself flush, but she did as instructed. He used both hands to palm her bottom, and the next second his hot breath feathered over her.

Wet.

She was instantly wet and aching.

And then wet and aching didn't *begin* to describe what she was feeling when his hot, agile tongue speared into her. And when he growled, low and throaty...Oh, the vibration!

She nearly lost it.

But this was supposed to be about give and take, what's good for the goose being good for the gander and all that jazz. So she bent, supporting herself with one hand while she grabbed hold of him, sucking his length into her mouth.

He tasted salty and male. He smelled like sex.

She was instantly on the precipice. And when he dipped his chin and caught her swollen clitoris between his soft lips, flicking it gently with his tongue, she knew she didn't have long. So with her mouth and her hand she did that "thing" he appeared to like so much.

And her reward? The swift upward thrust of his hips.

Oh, yeah...

And, just as she'd come to expect, the man didn't disappoint. He shoved a thumb inside her, laved at the aching bundle of nerves at the top of her sex, and when she began to tighten around him, she felt him jerk in her hand, felt him pulse. Hard.

And then he was falling over the edge. They both were. And it was sensual as hell, sexy as sin, the world shrinking down to just the two of them. Locked together. Giving pleasure and receiving it. The sights and sounds and tastes of completion melding together into one giant kaleidoscope of unbelievable sensation.

For long moments afterward, they remained like that, mouths on each other, breath shuddering from their lungs. Then Rock smacked her ass and she sat up, turning to glare at him. Which was silly, since she couldn't see her hand in front of her face.

She was about to open her mouth to scold him when there was a hard knock at the door. And before either of them had a second to think, much less do the whole naked-ass scramble, the thing swung open and harsh light spilled onto the bed.

"Jesus Christ!"

Uh, that'd be Bill's voice. Vanessa couldn't see him because one, she was blinded by the sudden light, and two, she was too busy flying through the air as Rock grabbed her around the waist and tossed her to the far side of the bed, throwing the covers over her.

"What the *hell*, dude?" Rock yelled, and, yeah, Vanessa seconded that opinion.

"Sorry. Jesus. Sorry, man." Vanessa could hear the embarrassment and was that…? Yes, that was definitely a touch of amusement in Bill's tone. Great. Just…perfect. "I didn't know…" Bill stopped there and even though she couldn't see him, she was pretty sure he was fighting a grin. "Uh, supposedly there's a guy at the front gate with this crazy story that involves you. So I was thinking…"

"I'll be down in five," Rock grumbled, the dissipating light an indication the door was already closing. *Thank God*. But before it shut all the way, Bill said one more thing, "Dude, are your boots still on?"

Chapter Twenty-two

ROCK SAT AT THE BACK WINDOW OF BKI HEADQUARTERS, concealed behind the tinted, leaded glass, and watched Boss lead the guy who was apparently claiming to have information about him through the back gate. The Knights knew discretion was the better part of valor. And as such, no one was allowed into the shop unless it was absolutely necessary. Which meant this little soirée was taking place out in the courtyard.

Already, those Knights currently in residence—all wearing leather and looking, quite intentionally, like nothing more than a gritty, and very dangerous, motorcycle club—were gathered around the unlit fire pit, arranged on the multicolored, mismatched lawn furniture. Each of the men wore an expression that fell somewhere between simple curiosity and overt suspicion.

Rock found himself falling somewhere between the two. Then his eyes landed on Vanessa in those goddamned sexy yoga pants, sitting on the green-cushioned chaise lounge chair, her gaze not on the man Boss was escorting, but instead on the ground in front of her, and he completely forgot about everything except the way she'd moved beneath him...above him, beside him. She'd been so sensual and sweet, so abandoned and giving. And, he was going to break her heart...

Because even though last night meant more to him than he'd like to admit—*oh, Lordy, did it ever*; he was going to remember it until his dying day—it didn't change the fact that they lived in a dangerous and deadly world. Deadly being the operative word.

Which brought him back to the part where he was going to break her heart. Because she might've played the tough-as-nails-operator card last night, challenging him to give in to his desires, saying she'd understand if, in doing so, it didn't change the way he felt about things, but the truth of the matter was she'd been deluding herself.

And the only thing he knew to do now was to nip this thing in the bud before it went any further, before the attraction and…and the intense *like*—for lack of a better word— she was feeling for him turned into full-blown love.

Because it could.

He'd been in love before and recognized the telltale signs. In her. In himself.

Mon dieu, he wasn't stupid enough to think *she* was the only one on the brink. He could love her in a heartbeat if he let himself.

"Have a seat," Boss instructed the mysterious man, interrupting Rock's spinning thoughts and jerking his wandering attention back to the group in the courtyard. And though their voices were muffled by the distance and the fact that the window Rock was sitting behind was only opened the tiniest bit, he had no trouble hearing the guy's gruff reply, "I'll just remain standing, if you don't mind."

Then the man turned slightly, and something about his face sent an odd sensation skittering across the front of Rock's cerebral cortex, halting his breath for a nanosecond.

Was it memory? Or some strange recognition of a brother-in-arms. Both?

"Suit yourself," Boss crossed his big arms, remaining

standing as well. "But I have to warn you, before you start going on with any stories about Rock, we don't believe the charges leveled against him. And if you're here to malign his memory—"

"You *shouldn't* believe the charges leveled against him," the man interrupted, and Rock's heart leapt. "They were complete bullshit."

"How do you know that?" Ozzie piped up from his position in a bright red Adirondack chair. As usual, a state-of-the-art laptop was balanced on one of the kid's knees.

"Because *I* was the one to kill those men."

Vanessa gasped, her eyes shooting to the rather unexceptional face of the mystery man—the guy had plain brown hair, plain brown eyes, and a profile that, while not unattractive, certainly wasn't anything to write home about either. But unlike his appearance, the words that'd jumped out of his mouth were anything but ordinary. They made the hair on the back of her neck stand on end, and she couldn't help herself; she slid a surreptitious glance at the dark window she knew Rock was hiding behind.

Holy cow! He had to have nearly puked his own heart upon hearing that news. She knew she had. In fact, she had to swallow, twice, before she could breathe properly.

If panting like a dog in the summer sun was proper breathing, that is…

"*You* killed them?" Boss asked, still standing, the equivalent of a giant human exclamation point. "Why would you do that?"

"Because that's what I was trained to do. What I was ordered to do," the man replied, the deep, nearly overwhelming sadness that pervaded his tone had Vanessa glancing uncomfortably away from his face.

As she looked around, she noted the courtyard was still wet from the previous night's passing thunderstorm, little puddles of glistening water standing in the small irregularities of the slate covering the ground and darkening the shingles on the roofs of the outbuildings. And the air? It still smelled damp and electric. Like perhaps another storm was rolling in. Something massive and dangerous and altogether too mysterious.

She shivered in response.

"What did you say your name was again?" Boss asked.

"Jonathan Dunn. And I was The Cleaner for The Project."

Hearing those last two words had stars dancing in front of Vanessa's vision.

Could it be...? After all these months, could they really be on the brink of clearing Rock's name? Of bringing him back to life? Or was Mr. Dunn completely full of shit? Some CIA operative sent in here to mess with them?

But he knew about The Project...Then again, maybe he *was* The Project. Maybe this was Rwanda Don, the freakazoid they'd been looking for. Maybe this...

Uh-oh. She'd better regulate her oxygen intake, and fast. Because her head was spinning.

Leaning her elbows on her knees, she let her head drop between her shoulders and concentrated on taking deep, slow breaths.

"Please take a seat, Mr. Dunn," Boss insisted. "It appears you've got a story to tell, and we're all eager to hear it."

And that was putting it a *touch* mildly.

The scuffling of Dunn's shoes on the slate and the

scrape of a metal lawn chair leg assured her the man had finally done as instructed. And then he started talking. And talking, and talking…

After five minutes of listening to him outline a story very similar to Rock's, she figured she'd tamed her breathing and was no longer on the path to going horizontal, so she glanced up.

Dunn sat on the very edge of his seat, his forearms braced on his thighs, his hands clasped together loosely, his face still the picture of heartache and misery. According to his story, he worked in the Albany field office of the FBI, and about a decade ago he'd been assigned a case investigating an organized crime ring. Apparently, that case brought him to the attention of the local crime boss—a man like the men Rock had described, a man who ran the show but was so far removed, hidden under so many layers of cover, that evidence linking him to any overt crimes could never be solidified. As a result of Dunn's involvement, and the subsequent arrests of quite a few of the crime boss's family members, the man put a hit out on Dunn's wife and daughter. Only, like everything that'd gone on before, the crime boss was savvy about it, and the deaths were never pinned on him. Which left Dunn with a broken heart and the fire of revenge burning in his belly.

Enter the CIA, The Project, Rwanda Don, and the promise for an opportunity to exact some of that revenge…

"Now I don't know why your guy, Babineaux, was blamed for those men's deaths," Dunn was saying, in his thick New York accent. "For the longest time, I couldn't figure out why a simple motorcycle mechanic would get pinned for the jobs. Then a friend of mine at the FBI informed me of the real nature of the work you all do

out here, and I began to wonder if maybe he'd pissed off
a higher-up who was looking to eighty-six him. Then
I found out the truth about that last man…" His voice
broke, utter anguish in his tone.

"What about the last man?" Boss pressed.

"He was innocent."

Bahm, bahm, bahm… She could almost hear the
three-note trombone slide in her head, and she held her
breath—screw the stars that started blinking in front of
her vision again.

Steady, who was looking dark and deadly over at the
picnic table while thoroughly cleaning his Smith and
Wesson .45 caliber ACP handgun—the Knights were
not above a little theatrics, and it was always good to let
an unfamiliar get a glimpse of what was in store for him
should he make one wrong move—asked, "How do you
know he was innocent?"

Dunn reached for his hip pocket, and Vanessa caught
the subtle movement of the men's hands. The Knights'
concealed weapons were going to make some quick
appearances should Dunn try to pull anything from his
pocket that was bigger than a credit card.

Thankfully, all he extracted was a thumb drive.

"This contains the supposed audio file of the interrogation of Fred Billingsworth. If you listen to it, it sounds like
he's confessing to a series of heinous crimes, just like…"
Dunn shook his head and stared off into the distance, his
mouth thinned. "Just like the others. But this one *isn't*
like the others. This one's a fake. A guy at the sound lab
at Quantico confirmed that after I got suspicious as to
why my kills had fallen on Babineaux's head. I started
questioning everything, had my man review *all* the audio

files on *all* the targets. But the only one that'd been tampered with was Billingsworth's. I...I don't know why, but Rwanda Don lied to me about Fred. Gave me false proof of his guilt. And as a result..." He stopped again, taking a moment to compose himself. "As a result I killed him."

Silence reigned over the courtyard, the steady drip of one of the clogged gutters on an outbuilding the only thing to be heard. Then, the silence was broken by Dunn shaking his head and whispering, "No. No that's not true. I *killed* those other men. But I *murdered* Billingsworth."

And the act obviously haunted him. Those other nine had been monsters. Dunn had probably convinced himself that what he was doing was, maybe not *right*, but perhaps *necessary*. But Billingsworth? Billingsworth had been an innocent.

And that made his death a horror...

She'd worked her entire adult life with men who made a living by getting blood on their hands. And if there's one thing she'd learned about them, it was this: they could live with the killing, as long as it was just and justifiable. But if it wasn't? Well, then they tended to have serious problems. Because the same inner strength that made them so honorable and dependable also had the tendency to make them incredibly tough on themselves and incredibly unforgiving of what they perceived as a personal failure, particularly if that failure came at the cost of an innocent life.

"Why are you here telling us this?" Boss asked.

"Because I couldn't live with the knowledge that you, Babineaux's friends, his coworkers, might actually think he was responsible for what happened when, in fact, it was me."

"So why not come clean to the powers that be?" Becky said from her seat beside Boss. "Why not come forward and clear Rock's name?"

Yeah? Why not? If you're feeling so guilty about—

"*What* powers that be?" Dunn lifted his hands, shaking his head. "I don't even know who I was working for over at the CIA." Okay, so same ol', same ol'. This Rwanda Don character was a frickin' ghost. *Unfortunately.* "I don't know who the hell to contact, because I don't know who the hell would listen to me. And I *won't* know who will listen to me until I find Rwanda Don."

Vanessa wanted to say, *good luck with that.*

Because between Boss's contacts in the intelligence community and Ozzie's crazy ability to crack any computer system and code, the Knights almost always got their man when they went looking for him.

But so far in the hunt for Rwanda Don? Nothing. Nada. Zilch.

"I *will* find him," Dunn declared vehemently. "And when I do I'm going to ask him why he..." Again he seemed to need a moment to compose himself. "Why he turned me into an instrument of murder and mayhem when that's exactly the kind of men we swore to obliterate." Dunn glanced around the group, meeting each set of Knights' eyes square-on. "But I swear to you, after I find Rwanda Don, after I have proof of The Project, proof that I'm not just some lunatic off the street, I *will* clear Babineaux's name."

Boss glanced over at Ozzie. "His story check out?"

Ozzie was staring at his computer screen. "All the stuff about the FBI, the case, and his family is public record."

Boss nodded, glancing toward the window Rock was

concealed behind before looking over at Ghost. A quick dip of his chin, and the Knights' acting sniper pushed up from his chair to stroll silently—it was eerie how quiet the guy was—toward the retractable awning the Knights usually kept rolled against the back of the shop wall. With the push of a button, the huge awning began to unfurl. At the halfway point, when it reached as far at its mechanical arms could stretch, it stopped. Ghost and Steady unraveled the rest of the tough, waterproof material, pulling it tight and securing the corners to permanent posts located at the far end of the courtyard. The result? A vinyl roof covering the entire area, protecting those in the courtyard from any prying eyes that might be in the surrounding buildings.

Then, the back door opened, and there was Rock. Looking big and strong in his faded Levi's, Pearl Jam T-shirt, and sweat-stained John Deer ball cap. Looking much more like a good ol' boy and much less like a hardened operator. Looking like the man who'd rocked her world last night, the man who'd stolen her heart.

And the expression on his face was indescribable. There was hope and concern and wariness. But above all else, there was pity. Because as much as he bore the burden of what had happened to Billingsworth, Dunn shouldered it more than a hundred-fold.

What a nightmare.

And Vanessa wanted to personally strangle whoever the hell this Rwanda Don person was for taking these honorable, dedicated, *patriotic* men and turning them into something less than what they wanted to be. Something less than what they'd signed on to be.

Rock's alligator cowboy boots clacked against the slate,

and Dunn glanced over his shoulder, then jumped up like his pants were on fire. "Jesus! You're alive!" he exclaimed.

"It would appear so, *mon ami*," Rock replied in that low, smooth drawl, and Dunn collapsed back into his seat. His legs folding beneath him.

"Oh my God!" the man breathed, shaking his head, staring at Rock in disbelief, his face completely draining of blood. "It's you. You're The Interrogator. I'd recognize that voice anywhere."

Rock grabbed the seat beside Dunn, looking into the man's bloodless face, and, *oui*, that sensation he'd felt earlier was definitely recognition. Not that he'd ever laid eyes on the guy, because he was certain he had not. But, still, there was something familiar there. And more than likely, it was because Rock could identify with the aura of sorrow and loss and determination that seemed to cling to him like a shroud.

Cut from the same cloth, they were. Both patriotic with a deep sense of duty. Both experiencing intense regret over Billingsworth's death. Both having been screwed over by the CIA and Rwanda Don.

And, as if on cue, Ozzie scratched his head and started attacking his keyboard. The *clickety-clack* was so loud it snapped Rock's attention away from Dunn and over to the kid.

"What's up, *mon frere*?" He'd seen that expression on the Ozzie's face more than a time or two and referred to it as bloodhound mode.

"Give me a second," Ozzie muttered, frowning at his screen. "When Dunn said you were The Interrogator and he was The Cleaner, it struck a chord with me. I think I…" He shook his shaggy blond head, growling, "Screw you, CIA database. You think you're so smart with your encrypted algorithms and backdoor defenses, but you're not smarter than ol' Ozzie."

Dunn glanced over at Rock, lifting a questioning brow. "*Oui*," Rock smiled, "he talks to his computers like they're alive. But, believe me, the kid's not insane. If there's a way to—"

"Got it!" Ozzie announced, lifting a hand to Eve who was sitting beside him. The woman—her eyes had been flying at full mast ever since they'd been down in Costa Rica, and Rock wondered how she kept the things from drying out like a frog's carcass in the July sun—looked at Ozzie's raised palm.

"Slap me some skin, woman!" Ozzie demanded, his dazzling smile lighting up the entire courtyard. Rock recognized that look, too. Ozzie was on to something…

Could it be? Has he really found—

"Oh," Eve immediately reached up and slapped Ozzie's hand, but the guy wasn't going to be satisfied with only that. He was feeling celebratory—and completely oblivious to the fact that Rock was on the edge of his seat waiting to hear the good news—so he hooked an arm around Eve's neck and smacked a loud kiss on her lips. When he released her, the poor, overwhelmed woman was beet red and, even through the haze of frustration and anticipation clouding his head, Rock heard a low growling noise.

Then he realized it was Wild Bill.

Ozzie must've heard it, too. Because the kid smirked before pursing his lips and blowing Bill a kiss. "Don't you worry, Billy boy." He wiggled his blond brows. "There's enough Ozzie to go around. So if you wanna come over here and gimme a ki—"

"For fuck's sake, Ozzie!" Boss thundered. "What have you found?"

"Oh," Ozzie turned his computer around, and on the screen was what appeared to be some sort of report. The sorry sucker had more than a few lines redacted. And even if the kid hadn't already been cursing about the CIA database, Rock would've known he was looking at some form of Company document just by the number of blacked-out paragraphs. No one was as efficient and/or slap-happy about redacting information as the spooks.

"What are we looking at?" Boss asked. Everyone, including Rock, leaned forward to try to read what words *were* still legible.

"This is a thesis, written about ten years ago by a budding CIA psychiatrist," Ozzie explained. "From what little I could gather from reading what remained of the text, it proposed a way to deal with an individual or group of individuals—which I took to mean terrorists, but it could very easily be homegrown bad boys—by splitting up the duties of investigation, interview, and elimination among a trio of operatives. It outlines a way to basically kill our country's enemies, not those we take out with bombs and drone strikes, but those individuals we happen to catch and can't necessarily prosecute by…erm, *traditional* means, without placing the responsibility of said duties on any *one* person's shoulders. This thesis proposes that a team of three agents, trained in each specific area, could be utilized to annihilate these threats."

Rock's heart was a riderless racehorse, galloping out of control. And when he glanced out of the corner of his eyes, it was to see Dunn breathing heavily and staring at Ozzie with a mixture of hope and dread.

"And here's the kicker," Ozzie sucked his teeth, nodding excitedly. "Guess what this thesis calls those three positions?"

"The Investigator, The Interrogator, and The Cleaner," Vanessa whispered quietly, and Rock looked over to find her staring at him, her eyes filled with unshed tears, her expression hesitantly hopeful.

Oui, ma petite, *this might just be it. This might be the lead we've been waitin' on...*

"Ding, ding, ding!" Ozzie shouted gleefully. "Give the girl a gold star!"

"But why three?" Boss queried. "Why not just let one guy do all the dirty work."

"Because," Ozzie said, turning the computer screen back toward himself, "according to this thesis, that kind of wet work has severe psychological effects on the person doing it. Basically taking a nice, normal, mentally sound person and, over time, turning them into a sociopath at best, a psychopath at worst. This thesis proposes that splitting up the work, never letting the guy who does all the investigating actually meet the target, never letting the guy who interrogates the target ever bear witness to the consequences, and never letting the guy doing the executing see the target as anything other than a monster, is a way to protect the psyches of all those involved. Sort of an intellectual and emotional checks-and-balances solution, if you will."

"Jesus," Boss ran a hand through his hair. "The Investigator, The Interrogator, and The Cleaner, huh?"

"Yup," Ozzie nodded. "And I, for one, don't believe in coincidences. At least not ones this big."

Neither did Rock.

"Fuck me," Boss sighed. "So now that we know what piece of shitty psychological mumbo-jumbo started this whole thing, all that's left to discover is who within The Company ran with it."

"Yeah," Ozzie frowned, and a thought occurred to Rock.

"Who wrote the thesis?" he asked.

"Ummm," Ozzie used his finger to scroll. "Says here it's a Dr. Donna Ward."

"Who is she?" he pressed, something scratching at the back of his brain, something he could *almost* put his finger on.

"Gimme a second," Ozzie caught his tongue between his teeth, typing frantically. Then he looked up, eyes bright. "She's married to Governor Ward. He's one of the politicians Billingsworth was investigating. Holy hell, we're really onto something here!"

"It's more than that," Rock said, his brain absolutely buzzing.

You could have heard a feather drop in the courtyard. Even the distant sounds of police sirens, the subtle trickle of the Chicago River flowing behind the outer wall, and the steady hum of auto traffic on the nearby Kennedy Expressway couldn't detract from the silence that hung over the entire group.

"What is it," Boss demanded, staring at Rock's face, "What the hell do you know?"

"I know who Rwanda Don is."

Chapter Twenty-three

EVE GLANCED AROUND THE COURTYARD AT THE HARD faces of the Black Knights, barely believing what she was hearing.

Geez Louise! They were all certifiable. Completely, totally, utterly insane. Of course, she'd begun to suspect as much way back in Costa Rica...

"You guys aren't really going to confront and interrogate the wife of the governor of West Virginia, are you?" she asked.

But if there was an expression that personified determination, each and every Knight was wearing it.

Okay, so I guess you are *really going to confront and interrogate the wife of the governor of West Virginia.*

Ozzie frowned at her like maybe *she* was the crazy one in the bunch. "She's not *just* the governor of West Virginia's wife," he said. "She's also Rwanda Don."

Because, as Rock pointed out, Donna Ward and Rwanda Don were anagrams—which the Knights found too fortuitous to ignore and too coincidental to chalk up to mere chance. Plus, once Rock and that new guy, the friggin' *hit* man, began comparing notes and discussing their training, they'd each come to the conclusion that, *yes, indeed*, come to think of it, Rwanda Don *had* seemed to use words and phrasing sequences more common in the fairer sex.

Although, for the life of her, Eve couldn't figure out what those might be. Or perhaps it was the glaring *lack* of words like *dick, cocksucker*, and *asswipe* that led Rock and Mr. Dunn to their conclusions...

And then there was the link between her husband and Billingsworth's investigation. Just that fast, the ball had started rolling. And Eve could only shake her head in an awed sort of consternation.

"Okay, so how do we get tickets to this thing?" Boss asked Ozzie, who was once again going at his keyboard with the concentration and rhythm of a concert pianist.

And call it fate or kismet or maybe even a touch of old-fashioned luck, but Donna Ward and her husband, friggin' *Governor* Ward, were in town, down at the Peninsula Hotel at a Party fundraiser.

And wouldn't you know? Dear ol' Daddy was supposed to be attending that same event.

"I, uh," Eve spoke up, glad, for once, that her family was so well connected. "I could get us tickets. My father is a huge campaign supporter. He could get us in."

Ozzie glanced up. "All of us?"

"However many tickets you need," she nodded.

"Remind me to kiss you again," he winked, then wiggled his eyebrows.

"Try it and you'll be walking funny for a month," Billy growled, to which Ozzie made a face and replied, "Touchy, touchy."

Eve felt the need to shake her head, really quickly, like a dog shaking off water. Who'd have ever thought she'd be involved in all of this?

Not her, that's for sure. And even though she was scared out of her head, she had to admit there was a little part of her, a part she'd never guessed she possessed, that found it all very exciting.

I mean, come on! I'm about to aid and abet a group of spies in the interrogation of a U.S. governor's wife!

It didn't get more James Bond than that. Well, if they'd give her a gun, it'd be more James Bond. Maybe she'd talk to Billy about—

Boss cut into her thoughts. "Okay, then. So how the hell do we get our hands on her? She's not likely to just come with us. And there will be security at this thing, so it's not like we can cart her off without drawing an assload of heat."

"From what I can gather from these political gossip boards," Ozzie began, and Ghost muttered, "Jesus Christ, political gossip boards? What's next?"

"Oh, you'd be amazed at all the juice out there on the Internet," Ozzie wolf-whistled. "I read this one post about the mayor of Newark that'd—"

"Ozzie," Boss interrupted, "get back to the point."

"Oh, yeah, sure," he nodded. "So, according to these gossip boards, Dr. Ward likes to snag a secret smoke after each fundraiser. Out in an alley, in a tucked-away bathroom somewhere. You know, out of sight of the high-falootin' sorts."

"Doesn't appear her smokes are very *secret* considering it's all over the Internet," Ghost muttered.

"Hard to keep much a secret nowadays." Ozzie grinned before adding, "We can grab her then, and I'll knock out the city surveillance cameras on that block, you know," he shrugged, "just in case our activities become nefarious." Oh, geez Louise. They're activities might become nefarious. "And we can park the Hummer out back in case we need a getaway car."

Getaway car…Eve's blood pressure rose with each sentence out of Ozzie's mouth.

"And what if she doesn't go for a smoke?" Becky asked.

"Considering the best-laid battle plans never survive contact with the enemy," Ozzie answered, "we'll just do what we do best."

"Which is?" Dunn asked.

"Improvise," Ozzie and Steady replied simultaneously.

"Okay," Boss slapped a hand on his knee. "So, we confront her in the bathroom or alley if we can, or pick a place on the fly if we can't. And we hope like hell Rock can use his woo-woo head-shrinking skills to get her to crack." He turned to the man in question.

"I'll crack her," Rock assured them, his face set in hard lines.

"Donna Ward won't stand a chance," Vanessa smiled at Rock so softly, so sweetly.

Eve watched Rock's face soften and, if she wasn't mistaken, that was the man's heart she saw reflected in his pretty, hazel eyes. Then, suddenly, as if he realized he was letting everybody in the courtyard see too much, he shook his head and glanced away.

"Thanks, *chere*," he muttered before standing and marching toward the shop. He stopped just before he reached the back door, spinning back toward the group. "Are you all sure you want to do this?" There was no mistaking the hesitation and…yes, that was anguish plastered all over his face. "You could get in serious trouble if this thing goes sideways." Which was what Eve had been thinking all along. "And you've all…" He took a deep breath and shook his head. "You've all risked so much already."

"Shut the hell up, *pendejo*," Steady growled. "Even if you had died on that porch in Costa Rica, we'd still be bustin' our ass to clear your name. All for one and one for all, hoo-ah?"

"Hoo-ah!" the Knights shouted in unison, and Eve nearly jumped out of her skin.

Holy moley, and here she was again, having to slap herself on the forehead.

So much for thinking you were closer to growing that set of balls...

A few more logistics were discussed and then the Knights broke apart. Eve went to push up from her chair when Billy stopped her with a warm, rough palm on her shoulder. She glanced up to find him standing beside her. And with his dark-chocolate hair falling across his forehead, his warm, brown eyes watching her so intently, he looked very much like the boy who'd laughed and kissed and taught her so much all those years ago.

Then he spoke, and his harsh tone obliterated that little fantasy right then and there. "You sure you're cut out for this tonight?"

She felt the pilot light on her temper ignite. "I'm made of much tougher stuff than you think," she declared, scrambling to her feet so they were on a more level playing field. She'd always lamented her height, her giraffe neck and gazelle legs, but she'd learned to use it to her advantage. Most men were intimidated by an Amazon woman.

Unfortunately, Billy had never been most men. He grabbed her arm, giving it a squeeze. "This is *important*, Eve. Men's lives are at stake."

"Stop manhandling me, you big brute!" She jerked her arm away, glaring. "And don't you worry about me. After all, this is *my* pond we're going to be swimming in. So you'd do better to worry about yourself." And, with that, she spun on her heel, stomping toward the shop, feeling his piercing gaze on the center of her back the entire way, trying not to let the fact that he had absolutely *zero* faith in her cut her to the marrow.

"Have you seen Rock?" Vanessa yelled over the din of Bon Jovi's "Wanted Dead or Alive." She was very sure they had Ozzie to thank for *that* particular musical number—the guy sometimes had a sadistic sense of humor.

All around her, the shop was buzzing with activity. Everyone, even Jonathan Dunn, was in various stages of readiness for the fundraiser. Tuxedo jackets hung on the backs of chairs, a pair of high-heeled silver pumps lay on the conference table, and Becky, in fire-engine red chiffon, sat at the bank of computers with Ozzie, watching the guy compile what information they'd been able to find on Dr. Donna Ward into a nice tidy dossier. Eve stood behind her in a stunning blue evening gown, bobby-pinning her hair into a sleek bun.

"I, uh," Becky had to shout over the music, "I think he's up in his bedroom, clearing his head!"

And that made sense.

Unquestionably, this was going to be the most important interrogation of his life. He needed to outwit and outmaneuver the mind that'd dreamed up The Project, and he needed to do it double quick. Because it wasn't like they'd have a ton of time with Donna Ward before someone came looking for her.

For a split second, she debated disturbing him. Then decided *to hell with it*.

"Thanks!" she yelled at Becky before lifting the floor-length skirt on the purple, sequined halter dress Becky and Eve had chosen for her during their madcap dash to

Neiman Marcus. She padded up the metal stairs to the third floor on bare feet—she wasn't going to slip into her heels until she absolutely *had* to. When she reached the landing, she dug a finger in her ear just to make sure it didn't come away bloody.

Ozzie had his stereo system volume level set to *rock concert*, and she was amazed he didn't suffer perforated eardrums. And though she could still hear good ol' Jon wailing away about being a cowboy and riding on a steel horse—*huh, kind of appropriate*—at least she wasn't pushing up against a wall of sound, which meant she could hear herself think.

And what was she thinking, do you suppose?

Well, nothing new there. She was still thinking about Rock. About that hint of uncertainty she'd seen in his eyes out in the courtyard when they came up with the plan to have him interrogate Donna Ward...

The last thing he needed right now was to be second-guessing himself and his abilities. And she was nothing if not good at pep talks. After all, she'd been giving herself pep talks regarding him for *months* now.

Knocking on his door, she waited until she heard him murmur, "*Oui?* Come in," before turning the knob and pushing into his bedroom. And there he was, doing nothing more than softly strumming his guitar as he sat on the edge of his bed—that big, messy bed with the sage-green comforter they'd done so many fantastically naughty things in—and her heart nearly leapt out of her chest at the sight of him.

He looked so good, so handsome and delicious and downright *wholesome*. And maybe it was the jeans and the boots and the big, shiny belt buckle, or maybe it was the sweat-stained John Deer ball cap he had turned around backward. But looking at him, she thought he belonged out on a tractor somewhere or sipping iced-tea while rocking slowly in a porch swing. Looking at him she was reminded of a song by Waylon Jennings her father used to play on vinyl. Something about a rambling man and standing too close to the flame. Something about once the rambling man messes with your mind, your little heart not beating the same…

Holy cow, Waylon. You were sure right about that.

Because ever since she'd met Rock, her heart had certainly taken up a new rhythm. One that flitted and fluttered like a drunken bird most days.

"You look beautiful," he said, letting his gaze run down the length of her purple-sequin-encased body. She felt the path of his eyes like a physical touch.

"Thank you," she whispered, suddenly hoarse. "So do you."

He lifted a brow, one corner of his mouth quirking. And, yeah, that sounded really lame. "So, what's up, *ma petite*?" he asked, dragging her wayward mind back to the situation and the reason she'd barged in on him.

"I…uh…I just," she cleared her throat and wrung her hands together. Now that she was here, about to offer him what she hoped would be a little reassurance, she felt silly.

Rock had come by his nickname naturally, because he was so solid, so dependable and unfaltering. Which meant the last thing he probably needed or wanted was affirmations and platitudes from her. Undoubtedly, he only craved a little peace and quiet to strum his guitar and mentally go over the strategy he wanted to use on Rwanda Don…er…Donna Ward.

And here she was disturbing him.

Still, she had to say *something*, because she could tell by the way he squinted up at her that he was beginning to think she might be going just a little batty. And, the truth was, when it came to him? He was probably right. As he'd say, she was crazier than a road-runnin' lizard.

Geez, Van. Get it together.

"I just wanted you to know that you're going to get that confession," she blurted and fought the urge to roll her eyes even as she pressed doggedly ahead. "You're going to get her to admit to being part of The Project. You're going to find out who she's working with. You're going to find out why they burned you. And you're going to clear your name."

"I know I will," he nodded, grabbing his hat brim and yanking it around until it faced forward. "I've been studyin' all the information we found on her, and besides havin' a pretty substantial God complex, the woman seems obsessed with the notion of beating the bad guys, of doin' good and leavin' her mark on the world. When I confront her with the true evil of what she's done, she's gonna wanna defend herself. Pretty vociferously, I would imagine. Still…" he cocked his head, then narrowed his gaze, for all the world looking like he could see inside of her, "I don't think that's really why you came up here, now is it?"

And, holy crap! He wasn't just mucking around in Donna Ward's head; he was mucking around in Vanessa's as well. How did he *do* that?

And until he called her on it, she hadn't really been aware the true reason she sought him out was because *she* needed a little reassurance. Some sort of sign from him that last night meant something. That regardless of what he claimed, there *was* something more between them than a big, heaping helping of red-hot lust.

"A-about last night…" she began hesitantly.

"What about it?" he asked, and for the first time in her life she couldn't read what emotion lay behind his tone. Probably because his voice was flat. Flat like a pancake, flat like a fritter. Flat, flat, *flat*.

And now her heart was threatening to come crashing out of her chest for a whole new reason, because she could think of only one explanation for the lack of inflection.

Don't! she wanted to scream at him. *Don't say it didn't mean anything to you! Don't say you weren't moved!*

She opened her mouth to do just that. But, *thankfully*, she was saved from making a colossal ass out of herself, from being dubbed Queen of the Needy Bitches, when Ghost, dressed in a tuxedo and looking very dapper indeed, knocked on the doorjamb.

"Sorry to disturb, folks," he said, his black eyes taking in the scene, taking in her heated cheeks and Rock's blank stare.

"*Non*," Rock shook his head, setting aside his guitar, "it's okay. Is it time?"

"Yup." Ghost nodded. "Squeeze into that penguin suit, my friend. We're about to saddle up."

"Be down in two," Rock said, and Ghost nodded before turning away, his black patent-leather shoes making no sound on the hall floor.

"Rock, I—"

"*Chere*," he cut her off, "now's not the time for this."

And, yeah, she knew that, but she just couldn't help herself. She needed to know what he was feeling, what he was thinking in that stubborn, denial-prone head of his.

"I know, but I—"

"Rock!" This time it was Boss hollering from below who interrupted Vanessa. "Get your ass down here. Time's wasting!"

One corner of Rock's goatee lifted as he shook his head. "Becky accuses the man of bellowing like a bull. I think she's right."

Watching him push up from the bed, she decided to bite her tongue—for now.

But once this thing was over?

Oh, boy, you better believe she intended to call him on the carpet. She was done being patient and sweet. They were going to settle this thing between them, one way or another...

Chapter Twenty-four

The Peninsula Hotel, Chicago...

CRACKING THE BATHROOM WINDOW, DONNA WARD kicked off her killer pumps—killer as in they *looked* killer, and killer as in they were total foot assassins—before she boosted herself up on the wide, peach-tiled windowsill and fished out the lone cigarette and the tiny BIC lighter she stored in her clutch.

And, yeah, yeah, medical degree or not, she knew she shouldn't smoke. But nothing soothed her like a long drag on a Marlboro, so she allowed herself this one teeny, tiny vice. Slipping the filtered end between her lips, she glanced at the door, assuring herself she was alone, before flicking the wheel on the lighter. Orange flame shot up, and then?

Heaven...

That first puff, that initial drag was always the best, the smoky taste of tobacco, the little buzz at the back of her head. She inhaled slowly, savoring every second, stretching her neck from side-to-side to work out the kinks.

Marcus did well tonight.

And he'd looked very handsome up there giving his speech, so wholesome and all-American. That's what had initially attracted her to him all those years ago, that choir-boy face and perfect politician hair. Of course what *kept* her attracted was his ambition and determination to leave his mark on the world.

The only other person she knew who was more driven than herself was Marcus. And she liked to think she'd helped him get to where he was today. Liked to think he'd help her, too, once he made it to the Oval Office. Marcus had believed in the viability and necessity of The Project when she'd written that thesis. And he'd been just as dejected as she'd been when the CIA withdrew the funding for it.

Of course, he'd never approve of her going it alone all these years, but what Marcus didn't know wouldn't hurt him. He'd have been especially furious to find out she'd used some of the funds she'd...*appropriated*—she didn't care for the word "stolen." It had a criminal connotation and she was certainly no criminal—in order to fund his campaigns, but Rock's and Billingsworth's deaths assured her he'd never find out.

And yes, she thought as she took another drag on the cigarette, *it's terrible it had to come to that. But the lives of those two men when compared to the lives I'll save once Marcus is in power and reinstates The Project are immaterial. It's for the greater good.*

After her brother's death, she'd done everything for the greater good. Everything she planned to do in the *future* would be for the greater good. But first, she needed to help get Marcus into office. And without the funds from The Project to bolster his bid for the Party nomination, Marcus needed to shine brighter than ever to in order to drum up financial support. And, as his wife, she needed to shine with him. Which meant she probably shouldn't get caught smoking in the bathroom like some high school delinquent.

Allowing herself one last, long drag, she held the

smoke in her lungs, luxuriating in the sensation, before she blew it out the window. Hopping down from the windowsill, she stubbed the cigarette in the sink and ran cold water over the tip before tossing it in the trash. Frowning, she slipped back into her pumps, checked her hair in the fancy gilt mirror above the long line of sinks, spritzed some Binaca onto her tongue, and turned for the door.

She was in the process of tossing the little tube of breath freshener into her clutch when she pushed into the long hall. Which was probably why she didn't see the man who stepped up behind her, throwing a baseball glove-sized hand over her mouth.

Adrenaline instantly surged, but before she could fight back, an entire mob of people in eveningwear were rushing her back into the bathroom…

"Move her toward the back of the room," a deep, smooth voice instructed, a voice she'd recognize anywhere.

Her heart began racing out of control as her eyes searched the group of people in front of her. It appeared as if an entire wall of humanity was pushing her past the row of stalls. She lost her shoe on the travertine tile floor and dropped her handbag as she struggled against the crowd, but there was no breaking away from the flesh and blood vice wrapped around her arms.

And, then…

There he was. Rock Babineaux. Dressed in a slim-cut tuxedo, altogether *too* much alive.

Goddamn CIA! They screw up everything! was her first thought.

They'd screwed up when they stopped funding for The Project. They'd screwed up when they let her go as a result. And now they'd gone and screwed up by not killing Rock.

Of course her second thought obliterated everything before it. Because her second thought had ice water rushing through her veins.

Oh, God, how did he find me?

"Take your hand off her mouth, Boss," he said, coming to stand in front of her, the people with him fanning out behind him.

Boss...The Black Knights. He was here with the Black Knights...

The ice water in her veins froze solid, and goose bumps pebbled her skin.

The hand that was over her mouth lifted away, but the big arm wrapped around her, holding her in place, remained iron tight.

"You," she breathed then realized her mistake before she took it too far. Shaking her head, she donned a baffled expression. "Who are all you people?"

"Cut the crap, Rwanda Don," Rock hissed, leaning forward until their noses were barely an inch apart, until she could see the forest green striations in his pretty hazel eyes.

Rwanda Don...How in the world had he pieced it together? Her stomach climbed up her throat to sit at the back of her mouth.

"Who..." She swallowed loudly, shaking her head, knowing her eyes were big and round. If she could just play dumb until help arrived, she could take some time to regroup, time to figure out how they'd made her, and time to decide the best way to destroy whatever evidence they'd found and discredit the entire lot of them. She had friends in very high places, after all. "Who's Rwanda... Rwanda Don?"

A look of disgust passed over Rock's face, and he sighed heavily before settling back onto his heals.

"I guess we're gonna do this the hard way, *non?*" he said, shaking his head.

"I...I don't know what you're t-talking about," she murmured, feeling a frightened tear slip from the corner of her eye to trail down her cheek.

What was the hard way? She didn't dare contemplate it...

Rock looked at the woman who'd ruined his reputation and tried to have him killed and had a hard time seeing the shadowy Rwanda Don in her. The coiffed, ash-blond hair, the Botox-ed forehead, the demure string of pearls laying against her slightly aging neck all screamed *staid politician's wife*. But the look in her eye...?

It was frantic and scared and altogether *knowing*.

She was Rwanda Don all right. Now he just needed to make her admit it.

And he knew just how to go about doing it.

Taking a deep breath, dragging in the scents of industrial cleaner, high-class perfume, and fresh cigarette smoke, he began with, "We've read your thesis."

"Wh-what?" she asked, pulling off the whole timid, middle-aged woman shtick with aplomb. Which was probably because, despite the psychology degree, the famous husband, and the super-secret spy life, the fact remained she *was* just a timid, middle-aged woman.

A timid, middle-aged woman who suffered from a God complex and more than a little bit of crazy. And she was no match for a man with his training and ability.

"The one outlinin' the jobs of Investigator, Interrogator,

and…" he snapped his fingers, the signal for Dunn to step from the back of the group. This was the first part of his strategy. "…Cleaner."

Her gaze flickered when Dunn came to stand beside him, her nostrils flaring slightly.

Oui, *you know exactly who he is*.

"That's supposed to be classified information," she whispered, cornflower-blue eyes big and watery. "I don't know who you are, or how you came about—"

"You know exactly who we are, Rwanda Don," Rock interrupted. "Rwanda Don…Hmm, you weren't very smart about choosin' that code name were you? Donna Ward, Rwanda Don…a boring, unintelligent little anagram."

At this her nostrils *really* flared. And, ah, the second part of his strategy seemed to be working. Her God complex didn't suffer well under attacks on her mental acumen.

"We also know Fred Billingsworth was killed because, ostensibly, he'd discovered somethin' unsavory about you, or maybe your husband, or maybe your involvement with a highly illegal operation known as The Project."

She was working hard to control it, but her breathing was accelerated. To anyone without a trained eye, she still just looked scared and confused. But to him? Pay dirt. He was pushing the right buttons.

The Knights, bless them, were silent and still as apparitions behind him. Creating a wall of support for him and a wall of opposition for Donna Ward.

"But it doesn't really matter *why* Billingsworth was killed," he continued. "All we need to know now is who you were working for. Because even though you may have orchestrated Billingsworth's death to cover up some sort of scandal on you or your husband's part, your boss has to have decided to go to bat for you since the instant you pointed the CIA toward my PO box," and he really wished he'd thrown those files away or else been far more careful to make sure no one ever followed him when he made a deposit in said PO box, "and the instant my Burn and Delete notice came over the wires, The Project was finished."

Her eyes flickered again. The skin of her cheeks tightening. And for a second he was confused. What was…?

There was something there. Something he couldn't quite put his finger on.

"I-I don't know what you're talking about," she insisted, her voice shaking. He had to fight not to roll his eyes. "Yes, I wrote that thesis. But I have no idea about the rest of it."

"Ozzie," he interrupted, and the kid stepped forward. "Will you read from the document containing the specifics of Rwanda Don's," continuing to use her code name was the third step in his strategy, "dismissal from the CIA."

And hadn't that little bit of intel been a punch in the gut? He'd been recruited by the CIA, trained by the CIA, but who the hell had been running his operations all these years? Who the hell had tapped Donna Ward after The Company axed her? And who the hell had burned him? The NSA?

"Dr. Donna Ward," the kid read aloud from the dossier in his hand, and Rock watched Dr. Ward's eyes flick down to the stack of papers, "is hereby terminated by the Central Intelligence Agency for conduct unbecoming. Her ideas and theories are considered subversive and destructive. She has no respect for the authority of this institution and is therefore deemed unfit for continued employment. Her security clearances, from this day forth, are terminated. She is to be considered—"

"That's enough," Rock cut in, catching the slight color change in Donna Ward's cheeks. Her blood pressure was rising. Getting sacked from The Company really burned her. "So we know you're no longer with the CIA. They were too smart to keep you on. They knew you were a loose cannon." Poke, poke, poke. Just like he'd been taught. "But, that begs the question, who *are* you workin' for now? NSA? Who's crazy enough to employ you and—"

He saw her break right before she strained against Boss's arm, saw the look on her face morph from doe-eyed innocence to an unattractive snarl. "What makes you think I *need* the government's help?" she hissed, veins standing out in her neck, eyes bulging. "After those idiots at the CIA rescinded funding for The Project and terminated my employment, I just kept at it on my own, running the operations myself. I did it all myself! And it was good work! Those men needed to die. They were filth! They were—"

She was screaming now, and Rock looked up at Boss, nodding. The big guy slapped a wide palm over her mouth as she continued to try to spew her insanity. But other than her muffled curses, the bathroom was dead silent.

No one moved; no one spoke. Everybody was stunned by the bomb she'd dropped.

So…he hadn't been doing ultra-black work for an ultra-clandestine branch of the government. *Non.* He'd been operating on the orders—kidnapping and interrogating American citizens—of a crazy civilian psychologist. Which meant he was exactly what they'd accused him of being…a rogue operator. The only difference was he'd been duped into the role.

Mon dieu. He couldn't breathe; the bathroom was spinning. But then he felt a reassuring hand at the small of his back, Vanessa, and he knew he had to pull his shit together. Now there were more questions that needed answers.

Swallowing, his mind racing, he asked, "Who did you get your information on these men from? You couldn't have come upon their files on your own."

Boss lifted a brow, and he nodded, giving the big guy permission to remove his hand from her mouth.

"Not everybody within The Company thought my ideas were subversive and destructive," Donna Ward whispered, all the fight having suddenly drained from her body. She was caught; she knew it. So now was the time to play to her second weakness, the fact that she thought her actions righteous and just.

"You had an accomplice?"

"I like to call him a partner," she said.

"Was he the one who took that shot at me down in Costa Rica?" he asked, feeling the weight of the consequences he was going to face for having been a part of her crazy scheme pressing down on his shoulders. But he'd deal with that later. For now, he needed to get all the information from her he could.

"No," she shook her head. "That would be the hit man he hired. But it was for the greater good, Rock." She looked at him imploringly, and it appeared her delusions knew no bounds. "Can't you see that? I needed to clean house, tie up loose ends so The Project had a chance of going on some day. Surely you can understand how badly we need to keep fighting, keep taking out those animals." She shook her head, another tear slipping from her wide eyes to roll down her cheek. "If only Billingsworth hadn't started asking me questions about the money, and if you hadn't started asking questions about Billingsworth, none of this would've happened."

It made Rock sick. His role in her deranged logic made him sick.

"What money?" he asked, having to swallow the bile that climbed up the back of his throat.

"My partner," she frowned, "the man at the CIA who found the targets for The Project, signed on to help not because he believed in our cause." And the way she used the word "our" made Rock want to vomit. "But because he wanted the money from the illegal accounts these terrible men had squirreled away. I agreed, of course, because I needed the intelligence he could gather, but I never thought to take a penny until Marcus needed a little extra to run a television ad campaign."

And, suddenly, the picture, the whole sordid mess of it, was clear. "And Billingsworth discovered the questionable origins of this money used to bolster your husband's campaign, which would've eventually led him to The Project, so you had him killed."

"He was going to wreck *everything*!" she lamented. "I couldn't let that happen. You can understand that, can't you?"

The woman was a serious piece of work. That she could be a practicing psychiatrist was almost too terrifying to contemplate.

"Can't you see," she went on, "that his life was nothing when compared to the lives we saved by getting rid of the type of men who killed your parents, Jonathan's wife and daughter," she let her eyes slide to the man in question, "and my brother?"

And, yes, Rock had discovered what he'd assumed had been the impetuous behind her penning that thesis all those years ago. It had to do with her twin brother. Apparently, he'd been caught sleeping with a local drug kingpin's mistress, and the kingpin had the guy shot in the head. But, like most kingpins, the dirty work was done by someone else, so he never received so much as a minute in jail.

Rock remembered that drug kingpin very clearly since he was the first target Rock ever interrogated. Rodrigo Vasquez.

"But he was an innocent man," Vanessa whispered, obviously no longer able to hold her tongue. But her hand? God love the woman, she still had it pressed against the small of his back. A tiny, warm touch of assurance despite everything she was learning about him and the truth of his second job.

"It was the only way," Donna Ward explained.

Dunn lunged, and had Steady not been standing directly behind the man, Rock had no doubt the guy would've gone for Donna Ward's throat. As it was, Steady managed to hook both hands around Dunn's shoulders, wrestling him back toward the bathroom's door with Dunn yelling hoarsely, "You turned me into a murderer. A murderer!"

"That's enough," Rock said, reaching into his tuxedo jacket to click off the recorder he'd stored there. "We have everything we need."

"What the hell are we going to do with her?" Ozzie asked. "We can't let her go and then confront her boss like we'd planned. The crazy bitch doesn't *have* a boss."

"I'm not crazy," Donna Ward insisted, the wild look in her eyes proving her words false. "I'm not—"

Boss slapped a hand over her mouth again.

"We take her with us and turn her over to General Fuller," Steady announced, and Rock disliked that option with every fiber of his being, but he knew it was the only one that was viable, proven by Steady's next words. "We don't know who her accomplice in the CIA is. We don't know what she's capable of doing if we release her. Not to mention the fact she'd probably go to ground like wounded rabbit. No. We have to take her."

Rock knew Steady was right, and now Donna Ward was struggling in Boss's grasp again, her eyes rolling around like pinballs.

"What about the local authorities?" Eve asked quietly, and Rock would be forever grateful to her for getting them into the fundraiser. This mission would've been far more difficult, their ability to maneuver through the hotel nearly impossible, if not for the security badges now clipped to their clothing. "Couldn't you just hand her over to them along with that tape you made?"

Boss answered for Rock. "The local authorities wouldn't know how to make hide nor hair of all this. Plus, it started with a treasonous idea within the CIA, and those folks are known for covering their tracks. So, since we don't know who her accomplice is, and unless we want Rock and Dunn to find themselves food for the fishes at the bottom of Lake Michigan, it's better we take this all the way to the top." He turned to Rock, "I'll call General Fuller and tell him you're coming."

Rock nodded, a hard knot of regret vying for space in his chest beside the hard knot of remorse.

"Hallway's clear out to the alley exit," Ghost announced from his position by the bathroom door. "If we're doin' this thing, the time is now."

Chapter Twenty-five

ROCK GLANCED AT THE CROWD GATHERED IN THE chopper shop, looking so incongruent in their fancy evening-gwear against all the heavy machinery, and he felt like he'd just come back from one of those ball-busting, seventy-two-hour insertions into the mountains of the Hindu Kush. The ones he'd done back when he'd been with the SEALs and one of his many suck-ass jobs requiring him to scour caves and bunkers looking for Taliban insurgents.

He was body-weary from too much adrenaline coursing through his system and mind-weary because Donna Ward's interrogation was the most disturbing of his life. You know, considering her revelations meant everything he'd always thought of himself, the man he was and the jobs he'd done, were all a big stinking pile of hogwash.

Or, maybe he could look at the bright side, in that her interrogation was very likely the *last* interrogation he'd ever have to do. Because for the last five years, he'd unknowingly been involved in illegal, non-government sanctioned activities, and he was going to have to pay for that. One way or another...

"You have everything you need?" Boss asked, his face lined with concern.

"*Oui*," Rock nodded, looking over at Dunn who was sitting on the metal steps leading to the second floor. He and Rock were the only ones who'd changed out of their fancy duds. The reason being their plan was for Dunn to drive Donna Ward back to DC in his Explorer while Rock rode behind on Patriot, and tuxedos weren't necessarily conducive to either task. "You sure you're okay with these arrangements, man?" he asked Dunn. "'Cause I could always ride with you instead—"

"No way." Dunn shook his head. "I've got some phone calls to make, some arrangements to take care of. And this way you'll get in one last ride."

Rock nodded again, thanking the man with his eyes. He respected the shit out of the guy for doing this, for turning himself in. Because the consequences Dunn stood to face were far more severe than the consequences Rock stood to face. Dunn *had* been the one to do the actual killing after all…

"You sure that's a wise move?" Boss interrupted. "The Feds are going to be scouring the entire country soon, looking for Dr. Ward. We could always have Fuller fly here."

Rock shook his head. "Dunn's windows are tinted, and everyone not only thinks I'm dead, but *graveyard* dead, so it's not like there's an APB out on me or anything. I'd really like to take this last ride, Boss. There's no tellin'—"

"Wait a minute," Vanessa interrupted, her dark eyes wide. "What are you talking about when you say *one last ride*? Surely you don't think you'll be held responsible for any of this. You were duped." She swung around to Dunn. "You both were."

"Doesn't matter what we *thought*," Dunn said, not looking at Vanessa, but staring straight at Rock. His eyes shone with bone-deep sadness, and Rock ached for the guy. For what Donna Ward had turned him into. Rock's heart was an anchor in the center of his chest. "Ignorance isn't an excuse," Dunn finished. And wasn't that the truth?

They *should* have asked more questions. But shoulda, woulda, coulda, it was all a done deal now.

"Boss…" he turned, and the torment on his old friend's face wrecked him. He wished like hell he didn't have to put the man through this and, more than that, he wished he hadn't put this black spot on the reputation of Black Knights Inc. But there was no going back to erase the past. So the most he could hope to accomplish was to do the right thing for BKI's future. "I'd like you to give us about eleven hours to make the drive. And then I'd like you to call Fuller. Tell him to meet me at the old spot down by the Potomac." The little, rural shack by the river where he and Boss had first run the idea for Black Knights Inc. by the general. "Can you do that?"

"You know I can," Boss said, a hard muscle ticking in his jaw. "But I wish there was another way."

"There's not. You know there's not, *mon frere.*"

Boss jerked his chin, once, the big guy's eyes overly bright. And, *mon dieu*, Rock was having a hard enough time keeping his shit together as it was. Seeing Boss losing it, even a little, was a steel-fisted blow straight to the gut.

"Wait!" Vanessa yelled, panic in her voice, her eyes frantic. "Wait! What are you guys saying? Are you saying you're going to prison for this? No!" She adamantly shook her head. "No! It's not right! It's not fair!"

Ah, chere, *there's my proud, dauntless lioness…*

"Surely you know by now, *mon ange*," he murmured holding her gaze, "there's nothing fair in this ol' life." He was so goddamned sorry…about everything.

"Rock," she ran to him, the anguish on her pretty face breaking his fucking heart. "Richard," she pleaded once she reached him, laying a beseeching hand on his arm, and that just made it all so much worse. "You don't have to do this. They think you're dead. You could just stay dead," she was panting, her voice unusually high. And it was obvious she'd forgotten they had an audience. The Knights were looking on with various expressions of discomfort and heartache, but Rock didn't care. His only thought was to soothe the woman standing in front of him. "You could get a new name. Move to a different country. I'll come with you." Oh, sweet Jesus, she was killing him. "I'll change my name, too. There's nothing to keep me here. No parents. My aunt died last year. We can—"

"Stop it, *chere*," he grabbed her upper arms, giving her a gentle shake. And it only managed to cause the tears that'd been standing in her eyes to spill over and slide down her soft cheeks. "This has to be done."

"No," she shook her head, her shiny, black hair brushing her shoulders. "No it doesn't. You could just run. Run *away*, Rock—"

"That's not the honorable thing to do."

"Screw honor!" she wailed, now crying in earnest. "What about *life*? We could have a life together. You and I. I love you, Rock!" She threw her arms around his neck and—*oh, dieu*—suddenly she wasn't the only one crying. One mutinous tear slipped from his right eye, slid down his cheek and landed in her hair where her head was tucked up under his chin. She loved him. It was what he'd been afraid of and maybe secretly yearning for all along…

Dunn pushed up from the stairs and strolled toward his vehicle parked just inside the shop—Donna Ward was already tied up in the backseat—and the Knights began to move toward the stairs, trying to be inconspicuous about quitting the scene in order to give him and Vanessa some privacy. But Rock caught Boss's eye, subtly shaking his head and making his intent clear.

Stay, mon ami. *I need your help.*

Boss nodded and hung back by the stairs as the rest of the Knights disappeared onto the second-floor landing.

Rock gave himself a moment…just one moment to hold Vanessa close, to drink in the minty-sweet smell of her, to press her warmth and lushness and, yes, *love* against his heart. Then he did what he had to do. For himself, for his sanity, but mostly for her wonderful, brave, far-too-open-and-giving heart. He couldn't do this knowing she'd mourn for him, for his loss, the way he'd mourned for Lacy. He had to make sure if she had any pain at all, it was as quick and as insignificant as he could make it.

So, grabbing her shoulders, he softly pushed her away. Her face was a mess: red, blotchy, covered in tears, and so goddamned beautiful it nearly brought him to his knees. "You know what I told you out in the jungle," he said, making sure his tone was kind but also hard and immovable. "That hasn't changed."

"Don't say that," she shook her head, sniffling. "You don't mean it. Not after last night. Not after we—"

"I *do* mean it," he insisted quietly but firmly. Still, her next words told him she wasn't really listening.

"They won't be able to put you away for very long," she said, wiping a shaky hand over her wet cheeks. "You didn't do the killing. You just did the interrogating. So, what can they charge you with? False imprisonment? Surely you'll be out in a few years, and I'll be here waiting on you. I'll be here—"

"Vanessa," he gave her another little shake, the air in his lungs on fire. Because even if he *had* changed his mind, even if he *had* done something colossally stupid and allowed himself to fall for her, there was nothing to be done for it now. She couldn't spend her life waiting on him. She had to go on living. She wanted a family, a husband and children. And there was no way he could give her those things. Not now. So he gave her what he could...

He gave her her freedom.

"I don't love you," he said, lowering his chin and holding her watery gaze, knowing his own was probably just as watery. "I don't love you, you hear me? So there's no use in you waitin' on me. You need to move on. Find someone else."

But even contemplating the thought cut him to the bone.

"No," she shook her head, hiccupping, her voice rising in a wail. "I don't believe you! You're lying!"

He looked over at Boss. The man's face was the picture of sorrow, but he nodded and jogged over to them, gently taking Vanessa from his arms. It took everything Rock had to let her go.

"No!" she screamed. "Don't do this, Rock!"

And he had to get out of there before he did something completely stupid, before he did something completely undignified and unethical and took her up on her offer to just run away. Fred Billingsworth's true murderer needed to be brought to justice, and he and Dunn were the only men who could do it.

"No, Rock!" Vanessa wailed, but he couldn't stay a second longer or he didn't know if he'd be able to make himself leave at all.

Jogging over to Patriot, he grabbed his leather jacket from where it lay over the seat. The back patch read *Black Knights Incorporated: May the Road Never End*... A hard lump formed in his throat. Today was going to be his last day as a

Knight. And tomorrow? Well, tomorrow he highly suspected his road was going to end…at least for a good, long while.

Shrugging into the jacket, he threw a leg over the bike and unhooked his helmet from the handlebar. Unfortunately, shoving the helmet over his head did nothing to drown out Vanessa's cries. And each tearful wail, each begging plea not to go, was a razor-sharp arrow to his heart.

This was slaying him. *She* was slaying him.

Pushing the button on the hydraulics, Patriot lifted to riding height, but before he started the engine, he glanced over at Boss. "It's been an honor, *mon ami*," he said, placing his hand over his thundering heart.

Boss dipped his chin, his Adam's apple bobbing. "The honor has been mine, my friend."

Rock nodded and tried to ignore the fact that the foundation of his life was cracking and crumbling beneath him. Then he let his gaze linger on Vanessa, fighting like a tigress, struggling in the big man's grip to no avail.

"*Chere*," he said, and she stopped squirming, looking up at him with puffy, pleading eyes, chest rising and falling rapidly. "Live your life. Live a *good* life. And know that I'll always cherish the time we had."

And before she could answer, he turned away, cranking over Patriot's big engine while simultaneously pushing the button on the handlebars that activated the huge garage door. It rolled up. It's loud whir barely discernible over Patriot's throaty grumble.

Without a backward glance—he couldn't bear to see everything he was leaving behind—he followed Dunn's SUV and motored out of the shop, away from the past he'd grown to love, and off to put himself into the hands of some of the very people who'd tried to kill him.

Chapter Twenty-six

Three weeks later...

"YOU'VE GOT TO COME SEE THIS," BECKY SAID, HANGING onto the doorframe of Vanessa's bedroom, alarm in her tone and in her face.

"What is it?" Vanessa asked, in the process of making her bed. Every day was the same, she got up, she made her bed, she went to work, and she pretended her heart wasn't shattered into a thousand tiny, bloody pieces. And every day the Knights tiptoed around her, handling her with kid gloves, pretending one of their own wasn't the *reason* her heart was shattered into a thousand tiny, bloody pieces.

"Donna Ward and her CIA partner were both found dead in a hotel room this morning," Becky said. "The victims of gunshot wounds to the head."

"Jesus." Vanessa skirted the bed to follow Becky down the hall toward the media room. "Not that I'm all that upset by their passing or anything. Donna Ward was a horror show, and I can only imagine her partner was, too. But still...*Jesus*."

"It gets worse," Becky said as they walked into the media room where all the Knights were gathered around the wide-screen television—it was set to the morning news. For two weeks they'd been kept in the dark about Rock's situation, General Fuller remaining frustratingly mum on the subject despite Boss's dozens of phone calls demanding answers. Then, last Friday, Fuller finally called to say Rock and Dunn were being released, and Donna Ward was undergoing psychological evaluation pending release while her accomplice at the CIA was stripped of all titles and security clearances.

"It's been decided by the powers that be," Boss had informed the group, and he'd been talking about *the* powers that be, "that it would be too damaging to the reputation of the intelligence community to hold trials, thereby dragging into the light the origins of The Project and the CIA's initial involvement in said scheme."

"And Billingsworth?" Ozzie had asked.

"A casualty of the system," was Boss's terse reply. "His murder is officially listed as *unsolved*."

Which Vanessa felt was a grave injustice, but she'd worked for the government too long to really be surprised.

Rock's name had been cleared of any wrongdoing, his record once again lily white. Dunn had been instructed to return to his job at the FBI as if nothing had happened. And Donna Ward? Well, Vanessa had hoped like hell that *psychological evaluation* proved her unfit to reenter society whereby she'd be confined to a psych ward for life.

Only, according to the news report, at some point she must've been released.

"...late last night. And it appears Dr. Dunn and former CIA agent, Dennis Wheeler, were both shot in the back of the skull at close range before their assailant, an as yet unidentified man, turned the gun on himself," the pretty blond-haired news reporter was saying. "Local police suspect—"

Vanessa's heart sunk. "Unidentified man? Who is she talking about?"

Though Rock had been released, he hadn't returned home. Instead, he'd called Boss to say he planned to return to Terrebonne Parish, Louisiana, claiming he needed some time to clear his head. But Vanessa suspected he'd gone back to visit his parents' and Lacy's graves. After all that'd happened, all the twists and turns his life had taken due to the events surrounding their deaths, she figured he was seeking some perspective.

But could he have decided Donna Ward and the CIA agent needed to be—

No. Rock isn't the killing kind, she assured herself. *And he's certainly not the kind to turn his weapon on himself.*

Then a lightbulb blinked on over her head, and she answered her own question. "It's Dunn, isn't it?"

"Yeah," Boss nodded. He was standing in the middle of the room with his arms crossed, legs splayed, and he didn't look away from the television screen when he added, "I figure it's Dunn."

"Jesus," Vanessa whispered and realized her vocabulary needed some work. She'd used that same expletive three times in as many minutes.

"Jonathan Dunn could live with being a killer," Becky mused, sidling up beside Boss, sliding an arm around his waist. "But he couldn't live with being a murderer. And he couldn't let the woman and man who'd turned him *into* a murderer live either. It's so…so senseless and sad."

"I'd say you're right," Boss agreed, bending to place a kiss by her temple. "On all fronts."

Vanessa had to turn away. Ever since Rock left, Boss and Becky's obvious love for one another, not to mention their overt affection, well…she was ashamed to say it got to her. Reminding her of everything she'd hoped to have and everything she'd lost when she'd gone all-in with Rock.

"Hey," Steady whispered, coming to throw an arm over her shoulders, giving her a gentle squeeze even as he handed her a mug of steaming, so-thick-it'd-stand-up-on-its-own coffee, "you okay?"

And there they were again, the kid gloves…

Geez, she was a real piece of work. A real piece of sorry, lowdown, heartsick work.

"I guess you probably already know the answer to that," she told him, taking the coffee, inhaling the dark, rich aroma. She didn't have an ounce of pride left after that show she'd put on down in the chopper shop, so there was no use lying.

"He's a fool."

"No," she shook her head, taking a tentative sip and wincing, not at the heat, but at the grow-a-patch-of-hair-on-your-chest flavor. "Not a fool. Just stubborn and guarded and unwilling to put himself in a position to get hurt again. Unwilling to let me put *myself* in a position to get hurt like he did."

"Well, then he's a goddamned, misguided coward," Steady hissed.

Before she could open her mouth to defend Rock, a gentle whirring sounded from below. It was the big garage door on the shop.

Boss turned away from the television. "We expecting anybody home today?"

He asked the question of the group, but it was Ozzie who answered. "Nope. Only person scheduled to be coming back in the near future is Mac. And he's not due 'til tomorrow."

"Anybody unaccounted for from last night?" Boss queried, because it wasn't unusual for one or more of the Knights to spend his evenings *elsewhere* when he was in town.

"We're all here," Steady offered.

Suddenly everyone knew who was coming home, and it was a race to see who could get downstairs first. A race, that is, except for Vanessa and Steady. The Black Knights' in-house doctor continued to stand there with his arm around her shoulders as the coffee turned to acid in her stomach.

"You don't have to do this if you don't want to," he said, taking the mug from her hands. It was then she realized her fingers were shaking and she was threatening to dump hot java all over the newly waxed wood floor. "You could just go to your room until you're ready to see him."

"No," she shook her head, taking a deep breath. "It's better to get it over with."

Steady smiled encouragingly, giving her a reassuring chuck on the chin before lowering his arm and taking a step toward the door.

"Steady?" she stopped him with a hand on his wrist. "I want you to know, Rock never lied to me. He told me he could never love me, but I...I didn't believe him." She ducked her head, staring at her shoes. "That was...that was arrogant of me, I guess."

"Or maybe just hopeful," Steady offered, and she glanced up into his beautiful, swarthy face to find the expression in his eyes understanding, understanding and *kind*. When he finally decided he was done sowing his wild oats, Vanessa figured he was going to make some woman very happy.

"Yeah," she nodded, the lump in her throat causing her breath to hitch. "Yeah...maybe just hopeful."

—∿∿—

Rock backed Patriot into his spot in the shop, pushed the button on the hydraulics, and switched off the grumbling engine. His spot...

Dieu, when he left three weeks ago he was certain he'd never see *his spot* again. But so much had happened in the interim. Then again, so much had *not* happened, too. Because after spending two full weeks with the CIA, having each one of his Project missions picked apart and analyzed under a microscope, he'd simply been given his walking papers. Well, those and a direct order to take what he knew of Donna Ward and The Project to his grave or else he might find himself on the receiving end of yet *another* visit from some fabled black stealth Chinooks.

Um, no thank you very much. One such visit in an operator's lifetime was plenty.

"Aren't you a sight for sore eyes, you crazy Cajun sonofabitch!" Boss thundered, clomping down the stairs from the second floor, the rest of the Knights right on his heels, sounding like a herd of buffalo. Except...

Where's Vanessa?

"Feels like I just left, but also like I've been gone a year," he said, pulling off his helmet and hooking it over the handlebars before swinging from the back of the bike.

He was instantly in the center of a group hug, arms and legs squeezing him from head to toe and, "Ozzie, get your hand off my ass," he growled.

"Oh, is that what that was?" Ozzie chuckled as the group stepped back en masse.

And there they were, the people he'd grown to love.

Yes, *love*. There was no more denying it. Because no matter how hard he fought it, the truth of the matter was, these men and women were his family, and he loved them like crazy. It was just too bad it'd taken almost losing them for him to realize what a goddamned, hardheaded fool he'd been.

And speaking of goddamned, hardheaded fools…

"I guess you heard about Dunn," Boss said, and Rock raked in a deep, weary breath.

He hadn't known Dunn for long, but in that short time he'd come to respect the man. And though he never cottoned to anyone taking their own life, he could understand how Dunn had come by the wrongheaded belief that the world would be better off without him in it. After all, he'd been psychologically programmed to take out murderers. And with Billingsworth's death, he himself *became* a murderer. It was all so sad, and had Rock known what was in the man's head after they were released, he would've done everything in his power to stop the guy. Unfortunately, he'd been clueless.

"I heard," he shook his head. "It's a cryin' shame."

"Yeah," Boss nodded, the group observing an impromptu moment of silence in Dunn's honor.

Then Rock asked the question that'd been eating a hole in him ever since he pulled in. "Where's Vanessa?"

"Here." Her voice sounded from the stairs.

When he looked up to see her slowly descending toward the shop floor, trailing Steady, his heart damn near leapt out of his chest. She was so beautiful. So dark and exotic and courageous and smart and wonderful. Everything he'd never dared to dream and didn't come close to deserving. Everything he was done pretending he didn't want.

"If ya'll will excuse me," he said to the group still gathered around him, "I've got some unfinished business to attend to."

Like Moses at the Red Sea, the Knights parted for him. He was at the stairs in two seconds, catching Vanessa around the waist before she could step from the last tread. Without warning, he didn't *dare* give her any warning or she'd probably lay into him like she damned well should, he kissed her. And when her mouth opened on a surprised squeak, he *really* kissed her.

She stiffened, going stick-straight in his arms for a couple of interminable seconds during which time he feared he may have messed everything up so badly that there was no way to repair it. Then the most wonderful thing happened...

She kissed him back. She wrapped her arms around his neck, hooked an ankle behind his knee, went all soft and sexy like he'd been remembering in his dreams, and she *kissed him back*.

Someone started to applaud—Steady?—and Rock pulled back, smiling down at her.

"Rock?" There was a question in her big, dark eyes. A question he was good and well ready to answer.

"*J'taime, mon amour*," he told her, *I love you*.

"Oh, Rock," she sobbed, burying her face in his shoulder, but not before he'd seen the tears standing in her eyes.

"Shh," he whispered, cupping the back of her head.

"I h-hate crying in-in-in front of everybody," she sobbed quietly into his motorcycle jacket. "I'm sssssupposed t-to be tough."

"Woman," he crooned, kissing her ear. "You're the toughest, bravest person I know."

She shook her head, her face still buried in his shoulder.

Turning toward the group, "We, uh," he jerked his chin and eyes upward. "We're gonna go—"

"Yeah," Boss cut him off. "Get lost, will ya? We're already sick and tired of looking at that ugly mug of yours."

Rock chuckled, nodding, before he bent and hooked an arm under Vanessa's knees and hoisted her up against his chest. She squawked out a protest, but he ignored her as he took the stairs two at a time, the Knights clapping and whistling in his wake.

~~~

Sometime later...

"Hmmm," Vanessa moaned blissfully, rolling off Rock who was still winded and sweaty. "That was nice."

"Nice?" he lifted his chin, frowning over at her until his goatee drooped. "Just nice?"

"*Deliciously* nice," she clarified, leaning toward him to nibble his earlobe.

"Hmmm." He let his head drop back to the pillow, turning his chin to give her better access to that ear. She loved when he did that. She loved him. And, miracle of miracles, he loved *her*. If she were any happier, she'd probably explode into a cloud of Valentine chocolate–box dust. Just...*poof.* "Now *that's* nice," he said, his arm snaking around her shoulders to pull her close.

For a few minutes they nuzzled and snuggled and laughed, then she pressed back, leaning up on her elbow in order to prop her cheek in her hand. "Rock?"

"Call me Richard," he murmured, eyes closed, dark

lashes creating a fan of shadows on his cheeks. He was sliding a lazy hand up and down her hip. "I love it when you call me Richard."

She bit her lip, smiling. "Richard?"

"*Oui, chere?*"

"Why did you change your mind?"

"Change my mind about what?"

"About loving me?" At this, his eyes snapped open and he searched her face. For some reason, her heart began to flutter and she pressed ahead quickly, "See, I figured you'd gone back to Louisiana to reassure yourself that loving someone hurt too bad. That letting me love you would eventually hurt *me* too bad. I imagined you standing over Lacy's grave and—"

He placed a finger over her mouth, nodding his head. "*Oui*, I went back to Louisiana and I visited Lacy's grave. And maybe I did it to try to bolster my stance on love." Now her heart wasn't fluttering, it was pounding. "But you know what happened as I was standing there in the sunshine with the Spanish moss hangin' down from all the trees, the birds chirpin' and the squirrels playin'?"

She shook her head, unable to look away from his sparkling eyes.

"I realized all I was rememberin' were the good times, the happy times. With Lacy, with my parents. And it occurred to me, that though their deaths were painful, I wouldn't give up the times I had with them for anything. The sweet times, the *lovin'* times are worth everything else that comes along in this ol' life, even the agony of loss. And that's when I knew I'd been a fool. See, I didn't change my mind about lovin' you, Vanessa. I've loved you all along." Oh, and weren't those just about the sweetest words ever spoken? "I just changed my mind about admitting it to myself, and about letting *you* love *me*."

"That's a really good answer," she told him, her smile so big it was making her cheeks hurt.

He shifted onto his side then, his expression growing serious. "I'm so sorry I hurt you, *chere*."

She tunneled her fingers into his short hair, leaning down to kiss his lips. "Ah," she whispered, "but, like you said, all the good times to come, all the *loving* times to come are going to totally make up for it."

"*Dieu*, I hope so," he muttered, palming her ass and rolling them until she was on top of him. "And I never thanked you for comin' after me, but I want to thank you now. I'd be dead if you hadn't done what you did. It's because of you I'm here now."

"Well I'll be damned," she said, shaking her head and laughing.

"What?"

"Boss said you'd thank me for that one day, but I didn't believe him. Guess I should have, huh? That man's rarely wrong."

"I don't want to talk about Boss," Rock said, and her breath hitched when she felt him hard and throbbing between her legs.

"No?" she whispered, moving gently against him, loving the feel of him beneath her. "So then let's talk about how you can thank me for saving your stubborn ass."

"How's that?" he asked, trying to catch her lips, but she eluded him.

"You can thank me by taking me out. On a date."

"I'll take you to moon if that's what you want, *mon ange*. Now, kiss me."

"Nope," she shook her head, giggling when he frowned. "I don't want the moon."

"*Merde*," he grumped. "You're gonna make me dress up in a monkey suit and take you somewhere fancy, right? Like Alinea? Or what's that frou-frou Italian place Christian likes so much? Spiaggia?"

"The Cubs are in town next week," she said, fighting a grin as he got very still beneath her. Still, except for that one hand that continued to rub her ass unconsciously.

"You're a baseball fan?" She could hear the hope and excitement in his voice as clearly as one hears a struck bell.

"Aren't you?"

"Marry me," he said, and she couldn't help it, she laughed.

"How about we start with a baseball game and see where it goes from there?" she said, groaning when he kissed his way up her throat to nibble on her chin.

"That's sounds like a wonderful plan, *chere*," he murmured before claiming her lips. But in her head, she knew she was eventually going to get Rock to that altar. And, oh, what a wonderful story they would have to tell their grandchildren. The story of a woman who was scared of the dark and a man who was scared of love, who'd come together to overcome all their fears…

Acknowledgments

As always, I must give props to my husband. This past year has been a doozy. Full of ups, downs, and even a few sideways. But, you've been by my side through it all. My heart, my inspiration, my rock…

A big shout-out to Catherine Mann, fellow romantic suspense author. Cathy, you agreed to read the manuscript of a total unknown, then dared to go a step further and endorse the book in front of the world. I am forever honored and grateful.

A resounding *huzzah* to all the folks at Sourcebooks. It takes a village to launch a debut series into a bestselling one, and the hours each of you spent on these books both awes and humbles me. Thank you.

And, last but certainly not least, *thank you* to our fighting men and women, those in uniform and those out of uniform. You protect our freedom and way of life so we all have the chance to live the American dream.

About the Author

Julie Ann Walker is the *USA Today* and *New York Times* bestselling author of the Black Knights Inc. romantic suspense series. She is prone to spouting movie quotes and song lyrics. She'll never say no to sharing a glass of wine or going for a long walk. She prefers impromptu travel over the scheduled kind, and she takes her coffee with milk. You can find her on her bicycle along the lake shore in Chicago or blasting away at her keyboard, trying to wrangle her capricious imagination into submission. For more information, please visit www.julieannwalker.com or follow her on Facebook www.facebook.com/jawalker author and/or Twitter @JAWalkerAuthor.